KINDLE ALEXANDER

Always
Copyright © Kindle Alexander, 2014
ALL RIGHTS RESERVED

Edited by Jae Ashley
Cover art and interior print layout by Reese Dante
http://www.reesedante.com

First Edition March 2014
ISBN: 978-1-941450-00-0

Published by: The Kindle Alexander Collection LLC

Always is a work of fiction. Names, characters, places and incidents are either the product of the author's imagination or are used fictitiously, and any resemblance to any actual persons, living or dead, events, or locales is entirely coincidental.

Licensed material is being used for illustrative purposes only and any person depicted in the licensed material is a model.

WARNING
This book contains material that maybe offensive to some:
graphic language, adult situations.

Trademark Acknowledgements

The author acknowledges the trademarked status and trademark owners of the following trademarks mentioned in this work of fiction:

Advil: Wyeth, LLC
American Medical Association: American Medical Association
Band-Aid: Johnson & Johnson Corporation
Brunello di Montalcino: Consorzio Vino Brunello di Montalcino
Cadillac: General Motors LLC
Chivas: Chivas Holdings (IP) Limited
Corvette (Stingray): General Motors, LLC
Day-Timer: ACCO Brands Corporation
Duke University: Duke University
Dr. Spock's Baby and Child Care: Benjamin Spock
Hugo Boss: Hugo Boss Trade Mark Management GMBH & CO.
Kleenex: Kimberly-Clark Worldwide, Inc.
Lamaze: Lamaze International, Inc.
Levi's: Levi Strauss & Co. Corporation
Lincoln Town Car: Ford Motor Company
Mickey and Minnie Mouse: Disney Enterprises, Inc.
National Geographic (magazine): National Geographic Society
Oral Roberts Christian University: Oral Roberts University
Pac-Man: Namco Bandai Games, Inc.
Pampers: The Proctor & Gamble Company
Rolaids: Chattem, Inc.
Rolodex: Berol Corporation
Twilight Zone: CBS Broadcasting Inc.
Tylenol: Johnson & Johnson Corporation
Yale: Yale University Not-for-Profit Corporation
Yves Saint Laurent: Luxury Goods International (L.G.I.) S.A.

Dedication

Aidan and Keagan, this one's for you.

To our amazing readers,
family and all our wonderful friends,
thank you from the bottom of our hearts.
Without your continued support and encouragement
we wouldn't be here.

Perry, you are missed every day.

Kindle, you are forever in our hearts.

True love is eternal, infinite, and always like itself. It is equal and pure, without violent demonstrations: it is seen with white hairs and is always young in the heart. ~ Honore de Balzac

Chapter 1

Present Day

The elegantly decorated hospital room looked regal and stately, much like the man lying in the bed in the center of the room. Kane Dalton entered in almost a dead run, moving as fast as his seasoned legs could carry him. Worry etched fine lines into his face. He paid no attention to the luxury surrounding him. Instead Kane's panicked gaze focused only on the man lying on the gurney with tubes and wires attached to several machines. Avery Adams had his eyes closed, taking short shallow breaths. He looked lifeless and pale, a far cry from the exuberant man Kane had grown to love beyond any measure of reason.

The tears that threatened finally broke Kane's resolve and spilled over, running down his cheeks. Thank God he'd made it there in time. Avery slowly turned his head, opening his eyes to look at Kane. Their gazes met and his heart lurched in his chest. The mental prayer replaying over and over in his head exalted its chorus, begging God to keep Avery safe and there with him for a little while longer.

Avery never lifted his head. Instead, he let those amber eyes pierce Kane's soul, just like they always had. For the briefest of moments, the world slowed, and he took the steps separating them. Kane wasn't sure of all the details, only that Avery had collapsed in his office surrounded by his staff, one of them being their daughter. She'd given him just enough bits and pieces of information to know the

1

problem had to do with Avery's heart, a long-diagnosed concern. Kane hadn't hesitated; he immediately dropped everything and drove himself to the hospital, not waiting for a driver to pick him up. His greatest fear now played out right in front of him.

They both ignored the hospital staff working feverishly to prepare Avery for emergency surgery.

"Baby, don't cry," Avery whispered as Kane clasped his hand.

"I'm not," Kane replied, searching Avery's handsome face. Kane willed himself to remember every single detail of this moment. A forever frustrating piece of Avery's hair had fallen down across his forehead. This particular piece of hair could never fully be tamed. Kane absently lifted a finger, moving the strand back with the others. It was a move he'd done a thousand times over the last forty years, but for some reason, this time the simple gesture caused the tears to fall with a little more force as his gaze landed back on Avery's.

"Give me a minute, please," Avery said to the room.

"Sir, we have no time. They're waiting for you in surgery" a nurse said, ignoring Avery completely.

"It wasn't a request." The force with which Avery said the words was in direct contrast to the pale older man lying in the bed. Every eye in the room turned toward him. Only the nurse had the nerve to answer.

"You have one minute before you're transported upstairs, sir," she said before she hurriedly shooed everyone else out of the room. Avery's eyes never left his.

"Kane, I'm going to be fine. I'm not ready to leave you, honey," Avery said, his voice back to the loving tone he always used with Kane.

"You don't know that." Kane leaned in, bringing his face close to Avery's, placing a simple kiss on his slightly parted lips.

"I do know it. I love you. I don't want to leave you. Forty years isn't long enough. I need at least another twenty," Avery whispered, and Kane's tears fell, dripping down onto Avery's face. Kane used the pad of his thumb to wipe them clean, but the effort was made in vain. The flow never stopped.

"I love you," Kane whispered.

"I don't regret anything. You made me the man I am today," Avery whispered.

"You made me whole," Kane replied.

"Kiss me before I go in," Avery requested, his voice weaker now than only moments before. Kane kissed him, meeting Avery's small swipe of the tongue with one of his own.

"Sir, we have to get you upstairs," the nurse said from the doorway. Kane stood when he saw Avery might fight for another minute. He never released his grip on Avery's hand.

"You fight for me," Kane said, trying to put on a brave face.

"Take care of our family. Make sure our grandbabies know how much I love them."

"Don't..." No more words would come. They both knew the gravity of the situation. Severe heart disease ran throughout Avery's ancestry. Avery had lived longer than any male in his family tree, but the odds were stacked against him. They both knew, at any point, time could run out.

"I love you, always," Avery said, his eyes still holding Kane's as they began to wheel him from the room.

"I love you, always." Kane forced himself to move and bent in to kiss his husband again. He willed himself to remember every detail of their tender kiss before Avery was pushed out from underneath him. He watched as they wheeled him away. Watched as the door closed with a firm click, and he still stood there staring at the thick oak wood. His life had just been pushed through that door, and now the helplessness was setting in. He could feel his body begin the slow steady tremble as he scrubbed his hands over his face, wiping away the tears in frustrated swipes. If only Avery would have eaten better. Stuck to the diet Kane had no problem sticking to. If Avery wouldn't have stolen those bites of cake and if Kane hadn't turned a blind eye... If Kane had made Avery walk more, work less, and disciplined him harder for straying off course. If only.

"Here, Daddy." Kane looked up, surprised to see Autumn standing in front of him. He hadn't heard her enter the room. She held a handful of tissues, and he accepted them, wiping at his face. He took the minute to pull himself together. He had to remember his children before he allowed himself to break down completely. Avery's only request had been to take care of their family, and their children needed him to be strong.

"They have a private waiting room ready for us. It's gonna be a while." Kane looked down at Autumn. Their daughter had always looked so much like Avery—she had his eyes and mannerisms. The thought tugged at his heart and filled him with pride at the same time.

He wrapped an arm around her lean shoulders, letting her guide him out the door.

"He said he would be back. He wasn't done with us." Kane smiled, trying for playful, possibly falling short as Autumn wrapped both her arms around him, giving him a tighter hug as they walked down the quiet hospital hallway.

"I know. Robert's here. Daddy, he's got the best care he can get." His strong, smart, beautiful thirty-four-year-old daughter was worried. He could tell by the small quiver in her voice.

"I know, baby...I know." They entered the small waiting room provided for high profile guests. Avery was almost as high as it got in this small community they lived in.

"I brought fresh water and a fruit tray. There's a restroom right through this door. Can I get you anything else?" a young woman asked from the doorway.

"No, we're fine. Thank you," Kane said, going straight to the window along the back wall. A nice view of a park sat right outside. Normally, Kane would have loved that. He had always loved taking his children to the park to play, but today he stared outside, not caring about the view in the least. Autumn pushed a chair up behind him.

"Sit, Daddy. You have to take care. Dad's gonna need you to take care of yourself, since he can't. He fusses over you as much as you fuss over him, and I'll be in trouble if he finds out I didn't do what he thinks I'm supposed to do for you." Kane let her fuss in Avery's place. A distraction to keep her mind occupied. Avery did that too. When something weighed heavily on him, he always threw himself into another project whether it be cleaning house or yard work, he found something to expend his nervous energy.

Even though their children were well into their thirties, they were a tight-knit family. All four of them were very close still today, and if something happened to Avery, it would shake them all to the core. The sobering thought had Kane taking a seat, still staring out the window. He could hear the silent prayer still unconsciously ringing through his head.

"I remember the birthday party we had at the park in Stillwater. What was I, like six years old? I loved that birthday party," Autumn said from directly behind him. He couldn't help the smile that touched his lips as he thought about that day.

"That was Avery's very bad idea." His smile grew wider and a slight shiver ran up his spine as he remembered the blistering cold wind. Who had an outdoor birthday party, in early March, in Stillwater, Minnesota? No one but them.

"It's one of my fondest memories. Robert's too, we talked about it just last week. Here's a bottle of water." Kane stayed in memory lane, letting his thoughts get lost in the moment. The small prayer pushed back to the forefront, taking up residence in his mind.

Please, God, don't take him from me. Not yet.

"Daddy, tell me again how you and Dad met. It's my favorite story." Kane looked up as she pulled her chair closer to his at the window. She took his hand, threading their fingers together.

"Tell me. I haven't heard the story in years. I want you to tell me now," she said, nodding, frantic tears finally welling up in her amber eyes. Avery's eyes. She worked hard to try and distract him, as well as herself, and he needed to let her. He gripped her hand tighter as he thought back all those years ago.

Chapter 2

"How in the hell did I let them talk me into this?" Avery said aloud to no one as he walked through his somewhat small, yet highly decorated, one bedroom condominium in downtown Minneapolis. He knew the answer, but still let the question take hold in his mind. The weather was just too damn cold outside to think of anything else.

Avery hadn't been back to Minnesota for any real length of time since he'd graduated from college over fifteen years ago. Even then, his choice to attend school in Minnesota was more of a public show of support; a family legacy kind of deal. All Minnesota had ever been to him was a place his family spent some of their summer months vacationing in a grand timber-framed getaway sitting along the St. Croix River. They had ridden horses, played in the fields, and shared dinners outside on the patio watching the boats drift by, which was rare quality time considering his prominent fast-paced family lifestyle.

The Adams ancestry had claimed their Minnesota land back in the settlers' days. Thousands and thousands of acres bordering Canada and it was all passed down from generation to generation. The roots of Avery's family tree ran deep in this state from all the way back to the fur-trading and logging days. He still owned all that land today. The upkeep was expensive as hell, and he couldn't remember the last time anyone spent time there, but the Adamses were considered the first family of Minnesota.

This state was the foundation that catapulted his grandfather to win his bid and become the beloved two-term president of the United States. As it turned out, Washington DC was the only thing that could entice an Adams out of Minnesota. They had never fully returned, apparently, until now.

It was clear why the Democratic Party picked Minnesota for Avery to begin his political career, between his family's roots and the progressively liberal attitude of the state, he was a shoo-in. What he couldn't understand was how he had ever been talked into tossing his hat in next year's Senate race. His own father, Alan Adams, had grown up in the White House and never had anything good to say about the experience. Alan chose business over politics, taking their family wealth into the multi-millions over the course of his life. His grandfather and father were both movers and shakers in their own chosen fields, yet neither could outrun the heredity of heart disease. Their deaths at reasonably young ages were the main reason Avery lived his life in such a way that he never took anything too seriously. Again, apparently until now.

His mother had taken over the reins of the family's holdings. At the time, it had been a natural step. She already ran much of their family business during his father's overseas travels. His mom was progressive, one of the most influential women in the world, and stood poised to make her own mark in the worldwide fight for women's rights. Kennedy Adams was really quite untouchable and currently sat aboard a yacht, coasting the Caribbean, technically where Avery figured he should be at this very moment.

Instead, he had opened his new Minnesota law office. His official campaign office would open next week when they made the big announcement. No time for coasting the Caribbean in his near future. These decisions were made. Besides, overall, politics fit him far better than business. Avery had an innate ability of understanding the hardships of the world, reading a situation for what it was and connecting to those involved. For whatever reason, people liked him.

This wasn't a decision forced on him. He'd weighed the options and felt this path would serve him best. Avery wanted this. He wanted to give back to this great country. To help people, and move the United States forward again. It was an honor to be back in Minnesota.

No matter what the outside thermometer read.

He tossed his scarf around his neck and tucked the ends inside his overcoat before he ran his hands through his thick blond hair, pushing one stray piece back in place. No more sunny beaches for him. No more surfing or weekends spent sunning on his boat. Soon, his deep tan would fade and that seemed okay too.

Avery ducked out his front door, bypassed the elevator, and took the stairs down to the main level. Once outside, he let the crisp night breeze take his breath away. He had reservations at La Bella Luna, an Italian restaurant just down the street. It was part of the "be seen" phase of his political run, and apparently La Bella Luna was the current place in town to be seen.

The biting cold had Avery jogging the short distance to the restaurant after deciding a cab might be too girly of a move for the short walk, only a block or so away. A young, good-looking man met him at the front doors. He pushed them open before Avery reached the first step. Recognition hit the man's face, so did the big grin.

"Good evening, Mr. Adams. Can I take your coat?" Avery almost denied him, still freezing from his short stint outside, but the guy was worth the extra minute.

"Thank you, it's still so cold outside," Avery said, accepting the small ticket and giving the greeter a genuine grin as he ran his hands up and down his arms.

"Yes, sir. It'll be another month before we see a real warm up. The maître d' is to your right. I believe you're right on time for your reservation. We didn't know if the name was a coincidence or not. I promise the restaurant's warm and toasty. They placed you close to the fireplace." As the man spoke, he gave off some of those telltale signs he might be interested. The hint was something in the way the guy stared straight back at him, not in any overt mannerism. Just a casual indication, which was the way Avery liked best. He liked his men to be subtly direct.

All of the sudden, this night out was taking a turn in a positive direction. Avery would need to be discreet. Although running in Minnesota was a safe bet, no one in the Democratic Party knew for sure how this would go with Avery being unmarried and his sexuality in question. Hell, it wasn't in question for him. He was gay. But the days of the beach volleyball tournaments turning into all night sexual conquests were over. The new trends in nationwide mass media coverage required his sexual encounters be discreet or be plastered all over the news.

Yet, this greeter, built like a small brick house, was two buildings over from his condo. Why couldn't hot-greeter-guy make a quick stop by Avery's place after he got off work tonight? A quick in and out kind of thing, all under the cover of complete darkness. Avery could see no reason why that wouldn't work just fine for both of them. As the front door opened behind him, Avery gave a knowing wink and moved on to the maître d'. He'd have this all worked out before he left the restaurant tonight, of that he was certain.

Avery looked back over his shoulder as he was taken to his table. The greeter stood there watching him walk away. Good step forward in closing this deal. They made brief eye contact and Avery grinned. A good Italian meal and some hot sex afterward…damn, this was turning out to be a good night after all.

* * * *

"We're turning people away, boss," DeWayne, the maître d' said, pivoting on his heels as Kane passed by with a handful of dirty plates.

"No room anywhere? Are you certain?" Kane whispered back. He never stopped moving toward the kitchen. DeWayne reached out to push open the swinging doors, letting Kane go through first.

"Absolutely, boss." DeWayne stood there as a busboy hurriedly relieved Kane of the dishes.

"Our guests must be lingering. I'll get them moving. What else?" Kane asked, already on the move back out into the restaurant's dining room.

"Just that and the Adams reservation is the real deal." DeWayne grinned at that one, extending his hand for their customary "give 'em five" hand slap. He'd been with the restaurant from the beginning. Now, only a few short years later, they were officially serving the most upper-crust clientele this community had to offer. No one got much higher than the current guest at table thirty-four.

"You're positive?" Kane questioned, coming to a complete stop, letting the door swing back closed in front of him. He only then lifted his hand for a halfhearted slap.

"Abso-fucking-lutely!" DeWayne was former military from the Bronx. It had taken years to break him of the accent, which still came back with full force when they were behind closed doors.

"Get Markie right on him. Have someone take his other tables. I want thirty-four watched closely. We want him to come back. His presence is excellent for business." Kane's heart hammered in his chest with excitement, but the outward calm slid back in place. Always the professional, he diverted from his intended path of the wine cellar and flipped around, heading back toward the kitchen to alert the staff. An Adams in his restaurant! How cool was that?

"Yes, sir!" Dewayne called out, letting the door swing in his wake.

Since the restaurant was booked up tight, Kane now had two immediate objectives. One, get the diners who were finished, up and out the door to free the table space. And two, personally greet table thirty-four.

"Paulie, thirty-four is extreme VIP," Kane shouted, ducking his head inside the second set of swinging doors. They were now tucked deep inside the restaurant, preventing anyone in the dining room from hearing all the noise coming from the kitchen. With intense efficiency, the entire kitchen staff was in full work mode. Paulie ran a tight ship, and everyone toed the line, working together to process each meal as quickly as possible to La Bella Luna's exacting standards.

"Got it!" Paulie's scratchy old voice boomed, but he never looked up from the chocolate design he currently piped on top of his signature terra mousse dessert.

"We're turning people away," Markie said from somewhere behind him.

"I'm aware. Did DeWayne tell you about thirty-four?" Kane asked, letting those kitchen doors swing shut—he didn't want to interrupt their established flow more than necessary—and turned to Markie.

"Yes, sir! He ordered Brunello di Montalcino."

"I'll have it at the bar, waiting," Kane said, pivoting on his heel, making his way toward the wine cellar for the special request. La Bella Luna had the largest selection of Italian wines in the United States. If the wine was available on the market, Kane stocked it.

The behind the scenes hustle and bustle died away as Kane took the stairs down, two at a time, to the wine cellar below the restaurant. The idea of turning business away gnawed at him. He couldn't spend too much time reveling in the accomplishment of getting an Adams in the restaurant. He needed to focus on the table turnover. That would require finesse to convince the diners it was their idea to leave so quickly after they finished their meal. Lingering was a lovely problem to have, unless you were the one waiting for a reserved table.

A small smile crossed his lips. His little restaurant was booked up tight and turned people away. What a better problem to have than having empty tables every night, and quite an achievement for a small-town boy from Alabama. Kane absently worked the keypad, opening the cellar, before scanning the rows of wine, looking for the requested brand.

"Sir, you asked me to let you know when Mr. Adams arrived. He's here and greeted," Rodney, his bartender, said from behind him as he continued to scan the bottles. He and Paulie were the only other ones who were allowed access to the wine cellar.

"I've been told. Here, take this up. It's for Markie. He's working thirty-four tonight," Kane said, carefully handing the bottle of wine to the bartender before turning back to find his next selection.

"Ten-four, boss." Just like DeWayne, Rodney was ex-military. Both of their jobs in the restaurant were Paulie's doing. He always hired any veteran that came looking for a job. It didn't matter if they had a position open or not. Paulie took them in, worked with them personally until any hard accents and rough edges were hidden, and refined manners were in place. For the success of the restaurant, those were critical balances to achieve. The La Bella Luna clientele required a gentle, sophisticated atmosphere.

"Thank you," Kane said absently and grabbed the next bottle before following Rodney back upstairs. A quick stop by the bar had Kane uncorking the special bottle of Merlot, and he decided to serve the wine himself. The local chief of police celebrated his thirty year wedding anniversary tonight. Kane wound his way to their table, going through all the steps of proper wine serving protocol, until the bottle was accepted. Kane poured both glasses, the entire time discreetly keeping an eye on table thirty-four.

Markie was on his game, staying attentive yet subtle, but for some reason, the menu was still on the table. Enough time had passed that the dinner order should have been taken. He was certain Paulie would be in the kitchen, waiting, probably having a fit by now that the order hadn't come through. Kane squared his shoulders and relaxed his stance, as he headed back toward to the bar. He did a quick scan of his reflection in a back mirror, making sure his suit lay just right and his close-cropped hair wasn't out of place.

"You look fine, Kane," Rodney said, only glancing over his shoulder as he worked his drink orders.

"He's a big one, the town's buzzing about him being back home. Keep his glass full and make sure we get him a ride if he drinks too much," Kane said.

"Like you aren't gonna be monitoring that yourself," Rodney shot back with a smirk, keeping his voice low and out of earshot of other guests. Kane chuckled, Rodney was right, he would definitely be monitoring the Adams table tonight. Like so many times before, he wound his way from the back of the restaurant into the dining room to greet their very important guest.

Kane scanned each table as he passed by. He nodded in greeting, making sure not to interrupt anyone as he made eye contact with the various regulars. He stopped a couple of waitstaff as he went and quietly gave instructions to fill drink glasses or remove empty plates. He continued that pace until his eyes landed on the corner booth, the one with a blond head sticking over the top of the bench seat.

Mr. Adams faced away from the room with his eyes focused on the front door. Kane mentally willed himself to remember if this was a dinner reservation for one or two. The best he could recall, the reservation was a party of one, but things changed. Perhaps that accounted for the delay in taking the dinner order. Kane looked up quickly toward the front, didn't see anything out of the ordinary, and turned his gaze down to the table. He saw a half-filled glass of wine and watched as Markie arrived again to take the dinner order. *Good.* Kane slowed his pace, letting the man give the waiter his order before he approached the table.

Chapter 3

The restaurant was packed, but not as thoroughly as Avery expected for such a prime piece of downtown property. The restaurant easily took up two, if not three, full lease spaces, with no table set close to another. Three of the inside walls were filled with luxury, oversized booth-style seating. Each was plush, covered in the softest leather and could easily seat a party of six, yet more than cozy enough to fit a lone patron. Large planters and hanging lanterns separated each booth with measurable space. The tables in the middle of the restaurant were situated in much the same way. They were easily ten feet apart. Plants, wine racks, and Italian décor had been placed strategically around the fine room, making sure every person encountered the same bit of privacy.

He could see why La Bella Luna had done so well. It wasn't the cattle call, serve as many as you could kind of establishment. Each guest experienced fine dining of a magnitude Avery had become accustomed to in other parts of the world, but had never chanced upon here in Minnesota.

By the looks of the price-less menu, this would be an expensive meal. Avery figured he'd be dropping a hundred dollars on his meal and bottle of wine, but if the food was anywhere close to the magic of the ambiance, it may be worth the cost. Honestly though, for Avery's taste, high-end elegance didn't hold much appeal. However, the view at the front door was a different story and easily held most of his interest.

Focusing on the greeter probably wasn't the best move for his see and be seen instruction. But the hot-greeter-guy would open the front doors to the restaurant every time anyone walked up, making himself a slide show of broad, beefy chest and then nice firm ass. Avery would hold his gaze in between those greeting responsibilities. They smiled at one another, winked, and as every minute passed, he was closer to sealing the deal for later this evening.

It sure seemed like a safe bet he'd be having greeter-guy sex in the next few hours. Perhaps if he worked things right, sex might even happen sooner. Avery loved the idea of being discreetly tucked away somewhere in this restaurant, getting to know the greeter a little more intimately. The chance of getting caught always added a bit of intensity, making the sex slightly frantic. He liked it hard and fast, and this place had more than enough darkened corners to pull something like that off.

His waiter popped into his line of sight, again rambling off several specials for the night. Avery figured he'd stalled long enough; they were ready for his order. He paid closer attention this time, and as the waiter spoke, Avery guessed Italian might actually be his second language. If not, he was trained well. Avery picked one of the three specials, easily letting the dish's name slide off his lips. After he finished ordering, he inclined his head, his eyes returning to the front door. Greeter-guy had vanished while he gave his order. That left Avery staring at an oak door with nothing else between his table and the entryway to occupy him as the waiter slid quietly away. Now the error of sitting in this direction sank in. This wasn't the best move for a man who sat alone.

More importantly, Avery's conscience finally made its presence known. He had to scold himself. Damn, he hated putting the reins on his good time, but United States senator wannabes, who already had a questionable past, sure didn't sneak off and have bathroom sex in a public restaurant. That came after he was elected, certainly not before.

"Good evening. I wanted to introduce myself. I'm Kane Dalton, owner of La Bella Luna. I wanted to personally thank you for stopping in tonight. Please let me know if there is anything you need." Avery looked up to see one of the best-looking men he'd ever laid eyes on standing before him. *Fuck!* He lost his breath, his heart slammed against his chest. He should shake the offered hand, but he couldn't move. All he could do was stare stupidly as the man continued to speak. He had never expected to find this restaurant's owner so young and handsome. For some reason, he'd pictured a much older, portly gentleman, maybe a transplant to the region. God, had he been wrong.

Kane Dalton was masculine, yet incredibly refined. Long and lean and very well groomed, not a strand of his dark hair out of place. His face held a strong chiseled jaw, high angular cheekbones with a smooth, clear complexion all leading to a perfect nose and extraordinarily kissable lips. Kane's eyes were downcast; he'd withdrawn his hand and was working something at the table now. Avery felt denied with those eyes not on him as he stared openly at Kane, taking in all that he could of the gorgeous restaurateur.

He could see hints of a fine sculpted body underneath a suit that looked handmade just for him. He should say something; maybe compliment him on his fine establishment and the delicious smells coming from the kitchen. What he really wanted to do was learn more about this man who just completely captivated him. Kane had stunned him. So much so Avery paused again; his words wouldn't come. He spoke to people all day long, every day. But for the first time in his life, the easy flow of conversation eluded him.

He stared openly at the exquisite man who seemed to rip his soul wide open without so much as trying.

Avery watched as Kane took the bottle of wine from the bucket, never looking his way. Kane continued to speak with hints of a cultured Southern accent. His hands worked the bottle with care, gently wrapping a linen napkin around the base before he reached out and poured the wine. His movements were precise yet tender. Every part of this man showed a poised, sophisticated gentleman, and Avery immediately wanted those strong hands to caress him, to touch him with that exact same care.

Avery's breath hitched as he looked up, his eyes colliding with a sky blue gaze, and he stopped breathing altogether while his heart drummed violently in his chest. He was having a moment like he'd never experienced in his life. He couldn't think, he couldn't speak, all he could do was stare, and Kane seemed as unaffected as Avery was affected.

Avery could see Kane registered his lack of response. Kane nodded, giving a polite smile as he carefully placed the wine bottle back inside the bucket. Avery tracked every movement, willing himself to breathe before he passed out in the booth and embarrassed himself even more.

"Avery Adams, is that you? I can't believe it!" the shrill voice echoed, and a bubbly woman came straight to the table, almost pushing Kane out of the way. Avery was forced to look over at the woman he could not recall ever seeing before, and his gaze slid back to Kane.

"If you'll excuse me," Kane said with another polite almost bow. He never again made eye contact with Avery. From the angle Avery had chosen to sit, he couldn't continue watching Kane without being overtly obvious, but after a second of losing Kane's image, Avery decided obvious was better than not watching the man at all. He twisted in his seat to turn his head fully around and stared at Kane's retreating form. He noticed the small roll of Kane's shoulders, a universal sign of loosening himself up. The material of Kane's fine suit stretched over his back, and Avery realized his poised elegant Kane was indeed hiding a hard, tight body underneath all those clothes.

It took a full minute for Avery to remember the woman standing at the front of his table. He recovered enough to paste the grin back on his face as he extended a hand. He didn't even try to place her. He just needed her to move on so he could find a way to get the owner back over to the table. "How are you?"

"Well, I'm just fine. I can't see how you would possibly remember me. I'm Sadie, my parents own the land right next to yours. We played some together during the summers when we were younger. I heard you were coming back home. I just wanted to stop by, say hello. My husband and I would love to have you over for dinner sometime soon." The woman spoke, all smiles and moving hands. She pointed to a table across the restaurant, and for the first time since she'd shown up, he wanted to hug her. It gave him the perfect excuse to move across the booth and face the man sitting at a table in the middle of the restaurant who awkwardly lifted a hand in his direction. Avery did the same.

"What a nice invitation..." was all he got out.

"Great. My husband and I own several of the properties downtown. We just used your law firm on one of the more recent deals. I'll make sure I give you a call to get that set up just as soon as you can fit us in. Avery, it's super good to see you again." She didn't wear out her welcome and left in the same way she came...abruptly. Better for him, as he'd much rather scan the restaurant looking for the hot proprietor.

* * * *

Kane kept his cool, letting all those long-standing walls drop into place as he walked through the restaurant. His outward calm showed nothing of the panic raging through his mind. The only clue he gave that something might be wrong was when he bypassed his waitstaff, not listening or answering one of their questions as he made a beeline directly to the kitchen.

His pleasant facade was nothing more than his body's natural defense mechanism kicking into place. Calm, cool, and collected were always what he projected to the world when his heart and mind raced completely out of control. And dear Lord did the greeting with Avery Adams, aka table thirty-four, seriously qualify as one hell of a stressful situation.

Kane pushed through the first set of double doors, leaving the tranquility of the dining room behind. The second set of doors opened to the bustling kitchen. Paulie, along with their head chef, Antonio, worked together on one single plate, trying to achieve their desired perfection before sending it out the door. Kane suspected that meal belonged to Avery Adams. Paulie's policy was any new VIP was treated with care until everyone got a feel for their likes and taste.

"You don't look so good." At Paulie's words, Kane jerked his head up to see the concerned glance Paulie sent his way. Paulie never stopped in the middle of the kitchen during peak business hours. Yet, he did this time. Whatever was on Kane's face caused a scowl to cross Paulie's, and the man stopped in mid-motion of taste-testing a sauce. After another solid few seconds of silence, he lowered the spoon. "What's happened?"

"I don't know. Nothing," Kane said, replaying the entire exchange he'd had with Avery Adams through his mind, trying to see what he might have done to cause such a reaction.

"Don't nothing me. What's happened?" Paulie asked, his tone gruffer than normal and anger clear on his face.

"We need to make sure dinner for thirty-four's perfect. I think I've misstepped somewhere. Mr. Adams seemed a little put out with my greeting," Kane said. As he spoke, he moved closer to where they were working, taking a good long look at the meal. Paulie knew him too well, and Kane's complete calm no doubt scared the crap out of him.

"What did you say?" Paulie asked suspiciously. The whole kitchen slowed, watching them closely, but Paulie wasn't having any of that. It was as if he had eyes in the back of his head. At five foot nothing, Paulie ran an efficient kitchen, and he barreled around, clapping his hands, motioning everyone back to work. This time, he moved Kane out of the way for privacy and lowered his voice. "What did you say?"

"I don't know. Just my normal greeting, I think. I'm not sure. He just wasn't into me at all," Kane said. He ran his palms down the front of his suit, before looking down at his hands, willing himself to shake off the unwanted feelings.

"Maybe it's Markie—he's the server, right?" Paulie asked, his voice a sharp, graveled whisper.

"Yes, but I didn't see anything out of place. I was watching before I ever approached the table. He worked it like clockwork." As if on cue, Markie came through the kitchen door, pushing into them.

"VIP plate ready?" he asked, looking between Paulie and Kane, his face showing immediate concern at their huddled meeting. "What's happened?"

"Are you taking care of thirty-four?" Paulie asked, still somewhat hushed. Paulie's hard Bronx accent was more pronounced with each passing second.

"Of course I'm taking care of the table," Markie shot right back, looking between Kane and Paulie. "What happened? He seems fine to me."

"So he's talking and participating. You're engaging him?" Kane asked.

"Yeah, why?" Kane stared hard at the waiter. They never had issues with Markie. Kane cut his eyes back down to Paulie.

"Then it's me. Stay on the table, I've upset him. I'll stay away. Comp his bottle of wine. I'll make it up in your tip," Kane said, forcing himself to remember the restaurant. Slowly, sound, reasonable thought trickled back in place. He was a business owner, not an emotional mess from a simple awkward greeting.

He turned away from the others, first walking to the sink, before he changed course and headed toward the back kitchen doors. He needed a minute alone to gather himself. Something was very wrong with this whole table thirty-four deal, and if he didn't get a hold of himself, he'd never make it through the night without another problem. And Kane never had problems like this. He worked too hard to head off these kinds of complications before they ever occurred.

"I need a minute," Kane said over his shoulder.

"What cha lookin' at? Get to work!" Kane heard Paulie call out. "Markie see if you can salvage the table. Of all people, we don't need him giving us a bad review out there. Get cha asses to work, people!"

Kane left the kitchen and didn't stop until he hit his office. He closed the door behind him, locking it before he gave in to the chaos coursing through him. This wouldn't do. This would never do. He tugged off his suit jacket and paced the small room. What the hell just happened to him? How had he managed to offend Avery Adams, on his very first visit no less. He was completely baffled by the way he'd been dismissed; Mr. Adams had ignored his offered hand and hadn't bothered to say a single word to him. What had he done to upset Avery Adams?

He scrubbed his hands over his face and then down the front of his slacks. Why would an upset patron affect him in this manner anyway? He only needed to figure out how to turn the evening around and ensure they had a pleasant experience. It wasn't until that moment he realized his cock was rigidly hard. Not the simple irritating hard-on that happened from time to time in life, but something ready to explode, and he had no idea how or why he had this reaction.

Kane panicked and immediately bent over, making sure he was tucked in, not sticking straight out. Maybe that was what turned Avery Adams off. Relief struck when he found he was hidden under his clothing.

Dang it, I'm attracted to Avery Adams.

"Pull it together, Kane Dalton. This is not a game. This is your life, and your burdens are too heavy to mess it all up now, especially over a man I just offended," Kane lectured himself as he scanned the top of his desk. He must find perspective. It would never do to have someone as high profile as a United States president's grandson avoiding his restaurant. Shoving papers aside on his very organized desk, he found the letter from his sister. It had arrived that morning in the mail.

He reread the entire letter as he dropped down in his office chair. His sister had been her normal short and to-the-point self, but never sweet. His mother was dying. No one in his family wanted him there.

In fact, her last dying wish was to make sure he didn't arrive and soil her funeral ceremony, but they needed money for her burial. This particular sister never minced words when she wrote to ask him for money. Never gave anything personal about herself or the rest of his family. She just said what needed to be said.

When he'd received this letter, he hadn't let himself believe his mom was actually dying. Even after fifteen years of not seeing his family, he still loved her dearly. Through all his mistakes, Kane still honored her and his father, even from a distance. This morning, after reading the straight-to-the-point letter, he closed himself in his office and prayed like his father taught him to do when he was a young boy. Kane was specific in his prayer. He prayed for her health and well-being, but he also prayed for God's will.

Only after his lengthy prayer session had he thought to pick up the phone and call the hospital. His efforts were in vain; his mom had passed away last night. Kane hadn't hesitated. He'd left the restaurant in the middle of dinner prep and gone immediately to wire money to his family. He sent more than they'd asked for, he always did. Then Kane called a local Alabama florist asking for a large standing spray full of yellow roses to be sent to her funeral, no card attached. In his heart, he knew his family would see the spray as a slight against their wishes, but his mother had always loved her rose garden. It was something the two of them shared throughout most of his childhood. He wanted her to have her yellow roses, regardless of the harsh letter he would certainly receive about the embarrassment the arrangement caused.

The tears that hadn't come earlier finally fell. His guard was down. Maybe this was why he'd been off his game tonight. Kane brushed away the tears that wouldn't stop flowing and dropped his head in his hands. All the things he wanted to say to his mother would now remain unsaid. The memories of his past came barreling forward, robbing him of his carefully placed resolve. When Kane was eighteen years old, freshly graduated from high school, he never imagined his life playing out like this.

At the time, he'd been kicked out of his house, he had the Lord's Prayer broken over his head—literally, the framed picture that had been hung in a place of honor by the front door was shattered across his skull—right after his brother dropped him to his knees with a couple of solid right hooks and his father shoved him out the front door with nothing more than the clothes on his back.

He supposed his father's sermon of tolerance, patience, and love, given that same morning in the Southern Baptist church where he pastored, didn't apply to his own family members. Kane should have known better. And for the love of God, he certainly shouldn't have picked the Sunday afternoon lunch to tell his large family he was gay. He still cringed today thinking about his own stupidity.

Fresh out of high school, tossed on the streets of a town with a population of no more than a couple thousand people, didn't leave too many options. He walked for days, slept in barns and old broken down vehicles, and starved as he made his way to Birmingham. Nothing more than pity and kindness made an Italian pizzeria owner give him a job. Three advantages came with that job. He got to eat, make money, and meet Paulie, the pizzeria owner. At that point in his life, the first two were high on his list of priorities.

By the fall, Kane found out his father had sabotaged his full scholarship to Oral Roberts Christian University in Tulsa. By then, he had worked sixteen hour days, seven days a week, and saved up a pile of money, but apparently he couldn't buy his way into the university. Those had been dark days. Every goal and dream of his future washed away because he had opened his stupid mouth and trusted his family with the truth about himself.

With Paulie's unwavering support, Kane even pulled himself up enough to get a little self-assured. That attitude was what gave him the strength and courage to actually follow through and fly to Italy, Paulie's homeland. Paulie taught him when one door closes, a window generally opens, and his saving grace came in the way of that little man who ran the La Bella Luna kitchen like a drill sergeant.

Without question, Paulie had saved his life. Kane would have none of this if it weren't for him. Paulie had lost his own son in the Vietnam War, and just like he had come to expect from the man's generous spirit, he had no problem taking on Kane as his own. They didn't share too many things in common, except for the most important one, the love of cooking. Paulie taught Kane everything he knew, and Kane found he had an innate understanding of food, a natural ability to blend and create delicious combinations.

When Paulie suggested he study in Italy, Kane jumped at the chance and enrolled in culinary school. Lord, he'd been so far behind compared to the other students' abilities, but he worked hard those years and eventually caught up, graduating with honors and many job opportunities. Paulie came to Italy for his graduation, watched him walk across the stage. Paulie had been so proud of him. That should have been enough, but secretly, it wasn't. The entire time he was in Italy, he sent monthly letters home to his family, begging for their forgiveness. He wrote passages to his family, trying to show them he held on to his parents' strong Christian values while making a decent life for himself. No one in his family ever responded to any of his letters. The only thing he ever got back from them was his father's scribbled penmanship marked across the envelope—return to sender.

Kane had reconciled himself a long time ago that Paulie was his family now, but as he sat in this office, the ache of missing his mom returned. In all honesty, he probably should have stayed home tonight. Given himself the day to grieve instead of believing he could push through, make everything all right if he just kept working. That had to be his problem tonight, too much weighed on his heart.

He leaned back in his chair and looked down at his crotch. Finally, a positive for the evening, his cock had settled down. And he couldn't help the harsh chuckle he gave. The past always had a way of knocking the wind out of his sails. Kane made a decision right then. He'd take it easy tonight. Stay hidden behind the scenes and completely away from the Adams table. He would maintain a quiet presence for his staff until closing.

Kane had comped the wine, and he would send a bouquet of flowers tomorrow apologizing to Mr. Adams for what he'd done— whatever that was. Certainly by tomorrow he would have a clear mind and could easily see what he had done wrong. Feeling like he had a solid plan in place, Kane left his office only to be met right outside the door by Randall, his door greeter.

"Justice Sawyer's leaving and wants a word with you." Kane nodded and forced the smile back onto his face.

"Thank you. I'll be right there." Kane would wear this smile the rest of the evening. Everything was all right. Tomorrow would be a new day. He squared his shoulders and went to find the justice. He was always good for a nice compliment or two.

"Did you see Avery Adams? He's a fox," Randall said, right on his heels.

"We need to be careful with him. Make sure he has everything he needs tonight," Kane said, rounding the corner back into the restaurant.

"I plan to," Randall mumbled as he slipped past Kane. Justice Sawyer met him at the bar before he could say anything more to the greeter. The man's big grin and compliments to the chef did help ease Kane's weary soul.

Chapter 4

Avery sat quietly, staring at the large mahogany desk in the center of his masculinely-decorated office. Dark cherry wood paneling covered every wall, with deep hunter green shag carpeting and dark red plaids covering the furniture. The drapes matched the furniture and were closed up tight, forbidding any sun from daring to peek inside this office. Avery found the entire room impossible to think within, and it seemed to zap his entire will to work.

He rose on a huff and stalked across the office. He tore open the curtains, letting the sunshine in. Avery turned back to the office as if he expected a miracle with the influx of light. How had the sun not helped the room look any better? *Damn.*

Avery pressed the intercom, his direct line to his secretary, and waited for her to answer. She was sharp and equally as quick, and just as he expected, she answered immediately. Janice had been with him for years, moving to cold Minnesota from sunny California to continue being his assistant. That loyalty said a lot.

"Yes, sir?" Her voice boomed through the small speaker into the quiet office.

"Can you find an interior designer to meet with me tomorrow? I can't think with all this brown. It's sucking my will to live," Avery said, holding the intercom button down on the phone as he spoke.

"Sure. I figured that was coming. I can arrange to have the company who decorated your office—" Avery stopped her.

"No, someone new. As a matter of fact, I'll handle this myself right now," he said. He'd fly his designer out from California. Surely he could pay her enough to get her up here to make changes to this god-awful place, something better suited to fit his taste.

Ignoring the files on his desk and meeting requests from the attorneys who worked for him, Avery dug through his Rolodex searching for his personal designer's telephone number. A thought crossed his mind. The handsome restaurant owner was completely his taste. Perhaps if Kane Dalton would just sit in this office, he might magically take away all this brown, and there was no doubt the man would definitely make the room look more inviting.

Avery took his seat, leaning back against the firm leather, and abandoned his task of finding the phone number for the moment. Instead, he twirled a ball point pen through his fingers as he thought about Mr. Dalton.

Avery hadn't been able to get Kane out of his mind. He stayed transfixed by the man, completely captivated. Even now, with all these case files lying untouched and work piling up around him, he still let his mind wander to the night he'd had dinner at La Bella Luna. He'd taken up residence in the small booth that evening, unwilling to give it up for several hours as he sat and mingled with some of the patrons that recognized him.

Avery told himself he was doing what the Democratic Party asked of him. Their great strategic plan of being seen out in the community and all that, but he knew the real truth. He only had eyes for Kane and yet Kane seemed to have eyes for everyone else but him.

They never crossed paths again for the remainder of the evening. Avery left, not even taking the blatant offer made by the greeter. Yesterday, a large bouquet of calla lilies arrived, with an apology note attached on behalf of the restaurant. It was a simple, generic apology. The kind he himself gave over the years when he had no idea what he had done wrong, the gesture meant to soothe ruffled feathers. It gave Avery a clue as to why the owner hadn't come back to his table no matter how long he stayed or how much money he'd spent. Perhaps Avery's awestruck moment had been interpreted as hostile instead of the true fact—he'd been undone by the man standing in front of him.

"Mr. Adams, you aren't paying attention to me," Janice said from the doorway.

"Of course I am. I'm just pretending to ignore you," Avery immediately shot back, turning toward her with a sheepish grin on his face.

"Good! Then you're agreeing to double my salary with a nice six months of vacation every year?" she said, cocking a severely arched eyebrow. He ignored her comment and went straight to his agenda.

"Did you get me bi-weekly reservations at La Bella Luna?" he asked.

"See? You didn't hear a word I said. I move halfway around the world, to the coldest place on the planet, and you pay as little attention to me now as you did before. You don't need me. You could ignore anyone just as effectively," she said, and he could tell she was a little put out as she entered his office uninvited, taking a seat across the desk from him.

"Now, that's not true. You are far easier to ignore than most people I've met along the way. Now answer my question, am I scheduled?" Avery teased, kicking back farther in his seat.

"No, sir. They're booked up solid for several months. The best I could get was to randomly fit you in. I put the dates on your calendar," she said and pointed to his Day-Timer. He rarely looked at his calendar, as it was her job to keep him on task. He never made that easy for her.

"So when's my next reservation?" Avery asked. The twirling of the ballpoint pen came to an abrupt halt as his brow narrowed.

"Not for a couple of weeks. I think three weeks from tomorrow, but you could open your Day-Timer and check yourself," she said, trying for funny and falling short, at least in his estimation, but clearly not hers as evidenced by the big, bright smile she sported.

"Not soon enough. Do you have their number?" Avery asked, opening the drawers to his desk, trying to find the hidden phone book.

"I can get it, but Avery, what are you thinking? You know they said to be discreet. That look in your eye and the way you've been acting is anything but discreet," Janice lectured. She wasn't old enough to be his mother, but she held that motherly tone.

"And how have I been acting?" he asked, not really caring how she answered.

"Preoccupied. Not focusing on work, and if I didn't know better, I'd say perhaps even a man in love," she said, and gave a little chuckle as she tried to get the last thought out.

He ignored her completely.

"Screw discreet! Have you been to this place?" Avery asked, plopping the giant, oversized phone book on the desk, thumbing through the pages.

"No, but a better use of your time might be to go through these case files. You're sitting in on the meetings—" Janice started, but Avery cut her off.

"Stay on task, Janice. We're discussing La Bella Luna. The place has shockingly, unbelievably delicious authentic Italian cuisine. You need to go," Avery said, looking down the long list of restaurants in the city.

"But you've never been a big fan of Italian," Janice shot back.

"It's the atmosphere," Avery said, flipping a page before resuming his search.

"It's a guy," she said flatly.

"He's in the atmosphere." Avery did look up at her, giving her a cheeky grin as he tried to sway her with his charm, but she didn't bend. Besides, he decided a long time ago, it couldn't be easy to sit so straight in that formal business suit, legs crossed so properly, and not be in a bad mood most of the time.

"I knew it! Avery, just be careful. You have a serious chance to follow in your grandfather's footsteps..." Janice started with the lecture again.

"That's debatable." Avery stopped her by picking up the phone and dialing the number he'd located in the book.

"So the flowers weren't an apology?" Janice asked in defeat.

"No, they were," Avery said, clearly confusing her. As he waited for someone to answer the phone, he gave Janice his most cocky grin, a very clear watch-me-get-what-I-want expression.

"La Bella Luna, can I help you?" The deep rich timbre turned him on instantly, and his gaze strayed to the corner of his desk, Janice completely forgotten.

"Good Morning, this is Avery Adams. Who do I have the pleasure of speaking with?" He already knew the answer, he just wanted to hear Kane's voice again. Avery thought about Kane's hands and how competently he'd handled that bottle of wine. He imagined them using the same care as he picked up the phone from the cradle. The air in the room sizzled, his heartbeat picked up, and his body grew hard with need. He had never in his life been so immediately taken with another. Avery prayed Kane might be at least bi-sexual. Straight men were much harder to work into his bed—not impossible, but harder—and he definitely wanted Kane Dalton in his bed.

"Hello, Mr. Adams. This Kane Dalton, would you prefer I transfer this call to someone else?" The soothing voice on the other end of the phone became tense.

"No, you're who I was hoping to speak with. It seems you and I may have gotten off on the wrong foot, and I'd like to set things right between us," Avery said, adjusting his gaze to stare out the open window.

"I have no issue with you, sir," Kane responded back immediately.

"There's a large bouquet of rather expensive lilies sitting in my office that might say otherwise." He cut his eyes back to the flowers on the small conference table. Kane didn't respond this time, there was just silence. Good. Kane got a taste of his own medicine. "Listen, I'd like to book a regular table in your restaurant a couple of days a week. It doesn't have to be the same days each week, but I thoroughly enjoyed myself a few nights ago and got reacquainted with several families from my youth." He was met with more silence, then he heard the rustle of pages being turned.

"Sir, I'm sorry, but I just don't have—"

"I'll make it worth your while." Avery cut him off, his eyes still on the flowers, but seeing the man who sent them instead of the lovely blooms.

"It's not that, sir. We're just incredibly booked." Kane started with the excuses again, but Avery wasn't taking no for an answer.

"Please lose the sir. My name's Avery. I'd like you to use it." Avery's voice turned lower and huskier as he spoke from his deepest desires.

"Avery," Kane said as if testing the word. "We don't have the space available. We're booked solidly for several months."

"No one's that booked," Avery called him on the lie, and left it right there between them.

After a long extended pause, Kane finally answered, "You're right, let's get you in Monday and Wednesday evenings. Does that suit you?"

"You sure do," Avery said. Now that he'd managed a firm reservation, it was time to draw Kane in. Not surprisingly, he was met with silence. "I'll take whatever days you offer." *In fact, I'll take whatever you are willing to give.* As the thought faded, Avery realized those were actually terrible days to be seen out and about.

"Seven o'clock?" Kane asked, ignoring everything he said.

"Whatever works," Avery replied.

"All right, would you like to come in tomorrow night?" Kane asked. His tone was back to all business.

"Absolutely!"

"Great. Thank you for choosing La Bella Luna." Avery could hear the pages turning again on whatever Kane was working from.

"Thank you, Kane," Avery said. There was silence again. The breathing he heard through the phone was the only indication that the other man lingered on the line.

"I'll see you tomorrow night." With that Avery hung up. It took a full minute for him to remember his secretary remained in the office as he rested there with the small smile plastered on his face, still looking at the bouquet. God, it was amazing how badly he wanted this to work out with a man who gave zero indication he was even gay, much less interested. He finally cut his eyes back to Janice, who sat there in her stiff way, a smug look on her pinched face. Maybe her face wasn't pinched, but for this moment, he decided it was the best way to describe her.

"He doesn't know what's about to hit him, does he?" she finally said, bouncing her high-heeled foot.

"It sure doesn't seem so," he said, dropping the phone book back inside the drawer. Now that he had Kane Dalton within his grasp, it was time to work. He looked down at the stacks of files on his desk.

"Watch yourself, Avery," Janice said. Why was she still in his office? He never looked up at her.

"I always do." He picked the first file of the bunch and flipped it open.

"This one's more important than the others," Janice said.

"Perhaps. Maybe not. We'll see." Avery still refused to look up. Maybe she would get the hint sooner or later. He was done with this conversation.

"That smile you're wearing says it all. Just so you know, I'm with you no matter what. I work for you, not the campaign, not the party." Those words surprised him.

"Thank you. That means a lot. Don't tell my mother," Avery joked.

"Got it, mum's the word." Janice left the office, shutting the door behind her.

Chapter 5

"Fly out this weekend. You have to see this. It's beautiful here," Brian said on a telephone line filled with static. He was a pilot for a private jet charter company that currently worked for a large land developer in Dubai.

"I can't. You're halfway around the world. I can't be gone that long," Kane said, somewhat distracted while working the ledgers from last night's sales. Kane's entire focus shifted as he flipped through the pages, trying to find the to-date annual totals for the restaurant this year. The best he could tell, they were right on course, increasing steadily. If he could keep this pace, the property La Bella Luna sat on would truly be his in a matter of a couple of years. Then Kane could focus on buying the investors out and be truly independent for the first time in his life.

"Did I lose you? Or are you not listening?" Brian asked, irritation clear in his voice.

"No, I'm here, I'm listening," Kane responded, trying to remember what they were talking about.

"No, you're not. Look, Kane, I've been thinking. This isn't working out for me anymore," Brian said. It wasn't the whiney way he normally used when he tried to manipulate Kane.

"Wait, what? You just wanted me to fly out," Kane shot back.

"It was a test. You failed. I'm tired of being alone and you being distant all the damn time. I've followed all your stupid little rules. I've stuck around for years being monogamous and I still can't get you to open up to me. It's too much. You're too much. I think we need to end this and go our separate ways."

"Brian, no. I'll do better. Maybe I can swing flying out next week, during the week." Kane immediately went to his desk calendar, searching the days for a good time to leave. Brian was his first real relationship. His first time at having a regular sex partner, and he didn't want to let that go so easily.

"Don't worry about it. Look, I've met someone. I wasn't looking, I swear, he just came out of nowhere, and I don't wanna string you along. I know how important all your rules are to you. I can't live that life anymore. I don't want to live that life. You need to loosen up, man. I gotta go. Take care. When I get back, I'll pick up whatever I have over at your place. You know what? Never mind, just keep it. You never let me leave much there anyway. Take care." The call ended, but Kane sat there several long minutes before he placed the receiver back on its cradle. This shouldn't have come as a surprise. Kane didn't have time for a relationship, and for those few men willing to take him on with all his religious baggage, it was even harder.

It had been hard reconciling his religious beliefs with his body's most basic needs. At twenty-five years old, Kane had caved and had pre-marital sex for the first time in his life. Emotionally, that act had cost him, but physically it was exactly what he'd needed. Kane wholeheartedly believed in the sanctity of marriage before having sex. Just because you had one sin working for you, didn't mean you had to have two, but it seemed no one else on the planet agreed with him. Desperate need finally outweighed his morals, and as soon as he was alone afterward, he had cried. Like a girl.

"Kane, the flowers haven't been delivered." Paulie stuck his head inside Kane's office door, looked at him more closely, and walked all the way inside the office, shutting the door behind him. Concern was etched on his face. "What's wrong, Son?

"Nothing really, Brian and I just broke up. I'll call about the flowers." Kane cast his eyes down to the ledgers, trying hard to act as if it were no big deal. He didn't really know how he felt about Brian, he guessed he loved him. He'd said he loved him when Brian pressed him to. There was an ache in his heart, and he stopped what he was doing and ran a hand over his face, rubbing his eyes. First his mom, now Brian. Not a good week at all. He hadn't told Paulie about his mother, about the money he sent, or how heavily the problem with Mr. Adams's dinner had actually weighed on him.

Desperate for a mental stress relief, Kane reasoned that things generally happened in sets of three, so he should be done, and he reached for his Rolodex to follow up on the flower delivery.

"I'm sorry, Son, but he wasn't right for you. You know that," Paulie said, taking a seat across the desk. Kane could feel Paulie reading him, seeing straight through his carefully placed omissions.

"I know you didn't like him, but I did." Kane picked up the phone and began to dial. The time had to be near five, the flowers should have arrived, but there wasn't cause for alarm yet. They still had thirty minutes to set the centerpieces and entryway flowers.

"You've had a crap week. First your mother, now Brian. He's a piece of shit for dumping you this week, just like I always said he was," Paulie said, his voice losing the tender quality he'd used seconds before. He jerked off his chef's hat, slammed it against his knee, and scrubbed his hands through his short gray hair.

"How do you know about my mom?" Kane cut his eyes up to the old man as he punched the last number into the dial pad.

"And the money you sent? I have my ways," Paulie said, angling his hat, crooked, back on his head.

"Brian didn't know about my mom," Kane said as the phone began to ring.

"Exactly my point! A man in a relationship shouldn't feel the need to keep secrets. You should have felt comfortable enough to call him and let him comfort you." Paulie was on a roll, pointing his finger, his voice rising. The true, expressive Italian side of his personality always ready to pop out at any given moment. Kane lifted a hand, trying to stop him from turning this into a lecturing rant.

"It's over, so there's no need to keep rehashing." Kane was momentarily interrupted from the conversation when the florist answered his call. "Hello, this is Kane over at La Bella Luna. I'm calling about our flowers for today." He kept his eyes on Paulie as the young woman on the other end assured him they would be there soon, they were just a little behind today. He thanked her and disconnected the call with Paulie still clearly waiting for some sort of response from him. Kane had no idea what to say and finally sat back, again scrubbing the frustration away from his face. Paulie knew him too well.

"They say it comes in threes. That was my third, so maybe it's over," Kane said, peeking at Paulie through the spread fingers covering his face.

"What's the third one?" Paulie asked, speculation on his face.

"I thought you knew everything," Kane teased back.

"I do, but remind me. I'm an old man with an old man's brain," Paulie shot back, and Kane barked out a laugh at that one. Paulie was as sharp as a tack, nothing got past him.

"Sure you did, and whatever, there's nothing old about that brain of yours! The third one was the bad customer experience this week. It stuck with me. It's been a long time since we hadn't met a customer's expectations." Kane was back to smiling. Paulie always had a way of doing this to him. He just eased every burden Kane ever carried.

"You resolved it. Standing reservation, twice a week on our slowest nights doesn't seem too bad," Paulie tossed back, standing again.

"I don't know, Paulie. There just seems something more to it." Kane lifted his arms, pushing them above his head, stretching out the tension of the last few minutes.

"Well, buck up and get dressed. The kitchen's ready, waitstaff's arriving, and the dining room's almost perfect, we just need those damn flowers." As if on cue, the back door buzzed.

"That should be them," Kane said, rising.

"Get dressed, Son, and let that pantywaist go. You need better than that. I can't die until I know you're taken care of, and you weren't ever gonna be taken care of with that one," Paulie said, swinging the office door back open.

"First, you aren't gonna die. Second, I can take care of myself!" Kane called out after him.

"Pfft," came through loud and clear as the office door slammed shut. His suit rattled on the hook behind the door, reminding him it was time to change for the night. Honestly, if Brian had been so important to him, why had he taken such special care in picking out this evening's wardrobe to impress a man who couldn't even utter a simple acknowledgement? He couldn't deny he'd been attracted to Avery Adams, his hard-on that night spoke volumes, but why should it matter how he looked if he was truly emotionally attached to Brian? No more stalling. The restaurant would open in about thirty minutes.

It was show time.

Chapter 6

Two brand new designer suits lay on his bed. One, the latest in Yves Saint Laurent's fall collection, and the other, a classic black from Hugo Boss. Avery looked over both of them with a still damp terry cloth towel wrapped around his waist. He couldn't decide which would be better for tonight. The latest casual style or the fallback black he always chose to wear when he wanted to represent well.

Avery padded across the plush carpet to his walk-in closet, pulling out a light purple dress shirt, along with two of the new satin neckties delivered earlier in the day. Both were of the season's most current colors, and on a backward thought, he grabbed a hanger with a solid white silk dress shirt. He carefully paired the shirts with the coordinating suits and laid the ties on each one before switching them, only to switch them back again.

"Damn it," he muttered as he stepped back to look at both designs. He'd never had a problem dressing himself. Frustrated, Avery grabbed his telephone on the nightstand and called his personal designer in California.

"Hello," she answered on the first ring.

"Colleen, the black Hugo Boss or the gray Yves Saint Laurent?" Avery didn't try to add to his lack of polite pleasantries. He got right down to business.

"For your dinner tonight?" Colleen was the only person on the planet who knew how important this dinner was to him. She'd worked feverishly with the local department store to get several new suits to him. They were tailored to his exact measurements, proving she could move small mountains.

"Yep," Avery said, still eyeing both, his foot tapping out his anxiety while he awaited her suggestion.

"Gray, if you haven't worn gray there before," she said quickly and efficiently. "Did they send over the purple French cuff and the matching tie?"

"Really? Wear those together? Are you sure?" Avery said, reaching down to switch the shirts back.

"Absolutely. You'll look stunning. It'll set off your tan," she said.

"Okay..." he said hesitantly. This was Minnesota after all, not the downtown streets of Hollywood.

"Avery, really. When I saw it this morning, I thought of you." The phone beeped, the new call waiting technology always threw him off when the beep sounded through on the phone.

"Thanks, Colleen, I have to take this," Avery said.

"Have fun tonight! Let me know the details." He laughed, but didn't otherwise respond as he reached down to the receiver to click over and answer the other line.

"Avery Adams," he said with a chuckle, dropping the towel where he stood.

"Hello, Mr. Adams. I'm confirming your reservation tonight for dinner." The deep rich, masculine voice instantly sent his heart racing. His eyes were focused on the suit, but all he could see was the image of the man calling him.

"Of course, I'll be there, unless you need the table." The thought made him furrow his brow, wishing he could take those words right back. He'd prepared all day for this dinner. Haircut, professional shave, plucked in all the most painful places.

"No, sir, absolutely not. We'll see you at seven," Kane said. Avery could tell Kane was about to hang up and he jumped in before the man said goodbye.

"Kane, tell me the specials for tonight." Avery couldn't actually care less what they served. He just wanted to hear the voice on the other end of the line. Kane's cultured Southern drawl made his blood boil, but Kane's voice still held all the proper hints of a well-practiced Italian accent as he efficiently ticked off the evening's menu. Avery stood transfixed, listening to the tone, until he closed his eyes, just letting the voice rock his world.

"Our waitstaff will let you know if anything changes. Thank you, we'll see you at seven." The call disconnected, and Avery, a little slower at lowering the phone, finally managed to absently place it on the hook. He picked up the black Hugo Boss and hung it back in the closet. He tossed the towel in the hamper. Avery still had a couple of hours to kill before dinner.

With absolutely zero encouragement from Kane, Avery placed a single stem of the calla lilies Kane sent on the pillow next to his. The action made him laugh as he rolled his eyes at the absurdly romantic gesture. It was unimaginable how important this one night had become to him. On a chuckle, Avery headed to the bathroom to jack off. He needed his dick hard, but not until it was time, and now certainly wasn't the time.

* * * *

Greeter-guy met Avery at the door. The same sexy grin was in place, but he wasn't near as forthcoming as before. Avery got it. Being shut down after all the flirting they'd done during his first dinner at La Bella Luna had turned the guy off.

Avery was immediately shown to his table, the same booth as before, and he wondered if this was now his designated place in this restaurant. The same waiter greeted him, and asked if he wanted the same bottle of wine. The entire staff was a little more formal this time. Avery assumed they had to be on high alert, making sure everything went perfect tonight. The calla lilies came to mind. He scanned the restaurant as he took his seat. Calla lilies were in every arrangement in the dining room. Avery made a mental note, wondering if that was Kane's flower of choice.

The waiter stated the night's specials and, remembering his choices from his previous dinner, asked if he'd like those again. Avery truly began to understand why La Bella Luna was the talk of this town. Kane ran a first class operation. This little restaurant, tucked away in downtown Minneapolis was as good as any he'd ever been to and that said quite a bit after his upbringing.

Recalling his primary goal, Avery kept the pleasant, friendly smile on his face. He needed to ease some of this tension he'd created the first time he was here. Gaining the information he wanted required everyone be comfortable around him.

"Markie, could you have Mr. Dalton stop by the table?" Avery asked seconds before the waiter retreated from the table. Markie hesitated, confusion clear on his face.

"Sir, has something happened since you arrived? I'm supposed to make sure you're happy tonight. The owner feels like we let you down last time." The waiter spoke candidly to Avery, and the genuine concern never left his face. When Markie came off the regular script, Avery could hear bits of a hard northern accent, maybe from New York.

"Nothing's happened. I'm not sure how I gave the impression my last experience here was bad, but I enjoyed myself immensely," Avery said, nodding as he spoke, trying for a reassuring tone. He really needed the entire staff to settle down, and start talking. They had the information he wanted to know.

"All right, sir, but if that changes, you only need to just say the word and I'll get you taken care of," Markie said, taking a step backward before turning away. The young waiter didn't seem to believe him. Avery tracked him straight to the bar where Kane was hidden in an alcove working something on paper in a darkened corner of the long bar.

Avery had searched for Kane as he entered, but hadn't found him. Now, as the waiter spoke to Kane, he turned his head to Avery's table, their eyes met and electricity crackled between them. God, Kane was stunning. The man's gaze alone robbed Avery of all ability to think. Surely, he couldn't be the only one feeling this, right?

Avery held the connection, never lowering his gaze, even when Kane looked down and placed whatever he held in his hands back on the bar. Avery stared, memorizing every step Kane took toward his table. Kane visibly squared his shoulders, and his handsome face transformed from normal and natural to a polite, calm indifference. Right then, he knew that was Kane's game face.

"Good evening, Mr. Adams. It's a pleasure to see you again tonight. Markie said you would like to speak with me?" Kane's voice had changed just like his face. He was quieter than he had been on the phone earlier today. Avery watched as Kane linked his fingers together and stood before him, waiting for his answer.

Seconds passed as Kane waited for Avery's response. A lump formed in his throat, something he wasn't prepared for. Avery thought he'd been on firm ground when he entered the restaurant tonight, but that shifted to unstable with each second that ticked by.

He was amazed at how this man standing in front of him could rob him of any coherent thought. Maybe he shouldn't have been so adamant about his biweekly dinner plans; maybe he had overstepped his boundaries. But he'd never felt so drawn to another. Avery Adams was in uncharted waters for the first time in his life. Perhaps he should have left well enough alone.

Any doubt or reservation Avery had been able to muster fled as he looked up into Kane's blue eyes and realized he'd met his *one*. Kane was meant for him. A chance dinner at a Midwestern restaurant had produced his other half. Who would have thought? Avery finally smiled. Motivation was such a great focuser and Avery moved right in on what he wanted. Surely fate wouldn't put his *one* in front of him and make him straight. Avery cleared his throat in an attempt to gather his scattered thoughts.

"I wanted to let you know that I had no problems the other night. I enjoyed myself immensely. The meal was outstanding, the waitstaff superb. You have one of the finest establishments I've ever dined in. I'm truly sorry I gave you the impression I wasn't pleased," Avery said. He stopped himself from being more forthcoming and asking the questions he really wanted answers to: will you...date me, make love with me, marry me? Kane visibly flexed as he spoke, and Avery had no idea what that meant.

"Thank you, sir. You've lifted a great deal of weight off my shoulders. We hate for any of our guests to walk away unhappy." Uncertainty crossed Kane's face. He started to turn away, but stopped himself, clearly unsure if the conversation was over. And it wasn't, at least not from Avery's perspective. "Has Markie taken your drink order this evening?"

"Yes, he has, but I would like to ask you a question. Do you ever take time to eat? Would you like to join me for dinner? My treat?" Avery asked, again he was met with more uncertainty. The question must have thrown Kane off. After another moment of pause, Markie interrupted them, bringing the bottle of wine to the table. Avery went through the steps of tasting and accepting before Kane answered the question.

"Thank you for the invitation, but I must regrettably decline. Enjoy yourself, and this bottle of wine's on me." Kane's skin was pale, probably from the long winter months. The slight blush never left his cheeks as he nodded and left the table. Kane's response wasn't quite a rebuff, but definitely a no, without any excuse as to why. What did that mean? Yet somehow, Avery recognized those few short moments had set them on a new course. One Avery had no idea about, but was more than happy to play along with.

* * * *

Kane resisted the inner groan as Markie approached him for the fourth or fifth time that evening, letting him know the Adams table requested to see him. He couldn't help but frown as Markie's smirk slid into place. For that matter, every one of his waitstaff looked full of grins and giggles, as though this were some sort of game. It wasn't a game. Kane was tense, completely stressed out, barely hanging on to his carefully placed control and way past ready to snap.

He never allowed himself to get this strung out over any situation.

"Markie, can you handle this one for me? I'm busy," Kane said, preparing to spend the rest of the night in his office, far from the dining room, away from all the annoying grins and hushed snickering being aimed his way, and definitely nowhere near table thirty-four.

"No, sir. I asked, but he requested you," Markie said in his straight up Bronx accent. Now, Markie was just trying to get on his nerves.

"I comped his bottle of wine. He'll be fine if you handle his request," Kane said, gathering his tickets to head back to his office.

"No, sir, that's not the restaurant's policy. A customer wants you, you do what he needs. And that customer definitely wants you," Markie said and actually chuckled this time. That just flat grated on Kane's nerves. All he could do was gawk at the waiter for a few seconds in total disbelief before turning his attention to the bartender.

"Rodney, can you handle this one for me?" Kane stopped at the end of the bar, even more frustrated that Rodney wore the same smirk as Markie. Why did his carefully planned life feel as if it was all of the sudden spinning out of control? His mother at the beginning of the week, Brian this afternoon, and now he had a guest from hell at table thirty-four...and his staff had decided this was all a game to them. Really?

"We tried that last time, remember? He wants you," Rodney said, grinning at Markie as he poured two new drinks. Did they really just exchange winks? Seriously?

Kane took a deep breath and let out an exasperated sigh. Avery Adams bothered him. No, that wasn't exactly accurate. The truth—this was beyond an attraction, he was exceedingly drawn to the man, more so than he'd ever experienced in his life. But that wasn't the only problem. Avery Adams flustered him, made him feel unsure and tongue-tied. The calm he trusted to always fall into place seemed to disappear, and he was left a bumbling mass of nerves. He absolutely didn't want to go back to that table.

Kane's palms started to sweat, and he sighed heavily. After this time, he was making himself scarce for the next few hours. From the corner of his eye, he saw most of the kitchen staff standing in the small windows of the double doors beside him. La Bella Luna was full tonight, how was Paulie letting this happen? Weren't there dinners to prepare? Kane cocked a brow, turning inquisitively toward the window, only to see Paulie's smirking face gloating back at him. He had to be in an episode of the Twilight Zone. Drill Sergeant Paulie gave him a big grin and nodded him toward the table.

How had he lost complete control of his restaurant? He ran his sweaty palms down the sides of his slacks and pivoted toward table thirty-four. He squared his shoulders, his signature move to pull himself together. So far tonight, he'd been called over and asked about the linens, then about the type of wood used in the fireplace, and then Mr. Adams had wanted to know if the bricks on the wall separating the spaces were authentic. He'd been asked if the florist was the same as who sent the bouquet to his office and if Kane had personally picked the arrangements out himself for both here and the bouquet he'd sent to Avery. The last time was to taste the sauce on Avery's dish.

When Kane had suggested he retrieve a clean spoon, Avery insisted he use his and lifted the spoon to feed Kane. He'd turned fifty shades of red, if the heat he felt warming his cheeks was anything to go by, as he bent in to take that bite. And now, just like every other time he'd looked over at the table, Avery sat there staring directly at him.

This was hard, one of the hardest nights of his entire life. He found himself so physically attracted to Avery it hurt. But more so, he was astounded at how observant Avery seemed with his pride and joy, La Bella Luna. Avery could pick up the slightest taste differences in the flavors blended together to create their secret recipe sauce. He'd wanted Kane to tell him which was more dominating, the grana padano or the pancetta. How did the man know those things? And why did it turn Kane on so much that he did?

"Yes, sir?" Kane asked as he closed in on the table. His eyes focused on the picture directly behind Avery's head.

"I asked you to please call me Avery." Kane thought he heard a hint of a frown in Avery's voice, but he didn't glance down to find out.

"I know. Is there a problem?" Kane asked. Avery was so much more handsome and elegant than the picture behind the man's head. Avery's presence actually made his restaurant more attractive. And why did he have to think of that right now? He could feel his cheeks burning.

"I'm not sure I'm drinking the right wine," Avery said, which confused Kane. Unguarded, he lowered his gaze to Avery, and then down to the wineglass, before looking at the bottle. Had he heard right?

"I'm sorry?" Kane asked.

"I'm guessing you have a wine room somewhere in this place. You keep coming through the back door over there with bottles of wine. I don't think this is truly a Montalcino. I'd like to see for myself." Kane narrowed his brow, opened his mouth to speak, but closed it again. Avery was already scooting out of the booth, coming to stand right in front of him. Avery was definitely taller than him...and why did that matter? No! Bad thoughts! This was a customer, nothing more. His height and gorgeous body had nothing to do with it. He focused on the absurdity of the man's last statement. Did Avery think they'd changed wines on him? Nothing else made sense.

"It shouldn't take but a minute." Avery actually extended his hand for Kane to show him the way. And even more surprising, Kane did. He turned, walking toward the wine cellar, not understanding any part of what they were doing. Did Avery want to see the aged bottles of wine surrounding his selection? He was so confused. He'd never heard of such a thing. Kane hit the swinging door behind the bar, held it open, and took the stairs down to the basement, still completely baffled.

* * * *

Avery followed closely behind Kane as they made their way down the steps to the wine room. Neither spoke, and he stayed a somewhat respectable distance all the way down. He also gave himself kudos for resisting the urge to lean in and smell Kane's cologne. What Kane seemed to have no idea of, and yet every other employee in the restaurant seemed to know, was that Markie had given Avery all the information he needed where Kane Dalton was concerned.

Twenty bucks obtained the necessary facts, and for the remainder of the evening, the rest of the waitstaff kept tossing him speculative looks. But it was well worth the price. Kane clearly had created a small, tight knit family among his staff. They sized Avery up, and at some point, must have deemed him worthy based on the kitchen staff he saw giving the thumbs up through a side door window.

Once Markie figured out what was what, he'd actually played with Avery a little. Telling him everything about Kane, except the most important piece of information. Avery paid another twenty to learn Kane was in fact gay. Relief flooded through him like he had never experienced before in his entire life. Fate was a funny creature. Avery could totally see his heart's desire being stiffly straight. But fate had smiled down on him this time, and now he was more determined than ever to get Kane on board with his plans.

From the time of Markie's final bit of information to this moment, he had decided to mess with Kane. The man deserved a degree of hell for making him work so hard for the smallest amount of attention. Avery actually began to whistle a tune as they walked the length of the bottom corridor to a set of heavy oak doors obviously leading into the climate controlled wine room.

The room was impressively filled with hundreds of bottles of wine. There were no markings on the walls, no way to understand the organization of the rows, but Kane knew and walked straight to the middle of the back wall, searching the bottles.

It was time to make his move and Avery didn't hesitate. For three days, he'd thought of little more than this moment. They were finally alone. He came up straight behind Kane, not quite touching him, but close. He lifted his right hand to the wine rack. Kane was an inch or so shorter than him, just enough that Avery could lean in and whisper into his ear. He still hadn't touched Kane and that cost him. His cock would certainly make him pay for the denial of even the slightest brush.

"Come home with me tonight," Avery whispered on the exhale, and then breathed Kane in on the inhale. Kane's scent coated his senses and ran rampant across his soul, settling squarely in his already hard cock. "You have to feel it. I can't be alone in this."

When Kane didn't immediately move away, Avery took the step separating them until his chest was fully pressed against Kane's back. His dick got the brush it needed and twitched in excitement, begging for more.

* * * *

Kane's heart pounded against his chest, racing so badly he couldn't hear himself think. Avery's breath coated his skin, danced across his ear, neck, and jaw, soothing as it created havoc all at the same time. The length of Avery's body moved against his. He could feel the hard cock pressing into his ass and every one of his nerve endings exploded into overdrive. Goose bumps sprang up across his arms, his breath hitched, and Kane desperately needed perspective.

Kane wanted Avery, wanted to do exactly what he suggested, but it was a bad idea. He fought emotions he shouldn't feel. Kane attempted to make his escape, sliding first to the right, only to find Avery had caged him in. Instinctively, he turned to the left. He had to get out from under this seductive assault or he was going to spontaneously combust.

Avery blocked his escape with his left arm, keeping him right there—stuck between the bottles of wine and Avery's hard body with his brain too stunned to think.

"Let me kiss you." The breath was back across his skin, this time from the left. The whisper-soft caress of air became his undoing. Avery slowly turned him around. The move proved to be all the incentive Kane needed, and he lifted his head. Avery's amber eyes held his. He was lost in a sea of turmoil at the emotion coursing through his veins. He swallowed before lifting his lips. Avery met him halfway.

The kiss wasn't a sweet searching brush of the lips. They both immediately opened, creating a swirl of tongue and teeth as they desperately kissed one another. Avery backed him against the bottles, circling an arm around his waist, drawing him tightly against his body and kissed Kane like he had never been kissed before.

Avery took complete control, dominating Kane in every way, and he let the man have his way. He lifted his hand to Kane's face. Avery's strong thumb stroked across his jawline then turned him to where he could delve deeper inside his mouth. The move caused nerves to explode again across Kane's skin and through his brain. His breath hitched, and he was forced to pull away, giving in to his need to breathe before passing out won in the end.

Avery latched on to his neck and stayed on him. All Kane could do was lean his head back feeling the bottles shift behind him, giving Avery full access to his jaw and ear. Kane heard himself groan when Avery's teeth nipped the soft skin under his ear. Avery ground his hips forward and Kane involuntarily met him thrust for grinding thrust.

"Come home with me. No, fuck home. I want you right here." Kane couldn't think with the sexy low voice whispering across his ear. Avery's hands were on him, seeking, and he pulled Kane's shirt from his slacks and unbuckled his belt. He was surprised to find his own hands working himself free, not Avery's. Loud beeps stopped Kane in his tracks as the security code to the wine cellar was entered.

The door opened. Avery stayed right there, keeping his back to the room, covering Kane. Kane's eyes darted up to Avery's, they connected and held. Avery only stopped kissing him. He continued the gentle massage on his cock, staying right there in Kane's face. Those eyes pierced his with an intensity that somehow matched the pounding of his heart.

"Sorry, boss, I need to get a bottle of red for a table," Rodney said, like it was the most natural thing in the world to walk in the wine room and catch Kane, or anyone for that matter, making out with someone. Kane started to speak, he opened his mouth, but nothing came out. Instead, his eyes stayed glued to Avery's.

"Don't worry, I'll cover for you." Rodney left almost as fast as he'd arrived.

They continued gazing at one another. Neither spoke, neither moved, they just stared for several long moments. Avery's intensity never wavered. Helplessness settled in. Kane could feel his soul being extracted from his body. His heart followed, no longer his own, but given to this man he didn't even know. In a matter of a few short minutes, he had become one with this man in front of him. Confused, he looked closer at Avery, seeing only shameless intensity in his eyes. He had no idea if Avery experienced these same feelings, and he surely wasn't going to ask.

Instead, he cleared his throat, removed himself from Avery's hold and tucked himself back inside his slacks, trying to find some control. It was a monumental experience to have finally given your heart away so freely, especially to someone you didn't know. The whole experience unnerved Kane.

"Meet me tonight. I can come to you," Avery said. He didn't stop Kane from adjusting himself, but he didn't move away either.

"It'll be late before I get off," Kane said, to his own surprise. He absolutely didn't do casual sex. That was one hundred percent against his beliefs, but here he was taking whatever Avery offered.

"It doesn't matter the time," Avery said, and Kane nodded. This time Avery let him sidestep away. The distance helped with his perspective as he looked down his body, making sure his clothing lay right. He buttoned his suit jacket to hide his erection.

"I messed up your hair," Avery said from behind him. He was close again, not as near as before, but close. "Kiss me again before you go."

"Not here," Kane said, afraid of his own lack of control.

"A small kiss, something to tide me over until tonight." Avery leaned in, and Kane obliged. He forced himself to keep it small, to end the connection after a couple of swipes of the tongue. "I live a few buildings over, but I can come to you after you're off."

"Your house is fine," Kane said and ventured a look up into Avery's eyes. The intensity was still there. Just like before, those eyes had a way of robbing him of any sensible thought he might have, so he forced his gaze away and his body forward, moving them from the wine room.

"I'm completely open to wherever if it changes. What time do you get off?" Avery asked.

"Around two. Is that too late?" Kane never looked back as he moved them down the hall.

"No, whenever, even if it's later. I'll write the address down for you. Please don't stand me up," Avery whispered, sliding a hand back around Kane's waist, tugging him back against his body, before he took the first step up the stairs. Kane only nodded and closed his eyes, allowing the embrace. After a full minute, Avery let him go with a warm press of lips on the back of his neck before they walked back upstairs.

"I need to brush my hair," Kane said, pushing the dining room door open for Avery.

"Don't stand me up," Avery repeated. Kane never looked back, only nodded as he retreated to his office. He needed time. Avery Adams had gone from being the guest from hell, to kissing him like he'd never been kissed before. A kiss that extracted his soul and had him agreeing to a one-night stand. He was going to need lots of time to figure all this out.

Chapter 7

The time ticked by, and energy Avery didn't know he possessed coursed through him. It was already a little past two in the morning. As he watched the minutes pass, Avery wondered about the wisdom of the way he left the restaurant tonight. He had written his address and phone number down on an order ticket at the bar and waited to hand it to Kane personally. The later it got, the more convinced he became that hadn't been the best decision. Maybe he should have stayed until Kane got off for the evening, just to ensure the man didn't change his mind.

Avery had wanted time to prepare for Kane coming over. He changed his clothes several times before finally deciding on a pair of worn Levi's and an old sweatshirt from his years at Yale. He was barefoot and underwear free. He paced his strategically darkened living room. Candles were lit, music played softly in the background, and a bottle of wine sat chilling in an ice bucket.

Much like with that devastating kiss in the wine cellar, Avery had no idea where his need to romance Kane came from. He couldn't remember ever requesting a kiss, let alone stopping at just a kiss. Not really a kisser to begin with, he certainly never lit candles and played romantic tunes waiting for someone to arrive. But with Kane, he wanted things different. What those were, he wasn't entirely sure yet.

All he knew was he wanted Kane more than he'd ever wanted anything in his life and this waiting only caused an uneasy desperation to build that he couldn't even understand how to process.

As the clock hit two twenty, Avery's internal panic began. He pulled the phone book from the drawer and searched for the restaurant's telephone number. He picked up the phone, but changed his mind. He decided to go there. When he put his address in Kane's hand, he made him promise again not to stand him up. He kept telling himself that Kane must have felt the draw between them. How could he not? But that didn't help his frantic heart. Avery grabbed his jacket, planning to go find Kane. He jerked open the door and came to an abrupt halt. Kane stood there, his fist in the air as if he was about to knock. Instant relief flooded Avery, and he reached out, grabbing Kane by his coat lapels, dragging him inside the condo.

"I didn't think you were coming," Avery said, and Kane looked down at his watch.

"I told you I got off at two," Kane said with that same sound of confusion in his voice he'd had at the table earlier.

"I know, but it's almost two thirty." They stood together in the entryway with Avery peeling off Kane's jacket as he spoke. The desperation of a couple of moments ago made him fumble with his task, but his most urgent goal in the world seemed to be to get Kane naked as quickly as possible. If he were naked, he couldn't leave. Avery didn't think, he just reacted and worked at undressing Kane.

"I had to walk over," Kane started, but Avery was past the point.

"You look good in regular clothes. I wondered how you'd look in jeans. You're hot as hell in those suits you wear." Avery tugged Kane's T-shirt up and over his head, smiling at the well-defined chest and arms now within his grasp. Kane didn't respond to the praise and Avery worked his jean buttons open.

"Button fly is only cool on commercials," Avery said with a small chuckle as he peeled back the layers of buttons until he pushed Kane's jeans down his ass, getting stuck on his thick thighs. For the first time since Kane entered, Avery looked up at his face. He saw uncertainty there, and Avery mentally counted backward, trying to remember the last thing Kane had said. He'd been so wrapped up in himself, he'd failed to do what he intended—romance Kane into his life.

"You're a boxers guy. I figured you would be," Avery said, biting his bottom lip. He kept his eyes on Kane's, his hands roaming the swells of the chest in front of him. Kane stayed silent, with his jeans pushed down to his upper thighs. *Damn.*

"Don't look at me like that. Be in this with me. Be right here with me," Avery said, pulling his own shirt over his head, tossing it aside with Kane's. "Take off your shoes…"

Avery leaned forward, threaded his fingers through Kane's hair and drew him forward for a kiss. He forced himself to slow down some. He pulled Kane against his body, wrapped him in his arms, and kissed him like they'd kissed in the wine room. Avery was already so turned on. His body's need for this man crushed every other thought coursing through his brain.

He could feel Kane slowly loosening up. Kane followed Avery's lead, wrapping his arms around him, running his fingertips and palms over the skin of his back. Damn, that was such a turn on. Avery didn't want to rush Kane, but after what he hoped was a sufficient amount of time, he turned up the heat on the kiss, working his way along Kane's jaw to his ear. He licked and nipped as he went, until he plunged his tongue in the inner depths of the shell. Kane's small moans and the grip on his body encouraged Avery to continue. He could definitely feel Kane's hardening arousal pressing against his.

"Take your shoes off. The bedroom's ready for us," Avery whispered. It cost him, but he stopped the flow of his lips and ran his nose along the length of Kane's neck until his face was buried in Kane's hair. He closed his eyes, breathing Kane in as the man worked his shoes off and then tugged at his jeans. God, he loved Kane's masculine, spicy scent. Finally Kane put his hands on Avery's waistband, pulled open the buttons on his jeans.

"You don't wear underwear," Kane stated. He pulled his head back a little. Only as far as Avery would let him, and he felt denied when Kane's scent wasn't the only thing he could breathe in.

"I do, just not tonight. I'm a briefs guy." Avery grinned at Kane's hesitant smile. "I didn't plan to do this in my doorway. I planned to have you come in, have a drink, unwind from the night. I just feel something in this. Something I need, if that makes any sense. I can't seem to control myself when you're within reach," Avery said, drawing Kane's head back to his shoulder so he could nibble on his ear.

"I don't need romance," Kane said, his voice hoarse. Avery prayed that was need speaking.

"Make no mistake, I will romance you, Kane Dalton, just not now. Right now I need to fuck you. Fuck you hard, and soft, and then do it all over again." Avery ran his nose over Kane's ear and back into his hair, breathing him in as if Kane were his only life source. "Take off my jeans. Touch me. I need to feel your hands on me. I crave your touch. Please."

* * * *

Avery seemed genuine, not like the player playing his game. Somehow the thought helped Kane justify this one-night stand. Kane mustered his nerve, forced himself not to consider the repercussions, and pushed Avery's jeans down his long legs until he kicked them off. Kane followed the pants to the floor, dropping to his knees, and looked up, his eyes landing on Avery's as he wrapped his fingers around the base of his shaft and directed the broad tip of Avery's cock to his mouth. He hoped the action came off as a bold move. Kane opened, sliding Avery deep into his mouth. A small taste of pre-come hit his tongue. Kane closed his eyes as Avery tangled both hands in his hair, guiding Kane in the rhythm he'd created.

"Damn, that feels good." Avery breathed out the last word on a groan.

Kane opened wider, willing himself to let Avery go as deep as he could. He slid his hands up Avery's thighs, then to his sac, cupping and starting a slow massage on his already retracting balls. His reward was the sound of a deep sensual moan from above. He cast his gaze up, meeting that intense amber stare yet again. He slid his hand around to grip the firm globe of Avery's ass. His fingers breached the crevice, sliding down to the rim. Avery tensed slightly at the contact, telling him everything he needed to know. Avery wasn't a regular bottom...and neither was he.

"Fuck, I'm already gonna come." Avery jerked himself away, ripping from the hold seconds after Kane slid his finger past the rim and massaged the gland inside. He took several steps backward and, for the first time tonight, created distance from Kane. Avery gripped himself tight with both hands, trying to stop the orgasm from overtaking him. "Not in my entryway. Not this way."

Kane stayed there on his knees, his eyes glued to Avery. At this point, he was completely unsure what to do. He couldn't ever remember being stopped in the middle of a blow job. He wasn't an expert by any stretch of the imagination, but in his experience, sex was a take what you could get kind of deal. No one ever worried whether Kane got what he needed. The release was the only important outcome to achieve. But apparently not with Avery, he seemed intent on making tonight special.

"Get up. Come with me, but don't touch me. It'll be my undoing. We're doing this right if it kills me," Avery said. He stayed a distance from Kane, but kept his eyes on him as he stood.

"You have to tell me where to go. I don't know your condo," Kane finally said as he got to his feet and picked up their clothes.

"I'm afraid you'll vanish if I turn away," Avery said, that intense expression returning.

"You don't have to say things like that," Kane said, his arms full of their clothes. He took a step inside the living room, draping the items across the closest chair, marveling that he'd still only made it a few feet inside the condo.

"I'm not doing it for your benefit. I'm saying how I feel. I can stop if it makes you uncomfortable," Avery said, tracking every step Kane made. He still had a death grip on his cock.

"This whole thing has me a little uncomfortable," Kane finally said. Between the kind words, and the way it looked like Avery still tried to hold off his release, Kane was being drawn in deeper. He had tried to talk himself out of what he'd felt in the wine cellar with Avery. He'd justified his decision to come here tonight as the one-night stand rebound from Brian. Now, Avery's every word increased his battle to keep this night impersonal.

"I can see that. How do I stop it?" Avery asked, finally letting go of his cock. He was so beautiful, standing there naked, his gorgeous cock bobbing in front of him as he waited for a reply. Kane realized Avery kept his distance on purpose to make him feel more comfortable. Dang, he couldn't help his heart connecting a little more in this moment.

"You can't. I don't do this," Kane said, waving his hands between their bodies. "This whole one-night stand thing. It's against my beliefs."

"Good...but never?" Avery asked, his usual intensity clouded by confusion. Kane got it. He was the odd one, not Avery.

52

"No, never," Kane simply responded. His own nakedness finally sank in, and he could feel his cock slightly deflating as he became more uncomfortable with the conversation.

"Are you in a relationship?" Avery asked.

"Not anymore."

"Since when?" Avery wasn't taking the subtle two word hints that he didn't really want to talk about this. Kane weighed his options, trying to decide what was best to say. In his mind, nothing appeared appropriate and he decided to answer honestly.

"Today," Kane finally said in little more than a whisper.

"Why today?" Avery asked, and Kane swallowed the answer down. He absolutely couldn't tell Avery he was unable to hang on to his man. "Was it because of me?"

"No." Kane shook his head, still not admitting the truth.

"You could have lied. I'd like to believe it was me," Avery said and smiled. He still kept his distance from Kane, but his cock was deflating, hanging freely between his legs. Great. Not only could he not hang on to Brian, he couldn't keep Avery hard. This so wasn't going the way he'd expected, and he took a step behind the chair. He still had a partial arousal going. It wasn't cool to be the only one.

"I had no idea you were gay until you cornered me downstairs. How did you know I was?" Kane asked.

"I paid Markie for the information right after I got there tonight. I couldn't wait to know. You're all I've been thinking about since I met you," Avery said, taking a step or two toward Kane.

"I was convinced I'd completely insulted you somehow." Kane used the chair between them as a protective barrier.

"I know, I just don't know why you thought that," Avery said.

"You never spoke. You never acknowledged me when I greeted your table," Kane said.

"You stunned me," Avery said, stepping closer as he reached up to run his palm across Kane's cheek, his thumb lingering. Kane had no idea how to respond, so he stayed quiet.

"If you don't do one-night stands, how many men have you been with?" Avery asked. He seemed content to keep the chair between them. Avery had gone completely soft, but slid his palm down Kane's arm to take the hand lying on the chair. He entwined their fingers together. That was so not a question he wanted to answer, so he chose to stay silent.

"You don't lie very well, do you?" Avery asked, grinning now.

"No. It's in the way I was raised." Finally, something he was willing to answer.

"More than ten?" Avery asked. Dang, why were they back here? "More than five?"

Kane stayed silent.

"Just tell me how many," Avery said, pulling Kane from behind the chair, to stand before him. Avery loosely wrapped an arm around his waist, keeping their hands intertwined.

"Two," Kane whispered and looked away from Avery. He'd just confessed his ludicrously small number to the worldly grandson of the president of the United States.

"Two? How old are you?" Clearly Avery had a hard time believing him. He could lie. *Just lie, Kane! You'll never see him again.*

"Thirty-three, how old are you?" Kane shot back, feeling defensive now. He needed to leave. Hell, he shouldn't have even come here in the first place. Why weren't they having sex right now?

"Thirty-five. How long have you been out?" Avery asked and held on to Kane as he tried to pull away from the embrace. He was seriously starting to regret this decision. Humiliation never occurred to him as a possible outcome. He wanted out.

"I was eighteen when I told my family," Kane said, and this time, he tore free of the hold, looking through the clothes for his underwear.

"Two men in fifteen years?" Avery asked. Kane immediately began pulling all his clothing from the mix he'd picked up from the floor. He bent forward to slide his underwear back on, but Avery stopped him, actually taking the boxers from his hand. "Are you here to get back at your boyfriend?"

"No," Kane said and laughed. For the first time in several minutes, Kane looked deeply into Avery's eyes. The truth? Something he hadn't admitted before right this minute—he was here because he'd never been kissed like he'd been kissed by Avery in his wine cellar. Avery had somehow branded himself on Kane's heart in those few short minutes. Kane was compelled to see what more was there between them, even if it were just one night. Brian hadn't even been considered until Avery brought him up. How had he not thought of the man he had dated for the last four years?

Avery studied Kane, examining him as if he were being dissected under a microscope until he held Kane's boxer's out to him. "I'm shallow enough that I want to have sex with you anyway, but you need to tell me now if this is it between us. I want more than tonight, but if you don't, tell me."

This turned into a night of so many firsts. No one had ever said anything like that to him before. What did wanting more mean? He took the underwear and dropped them back on the pile of his clothes while he stood there silently contemplating his answer. He stared at Avery, trying to discern if he spoke the truth, but he sucked at detecting lies. Avery's face hardened as he watched Kane. He started to move forward but physically stopped himself and waited for Kane to answer.

"My last two boyfriends broke up with me because I'm too intense. I work too much and I have strong religious views." That truth pained Kane to say, but he hoped it answered Avery's question.

"I like intense. I respect work. Religion can be good. What kind of religion?" Avery asked, back to wrapping Kane in his arms.

"I'm a practicing Christian. Not currently in a church," Kane said. He was naked in the living room of a man he'd known for less than a few days, talking about religion. He wondered how many Southern Baptist rules he was currently breaking.

"Was your father a pastor?" Avery had hit the nail on the head and Kane only nodded. He was laying himself open for Avery to reject him, but he couldn't stop himself. He hadn't given Brian this much information for the first year and a half they'd dated.

"Do they support you?" Kane shook his head and looked down at the floor. That was baggage and more than needed to be discussed right now.

"Come on. I want to start this night over. I have a robe you can wear," Avery said, pulling Kane toward the back of the condo.

"You don't have to do this," Kane said, reluctantly following behind him.

"Actually, I do. I wanted to before, but I got desperate. I just don't want you back in your clothes. You need to be wearing something where I can get to you easier." Kane followed until he stood just inside the master bedroom door. Avery went to a closet and pulled out two robes, handing him a black terry cloth one.

* * * *

55

Avery purposely slowed them down. He and Kane sat in his living room for the next couple of hours getting to know one another. He kept Kane close, working hard to loosen the man's reserve. His overall plan was to ply Kane with wine as they spoke of their lives, mainly Kane speaking of his life. Avery learned how Kane met his mentor, Paulie, whom Avery unknowingly met tonight. Paulie had come to his table and introduced himself right before Avery and Kane had gone downstairs. He hadn't known the importance of their meeting. Though he'd picked up on Paulie being protective of Kane, he hadn't understood that Paulie was all Kane truly had in the world to call his family.

Kane only spoke in brief bits and pieces about his biological family and those were just of his childhood and the years he'd spent in the church. Avery had an instant dislike of the Dalton family, but kept that to himself, at least for now.

Avery did his fair share of talking about his grandfather and father. When Kane prodded, he spoke of his childhood and studying abroad. They sat close together on the sofa and exchanged stories as the night turned into morning. As time went on, Avery slowly began to touch Kane, small gentle caresses that were eventually returned.

Avery found what he suspected to be true: Kane was smart, articulate, and after a few glasses of wine, relaxed. Kane suited Avery well. They would be good together. While Kane would be good arm candy and present a poised, sophisticated image, Avery knew the country wasn't ready for a gay statesman. Yet Avery couldn't help but speculate how Kane would be the perfect gentleman to have on his arm if he did run for office.

Avery never spoke of his plans to run for office. Even when needled by Kane, he didn't truly admit why he'd moved back to Minnesota. He didn't want to scare Kane off before he figured out what was going on between them. Homosexuality was becoming more accepted. Avery could feel the movement just beginning to pick up steam, but they were still decades away from this country being anywhere close to ready for a couple like them.

Avery leaned back against the sofa and rested his head in his hand, just staring at Kane while he spoke. Why in the world was Avery sitting with a man he'd only met a few days ago, speculating about them as a couple, and already moving them years down the road? Except, he knew the answer. It was the draw, the deep connection between them that pulled him in. These feelings were so new and fresh, yet unbelievably real.

He'd heard the *soul mate* catch phrase tossed around a lot recently. It was the newest, latest way to describe love. Somehow everything inside him registered those words with Kane. His soul mate. The person who shared space inside his soul. He couldn't help the small grin he gave or how he scooted closer to reach out and run his fingers through Kane's silky dark hair. As the candles flickered, Avery slowly lifted the short pieces and realized auburn might be the true color of Kane's hair. He loved auburn hair. God, he was so physically attracted to this man. Avery started to move forward again as though drawn by a magnetic force.

Slow down, mister. You'll scare him off before you even get a chance.

Avery managed to hold himself off until somewhere after four thirty in the morning. He stifled a yawn and set his wineglass down on the coffee table, then made the move to take Kane's glass and placed it next to his before scooting closer to him on the sofa.

"I need to remember to call your last boyfriend and thank him. You wouldn't be here tonight if he hadn't ended things today," Avery said. He was as close to Kane as he could get. "I can follow your lead in this. We can wait if you want, but I want to try this relationship thing with you, see how it goes. What do you say?"

Kane grinned, way more relaxed than Avery had ever seen him. He wanted to believe it was him, but he wasn't so certain since Kane had drunk six or seven glasses of wine in the span of an hour and a half. Avery hadn't let Kane's glass get empty.

Kane leaned forward on his own and nuzzled Avery's neck. Avery tilted Kane's head back, running his fingers through his hair, holding him there, enjoying the feel of Kane's warm mouth on him. "I don't want to leave tonight. I wanna make love and be made love to."

"Is it always like that for you? Do they make love to you?" Avery asked, lifting Kane's face by the chin, looking into his eyes.

"No, it's just in my head that way," Kane confessed, his words were slurred with a crooked grin in place. Would he be embarrassed by the admission in the morning? Avery hoped not. When had talking become the best foreplay on the planet?

"Mmmm…I like the idea of tender and sweet with you." Avery leaned in and took Kane's lips in an indulgent kiss. The kiss lingered until picking up steam, and Avery pushed the sash of Kane's robe free.

As much as he wanted to touch Kane, he only ran his fingers across his muscular torso once before he rose from the sofa and extended a hand down to Kane. "Come to bed with me."

Chapter 8

Kane stood, only then realizing he was drunk. The shake he gave to his fuzzy brain caused him to stumble a step, hitting the sofa with the back of his knees. Nothing cleared the fog clouding his thoughts. Why hadn't he considered this as he sat there drinking so much?

Avery led him away, seeming to not notice his balance issues. He held Kane's hand as he walked them back to the bedroom. This whole seduction scene was something Avery totally had down, and something he completely hadn't expected when he walked in the door tonight. Kane had been a sure bet. In Kane's mind, they should have been going at it for the last couple of hours, but instead Avery sat in his living room, talking to him, and actually listened to his answers without judgment or criticism. Avery wanted to know about Kane and had slowly, yet completely, gotten him drunk. Without question, when tomorrow rolled around and he thought over the events of tonight, he'd have to remember Avery was a sly one.

"How do you like it?" Avery asked. Kane felt like the question was more a formality. They had broached this subject earlier.

"However's fine," Kane said, coming to stand in front of Avery's bed.

"You're versatile?" Avery asked, sliding his hands through the open lapel of Kane's robe and running his fingers and palms over his chest.

"Not normally, but I felt you tense earlier when I touched you. I'll bottom, just take it slow," Kane answered honestly.

"I want us to go both ways." Avery finally pushed the robe off his shoulders, letting the terry cloth fall to his feet. He ran his fingertips up and down Kane's arms before he moved them to his stomach and tickled his way over each defined muscle. "I couldn't tell under that suit what you looked like, but I imagined you just like this."

Avery reached up and threaded his fingers through Kane's hair to pull him forward as he pressed their lips together. He slowly guided them back a step or two to his bed, as he lowered his hands, unwrapping his own robe as they moved. Kane kissed him like he had a right to be there, pushing Avery's robe to the floor. Kane claimed Avery's body and soul in that kiss, embracing him so tightly in his arms they fell together awkwardly onto the bed. Kane held Avery close, not letting him go. He would never get enough of the man in his arms.

* * * *

Avery would have moved them along where Kane seemed content to kiss and be held. Cuddling was something new, something he hadn't considered much before now. Avery needed to remember this for the future. Kane responded to every single touch Avery made. As he deepened the kiss, he wondered if Kane might be lonely in his life. What an incredibly odd thought to have, considering he had his tongue shoved down the man's throat.

"Let me make love to you," Avery whispered as he gently bit Kane's shoulder. Kane answered by taking his mouth in another deeply erotic kiss. Kane's kisses were what wet dreams were made of. He just lay there, sprawled across Kane's chest, kissing him. Kane lay on his back, legs wide open, and Avery was lost to the moment. He glanced down at Kane's cock, hard and ready, pre-come leaking onto his flat stomach. The sight made his mouth water. He wanted to taste the glistening fluid dotting Kane's skin. Before he knew it, he had drawn his fingers through the wetness and brought them to his lips.

"Mmm…so sweet, Kane." His eyes met Kane's, and he saw vulnerability flash in those blue orbs. He was going to do everything he could to remove any doubt from those beautiful eyes and prove to Kane he meant every word he said. He gave a reassuring smile before sliding a hand down between Kane's legs to begin the slow steady massage of his rim.

Kane was tight, probably as tight as Avery. They would both need to take care with the other until they were ready. Avery planned to fuck Kane, those plans hadn't changed, and he slowly pushed a finger inside. Their lips stayed together, Kane's arms tightly encircled him, making his movements almost clumsy. Avery reached across the bed to palm the bottle of lubricant he'd laid out hours ago. The condom packets were placed close by, but Avery ignored those. He'd made a practice of protecting himself for the last few years, but not tonight.

Hopefully not ever again.

"Baby, you have to let me open you." Avery tore free from the kiss and pushed back, trying to break from Kane's hold. Kane wasn't having any part of his plan and followed him, rising up to continue the kiss. Avery finally managed to break his grip, resting back on his knees between Kane's parted thighs, staring down at him. Kane's lips were full and red from their kissing, his skin flushed and heated as Kane stared back at him from under heavily hooded eyes.

"You're beautiful," Avery said as he took in every inch of Kane's exposed skin in front of him. "That was my only thought when I looked at you in the restaurant that first day. You took my breath away. You stole my words. I couldn't speak."

"I thought I messed something up terrible. You just stared at me," Kane said. Avery flipped open the top to the lube and poured the slick liquid on his fingers. Kane leaned up and kissed him sweetly on the lips before he settled back in place.

"I couldn't form words. You stunned me," Avery said as his fingers wrapped around Kane's thick cock, giving him a few strokes. Avery watched when Kane's leg fell to the side, giving him an unobstructed view of his perfect pink rim. He gave Kane's dick a few more strokes before sliding his hand down Kane's perineum, applying light pressure. Avery pressed his slick fingers against the tight ring and inserted a finger. Kane's body arched as Avery easily found the spot, curved his finger, and worked Kane from the inside out.

"That feels good," Kane moaned.

"I hoped it might." Avery grinned, adding more lubricant, before inserting a second finger. With his other hand, he again began the slow stroking of Kane's cock.

"I'm relaxed, really relaxed. Make love to me," Kane pleaded, and his eyes closed as Avery pushed in a third finger. Kane was such an extraordinary find. Avery was so completely taken with him that the emotion of the moment ran rampant over his heart. He leaned down, and kissed the wet tip of Kane's leaking cock.

"Oh, God, that feels good." Kane's eyes focused on Avery's lips brushing against his broad head. The intensity of the Kane's gaze shot straight through his body, landing squarely in his balls. Avery's cock wept with the need coursing through him. He kept his eyes on Kane and watched as he writhed and rolled his hips working Avery's fingers in and out of himself. Avery gripped the base of Kane's prick and dipped his head, sinking that beautiful cock into his mouth, taking him deep, moaning his pleasure around the velvety head. His greedy tongue explored his lover's weeping slit, swirling and lapping at the salty tip. Kane's dick twitched in his palm as the taste of pre-come flooded across his tongue. Kane's essence was so damn sweet.

"Don't come yet. Hold it, Kane. I want to feel you come when I'm in you," Avery said, scissoring his fingers in Kane's tight channel.

"I'm close," Kane moaned and lifted back up, grabbing Avery's cock in his hand. He moved in closer, positioning Avery at his entrance. "I need you in me now."

"I thought you wanted tender," Avery said. The feel of Kane's hands on his already aching dick robbed him of his sense of reason. He drove his hips forward, seeking the warm friction of Kane's palm on his cock. The fingers he had working Kane's ass faltered. If he wasn't careful, he'd lose his load, right there.

"I do. Just need you inside me," Kane whispered, raising his body until soft lips took his. Kane nibbled his lower lip, drawing the tender flesh into his mouth, nipping and suckling until it slipped out as he lowered back down on the bed. Kane's eyes stayed on him as he gripped the back of his thighs, pulling his legs toward his chest. "Now, I'm ready now."

Avery positioned himself, pushed through the tight ring of muscle, and met with resistance. He broke out in a sweat, his hunger to claim Kane coursing through his body with every beat of his heart. The only need greater than his own release was his desire to give Kane exactly what he wanted. He needed to make love to Kane even if it killed him and at this point, it just might. "I don't wanna hurt you."

"You won't." Kane's grip on his legs visibly tensed, and he pulled his legs tighter to him. Avery rested his hand on the back of Kane's thigh and pushed in. Snug heat gripped him as he sheathed himself in Kane's snug passage. Avery clenched his jaw; nothing had ever felt this good. Nothing. Avery's head dropped forward between his shoulders, he wanted to bury himself so deep in Kane he actually ached. He took big, deep breaths, drawing air into his lungs while allowing Kane's body to adjust to his.

How is this already the best experience of my life?

"Ahh." Kane's hips began to roll, forcing Avery to move. It wasn't the best option, he was already too close. Avery fought the urge to pound into that delicious heat. He steeled himself, easing forward in a slow, gentle thrust of his hips.

"Love the burn of you stretching me," Kane said, wrapping his legs around Avery's waist, lifting his hips, urging him on. Kane's strong fingers dug into Avery's shoulders as his lover kept him close, writhing beneath him.

"Yeah." Avery concentrated on keeping his load contained, the feel of Kane's body enveloping him, holding him just right there while making love to him completely overwhelmed him. He was in over his head and he knew it. He welcomed it, in fact. This was the man for him, *always*.

"Feels amazing," Kane panted, his voice husky with need, his warm breath heavy in Avery's ear. How could just the sound of the man's voice drive him to desperately want to buck his hips and end this agony?

"Yeah," Avery managed between clenched teeth. Kane lifted Avery's head, brought their lips together, and kissed him rough and sweet as he increased their pace. Kane's canting hips opened his body wider, letting Avery sink farther into his tight, hot channel.

"Fuck!" A slick sheen of sweat formed on Avery as he fought for control, his grip tightening on the bedspread. They never stopped moving, the erotic friction never slowed, their pleasure building in a heated frenzy.

"You feel so good, babe." Avery finally reared back, breaking the embrace Kane had on him. He pushed himself up on one hand and reached between their sweat-slickened bodies. Avery wrapped his fingers around Kane's cock and pumped with purpose.

"Come for me, Kane." The command ground out between gritted teeth as Avery's hips pistoned wildly in and out of his lover's body.

Kane threw his head back, his mouth open in a silent scream as he came. Damn, he was so beautiful to watch. His release wasn't an earthshattering roar, but more the quiet elegance he'd learned was just Kane's way. Avery drove himself harder and deeper into Kane. The prickling spiral of heat gathering in the base of his spine spread quickly to his balls, causing his thrusts to falter.

Kane was indeed Avery's perfect gentleman. That thought and the scent of his lover's climax combined with the contracting of Kane's muscles was entirely too much to endure and sent him toppling over the edge. "I'm gonna..." He screwed his eyes shut as his orgasm burst from his body, shooting deep inside Kane's ass, staking his claim with his seed. This moment was too good, too right, and the bliss overwhelmed him, his arm gave out, and he fell down on Kane's body, satiated. And completely head over heels in love.

Chapter 9

Kane woke slowly, but tried to resist. He grinned, thankful he'd taken the time to buy new pillows and burrowed deeper in the plush softness. Time passed slowly as his brain finally began to override his need to sleep. He didn't remember buying anything new. He sat up immediately, looking around the room. Not his room. A second more ticked by before he recalled he was still in Avery Adams's bedroom. That had him jerking his head toward the other side of the bed, before scanning the room. Avery was nowhere to be found. His eyes landed on the alarm clock that sat on the nightstand—ten thirty in the morning. He fell back on the mattress.

Taking account of the different aches in his body, Kane started with his ass and then worked his way to his head. His mouth felt like it was full of cotton, he clearly had a hangover, and was late for work. He shoved all that aside and listened intently, trying to find Avery in the condo, but he heard nothing. Either Avery was extremely quiet or gone. He didn't know him well enough to even guess, so he sat up again and reached for the phone. He would search for Avery after he called the restaurant and made his excuses for being late. A bottle of Tylenol, a glass of water, and a note rested right beside the phone.

Anchoring on his elbow, Kane downed the pills first, before he flipped on the lamp to read the note. The light pierced his brain, not in a good way, before his eyes adjusted to the bright glare.

> *K,*
> *I don't think you're a big drinker. I could be wrong, and yes, I did get you drunk to help get you through last night. Get me drunk tonight? Call me when you wake. I'm at the office. I didn't want to disturb you.*
> *Always,*
> *A*

Kane read the note once, then twice, before he felt the silly grin on his face. The aches in his body completely forgotten as he read the note for the third time. The smile never left his face. *Always...* For some reason the word did seem to fit last night. The idea of them being just a one-night stand didn't capture their essence near as closely as the word *Always*. Worries that this man could be nothing more than a player setting his game resurfaced, but he shoved them aside. If this was how Avery Adams played, then let the games begin.

It took a second more for Kane to put his responsibilities over his heart's desires. He called the restaurant first and left a message on the answering service when no one answered. Then he called Avery, who picked up on the first ring.

"Avery Adams."

That was a tone of voice he hadn't heard before. Strong, self-assured, very much cut to the chase. Kane gave a pause. He had no idea what to say. When nothing came, he forced out a croaked, "Good morning."

"Good morning. I hoped it was you." Avery's voice changed instantly back into the kind, caring man from the night before.

"You left me sleeping," Kane said, still searching for something to say.

"You were completely out when I left. I showered, dressed, turned on the news and you never woke. I figured you needed it. Did leaving you sleeping mess up your day? I considered that, I just had no idea when you went in to work," Avery said.

"No, not really. I'm usually there by now, but I don't have to be. Paulie's got it, I'm sure."

"How do you feel?" Avery asked, his voice lowering an octave.

"My hurt heads?" Kane answered, not going where he thought Avery might be leading.

"What about the other parts?" Avery asked in his sexy voice, and he could feel the blush heating his cheeks. He never openly talked about sex.

"I'm a little sore. Not bad," he answered honestly.

"Good. What do you think about tonight?" Avery clearly went after what he wanted.

"I have to work," Kane said.

"Come over after, like you did last night. I'll make sure you get up in the morning. We can set the alarm," Avery said, efficiently attempting to tie up any loose end he could see in his overall plan.

"All right, if you change your mind, call the restaurant," Kane said, finally pulling himself up to sit on the side of the bed, neither his ass nor head seemed comfortable with the move.

"I promise, I won't. Have a good day. You've made mine better already." Avery's voice was fully in that sexy low thing he pulled off so well.

"Me too. I'll talk to you later," Kane said and hung up the phone. He only sat there a minute before he forced himself to begin his day.

Chapter 10

"Someone got laid last night. Dude! About time," Rodney said as Kane walked through the restaurant, officially three hours late. He had to give Rodney credit, his hands never stopped working the glasses into the ceiling rack of the bar. His eyes did narrow, examining Kane's face as he got closer. "You drank, too? A fuck and alcohol. Whoa, man! Give me five!"

"You don't know that," Kane said, shoving his sunglasses up on his face, ignoring the outstretched hand. He'd only worn them in a lame attempt to hide his bloodshot eyes. Of course, a bartender could pick up on someone with a hangover—it was usually his handiwork that created the situation.

"I absolutely do know. You're late, wearing sunglasses, squinting, and walking funny. Let me see your eyes," Rodney said, rounding the corner to get a better look.

"Paulie! Your boy's here," Rodney called out to Kane's retreating back.

"I seriously think you need to be fired," Kane said, pivoting back on his heels, shocked at what Rodney had just done. What the heck was Rodney thinking calling Paulie out here!

"Whatever. Paulie, he's been drinking. He needs to be in trouble," Rodney called out, crossing his arms over his chest, grinning big as

Paulie came through the kitchen door, drying his hands off with a kitchen towel.

"Rod, leave the boy alone. He needed a good drunk fuck," Paulie said, his gravelly voice completely amused.

"I'm standing right here. I can hear everything you say," Kane said to both of them.

"He's walking funny, too," Rodney said, hitting Paulie in the shoulder. "Show him how you're walking funny, Kane."

"That's it. This is completely inappropriate. I don't ask you about your sex life, I don't need you asking me." Kane went straight through the back doors to his office.

"I wasn't askin'. See how he's walking, Paulie?" Rodney made a big production, calling out after him. Kane could hear Paulie's cackle all the way back to his office. For good measure, Kane slammed his office door and then winced at the loud bang. Why had he done that? Not a smart move considering his present condition. Kane dropped down in his desk chair, pulled out a few more aspirin from his desk drawer, and downed them dry. The clock chimed noon, sounding very much like church bells reverberating right through his office. He let out an unsteady sigh, and prayed the medicine kicked in soon; he never let himself drink that much. He hadn't been at the restaurant for ten minutes and this already felt like an incredibly long day. The knock on his door had him narrowing his brow.

"Who is it?" Kane barked.

"Philip," the new waiter called out.

"If you're alone, you can come in," Kane said, pulling the receipts from last night's totals.

"Rodney said you needed this?" Philip said, bringing him a large piece of foam packing material from the wine bottles shipped into the restaurant.

"What for?" Kane looked up, clearly confused, but took what was being offered.

"He said you needed it to sit on." Philip looked sincere, but the bark of laughter from the other side of the door showed the kid had been set up. Kane stifled a chuckle, because Philip still didn't understand what he had done, or why it was so funny to everyone now gathering in his doorway. Kane tossed the foam and the kid out of his office and slammed the door again with a smile on his face.

* * * *

Avery sat on the end of the bar at La Bella Luna, perched on the barstool he'd taken up residence on for the last couple of hours. Out of nothing more than desperation, and his inability to stay away from this man, he'd shown up at the restaurant around nine thirty. Kane and his crew didn't seem to mind him being there, so that was where he stayed—at the bar, out of the way of the busy dining room. Rodney kept him company as he could and supplied him with endless information about Kane. The more Avery heard, the more he liked.

Kane, for his part, pretty much ignored Avery—other than the first few minutes after his arrival at the bar. Kane went on about his night, running the restaurant like a well-oiled machine. There was nothing Kane couldn't do, no part of the operation he didn't jump in and help along when needed. If the kitchen got behind, he cooked. If the bar needed help, he mixed drinks. Kane cleaned tables, served food, and sat customers all with the patience of Job.

Rodney kept Avery's signature drink, Chivas and water, full, and Avery had drunk several glasses over the last few hours. He was a believer in the benefits of drinking before bottoming. If this continued between him and Kane, he'd get more accustomed to the invasion, but for now, he needed the liquid encouragement and relaxation.

Avery popped a few peanuts in his mouth as Paulie came out of the kitchen, pulling off his cap, and took a seat beside him. He didn't remember Paulie being so short or wrinkled when they'd previously met at Avery's table. Avery wondered if he might have been in the military at some point. He'd guess a sailor. His arms were tattooed up and down, his voice was harsh and gravely, and he was very direct, in a good way.

"So you're interested in my boy?" Paulie asked, angling up on the stool beside him. Rodney placed a whiskey in front of the man before he ever fully took the seat.

"Yes, sir, I am," Avery said, matching Paulie's sideways glance, trying to hide the grin forming. For all of Kane's baggage with his biological family, he sure had a group of solid people in this restaurant all looking out for him.

"Are you a good guy or one of those hippie free-lifers?" Paulie asked, the disgust clear in his voice. Avery barked out a laugh, so did the bartender, but Paulie's expression made it clear he didn't see the humor.

"Well, sir, I'm not a hippie, I don't guess. My ancestry might actually roll over in their graves had I chosen an anti-government stance. I might have had a moment or two of free love, though, along the way. I can say, since I met Kane, he makes me want to be a better man." Rodney reached out a hand to give Avery a quick good-answer slap.

"Kane Dalton's a good man, better than anyone I've ever known. He deserves that back. I heard you were here to get into politics. How's that gonna work?" Paulie asked, taking a big long drink of his whiskey without a single wince at the burn as he swallowed. Clearly whiskey was the man's drink of choice.

"Paulie, give the guy a break. It's their second date," Markie said, sliding a drink tray onto the bar.

"Date?" Paulie gave a grunt. "Nobody ever goes on a real date anymore! My Marjorie and I, now we had some good times out together. Kane deserves to be taken out on the town."

"Paulie," Kane warned, coming up from behind. He carried a rack filled with glasses. The restaurant was officially closed, and they were in cleaning mode now.

"Paulie! Paulie! Is there a parakeet around here? You do deserve to be taken out. There's nothing wrong in saying it, and I think this pretty boy has it in him to take you out, show you a good time." Kane cut his eyes over to Avery, clearly embarrassed. Avery just grinned back. This was a family. A tight family and he loved to watch them interact.

"I'm sorry," Kane shot out when Paulie was done with his rant.

"No need," Avery said. He tended to agree with Paulie, and he was definitely up to the task of taking Kane out on the town. By this time, most of the restaurant staff had gathered around them at the small bar. Rodney worked to supply everyone a drink, seeming to know what each person wanted without asking. Paulie was their patriarch, and Avery wondered if perhaps they were all a little misplaced in the world, but together they'd found a unit.

"Paulie, you know who his granddad is, right? He's President Adams," Kane interjected. The statement came out of nowhere and didn't fit the conversation at all. Kane had just tried to change the subject. Sneaky man.

"No kidding?" Paulie took the bait, turning fully on his barstool to face Avery. "Now that was a good man. A statesman. Our last true statesman. Best president we ever had."

Paulie went off on the wonders of Avery's grandfather's administration while Kane looked at him, raised a finger, and mouthed to give him a minute. Avery nodded, kept the amused smile on his lips at the old man who never stopped his lecture on the wonders of Avery's grandfather's policies. Kane held true to his word. He came back in a few short minutes, a duffle bag in one hand and coat in another.

"Lock up for me tonight?" Kane asked Rodney.

"Absolutely," Rodney immediately shot back, giving Avery a wink. Avery pulled his wallet out, tried to pay. He'd had four or five drinks over the last few hours, but all three men were immediately on him. Apparently his money wasn't any good at the bar, which was a first for Avery.

"Go on! You two have some fun. The night's still young," Paulie called out, waving them on. Kane seemed more than happy to oblige, already halfway across the restaurant before Avery had his wallet tucked in his back pocket and his coat shrugged on.

"Good night, thank you." Avery jogged the steps until he reached Kane who now held the front door open for him.

"I was gonna change, but I didn't take the time. I'm sorry about that in there. He's getting old, too old really, to be doing all this," Kane said as soon as they got a safe distance from the front door.

"No, it's fine. They're protective of you. I admire that," Avery said, dropping his hands in his pockets. Kane seemed immune to the cold as they walked stride for stride toward Avery's apartment.

"He is, for sure. He's been like that since the beginning. He took me in when my parents kicked me out. I owe him everything. I'm not sure where I'd be today without him," Kane said. Avery jogged ahead, opening the front doors to his building for Kane. Security sat at their station, acknowledging him with a nod as Avery shivered in the warmth of the lobby. After a couple of steps, Avery reached out and took Kane's hand in his, entwining their fingers. Kane's hand was warm against his, and he imagined his body would be too. Neither spoke a word as they walked, hand in hand, toward his bank of elevators.

"I like your restaurant. Those are good people," Avery said, trying to find something to say. His entire body was focused on finally being able to touch Kane again. "You won't have to get me too drunk. I did lots of that work for you."

"Good, then we can get right down to business," Kane said quietly, looking around to make sure no one was in hearing distance.

"What? Was that a joke? Did Kane Dalton just lighten up enough around me to joke?" Avery teased, stepping in closer, standing chest to chest with Kane.

"Ha ha," Kane said, grinning. He didn't step back, just stood there with his head tilted slightly up, looking Avery in the eyes.

"I like when you smile, and when you laugh. You've done more smiling tonight than the first two nights I saw you." Avery's gaze lowered to that sexy mouth. Images of his cock sliding between Kane's perfect lips had stayed with him most of the day. Now they turned his half arousal into something hard and solid.

"I'm nervous around you," Kane admitted. Avery liked how Kane just spoke the truth. There was no cat and mouse with him. He didn't hide himself or make Avery guess what was going on inside his head.

"Good. I don't want you to think I'm the pushover I've clearly become when I'm around you. When's your next night off?" Avery asked. The elevator dinged and opened, and he stepped inside, pulling Kane in with him.

"I don't really take nights off. Remember, I told you, they say I work too much."

"Well, working too much and never taking a day off are two different things," Avery said, pushing the button to his floor. He rested against the back wall, pulling Kane between his legs, wrapping his arms around his waist. This time he pulled him close enough to feel Kane's arousal was as hard as his.

"I want to take you out. Paulie's right, you deserve some wining and dining," Avery said, leaning in to kiss his lips.

"You don't…" Kane started, but Avery cut him right off.

"Shhh…yes, I do. I heard about a dance club over in St. Paul. Maybe we could go this weekend," Avery suggested.

"I'll have to see if I can get Rodney to take over my shift, but maybe. If you really want to."

"I want," Avery said, going in for the kiss. He was denied as the elevator doors chimed again, this time for his floor, and Kane turned, moving out from under his hold and toward the opening. Avery let Kane lead them off the elevator, but stopped in the hallway jerking Kane against him. He loved when Kane stumbled back in surprise as he fused their mouths together. Avery loved kissing Kane. He slid his arms around him, pushing him back a step or two until they hit the front door of his condo. He fumbled for his keys, kissing Kane all the while until he was forced to look down to place the key inside the lock.

"I thought about you all day," Avery said, turning the knob while wrapping a strong arm around Kane's waist, keeping him from stumbling backward as he shoved open the door. "Did you pack this bag to stay all night?"

"No, I planned to change, but I didn't want you stuck there listening to Paulie any more than you had to," Kane said, his head leaned back, giving Avery complete access to his neck as he slowly backed him into the apartment.

"I'll listen to him all day. He loves you," Avery said, kicking the door closed behind him.

"I love him, too," Kane said, dropping his coat and duffle bag to the floor. He slid his hands under Avery's jacket, pushing it from his shoulders. The composed, elegant Kane wasted no time unwrapping Avery from his clothing like an eager child on Christmas morning revealing a long-awaited toy. Somewhere in the last thirty seconds, they had switched places and Avery could barely keep up.

"I can't believe I fell asleep before I got my turn last night," Kane said, shoving Avery's undershirt and sweater over his head before letting it fall to floor.

"You were drunk," Avery said. He tried to undress Kane, but he couldn't seem to gain control for even a minute. Kane was a man on a mission.

"You're pretty tipsy, now," Kane said as he shoved Avery's slacks and underwear down until they fell freely to the floor.

"So you can use me all up," Avery managed, kicking his feet free of the clothing. Only then did Kane have him in his arms, kissing Avery as if his very life depended on their connection. Kane's hands caressed their way across his body until he flicked Avery's nipple between his fingers. The move sent Avery's hips in an involuntary roll. Kane released him and pushed him back. Avery was surprised to find they had already made it to his bedroom, and he landed back on the bed. Kane stared down at him sprawled out across the covers. A sexy, evil grin lit his lover's face as he began to pull off his clothes.

"And I *intend* to use you all up."

Chapter 11

No amount of talking could divert Avery from his plan to pick Kane up for their date. Since he'd been with Kane every single day and night for the last five days, they had done quite a bit of talking on the subject. Kane was a classic gentleman to the extreme, and that endeared him to Avery's heart like nothing else had ever before. Which was odd because if anyone had asked Avery a week ago what he wanted in a partner, old fashioned wouldn't have even made it into the top one hundred attributes. But number one on that list would have fit Kane to a T: a good-looking, sexy lover! Kane never seemed to get enough—just the way Avery liked it.

The area of St. Paul where Kane lived differed greatly from the polished, sophisticated almost-boyfriend that Avery had gotten to know over the last week. Kane's demeanor seemed out of place in the loud, colorful part of town that housed the brownstone quad-complex he shared. The building included four smaller apartments made out of an older brick home, and these type homes were stacked side by side for the entire length of the block. Completely different than the man who wore handmade suits and designer jeans every single day.

Avery parked his Stingray at the curb, taking care to lock the doors. He loved his brand new car. After a minute's pause and a simple prayer that the Corvette would still be there when they came down,

Avery made his way inside the building. Kane lived on the top floor, four flights up, and Avery huffed all the way upstairs.

Knocking on the door, he waited. After what felt like forever, he knocked again. Kane answered in a rush, opening the door before hurrying off again. "I'm late. I didn't get out of the restaurant when I wanted too," he yelled over his shoulder. Avery watched his retreating back as he pulled a polo over his head and disappeared through a side open doorway. Avery stepped in, a little surprised. His image of Kane fit perfectly with this living room. Although the room was small, he kept everything immaculate and completely color coordinated. Every picture, lamp, and table fit together. Nothing was out of place, and everything was so neat and tidy, Avery thought he might be able to eat off the floor.

"I like your place," Avery said from the entryway. He cocked his head, bending to get a better look down the hall. From this angle, it appeared as though there were only two doors at the end of the small hall. He stood in the living room, and the small kitchen was just to his right. He wished he could see Kane's bedroom. A bedroom said a lot about a man.

"Thanks, it's small, not the best part of town, but I've lived here a few years now," Kane shouted back. "I'm sorry I'm late."

"It's fine, we aren't on a time schedule. This is like downtown St. Paul now, isn't it?" Avery said, losing the battle with polite manners and taking a couple of steps farther inside the home.

"Yeah," Kane said, rounding the corner while raking his fingers through his hair. Avery liked that move, which Kane seemed to do quite a bit. Perhaps a nervous habit? Avery found he loved to run his fingers through Kane's short, thick strands when they lay in bed together. All in all, Kane had some great hair.

"Why are you standing here?" Kane asked, and Avery realized there wasn't a good explanation for where he stood. He wasn't in the living room any longer. He'd inched his way to stand almost in the hall. Silence ensued between them. "What? Did I miss something?"

"It's just rare to be this close to a bedroom and not be in it." Avery grinned, dropping his hands in his slacks pockets.

"Is that new for you?" Kane threw out, sliding on the shoes by his front door.

"New for us," Avery shot back.

"You can take a look around. There isn't much to the place. This is kind of it," Kane said.

"Nah, I think I need to stay here. You look too good tonight. We won't make it out the door if I step any farther in this house, and I really wanna take you out," Avery said. Kane gave a little sideways smile, running his fingers back through his hair as a small blush crept into his cheeks. He walked across the living room toward a coatrack by the front door.

"Thank you, you look nice, too," Kane said, reaching for his jacket.

"What? This old thing?" Avery held open the lapels of his brand new suit. Kane laughed as Avery posed with his suit jacket open revealing a partially buttoned silk button down. As Kane watched, Avery executed a perfect full circle turn on his heels before doing an exaggerated strut down a make-believe catwalk, all headed toward Kane.

"It's a hundred percent silk dress shirt that I bought just for you. Thoughts of you dancing against me, rubbing those sexy hands across my chest made me buy this without a second thought." He turned like he was going to give Kane a kiss, and instead flipped around and wiggled his ass. Avery was forced to jump backward or be slammed with the door as it was pushed open in front of him. Avery watched as Kane's entire demeanor changed when he saw whoever was at the door.

"What are you doing here?" Kane asked, and Avery stepped around the door to see a nice looking, much shorter man, who clearly had a key to this apartment, standing in the entryway. The fun vibe of a minute ago was zapped from the room and Avery narrowed his brow in speculation.

"I came for my things. Who's this?" So this must be the ex-boyfriend. Jealousy struck Avery hard. He wanted this guy out of the house and gone, right now.

"Avery Adams, his date. Who are you?" Avery answered for Kane, sticking out his hand for a handshake.

"Brian Walton, his boyfriend." Avery wanted to snap the guy's arm right off his body.

"Really? Because I'm pretty sure I replaced you and thanks for vacating the spot..." Avery was on a roll, but Kane jumped in, taking the wind out of his sails.

"Brian, why are you here?" Kane asked. The entire conversation took place in the small entryway and Avery resisted the overwhelming urge to wrap an arm around Kane in ownership.

"I came for a few of my things, but we need to talk," Brian said. Avery watched something spark in the guy as he stared first at Avery, then back at Kane. Avery knew the look—competition. Shit. He'd made it worse with his cocky attitude. He'd only had a few days to solidify his position in Kane's life, this guy had had years.

"You should've called first. I have a date tonight, Brian," Kane said, stepping in front of Avery to take the doorknob.

"Date? Really? You?" Brian laughed in Kane's face.

"Call the restaurant and leave them your address. I'll have your things delivered to you." Kane's voice took on that super calm tone, the one he used in the restaurant. Avery found that voice meant so many things, none of which indicated Kane was comfortable with the moment. Avery didn't like it. He didn't like the guy laughing in Kane's face or the insinuation Kane couldn't get a date.

If Avery right-hooked him, how much trouble would he be in?

"That's all you have to say to me? Four years together and you replaced me in a couple of days?" Kane didn't bite, but gently and thoroughly put his hand on Brian's chest and began moving him backward, the door shutting a little farther with every step taken.

"Remember, you met someone," Kane said.

"I had second thoughts. Don't do this, Kane, I'm sorry. There I said it," Brian said.

"Too late," Avery called out from behind Kane. Avery felt territorial and primal. He clenched his fists and dropped them into his pockets to keep from going after the guy.

"That's not for you to decide," Brian shouted back at Avery. That got his attention. Avery's eyes narrowed, and he ripped his hands free of his slacks, moving around Kane, toward Brian. Brian backed the rest of the way out of the apartment, holding up his hands. Kane's hands were on Avery's chest, pushing him back, so he slammed the door shut with his foot. Avery locked the dead bolt in a show of dominance.

"That's what you want?" Brian yelled through the door.

"Get out of here!" Avery yelled back, already unlocking the front door. Fuck the consequences; Brian needed an ass whoopin'. Brian didn't have to be told twice, though. He hightailed it out of there as Avery jerked open the front door.

"You dated *him*?" Avery said, heading to the top of the stairs. Brian was already three flights down. He'd zipped down those stairs faster than anything Avery had ever seen.

"Avery..." Kane said from behind him. He willed himself to calm. He'd won the battle and kept his man, but settling down was hard to do.

"Seriously, Kane, thank God I came along. You dated a weasel like him for four years?" Avery said, turning and looking at Kane incredulously. He had tried for funny, but fell short, and ended up being aggressive and insulting.

"He isn't that bad, Avery," Kane said. He reached back inside his apartment to grab his coat and locked the door before pulling it shut.

"He certainly is that bad," Avery said, openly staring at Kane as if he were the craziest man on the planet. Kane laughed and sidestepped Avery, heading down the stairs. Avery took them at a slower pace.

"Forget him. Let's get on with this date you keep talking about," Kane said, glancing back over his shoulder at Avery as he rounded the stairwell, taking the next flight of stairs down.

"I don't want him here anymore," Avery said, taking each step much slower. Kane was already close to the door.

"Neither do I," Kane replied, peeking up at Avery over the banister.

"I'm not kidding, Kane. I think you need to move in with me where he can't find you. He makes me uncomfortable," Avery said. By the one raised eyebrow on Kane's face, Avery had to mentally stop his rant and think about what he might have said that caused that look. He couldn't figure it out. The answer seemed so clear to him.

"What? I'm serious. Don't stay here anymore. At least move out for a while." Avery let out a sigh as he came to stand right in front of Kane. "I'm jealous," Avery admitted, taking the sides of Kane's jacket and pulling him against his body until they were standing chest to chest. Kane had to lift his head to look him in the eyes, and Avery loved that move. He took it as an invitation for a kiss, and he kissed Kane simply on the lips. Having Kane in his arms soothed his ruffled feathers, but he wanted Kane to agree with him before he let go of his anger.

"I get how you're a force to be reckoned with," Kane said.

"I'm sorry. I can't tell you who to be friends with, but I don't like him, I don't want him around, and I want you to move in with me," Avery said. The raised brow was back and he finally understood what he'd said that caused the look to begin with.

"I didn't know he was coming tonight. I'm supposed to be at work. I guess he'd planned for me to be gone," Kane said, stumbling over his words.

"Let's go, and just plan on staying at my house for a while. I'd feel better with you there," Avery said, wrapping an arm around Kane, trying to get him out the door.

"Avery, I was supposed to be at work." Kane tried again as if that answered some point Avery had made. It didn't. Avery let the argument go for now. By the end of the night, he'd have Kane in his house, exactly where he needed to be. Besides, it was just safer all the way around.

As they stepped outside, relief struck him hard. "Thank God my car's still here!"

* * * *

The music blared, the strobe lights flashed, and the disco ball spun, yet to Kane there was nothing more in the world than the man who slow danced in his arms. Something by Donna Summer screamed in the background, men in various states of dress crowded in beside them, but nothing could drag his attention from Avery. He lowered his head to Avery's shoulder and tucked his face in against the man's neck, breathing him in as they swayed to the beat of the sounds. Avery kissed him lightly wherever his lips could reach, and Kane closed his eyes, letting Avery's natural charm take him away.

"You're anything but boring. You know that right?" Avery said loud enough for Kane to hear.

"Maybe not boring, just intense and a workaholic." Kane didn't budge from his spot, but reached his lips forward to kiss Avery's neck. He never opened his eyes.

"Oh, you are those things," Avery yelled, and Kane chuckled.

"I know, but most people think that's a bad thing," Kane said. The song began to change, a faster beat, but they kept the slow steady pace. They were several hours in with more drinks downed than Kane had drunk in a long time. The hours ticked away, their first date coming to an end.

"I think it's sexy," Avery said. Kane's reward for such a crazy comment was to run his hands down Avery's now shirtless back to grip his ass, squeezing until he wrapped his arms back around Avery's waist, hugging him tightly.

"Have you ever done it in a public place?" Avery's lips brushed against his ear.

"Of course not," Kane responded. For the first time in several minutes, he looked up. The amount of alcohol he'd drunk caused the room to spin just slightly until his eyes settled on Avery's cocky grin. He was learning that smile usually meant Avery had an outrageous plan and Kane better buckle up, because he had no choice but to hang on and enjoy the ride.

"We aren't far from home," Kane suggested, putting a minuscule amount of space between them. Avery apparently took great offense to that, pulling Kane right back against him, locking him in his arms.

"We're closer to the bathroom, and it's your turn to top," Avery stated, clearly playing all the cards right now.

"People get arrested for that," Kane said.

"Not here. Come on, let me show you." Avery grabbed Kane's hand and pulled him across the dance floor. He was a man on a mission. No matter how Kane resisted, Avery held on until they hit a darkened hall where the restrooms were located. Avery pushed open a door and angled Kane in front of him as they entered. The light was dim, matching the mood of the dance floor, and there were a few men inside.

"Avery, no! Not here." Kane tried to make him see reason, spinning around in Avery's arms. Kane's face was tilted up as he tried guiding Avery back out the restroom door. One second he was successfully pushing Avery out the door, the next thing he knew Avery's tongue was shoved down his throat.

Kane lost his balance as he was pushed back against a wall. The wall didn't hold as Avery urgently assaulted his mouth. Kane pitched backward, stumbling several steps. Avery held on tight, making the whole thing harder when they both reached out to steady themselves. The maneuver had Kane losing his footing, and he landed ass down on the toilet. The spinning in his head was out of control. Dazed and confused, it took him a second to realize Avery was locking the stall door and working quickly to rid himself of his slacks.

"Baby, we don't have time to waste. Hurry," Avery said, pushing his waistband down, freeing his rigid cock. Avery's cock bobbed in front of him, begging for his touch. Kane reached forward, and after one simple touch, Avery was on him, pulling him to his feet, unfastening his slacks, and pushing them down his thighs. Clearly Avery was a professional at this sort of thing.

He found a small cabinet door tucked against the back wall. To Kane's drunken mind, it magically opened and inside laid a generic bottle of lube and some condom packets. His eager partner grabbed the lube, left the condoms, and pushed the bottle into Kane's hands.

"I want you to fuck me," Avery whispered and took his mouth in a hungry kiss. "Fuck me so I know I'm yours."

"You must like this bottoming thing," Kane said, grinning. He opened the bottle of lube, but apparently he wasn't fast enough as Avery grabbed the bottle and began pouring lube on Kane's cock and stroking down his length. Kane hissed as Avery's tongue pushed into his mouth again. This time the invasion was quick, and Avery tore from the kiss, looking Kane in the eyes.

"You have to be faster. Come on. We'll be caught," Avery said, turning around, facing the wall. Avery hadn't been joking when he'd insisted they needed to be faster.

"I thought you said it was okay," Kane kept his eyes on the door.

"In theory it is, until the cops come," Avery answered.

"Maybe we should go..." The words trailed off when he saw Avery's perfect ass sticking out at him, and he watched, mesmerized as Avery pushed two fingers into himself. The sight had him reaching for his own dick and stroking himself while he enjoyed the show. Avery was opening himself up for him. No one had ever done that in front of him and it was sexy as hell. He was on the edge, and he wasn't even inside Avery. If he weren't so worried about getting caught, he might just sit there all night and watch his lover work himself on his own digits. But they didn't have time. He stepped up behind Avery.

"Let me." He nudged Avery's hand out of his way, and using his well-oiled finger, he slid over Avery's rim, pushing in past the knuckle, easily finding the gland. Avery arched back on the move.

"Put it in, Kane, I'm ready!" Avery gazed at him over his shoulder, then reached back to help guide Kane's hard cock to his entrance. His lover sank back; warmth gripped him as Avery's channel stretched around him. They both moaned loudly as Kane filled him.

"Fuck me like you mean it," Avery growled. For Kane, it was exactly what he needed to hear. The feeling of being buried deep in Avery's ass had his knees shaking and his lips quivering. He dug his fingers into Avery's hips and pushed deeper into that tight, constricting heat.

"You're so tight...feels so good," Kane moaned.

"Come on, Kane, I need it hard!" Avery pushed back on him, meeting Kane thrust for thrust. He rammed his hips forward, losing himself in the feel of Avery's body yielding to his. As he withdrew from Avery's snug channel, Kane grabbed for the small bottle sitting on the back of the toilet and poured more lube on his dick. Kane made a mess, but the slickness was what he needed to do the trick, allowing him to slide deeper and fill Avery completely. *Yes!* He began a steady pounding against Avery's ass. The sound of skin slapping against skin could be heard with each thrust forward.

"Yes!" Avery gasp, raising up, driving Kane's body deeper into his. Avery ground against him, his lover's hands banged loudly against the metal stall he used for leverage. Kane continued fucking him in long hard strokes and awkwardly kicked at his legs trying to spread them farther apart. The tangled slacks at his feet only allowed for so much.

Avery wasn't quiet as shameless whimpers and guttural moans echoed off the walls of the small cubical. Kane held most of Avery's weight as he crumbled against him, his lover's back pressed against his chest as he dropped his head on to Kane's shoulder. Kane never stopped the sensual assault, reaching low to stroke Avery hard and fast. The smell of Avery, sweat and sex, filled his nostrils. Such a potent scent, one that clouded his brain and settled deep inside his balls.

"Ahh...Kane." Avery passed the point of sensible. He begged and pleaded, his words making little sense. Kane continued impaling him, driving deep inside him.

Minutes felt like hours. The whole experience was perfect and this moment was so right. Avery's eyes were closed, lips parted, pleasure clear on his face. Kane loved all the eager sounds coming from him, reveled in them. His lover tensed and fell forward, his dick twitching in Kane's hand as liquid warmth spilled over his fingers. Avery's passage tightened, drawing him in and constricting around him, milking him. That was all it took. He dropped his head on Avery's back and sank his teeth into Avery's salty skin, barely pulling free in enough time to shoot his creamy load across Avery's ass.

* * * *

Slowly the earth settled back. Avery had his cheek pressed against the cold steel bathroom stall, drool gathering in his open mouth. What the hell just happened? When he suggested a bathroom run, he had no idea his entire world was about to be completely rocked. What a ride! Kane Dalton fucked him like he had never been fucked before in his life. And he hadn't even been drunk. He'd switched to water hours ago. Damn!

"Baby, you gotta get up," Avery said, twitching his shoulders where he felt Kane pressed up against him.

"I told you it would be good," Kane said. Avery laughed at that one. They had to be a complete mess. The evidence of Kane's orgasm ran down his ass cheek.

"I think that was me telling you that, and you saying, no, we'll be caught," Avery said in a teasing voice. He reached over, grabbed the toilet paper, and attempted to clean his ass.

"Well, I knew it was one of us. Let me clean you," Kane said, wiping his hands on a wad of toilet paper before taking over the task. He was sloppy, clearly still very drunk and totally in that satiated after-sex moment. It took a minute, but they cleaned themselves up the best they could and dressed between small kisses and silly grins. It wasn't until Avery opened the door that he found they had an audience.

"Dude, that was some serious hot shit coming out of that stall!" The guy standing right outside their door was young, a punk rocker with a foot long, multi-colored Mohawk. Avery grinned, sliding an arm around Kane's shoulders, drawing him in close to his side. Kane matched him, wrapping an arm around his back, the other over his stomach.

They kept that awkward hold as they found their jackets, Avery's shirt long gone on the dance floor. They stayed glued to one another until they reached the front doors of the bar where Avery had to fish out his valet ticket. He moved right back into the circle of Kane's arms, letting his lover's warmth consume him. Avery never remembered holding anyone this close for the world to see or feeling totally comfortable as he did right that minute.

"Our sex is always good," Kane whispered, laying his head on Avery's chest, right below his shoulder.

"The best," Avery whispered back, kissing the top of Kane's hair.

"You were hot tonight. I loved dancing with you," Kane said.

"I want more of this. I want you to stay at my house," Avery said. Kane's head jerked up, but Avery pushed it back against his chest. "You don't have to call it a move-in. I get that it freaks you out, but I'm just a couple of buildings down from the restaurant. It's a safer neighborhood, and Brian can't get to you."

Kane slowly lifted his head, looking closely at Avery. "I only live there because I try to pour everything back into the restaurant. I wanna expand. It's cheap there."

"Babe, my place is even cheaper," Avery said, looking down at the beautiful upturned face. As usual, he couldn't resist leaning in and placing a simple kiss on Kane's perfect lips.

"Now, I can tell you're going to argue. But, Kane, it just makes sense. You don't have to give up your place. Keep it as long as you want, just stay at my house. We didn't even get Brian's key from him. It'll make me feel better. Besides, I already cleaned out drawers and closet space for you. The shoes you left over there are lonely for your other things."

"I just met you," Kane said, not responding to his teasing.

"I don't care. I like the idea of moments like this with you. *Always*," Avery said, nodding as he let the word sink in. "You fit me perfectly. And I knew you would. From the first minute I saw you, I just knew." Avery's words were packed full of the emotion churning through him. He kept his movements tender. "You get quiet when I say words like that. It makes me insecure."

"I like what you're saying, it's just so fast," Kane whispered.

"Amount of time doesn't matter. Let's do this, see where it goes," Avery said, staring intently down at him. Kane finally nodded, and relief caused Avery to tighten his grip on the man.

"Let's go home," Avery said as his car pulled in front of them, forcing them apart. Avery took a twenty from his wallet, tipping the valet as Kane walked over to the car.

Frustration shot through him as he looked over to find Kane already inside the car. He hated not being able to get the door for him. Really? Avery rounded the hood and refused to consider what a seriously lovesick fool he had become in such a short time.

He slid inside the running Corvette and looked over to his lover. Kane had his head back on the rest, and he swiveled the angle until he could see Avery. A crooked grin spread across his lips.

"I had fun tonight," Kane said. Avery reached down and linked their fingers before using the space between their palms to push the gear in place, apparently unwilling to let go of Kane for any length of time.

"Me too," Avery said to Kane's snore. He drove slower than normal all the way home, taking care of his precious cargo that apparently had sinus problems tonight based on the soft snores growing in intensity.

Chapter 12

The pencil twirled through Avery's deft fingers as he sat back to kick his legs up on the conference room table. He listened to the long-winded voter demographic breakdown given by a senior staff member of the Democratic Senatorial Campaign Committee. They were three hours into this Sunday afternoon meeting where Avery had been an hour and a half late. His mother, Kennedy Adams, flew in for the meeting and sat across the table from him. She sat next to Janice, who sat right next to his new campaign chairman, Dennis Joslin, and on his side of the table, sat another overdressed three piece suit that Avery wasn't really sure why he was in the meeting.

By design, this gathering was intended to be a closed-door, somewhat secret, and very private meeting where the Democrats and Avery ironed out their agreement to move him forward in the Senate race.

Based on everything said, the Democratic Party seemed clear: they had found their man in Avery. His preliminary acceptance and approval ratings were high. With a small amount of tweaking and a large amount of prepping, he should be a shoo-in. Yet, this was the part of politics he hated the most. The almost manipulative calculating, poll numbers on every type of survey known to man, the studies of household voting practices…God, Avery hated those the most!

For Avery, this was all major boring bullshit. He'd pushed up his shirt sleeves, loosened his tie, and poured himself a double Chivas, which he'd refilled once already. His legs were crossed, the heels of his dress shoes on the table, and he leaned as far back as the squeakless chair would go, resting his head on the headrest.

Avery kept his eyes on the speaker. One of his best lessons from law school was how to stare someone in the eye, let them believe you were truly listening to them, and tune them out completely. It was exactly what he was doing right now because his mind kept straying back to how sexy Kane was when he danced, and how he'd had to leave his warm inviting bed, with Kane wrapped around him, to come to this stupid meeting.

Kane had agreed to come back to his place tonight after work. Avery took nothing for granted where Kane was concerned and would ask to make sure Kane came back every night. He'd never just come on his own. Avery mentally frowned and then wondered if the look had crossed his face as the speaker faltered in his lecture. He couldn't help the facial faux pas, every time he thought about Brian showing up at Kane's place, completely unannounced, it thoroughly pissed him off.

Brian begging for a second chance had taken some of the wind out of his sails. Avery had pretty much convinced himself that he and Kane were a love-at-first-sight kind of couple. They were soul mates finally reconnected. Something made in the movies, most definitely a happily ever after. But Brian messed that up a little for him. He had longevity, where Avery only had a few days, and nothing really talked through between him and Kane. Not only was nothing talked through, they also had this monumental Senate race looming over them that Avery hadn't mentioned one word about. Quiet, reserved Kane Dalton, who was shunned by his family for being gay, wasn't just going to easily jump on board with this.

"If you can tell by this graph, we have isolated the problem areas here in green. We have hired Mr. Freeport here. He's a top campaign manager, his last four campaigns have won their districts, and if you stay on the plan we've outlined, you should have an easy landslide victory."

Avery continued to stare at the speaker, barely hearing anything he said until he realized all eyes were on him. He had to tick back in his head to remember the last thing said. With no luck, he chided himself. He was usually far better and much craftier at hiding the fact he ignored people. Damn! So, instead of answering, he paused a moment, biting at his thumbnail. If he moved forward with this campaign, he'd have to be careful with Kane. Public opinion was still very clear on its perceptions of homosexuality. Would Kane hide? Did he even want to hide Kane? No, he didn't, not at all. He was too proud of having finally found him.

Then how would a run affect Kane? Would it negatively impact La Bella Luna? Probably and no way Kane would take money from him. Kane wouldn't even allow Avery to pay for his dinner or drinks at night anymore. Kane's whole life was wrapped up in that restaurant.

"I've met someone," Avery blurted out. The silent stares changed from ones of thought to ones of surprise. His mother cocked her perfectly arched brow at him. He resisted the smile. He knew her thoughts were more directed toward wondering why this was the first time she had heard this. He shrugged at her.

"What exactly does that mean, Mr. Adams?" Dennis Joslin asked. "Like a someone to date? That's fine, actually even better. We can school her, fill her in, get her moving in the right direction." Avery's stare turned hard. Did he truly plan to do this? It was one thing to fantasize he'd met his mate, but another altogether different thing to truly tie himself to that person.

Avery knew the deal, understood the United States, and knew no one was ready for an openly gay political leader. What he did behind closed doors was fine, but he also didn't want to hide Kane. Under deep rejection, Kane still owned who he was as a person, even though his religious beliefs didn't always leave him comfortable with himself. As every day passed, Avery began to understand Kane thought his homosexuality was a sin. To ask Kane to hide would just make all that so much worse and unfair to both of them and their relationship.

Avery needed to talk to Kane.

"Excuse me for a minute," Avery said, dropping his feet to the floor, and abruptly standing. He walked straight out the conference room door without any explanation. He made a beeline for his office, absently slamming the door shut behind him. He didn't bother with taking a seat at his desk, he was too wound up. Instead, he reached over, picked up the phone, and dialed Kane's direct office line. He prayed he'd answer.

"La Bella Luna, can I help you?" Just the sound of Kane's voice calmed Avery.

"How are you today?" Avery asked. It wasn't the real question, but still something he wanted to know.

"I'm good, how are you?" Kane asked, and he could hear the smile in Kane's voice. He got it, he was smiling too.

"I'm good. Not sore anymore. That's good. I think it means I'm getting use to you being back there," Avery said.

"Are you okay? You sound a little tense." So Kane was learning him as he learned Kane. Good, it had to mean he cared.

"I'm good, just making a decision on some business. I have a question for you," Avery said. He sat back against his desk, his leg bouncing with anticipation.

"Shoot," Kane replied.

"All right, here's the question and I'm nervous so I'm just going to dump it out there. Pay attention," Avery said.

"Are you sure you're okay?" Kane asked again, concern in his voice.

"Are you listening?" Avery asked, ignoring Kane's question.

"Yes?"

"I'm into you. I mean really into you. Like always into you. Do you feel the same way about me?" Avery's heart thumped wildly in his chest, and he closed his eyes.

"Yes," Kane replied quietly. *Thank God!*

"Good. I'll see you later. I'll call you when I'm done here," Avery said, but Kane's voice stopped him from dropping the phone back on the hook.

"That's it?" Kane asked. Avery almost hit himself with the phone as he jerked it back up to his ear to hear what Kane said.

"Yes! Thank you for agreeing, it's what I needed to know. I'll explain later. Take care. I'll call you soon." Avery waited to hear Kane hang up before he did. Relief caused him to plop down in the chair closest to him. The dating game rules dictated they needed more time before giving declarations such as that one. But time was something he didn't have right now. Forcing himself up, he went straight back to the conference room. His decision made.

"Gentlemen, thank you for waiting, and you too, Mom, Janice," Avery said, giving his mom a warm smile before he continued. He didn't take his chair. Instead, he stood at the head of the table, looking down the row of people.

"I've met a man, not a woman. Someone I see a long-term future with." Avery kept his gaze focused, looking each person in the eye, refusing to look at his mother. This would mean more to her. He'd wait to talk this through with her later.

"They discussed this with you from the beginning, Mr. Adams. You can't be openly gay and have any chance of winning," Mr. Joslin said.

"I understand that, but it doesn't change the facts," Avery argued.

"Do you understand what we are telling you? There is no way you would be supported if you ran as a gay man. How long could you have possibly known him if you talked about this before and he wasn't a factor?" Mr. Joslin asked.

"The length of the relationship isn't important," Avery replied.

"So we hide him. You aren't the only gay man in office. We can find a nice filler woman to stand in. No one has to know..." Mr. Freeport was on a roll, the other two nodding along with him. He could see their minds ticking away with the possibilities.

"I'm not interested in hiding him. I'm not unsympathetic to the complications this poses or unfamiliar with the odds of running a viable campaign as a homosexual. Regardless, it doesn't change the facts, I refuse to hide him." Avery left no further room for discussion on the subject.

"Avery..." Kennedy Adams said from across the table. Finally, he looked over at her, and based on the look in her eyes, he couldn't tell where she was headed with her line of thinking, but whatever she had to say, needed to be said in private.

"Mother, I'm not hiding him," Avery said, just as stoned-faced and hard as he had said to the three political strategists in front of him.

"You honestly can't make this kind of decision on a recently found piece of ass, Adams. This affects more than just you," Mr. Joslin said. He was clearly disgusted with Avery's turnabout.

"Don't ever talk about him that way again." Avery turned his steely gaze in the man's direction. He understood all the time and effort they put into making this campaign a reality, but he'd climb over this table and beat the shit out of anyone who dared trash Kane.

"No offense, I swear, but come on, man. Everything's in place. You're the ticket back in. It's been sixteen years since we ran the White House. You know all this," Mr. Joslin said, changing his tactic. He appeared to believe acting like Avery's buddy would encourage him into the better decision.

"I do, but I'm gay. This country's too narrow-minded and I can't—and won't—put him through it. He's been through too much." Avery had just pulled himself from the race. He schooled his facial features, kept his game face in place, and let his internal emotions run rampant. This decision was huge and based completely on emotion over a man he'd known for a short time. But seriously, *what a man!* He allowed the thoughts of Kane to fill his heart and his mind, giving him strength.

"So that's it then. Everything's over? You just let us go on and on for nothing?" Mr. Freeport said.

"It's truly unfortunate. I would have loved to give this a shot, but I won't hide him. When you're ready to run an integrity-driven campaign, based on the honest truth of who I am, give me a call." Avery wasn't going to let them pin this on him in a negative way. It wasn't his fault the United States mentality was so incredibly shallow and narrow-minded.

He said what needed to be said and walked to the conference room door. No one moved. Janice looked proud of him and that meant something since he'd have to listen to her every day about this decision. His mother sat back in her seat, her eyes calculating. Anything could be going on inside that head of hers.

"Janice, will you show our guests out?" Avery left the room, taking long strides to the front door. He needed fresh air and perspective. This was right! Absolutely the right thing to do, he just wished he'd known Kane longer. Had the time under their belts to have commitments and those three little words spoken, but he also couldn't rip those possibilities from them. He wanted those words with Kane. He'd get those words from Kane. Kane was meant for him.

"Avery, wait!" Kennedy Adams said, her high heels clicking on the tile floor as she crossed the office toward him before he could get out the front door.

"I don't want you to try and talk me out of this." Avery rolled his eyes as he pivoted to face her.

"Son, this is a big step you're taking. Are you certain of everything you're doing right now?" she asked, coming to stand right in front of him. She was a tall woman, but he still had to lower his head to make eye contact. She looked like a worried mother, not the strong-willed business woman she had become.

"I am reasonably certain of what I'm doing," he said. She didn't look pacified by his response.

"And does this man know what you're giving up? He's good with this decision?" she asked, and Avery just stared down at her. Damn, she was good. She knew exactly the right questions to ask.

"No, he doesn't, and no, he wouldn't like me doing this. Mother, I need you to trust me on this. I know what I'm doing. I love him, and even if he isn't there with me yet, I want to give us the chance. Please go back in there and smooth those ruffled feathers. Have Janice cover the cost of their trip," Avery said. As he spoke, he reached out and took both her arms in his hands, drawing her close to him. He kissed her on the forehead before turning his searching gaze back to her. "I need to go. I'll see you back at the hotel in a little while. I'd like you to meet him, if it's not asking too much right now."

"Of course, I want to meet him," Kennedy said.

"Thank you." Avery didn't say another word. He took off out the front door. He had preparations to make and little time to do it in.

* * * *

The restaurant was packed solid. Every table was full and the waiting area was standing room only, with guests trickling outside on the front porch for a place to stand. This might just turn out to be the best Sunday night in La Bella Luna history. Kane worked feverishly to maintain the pace. As long as everything fell into place, he was sure they could pull this off.

Maybe all this positive attitude he was sporting had to do with the giant smile that never seemed to leave his face and the incredible sense of love radiating through his heart. It had only been a short time since he had started seeing Avery, yet everything about Kane was a changed man. They were the best days of his entire life.

"Kane, they're ten minutes behind in the kitchen," Rodney said, standing beside him as he ran a charge through for a client.

"Have they asked for help yet?" Kane asked, never looking up from his task.

"Not yet, but I think you need to get in there. Paulie's yelling at them all," Rodney said quietly as they stood together in the packed lobby. Kane nodded, finished with the charge, and wound his way around the tables until he dropped off the credit card and thanked everyone at the party for coming that evening. He kept his super calm composure in place, making his way to the kitchen. He barely got inside the first set of doors before Paulie let out a string of curse words to rival any sailor on a dock. Paulie had been that sailor back in the day.

"Kane, we need a bottle of Merlot, or whatever you suggest, for table twenty-one," one of his waiters said. Kane nodded as he stuck his head in the kitchen. It took a second for Paulie to see him. Every person in the kitchen was bent over their stations, working as feverishly as they could in hopes of not being targeted by Paulie's wrath.

"What are you grinning about? I got this under control," Paulie barked at him. Kane just nodded, still grinning.

"I got the wine, you're needed up front," Rodney said, shooting past him toward the wine cellar. Kane changed direction and went back the way he'd come.

He was deep in thought and bent over the hostess stand, trying to work out a problem with seating when the light dimmed above him. He glanced up to see who hovered so closely and was surprised to find Avery standing over him.

"I love that smile. Can I see you for a minute?" Avery asked.

"Can it wait? We're busy and behind," Kane started, but Avery looked crestfallen, and he immediately amended what he said. "Can you wait for me by the bar or back in the kitchen. Paulie won't yell so loudly with you in there."

"Sure, which one," Avery asked and reached out, taking Kane's hand, giving him a small squeeze. The gesture was sweet, but out of place, confusing him that much more.

"Would my office be better?" Kane questioned, and he could feel his smile faltering. Avery showing up during the height of business hours, reaching out, gripping his hand...Kane had sat through too many grieving church services. The hand squeeze was the universal signal for things are bad, and I'm so sorry. The smile completely faded as panic filled his heart.

"Your office. Come back when you can," Avery said, leaving as quickly as he'd come.

Kane worked to tie up his loose ends as dread took hold. The hopefulness of a few minutes ago fled, desperation filling its place. Kane had tried with Avery. He had broken out of his normal routines, opened himself up more than ever before. He tried hard to be the man worthy of Avery. Where had he gone wrong?

He'd left the restaurant on the busiest night of the week and gone out dancing. He'd had sex in a public place. Maybe that was it? No. Avery wanted that, right? Thoughts of Brian trickled in. If he couldn't keep someone like Brian, how in the world had he ever thought he could have Avery Adams?

Kane stalled for as long as he could. He didn't want to head back to his office. His blissful night had taken a full nosedive in a matter of thirty seconds. Maybe if he didn't go back to his office, he wouldn't have to hear the words and Avery would just leave. But Avery was a stand-up guy. He'd feel like he had to make it clear, this breakup wasn't Kane's fault, blah, blah, blah. The better plan was to get back to the office, let Avery say whatever he planned to say, and get him moving out the door sooner rather than later.

Kane's heart hurt on a level he'd never experienced before. Why did this seem to ache so much worse than both Brian and his mother?

"You all right, man?" Rodney asked as Kane walked past the bar, heading toward his office.

"Sure. Can you watch things for a minute?" Kane asked, barely looking over his shoulder or waiting for Rodney's answer. Kane pushed through the doors to find Avery pacing the hall from his office to the kitchen. *Crap.* Desolation filled his soul as Avery looked at him with worry. Kane kept quiet, dropping his sweaty palms inside his pants pockets as he decided to take it like a man, and forced himself to walk toward Avery.

"Is everything okay? Do you have time to talk to me right now?" Avery asked, and Kane nodded, coming to stop about five feet from where Avery stood. The sounds from the kitchen filled the small hall. Avery looked antsy and intense. Kane crossed his arms over his chest, trying to hold his heart inside. "Can we go in your office?"

"Please just say whatever it is you have to say. We're busy," Kane responded. His tone didn't come out harsh like he intended. Instead, he was more quiet and resolved. The super calm was completely in place. Kane knew what Avery came here to say, and he really didn't want to listen to any part of it.

Avery hesitated, seeming unsure. The emotions playing out across his face matched the havoc tearing through Kane's heart. After a second or so, Avery visibly squared his shoulders, firmed up his spine, and took the few steps separating them, wrapping Kane inside his arms. Kane resisted, but the smell of Avery's cologne, the feel of strong arms wrapping around his waist threatened tears, and he dropped his hands to his side. Crap, was he going to cry? He closed his eyes and dropped his head as Avery went in for one brief, swift, chaste kiss.

"I know you're busy, I just couldn't wait, I'll plan better next time. I turned down the Democratic Party today. They wanted me to run for the senate," Avery said, and Kane snapped his head up.

"I heard about you possibly running. You hadn't said anything. Avery, why didn't you run? Everyone's talking about you running…" Kane started but Avery cut him off, pulling him tighter against his body.

"I'm not running for office. Not anymore. Because of you," Avery said, smiling down at him.

"What? Avery, no," Kane argued, he was completely confused and too much emotion rolled through his brain to allow him to think properly. "I never asked you not to run."

"No, wait, Kane. Let me finish. Will you please hold me? Put your arms around me. I need you touching me right now." Avery lifted Kane's arms, draping them around his body. Kane was stunned as the magnitude of Avery's confession settled inside his heart.

"Avery, you can't give that up…" Avery looked frustrated and gripped the sides of his arms, pushing Kane back a step before he bent down to one knee. The whole action confused Kane as he looked down to see Avery extending a hand.

"No, Kane, you aren't listening. Let me finish. I need you to listen. I know this is too soon. And I'm not saying right now, but promise me, one year from today, that you'll marry me if you still want to be with me." Avery held a small black velvet box and flipped open the lid. Kane's eyes landed on the ring and then darted straight to Avery's face where an intense expression stared back at him. A minute or two passed with neither man willing to look away.

"Say something," Avery finally said.

"You barely know me," Kane shot back. A few minutes ago, he thought they were breaking up, and now, Avery was down on one knee. *What?*

"I said in a year. One year from today. I don't want to marry you tomorrow. A year will give us time. If either of us wants out, it's all right, but for now, this is a promise ring. You are promising to be mine," Avery said, carefully explaining everything while still down on one knee.

"We can't marry," Kane fired back.

"We can in the church. We can be married by your God's word," Avery said, pleading with him now.

"Avery, my God doesn't believe in us," Kane said. That had Avery faltering. He lowered his arms and stood, backing Kane against the wall both literally and physically.

"But he does. I know he does. I know you're meant for me. I know you're the other half of my soul. We are meant to be together. I know in one year we will be married, and I promise to spend the rest of my life loving you, taking care of and standing beside you. Say yes," Avery said, placing both palms on the side of Kane's face, slightly lifting his head to look into his eyes. "You're killing me, Kane. You told me *always* on the phone. You said you agreed with *always*."

"I'm scared," Kane whispered. He wasn't sure he'd ever said those words out loud before in his life.

"Me too. What we have between us is so strong. Please say yes," Avery said, placing a simple kiss on his lips.

"Okay," Kane said, his voice growing stronger with each word he spoke. "Yes, I will marry you in one year."

"Thank you, I'll hold you to that!" Avery grinned before devouring his slightly parted lips. Kane kissed him back with everything he held inside his heart. The barriers he'd constructed over his heart tore free. He was so completely in love with Avery Adams, and they hadn't broken up, actually quite the opposite.

Paulie stuck his head around the side wall separating them from the kitchen. They must have been heard, or more likely, Paulie eavesdropped, which was completely okay with Kane. His voice didn't match the smile he wore.

"If you two lovebirds can tear away from each other for a minute, table four has the wrong bottle of wine and Rodney's playing host. You traumatized the staff doing that dead man walking through the dining room just a minute ago. It's a bad day when the staff would rather come to me, than interrupt you," Paulie said, darting back from where he'd come.

"I asked him to marry me," Avery called out. Paulie's head shot back around the wall.

"Did ya now?" Paulie asked, coming forward to shake both their hands, taking it all in stride. Clearly that hadn't been a surprise to him.

He'd definitely eavesdropped. There was no way the old man hadn't heard them, but he pretended like he hadn't and shook Avery's hand before doing the same to Kane, ending with a big fatherly bear hug.

"In a church," Kane added, a bigger smile hitting his face.

"Great! True love prevails and table four needs their wine. And these pansy asses can't be left unattended for even a second," Paulie yelled, already rounding the corner back into the kitchen. Kane couldn't wipe the smile off his face. He leaned in to give Avery a peck on the lips, but Avery deepened the kiss.

"I got table four," Rodney called out as Kane wrapped himself around Avery, letting the world fade away.

Chapter 13

April, 1976 ~ Stillwater, Minnesota.

Kane stared at himself in the dressing room mirror for several long minutes, probably more like thirty, yet he never truly saw himself. He sat absorbed in nothing more than his thoughts. Today was his and Avery's big day, their wedding day.

His hair was cut short and perfectly styled in the latest trend. He'd even let Avery talk him into adding some very subtle lowlight auburn streaks to the front. He was surprised and rather pleased at how such an insignificant, almost unnoticeable change could make his blue eyes pop. At least that was how Avery described him after he was done. A smile came to his lips as he thought about how Avery had dropped to his knees in the entryway of their apartment and given him one of the sexiest and best blow jobs of his life because he'd followed through with that simple request.

Kane was also freshly clean shaven, plucked, tweezed, and clipped. Avery took care of all the elements of the wedding, including giving Kane a morning at the local spa. Avery had clearly missed his calling in life. His honey was a born party planner, handling every detail with skill and a decisive grace. Without question, he was certain this wedding extravaganza would fit Avery perfectly and be beyond spectacular. Just like he saw Avery—perfect and spectacular.

Avery chose handmade tuxedos for them both. The tailors performed fittings as late as a couple of days ago to make sure everything fit just right. Honestly, Kane had always spent money on his wardrobe, wanting to appear successful to his clientele, but this tuxedo was the most comfortable fit he'd ever worn.

Avery dictated every part of their wedding, but Kane drew the line at the tie. He chose a black silk necktie over the standard bowtie. His negotiating point, he caved, allowing for a slightly ruffled silk dress shirt. Avery loved the shirt he was wearing, saying Kane looked like a prince who rode in and swept him off his feet. It didn't take long for Kane to find he usually got lucky when wearing his prince shirt around the house. Avery was his perfect lover in every sense of the word.

His restaurant, La Bella Luna, was officially closed today, which was another first. In all the years he'd owned the restaurant, he'd never closed, not even on the holidays. Since the majority of the staff were misplaced from their families, having the restaurant open during Thanksgiving and Christmas was a godsend, helping to keep the depression away. Closing today said a lot. His entire little family from the restaurant was beyond excited about the upcoming nuptials.

Even though Avery claimed they would wait a year when he proposed, he began planning their wedding the same day Kane agreed to marry him. There had never been any doubt in Avery's mind that this day was going to happen. Once Kane realized the magnitude of what Avery had in mind, he immediately halted everything, making Avery promise to keep the wedding small and intimate. Based on Avery's standard, he did keep their wedding small, but by Kane's this was far bigger than anything he imagined. He was certain the chapel was packed tight with their guests.

To Kane, this day meant everything. It didn't matter this wasn't a legally recognized union, he was tying himself to Avery with the authority of a much higher power than any government. From the time he was little, he'd always dreamed of a God-blessed marriage. As a boy, Kane never had dreams of becoming a policeman or firefighter—he wanted to be a pastor of his own congregation.

Today, the attack of cold feet had everything to do with the monumental sanctity of this marriage in the Lord's name. This wasn't to be taken lightly, at least as far as he was concerned. He'd be committing himself to Avery for the rest of their lives, and regardless of how Avery argued, Kane couldn't let go of his childhood teachings.

It had been instilled in him from an early age that the Lord designed marriage to be a union between one man and one woman. At this point, Kane's biggest hope centered in not pissing God off any more than he already had. Kane would take their vows as seriously as anything he ever had in his entire life.

"You ready, Son? They want us for pictures." Paulie poked his head through the door of his dressing room, interrupting his thoughts. For the first time since he'd entered this room, Kane looked away from the mirror and over his shoulder toward the door. Paulie, who was dressed in his own handmade tux and bowtie, narrowed his eyes and stepped inside the room, closing the door behind him.

"What's wrong? Having second thoughts?" Paulie asked, coming to stand behind Kane's chair. They both stared in the mirror at the other.

"Nah, well, yes, but not for the reason you think," Kane said. He resisted the urge to bite at his freshly manicured fingernails. Paulie reached out and placed a loving hand on his shoulder, giving him a gentle squeeze.

"What's the reason I think?" Paulie asked quietly, compassion filling his rough voice.

"Second thoughts about Avery," Kane replied instantly.

"No, Son, I never thought that," Paulie said, shaking his head. "Not once. You two are like peas and carrots, you just fit."

Kane bit his lip. It was a question he'd been thinking about for some time. Finally, he just blurted the words out, "Does this marriage mock God?" His eyes were trained on Paulie, watching every single move he made. Uncertain and scared, Kane had no doubt desperation was written all over his face, but Paulie had never steered him wrong in the past, and he knew if anyone would be honest with him, that person would be Paulie. He chastised himself for not finding the balls to talk to Paulie about this months ago.

Behind everyone's back, Kane had spent months secretly pouring through the New Testament. He was a Christian and believed wholeheartedly in the New Testament, but no matter how much he researched, he found no clear answers supporting the beliefs he had been raised on regarding homosexuality. Finally, he had decided to let that be enough, but now, as their marriage loomed over him, he had to know for sure.

"Why would you think such a thing?" Paulie asked. "It's never wrong to marry for the right reasons, Kane. Committing yourself to

Avery in the name of the Lord is serious business, I give you that, but I can't see how God would be upset by this at all, for any reason. You deserve a happy life, Son. Sometimes I still don't think you understand that, but it doesn't change the facts. You deserve to be happy. God wants you happy. And Avery makes you happy, doesn't he?"

Kane was silent for several long moments, staring at Paulie, thinking over what he'd said. Paulie had used those same words countless times on him throughout the years, sometimes they eased him, sometimes they didn't. Paulie squeezed his shoulder, seeming to know, and patted him before stepping back.

"We've got pictures to take. That cameraman doesn't like to wait. He thinks highly of himself always talking about all his National Geographic prints like that's supposed to impress me. I was in the trenches of World War II. I saw enough national geographies to..." Paulie was on roll.

Kane checked himself one last time in the mirror and jumped in as Paulie stopped to take a breath. "Did anyone in my family come?" Kane asked, effectively stopping Paulie's rant, but he did look up at Kane, staring him directly in the eyes. After all this time, Paulie had grown to dislike his family with a vengeance, but today he didn't let that show.

"No, Son, they didn't come. At least I haven't seen them yet," Paulie said. Kane never really expected them to actually show when he sent the invitations. It just felt wrong for him not to invite them.

"I knew they wouldn't," Kane said and lowered his eyes, looking down at the floor. He just couldn't bring himself to meet Paulie's gaze for fear he would find pity. He was so freaking emotional today. He hadn't seen his family in fifteen years, why did he feel like crying today because they weren't here?

"You aren't in the wrong, Kane," Paulie said, brushing his hand across his signature buzz cut as if for some reason the short, almost nonexistent hair could ever mess up. And honestly, it wasn't so much a buzz cut as just plain bald, but Paulie acted like there was still hair left on his head.

"I don't know, maybe I am. I just haven't been able to figure out how to change the way I am or the way I feel." Kane glanced at his watch. "Are you ready?" he asked, motioning for Paulie to open the door. Avery had every minute of this day planned to precision. It wouldn't do for Kane to throw them off by being his normal analytical and apparently newfound negative self.

"Because it's not changeable, Kane Dalton! We've been over this." Paulie frowned again, pulling open the door with a huff. "You are so damned hardheaded, and you don't listen. I've been saying this since I met you. It's like changing a pumpkin into a carriage, you just can't do it."

"Thank you for standing by me today," Kane said, looking down at Paulie. He always had a way of making him feel better about things, and changing the direction of his wayward thoughts. Like he'd done so many times before, he gave a silent prayer of thanks for having Paulie come into his life. He kept step with Paulie as they headed toward the chapel.

"I wouldn't be anywhere else. You're family to me, Son. You gave me back a life, and anyway, don't I look good all gussied up in these fancy duds?" Paulie laughed, straightening to his full height. Kane could only smile as Paulie attempted to pull him out of his funk.

"You look great. I knew you would." Kane beamed, and Paulie grinned back, giving him a nod. Lord, it felt good to smile. He'd taken himself way too serious lately. "Avery's already here at the church? I've been weird lately. I'm surprise he showed."

"Yep, he's here. Even after all his rules that everyone needs to make sure you two stay apart, they're having a hard time keeping him from coming to see if you're really here. He's worried you're gonna bolt," Paulie said.

Kane laughed at the absurdity of that thought as he opened the big ornately carved chapel doors and let Paulie step inside before him. They both came to an abrupt halt. Kane had been involved in the wedding plans. He went to every meeting Avery asked him to attend, had a say in every part of the design, but nothing prepared him for this moment, for the sheer beauty Avery had created.

There were thousands of flowers, all in white. Hydrangeas, roses, peonies, and calla lilies were draped across every pew, altar, pillar, archway, and candelabra in the entire church. Dozens and dozens of large urn planters were filled to overflowing with bouquets of white calla lilies. The high windowsills had cascading blooms dripping off their edges. Thousands and thousands of white rose petals outlined the walkway they were to take to the altar. The chapel was breathtakingly beautiful and fragrant, and Avery had done this for just him. He loved flowers, they calmed his soul and settled him. Beautiful blooms were a staple of their home and this seemed very much a gift from Avery just to him.

"Your guy sure knows how to impress," Paulie said, looking all around the room. "Did you plan this?"

"No, I had no idea," Kane said, the reserve of a few minutes ago faded away as a smile bigger than Texas spread across his face. He couldn't take it all in fast enough.

"Come on, Romeo, the photographer's waitin'," Paulie said, grabbing Kane's arm and guiding him down the aisle.

* * * *

Details were being slung at Avery even as he prepared to walk down the aisle. He stood outside the designated chapel door, trying to contain himself. It wasn't often he denied himself, especially where Kane was concerned, but he'd reluctantly stuck with their plan, even when each minute that ticked by made the plan seem dumber by the second.

This whole not seeing each other the day of the wedding was Kane's big idea, not Avery's as everyone assumed. Kane had used that damn ruffled shirt to get him to agree they would sleep in separate places last night and not see each other until the ceremony. So, besides the fact Kane had them on a no sex regime for the past two weeks, he hadn't seen his mister for almost twenty-four hours, and *that* hadn't happened since their first kiss. The time apart wasn't good for his soul or his naturally sunny disposition.

"Avery, your backyard's ready," Janice said, coming to stand beside him as he impatiently bounced his leg, ready to get this show on the road.

"The ice sculptures arrived?" Avery asked, his eyes trained on the door.

"Yes, they just arrived. They're going to wait about thirty minutes to place them out," Janice said.

"And the quartet's there? They have the playlist of what Kane likes?" Avery asked.

"Yes, sir, double checked myself. You look nice, Avery. I'm glad you chose the bowtie. Reminds me of your grandfather," Janice said, and that drew his eyes down to Janice standing beside him.

"You look nice, too. Thank you for keeping this together today. Take care of anything else that comes up for me, okay?" The organ started, alerting him of the time, and he cocked his head back to the door, forgetting Janice. He resisted the urge to run his fingers through his hair, his hair dresser would kill him for messing up his so called masterpiece, but Avery was tense. He knew he wore that look on his face, the one that always made Kane anxious, and he physically schooled his features. He didn't want the first glimpse Kane got of him to fill him with even more worry than he already had. This was their day, their moment, and this event meant everything to Kane, so in return it meant everything to Avery, too.

He had worked hard to make today special for his Kane, and Avery understood the significance and devotion with which Kane would take his vows. It wasn't every day you committed yourself to one person for the rest of your life. To Kane, that was exactly what he was doing today, pledging himself to Avery forever. For Avery, he had tied himself to Kane the first night they'd made love. From that moment, he never wanted be without Kane and now he was finally having that same promise returned in front of their friends and family.

"Avery, are you ready?" the wedding planner asked as the organist began the processional.

"Yes." The word came out as he exhaled the deep breath he'd been holding.

"Remember, take slow steps forward. Don't rush it. Your mom is in the first pew and you will stand directly in front of her. In just a minute, I'll open this door and you'll begin," she said, timing her part perfectly.

Months ago, they'd found this Episcopal Church that openly welcomed homosexuals. Every decision made since then centered on supporting and belonging to this church. He and Kane attended Sunday mass here regularly. For Kane, this congregation was a dream come true. He had no idea churches like these existed.

Over the last several months, Avery found that Kane was as much at home in this church as he was in his restaurant. After getting past his initial hesitation, Avery found Kane truly enjoyed being here, and the members of this church loved having Kane around. When they weren't attending Sunday morning worship, Kane volunteered, spending countless hours just being helpful to the church and all of its members.

Another big step was building a house here in Stillwater. Avery's ancestry had claimed some prime property looking down along the St. Croix River. He chose to custom build their home, working endlessly with architects and builders, trying to make a perfect home for his Kane to live in. Kane insisted Avery spent too much money, and every time he gave input, it was designed to save them money. Avery nixed most of those ideas, stating very clearly this was their dream home, the perfect place for his prince to live his life in style.

Their house sat on a cascading hilltop looking down over the river. Kane loved the view, but no matter how Avery argued, Kane refused to move into the house until they were officially married. It made no sense and became the one thing they always argued over. They had lived together virtually from the beginning and still stayed together in the apartment close to the restaurant. Avery spent every single night at La Bella Luna just to be near Kane. He had his designated perch reserved at the bar. It was nothing for the members of this community to come in and see Avery serving food, clearing a table, or helping out behind the bar, but to Kane, all that time spent together was different. In his mind, he'd maintained the rent at his old apartment, therefore they weren't truly living together, and Kane wanted to start them off right in their new home.

Even thinking about the hours they had spent arguing over their move caused Avery to grit his teeth and narrow his eyes, but tonight everything would be different. Tonight, his prince was coming home. And he would be wearing that ruffled dress shirt. Damn, he was a lucky guy.

The wedding planner opened the door and stepped aside, motioning Avery forward, taking him away from his musings. The notes of the organ rang out and everyone in the church stood. Avery immediately cut his eyes to the left to see Kane as he entered. The plan had them entering at the same time, walking the aisles until they met together at the front. But he saw nothing over the sea of heads in the room.

Everyone who had been invited had come. All three hundred fifty guests on the list came for their wedding. Dignitaries, business acquaintances, and long-time family friends were all present, including the current vice president of the United States. Avery had avoided mentioning that one to his already nervous bridegroom.

There were no real sides of the church for Kane's family as compared to Avery's. Kane's list of attendees had been small, twenty-three plus their guests, and every one of them sat in the family section up front. Avery had only found out Kane had invited his biological family when they sent back a mean-spirited, ugly refusal to attend. One he decided not to share with Kane. Avery was certain Kane had to know they weren't here, and Avery had no idea how to make that better—except to devote himself to making sure every one of Kane's minutes were filled with happiness for the rest of the evening.

When Avery rounded the corner and headed down his aisle, he gave a few nods along the way as he recognized faces in the crowd. Paulie's voice could be heard above the murmur of the congregation. Avery couldn't quite make out what he said, actually there was no telling what Paulie was saying as he leaned in to speak to his mother who had the pleasure of being seated next to him.

Avery smiled at the lack of decorum, and he looked up again, his gaze connecting to Kane's for the first time today. He almost tripped over his own feet. Kane looked gorgeous. To Avery, he was the most handsome man he'd ever laid eyes on. Kane was almost too handsome to look at and still remain upright. His knees always went weak when he was around the man and today was no exception.

Avery was so glad Kane had chosen the silk tie. The style polished him up and made him perfect.

Kane's eyes held his. Emotion churned through that blue gaze, and Avery prayed Kane felt all the same deep emotional connections that coursed through him. Again, he resisted the urge to run his hands over his hair to make sure everything was in place. He prayed he looked his best in order to stand next to this fine man he was fortunate enough to be marrying. Avery was a couple of steps ahead of Kane, and instead of stopping at the priest, he continued walking directly to Kane.

As he came to a stop, he reached out, taking both Kane's hands in his, holding them tightly. It wasn't until Kane gave him a questioning look, that he realized they were completely off center of where they were supposed to stand. The guests chuckled, so did Avery, because apparently his soul mate had just robbed him of all ability to think.

"Hi. You're beautiful," Avery whispered as they moved together back to the front, taking their place before the priest. The notes coming from the organ came to an end. Kane's nervousness showed on his way too serious face. Avery gave him his best grin and winked, watching until his mister's facial features lightened and finally Kane smiled back. That sweet smile robbed Avery of any functioning brain cells left in his already fragile mind.

Avery kept a tight hold on Kane's hand. He had to touch him, like he had to breathe, and the feel of Kane's warm skin helped to settle Avery's nervous energy. It calmed him enough to focus on the female priest as she began the service.

Avery stayed quiet. He couldn't keep his eyes off his beautiful lover for the entire service. He moved when he was supposed to move and kneeled when he was told to kneel, but he never let go of Kane's hand throughout the ceremony.

When the vows began, Avery listened intently to each word Kane repeated from the pastor. Kane's voice broke as he said his vows, and Avery could feel how deeply Kane meant each word. From this moment forward, Kane would always be his and he would be Kane's. Avery swore he wouldn't let anything come between them, ever. That thought settled in his soul and brought a huge smile to Avery's face.

Avery began his vows, making sure his voice was loud and clear as he gazed into Kane's eyes with each word spoken. After the last repeated line of their pre-written vows, he continued talking.

"The first moment I saw you, I knew we would be standing here today. There has always been certainty between us. That day, in La Bella Luna, you stole my heart. Today, I give you my soul. And from this day forward, I vow to never be without you again. Kane, I choose you to be my partner in life, to be the person I share all life's ups and downs with. You are the one I want to laugh with, cry with, and grow old with. I promise to love you, honor you, and cherish you, not only on this precious day but, *always*." Avery stepped closer to Kane and lightly brushed his lips across Kane's before stepping away and turning back to the pastor. "I've said everything I wanted to say. You may finish."

She gave him an indulgent smile before continuing, "Avery and Kane have pledged themselves to each other by solemn vows with the joining of hands and the giving and receiving of rings. May the grace of Christ attend you, and the love of God surround you, the Holy Spirit keep you, that you may live in faith, abound in hope, and grow in love, both now and forevermore. It is now my privilege to announce you united as one in love and marriage. Those whom God has joined together let no man put asunder. You may kiss your groom, again."

Avery grinned as the room full of their friends and family cheered them on. He stepped up to Kane, lifted his hands, and gently took Kane's face between his palms. He angled him as he came in for the most sincere kiss of his life.

Chapter 14

The band played softly in the background as Avery danced slowly with Kane, holding him tightly in his arms. Avery led, Kane followed, resting his head on Avery's shoulder, his hair tickling Avery's nose as he breathed in his husband's spicy citrus scent. God, he loved holding him in his arms, and he especially loved all the small little nips and soft kisses he'd get between each breath.

Their wedding and reception was turning out to be a great success, at least as far as Avery was concerned. The wedding had been followed by dinner, dinner was followed by dancing, and the dancing continued for hours. Their guests seemed happy, content to stay and celebrate the union, just as Avery had hoped they might.

The oversized tent he'd rented easily fit all three hundred fifty of their guests. Flowers, large planters, and twinkling lights filled the tent. A buffet fit for a king ran along the right side, while the dance floor sat in the middle so it could be seen from any table. Mini wet bars were positioned strategically throughout the area, along with large ice sculptures, and white linen covered tables and chairs throughout all the open space. He'd spared no expense, hoping to make this a special memory for Kane. All he wanted was Kane's happiness.

It seemed like he had achieved his goal.

Avery was so eager to begin their lives in their new home he'd held the reception in their backyard. The party tent sat between the house and the St. Croix River. Valets greeted guests, parked the cars, and shuttled people from the front of the house back to the tent. This was all designed to have Kane one step closer to moving into their new home tonight. That pleased Avery far more than anything else they'd done this evening. No more separate homes or forced separation for fear of living in sin.

His usually ultra-conservative, straight-laced new husband had let his guard down and relaxed tonight. Those times were rare indeed. Kane's face was filled with joy and he seemed blissfully happy; he laughed easily and stayed close to Avery's side for the entire night. They held hands, giving each other little knowing smiles, quick pecks, and had begun ending each other's sentences, like an old married couple.

He was so in love with Kane, and had been since the day he'd first laid eyes on him. In the past, these special moments were shared in the privacy of their apartment, but tonight Kane opened up completely. It pleased Avery beyond measure to call Kane *his* in front of all their family and friends.

Another thing Kane had done that evening was show the political world he was a solid, competent, charming man. How he would make a perfect, well-balanced mate for any future political office Avery may consider running for. Avery saw the speculation from the few politicians attending tonight.

"I love you," Avery whispered against Kane's ear as they gently swayed back and forth to the music. He laid his cheek against the top of Kane's head and pulled Kane tighter against him as the band played. The evening was perfect.

"I loved the flowers in the church and the ones in here too. You remembered the calla lilies," Kane said, moving his head slightly forward to kiss Avery on the neck. The simple gesture sent goose bumps springing up across his neck and arms.

"I'll never forget your favorite flower. You sent me your favorite flower. I love that memory," Avery replied. "I have another confession. Actually, I planned to wrap all the paperwork with a big bow and give it to you as a wedding gift, but I can't seem to wait. I bought your investors out. La Bella Luna's now completely yours."

Kane lifted his head and the look of shock on his face brought a smile to Avery's lips. He kept Kane wrapped in one arm and urged his head back down to his shoulder. "No, I like you like this."

"Avery, that's too much," Kane said, his head barely lowering as he spoke.

"It's not too much. I love you. Paulie still has his shares, but now you hold the majority. And it makes me happy to give this to you, so please just say thank you. Don't argue with me right now," Avery said, leaning down to kiss Kane's beautiful lips. His half aroused cock grew thicker, not leaving much room in his trousers as Kane brushed against Avery. He willed himself to calm down, much like he'd done a thousand times over the last few hours. He wanted so desperately to be alone with Kane—to make love to his new husband.

"Thank you. We're married now and all I got you was a belt, but it's very nice Italian leather," Kane said, lifting his head slightly to look Avery in the eyes. The angle was perfect for a kiss, and Avery didn't hesitate to take advantage of the moment, loving how easily Kane accepted their PDAs now.

"You finally made an honest man out of me, Kane. It has to be close to midnight. Let's go home," Avery suggested, nodding his head as he spoke. Kane chuckled, hugging him tighter. Avery felt the full hard-on Kane had going on in his pants, and he grew even harder. "Let's tell Mom and Paulie goodnight and sneak out. No need to make a big to-do about it, everyone's having a good time. I don't want them to think they have to leave because we are."

"Okay," Kane agreed and kissed Avery again. They made their way off the dance floor, arm in arm, Kane tucked in tight around him. They didn't stop for any polite conversation, but Avery gave a nod here or there as they walked to the back of the tent where his mom sat with Paulie. They'd become fast friends over the last year, Paulie challenging his mom on a level she'd never experienced before. Paulie, for his part, couldn't care less that she was the CEO of a multi-million dollar empire, he treated her like he treated everyone else, and she appeared to love every minute of getting to know him.

"Mom, Paulie, I think we're gonna call it a night," Avery said. Kane stayed pretty much glued to his side, holding Avery tightly with both arms wrapped around him. He leaned over and kissed Kane's upturned, tired face.

"The night's still young. You've got an entire life ahead of you two. Stay," Paulie teased. Kane started to agree they shouldn't leave, but Avery put a stop to that nonsense.

"It's midnight, and I've barely had five minutes alone with him since the nuptials," Avery said, tightening his hold as Kane began to untangle himself.

"I'm real proud of you, boy." Paulie stood and shook both their hands, giving Kane another giant hug.

"Thanks, Paulie. Thanks for helping get all this together tonight," Kane said. Avery's mother was up, too, hugging Avery and then Kane. Kennedy Adams had become a staple in their lives.

"You two go. Don't worry about anything. We'll close everything down," she said.

"Mom, you don't have to stay. I've got it all arranged to let everyone be here as long as they want." Avery kept Kane close as he leaned down to kiss his mom's cheek.

"Thank you for being here and doing so much to help pull this off. It was perfect. Today was perfect," Kane added. The huge grin on his face lit up his eyes, causing them to twinkle. That smile made Avery feel like a million dollars. All the work, every bit of planning he'd done, had been so he could see that smile on his Kane's handsome face.

"It's not every day your son gets married to such a fine man. Where else would I be?" There were tears in her eyes and she hugged them both tightly. "I'm very proud."

Avery enjoyed the few moments with his mom and Kane, but ended the conversation as quickly as possible, tugging Kane along with him when it looked like he might try and stay with his mom and Paulie a little longer. The party was still in full swing, but there had been enough of an exchange between the four of them that the room finally clued in they were leaving. They got a thundering round of applause and Avery didn't do anything more than turn and wave as he ducked out of the tent, pulling Kane right behind.

"Thank God it's over," Avery said, bypassing the waiting shuttles. The warmth of the tent hid the crisp April breeze blowing off the St. Croix. Their new house was a few hundred feet from the reception tent and Avery willingly wrapped Kane back in his arms to help fight off the cold as they headed toward the back door.

"You're cold. We should have grabbed our jackets," Avery said, holding Kane a little tighter against the side of his body. He ran his hand up and down Kane's arms, trying to build warmth.

"It's not far," Kane said, dropping his head back on Avery's shoulder, letting the moonlight guide their path.

Avery bent down to kiss the top of Kane's head and looked back out over the distance. "I love the view. It's too dark to see, but you can hear the river churning. I sat out here for hours last night, wishing you were here. I couldn't wait for today. I hated being away from you. You've changed my life so completely, Kane."

"It's a beautiful place. You did really well, Avery," Kane said, looking up at Avery. That earned him a quick kiss.

"Baby, we did well. You did this with me. I love you," Avery replied, but didn't give Kane any time to respond. "You were stunning tonight. When we were dancing, I wanted to leave the dance floor and drag you from the tent. You were so breathtakingly handsome, and we fit perfectly together."

"I loved that dance. I'm glad we took those dance lessons," Kane said, walking up the steps to their oversized back deck.

"Me, too." Avery jogged up the steps, then across the patio, holding the door for Kane as he came in behind him.

"You're my husband now," Avery said, shutting the door and gathering Kane in his arms again, keeping them right there in the back kitchen entry.

"And you're my husband," Kane added, waggling his brow as Avery began the descent to his lips. Avery stopped right before his lips touched Kane's and cocked his head, looking closer before he pulled his head back. Kane had been in the process of opening for him, and his lips were still parted, ready for the kiss. "You look exhausted. Did you sleep last night?"

A look of confusion crossed Kane's face. "Not much, I was nervous."

Avery changed his intention and leaned in for a chaste kiss. He wanted to make love to Kane like he wanted to breathe, but he didn't like the fatigue he saw surrounding those beautiful blue eyes. Avery took Kane's hand again, pulling him down the hall to the stairs in the middle of the two story colonial. "Let's go upstairs, you need to sleep."

"I'm not sleeping on our wedding night," Kane insisted, walking much slower to the point of Avery having to work to tug him along.

"Yes, you are. I can't believe I didn't notice how tired you looked earlier. We would have been up here hours ago," Avery said, taking the stairs up to their room.

"Avery, I'm not that tired," Kane started, but stopped as Avery opened the door to their bedroom. Avery watched as Kane took in the space. His face lit up, and the look made everything worth it. He had gone all out in this room in his pursuit to please Kane. Rose petals were sprinkled across the bed and table. Bouquets of calla lilies sat on every surface of the oversized bedroom, and the wine he'd picked for them had been placed in a silver bucket by the bed to chill.

"I love you, thank you for this. I seriously can't believe you remembered the calla lilies," Kane said and brushed past him, stepping inside.

"How could I not? They remind me of you." Avery smiled and followed Kane into the room. "Do you like the furniture?"

Kane hadn't been in the room since the builders had finished the house's initial rough in. He'd told Avery he wanted this night to be special for both of them. And even before the foundation was poured, Kane had refused to come near the room, saying that Avery was tricky. He swore if he came up here with Avery, they'd end up christening the room. "It's so big in here."

"Our room runs along the entire side of the house," Avery said and turned Kane around toward the part of the room behind the door.

"You put your office in here." Kane's excitement was evident as he walked to one of the two desks in the back part of the room. He ran his fingertips over the surface, and a smile touched his lips.

"I put both our offices in here. I don't want to be separated from you any longer than I have to be." Avery closed the distance between them, wrapping his arms around Kane's waist. "I'm a man crazy in love."

"I love you, too." Kane turned in his embrace and slid his arms around Avery's neck. They stared at one another for a moment before Kane ran his fingers through Avery's hair and drew his head down for a smoldering kiss. One Kane deepened quickly. Avery pressed against the length of Kane's body and rolled his hips before pushing his hand between their bodies and unfastening Kane's slacks.

Kane gasped for breath as Avery's hands slid inside his boxers and wrapped around the thick length. Avery grinned when Kane's slacks dropped to the floor and a moan escaped his lips. His body responded instantly to the sound and smell of Kane's arousal. Avery had been feeling denied the last few weeks as they had abstained from sex. Holding off was clearly worth the wait. Kane's actions were frenzied; he thrust his hips forward, grinding hard into Avery's palm. Kane was a man desperate for his touch, exactly how Avery liked him.

"I know you're tired. I know I've pushed you…It's been a lot to deal with, let me make love to you tonight," Avery whispered the words in Kane's ear as he mouthed the soft skin along his neck, biting the warm flesh between each word. Kane responded by closing his eyes, dropping his head back, allowing Avery complete access to his neck. Kane's hands moved to his buckle, clumsily working the belt undone until he finally found his way inside Avery's slacks and pushed them down his legs. Kane's brow lifted and he grinned, and Avery knew he'd felt the assless underwear he was wearing.

"You like? I got these for you, just in case we found a place for you to take advantage of me during the wedding or reception," Avery breathed into Kane's hair. He closed his eyes, savoring the citrusy scent of his lover. He ran his tongue around the shell of Kane's ear and flicked into the opening, making Kane moan.

"Take me to bed." Avery pulled Kane's dress shirt over his head. Their ties had been lost sometime during the feverish kiss. He managed to get Kane's white undershirt off without tearing it open. He couldn't say the same for his own clothes, but Avery ignored the ping of buttons flying across the room when Kane's tongue found its way into his ear. Avery was pressed head to toe against Kane, and he still couldn't get enough. He craved every part of Kane touching every part of him. "God, I've missed you," Avery whispered.

"I've missed this. I've missed being with you. I love you." Kane's hot breath caressed his skin and the words embraced his heart.

"I want us to stay like this forever," Avery said, running his cheek and nose against Kane's dark silky hair. He was so lost to the man in his arms his knees went weak. He wasn't certain he was supporting himself or if it was Kane that held him upright.

"Me too." Kane's voice sounded strained. Avery released the grip he had on Kane's cock, stopping the slow strokes. He slid his hands up Kane's stomach and chest to cradle his husband's face in his palms.

"We can always make love, sleep for a little while, and then switch it around," Kane stated, his lips curled into a smile as he pushed Avery back against the bed. "If that's what you want, that is."

"Whatever you want. I don't think I can wait much longer, though." Avery's legs hit the back of the bed, causing him to lose his balance. Kane tumbled down with him, gathering Avery in his arms and kissing him deeply. They used tongues and teeth, devouring one another with their mouths. Avery coaxed Kane forward, scooting them up on the bed as he reached for the lubricant he'd happily placed in the headboard earlier that day. Kane's mouth never left his body, he just moved his lips and tongue to whatever part of Avery's body was closest.

"No…" Kane moaned and reached for Avery as he sat back on his heels, kneeling between Kane's parted thighs. Avery just grinned down at his husband and lifted his cock, bending forward to place a simple kiss on the glistening broad head. He began to stroke Kane in long sure pulls, adding the little twist at the end that he knew drove his lover wild. And like he hoped, the effects were immediate. Kane arched his long body, throwing his head back toward the pillow, and dug his feet into the mattress.

"That's it… Yes!" Avery tightened his grip on the base of Kane's cock when he saw his sac draw up.

"Not yet. It's too soon, baby," Avery said, watching as a look of desperation crossed Kane's face.

"No, Avery, I want you to make me come twice," Kane pleaded, thrusting his hips up hard into Avery's palm. "Finish me."

"No, I can't last that long." Avery tightened his grip and bent forward to lick the bead of pre-come gathering at Kane's tip. Kane spread his legs wide and bent forward looking up at Avery. Avery used his free hand to cup Kane's balls, slowly rolling them in his palm before sliding his fingers down and circling his tight rim. "You're tight, again."

"We haven't been together for weeks," Kane said.

Avery smiled down at him and lifted his brows. "Because of you." He let go of Kane's cock and popped open the bottle of lubricant.

Kane chuckled at his words. The forced abstinence was never in Avery's plan, nor was it something he ever planned to do again. He never kept it a secret how much he disagreed with that part of Kane's plan, and he'd tried to sway Kane every chance he got, but unfortunately his mister had unwavering patience.

"Loosen me." Kane's tone was husky, sensual, and Avery's cock jerked at the command. His lover's words held a hint of dominance, and he wanted nothing more than to submit.

"You'll come if I play down here too long," Avery said and pushed his finger inside his husband's tight passage. He easily found his prostate and began to massage. In that same moment, he reached up and gripped Kane's cock, stroking him hard and fast. He knew exactly what he was doing to Kane and loved making him beg. Kane dropped his head back against the pillow and lifted his hips, groaning loudly. He worked Kane until his second finger slid easily inside the tight passage.

He kept the firm grip on his lover's weeping cock and deep-throated Kane on the first try.

Kane's hips bucked, forcing his cock deeper inside his mouth. Avery relaxed his throat muscles allowing Kane to take what he needed while he worked the gland, massaging Kane open in order to add a third finger. Kane's fingers tightened in his hair, forcing him farther down on his rigid cock. He gasped for air as his husband picked up the pace and fucked his mouth hard, hitting the back of his throat.

"Now..." Kane growled, and Avery tore free of his hold, catching his breath. The look of sheer passion filling Kane's face had Avery's dick leaking. This man was his perfect partner. He was so sexy, Avery's need to be inside him almost won out, but he knew exactly what Kane needed, and he was going to make damn sure he took care of his husband.

"You're not ready. You like to be open," Avery said and never stopped the scissoring of his fingers.

"I am." Kane lifted his hand, cupping Avery's head. He pulled him down, then thrust his tongue deep into his mouth, kissing him with all the emotion inside him. Avery felt warm fingers wrap around him as Kane began to stroke his aching cock.

"Baby, now. Let's do this now," Kane breathed against his lips.

Avery wouldn't give in. He broke from the kiss and continued to pump Kane with one hand, massaging him completely open with the other. When he was certain Kane couldn't take another minute, he poured a generous amount of lube on Kane's rim and his cock before he pushed against Kane's hole. Heat engulfed him as Kane took all of him, making the moment perfect. Avery held perfectly still, allowing Kane's body to adjust to the penetration. Kane hissed and reached for him, tugging him down on his chest. He wrapped his thighs around Avery's waist and ran his hands up Avery's back, twisting his fingers in his hair.

"I love you," Avery whispered and slid his hands under Kane's back, gripping his shoulders as he slowly began to move his hips, pulling almost out and slowly pushing back into that delicious tightness, moving faster and harder with each thrust.

"I...love...you..." Kane whimpered.

Avery gritted his teeth and closed his eyes, burying his face in the crook of Kane's neck. He wanted this to last, but the force of Kane's muscles gripping him felt too good. "You're finally mine."

"And you're...finally...mine..." Kane declared, his hips rising to meet Avery's, thrust for thrust.

"I've been yours since the first moment I laid eyes on you. Today was for you, baby." Avery gripped Kane's shoulders tighter, holding him in place as he drove himself deep into Kane's body. His knees dug into the mattress as he tried to get better leverage. He couldn't get close enough to Kane, couldn't get deep enough in the man he loved. He slammed his hips wildly against Kane, their loud grunts and moans filled the room, and the sound of their bodies slapping together added to the heat of the moment. Avery managed to slide his hand between their sweat-coated bodies and pump Kane's hard cock. His rhythm was erratic, he couldn't keep the pace, not with the way Kane's tight ass grasped him, but he wanted Kane to come before he did.

His body strained, and he screwed his eyes shut, trying to prevent his release. He hung on until he felt Kane's cock twitch and hot jets of thick cream shot between his fingers and splattered on his chest. Kane shuddered and moaned beneath him, and his ass contracted around him. The smell and feel of Kane's release drove him insane. He grabbed Kane's thighs, pushed them back, lifting him higher, and plunged into him, pistoning his hips like a jack hammer. "Yes. So...good, baby." It wasn't a second more before his own release hit, and his cock jerked deep inside Kane's hot ass as he filled him with his come.

"You're amazing," Avery roared as he slumped forward, falling on top of Kane. It took several minutes for the pounding of his heart to ease and his breathing to return to normal. Kane was under him, supporting all his body weight, but he couldn't move. Avery lay there for a while, lost in the feeling of Kane's heart beating against his. His love for this man overwhelmed him; he was so lucky to have found his perfect partner. He pushed himself up and moaned when his softening cock slipped free of Kane's warm body. Avery hated the feeling of loss. He would stay buried in Kane forever if he could. Avery leaned in to kiss his new husband, yet his world lay softly snoring underneath him.

Avery gave a soft chuckle, staring fondly at the love of his life. Kane had been so tired, he'd passed out. He hadn't even felt Avery rise to clean them, or when he tucked the covers around them. Avery curled in tight, wrapping himself around Kane. They always slept snuggled closely next to one another. Neither moved too far from the other as they slept. Tonight they seemed even closer than ever before. Avery registered faint sounds of music blaring from the tent outside.

They'd done it. Tomorrow Kane would legally take his name, becoming the beneficiary on all that was his, then they would truly be one. That had been a trick that took Avery months to get Kane to agree to, but in the end, he had. Avery smiled a sleepy smile and closed his eyes. Everything was right in his world. Kane had finally become his.

Chapter 15

July, 1978 ~ Stillwater, Minnesota

"Babe," Avery called out, barely inside the kitchen through the garage side entrance, only to find it deserted. *Damn!* Of course this would be the day that Kane wasn't in here cooking away or cleaning their already spotless house. He could hardly contain himself as he dashed through the kitchen into the spacious living room.

"Kane, where are you?" This time he almost yelled the words.

"I'm up here!" he heard Kane reply. Avery centered in on the master suite upstairs. He took the stairs two at a time and hurried down the hall, rushing around the corner, keeping up his pace as he stepped into their bedroom. Kane had his eyes glued to a five-inch-thick microcomputer manual on his desk while pecking away at the small keyboard in front of him. Every few seconds he would lift his eyes and watch the screen, his brow narrowed. "Dang!"

"Dang, what?" Avery said, slowing his stride as he got closer to the desk where Kane sat. All of the sudden his stomach lurched and his heart began to pound in his chest as his excitement turned to uneasiness. He gripped the thick file folder in his hands as he leaned in to kiss Kane's perfectly pouty lips. *Damn!* Why was he so nervous now? He knew that answer. Kane was definitely going to fight him on what he held in his hands. Avery realized he wanted Kane to be on board with this more than anything in the world. He wanted this life for them, and the folder he gripped tightly in his hands made his wants a possible reality.

"I can't see how these things are gonna streamline anything. You have to research for hours to learn how to even type the information in correctly and one bad keystroke and the whole thing is messed up…" Kane hadn't really turned from the screen to kiss Avery. His eyes were still glued to the dark monitor with the green flashing cursor. The blinking cursor reminded him of the beat of his own nervous and overactive heart. Could that stupid curser be mocking him now? Avery rejected the crazy thought, but the longer he stood there, the more frantic he became, which was so completely outside of his normal personality.

"I think it's mocking me." Kane said exactly what Avery was thinking before dropping his gaze back to the manual.

"Can you take a break? I've got something I really need to talk to you about," Avery said, leaning back against Kane's desk. He stopped short of stepping in front of Kane, but came close. He needed Kane's full attention. What he had to say was very important to both of them.

Kane looked up at Avery, but looked immediately down again as he continued to type. Avery waited a second more, telling himself this wasn't a good time. He should let his husband keep working. The thing was, his heart wouldn't allow him to put this conversation off any longer.

"What's up?" Kane finally asked and that gave Avery all the invitation he needed. Avery laid the file folder he held in his hands on top of the manual Kane continued reading from.

"What is it?" Kane asked, all his attention now centered on Avery. *Finally*! Avery's heartbeat intensified as he reached over to drag his desk chair next to Kane's and sat down beside him. His mouth went dry as he started to speak, but he managed to smile at Kane and kept on task.

"Honey, I have something I've been following for a while. I never mentioned this to you, because I didn't want to get our hopes up," Avery said as he opened the file folder. He could see Kane's eyes were immediately drawn to the first page, narrowing as he began to read the print. That had Avery picking up the pace, talking without really thinking. He wanted to get this out before Kane had a chance to figure out where he was going with all this.

"Babe, look at me, not the file for a minute." Kane actually lifted his eyes and met his for a moment, but cut his gaze back down to the folder. Avery was forced to continue without being able to gauge Kane's reaction. His usual smooth-talking ways abandoned him, and he blurted out what he should have padded.

"The first test tube baby was born today. He's healthy and strong and I want us to try and have a test tube baby," Avery sputtered, and Kane jerked his gaze up. Their eyes connected for several heartbeats. Under normal circumstances, Kane's facial expressions would have been comical. He ranged from uncertainty as if he hadn't heard Avery correctly, then to shock, and now doubt was beginning to cloud his eyes. Avery didn't like that look at all.

"Avery…" Kane began, hesitation clear in his tone.

"No, now listen. The doctors have given this baby a clean bill of health. I've been tracking this from the beginning. The pregnancy and birth were normal. The baby's doing great. The doctors are saying he's healthy, normal, just like a new baby conceived the natural way. I made phone calls, Kane. I'm getting this information firsthand."

Kane didn't say a word. He only stared at Avery. With no response from his husband, he had no idea what to say. Avery understood this was coming out of thin air, he was blindsiding Kane, and there might be a moment of uncertainty, but dead silence with no discussion just wasn't like them. They had always been open and honest with each other and could talk about anything. Avery forced himself to calm down.

To say they hadn't ever spoken about anything like this was an understatement. They'd never really talked about having children. They were secluded here, tucked away in their little part of the world, living their lives together. It had never been even a small option that they might become parents, but Avery still didn't like the silence, and he knew Kane well enough to know what their obstacles were.

"Honey, is it even legal for us to do this?" Kane began and actually shook his head no before looking away from Avery and closing the file folder as though the discussion were over before it had even begun. That single action slapped at Avery more so than the craziness of the legality argument. Avery was angrier than he had ever been with Kane. They never fought, but the emotion pouring through him needed an outlet and it looked like right now Kane was going to be it.

"Dammit, Kane! I'm so sick of that look you get in your eyes whenever I suggest we do anything a normal couple would do. We're gay, we're in love, and we're married. It's not wrong. We're not wrong! Why can't you get that through your thick skull?" Avery rarely got this angry and never with Kane.

He was up and out of his chair, the rant flowing easily from his lips. Kane sat back, becoming more stone-faced and calm. Reason shouted those were Kane's natural defense mechanisms coming to the forefront, but he'd already worked this out in his mind. He'd followed this for the last year. Reason had nothing to do with this moment.

Kane didn't respond, merely sat back and stared at Avery. That had him pacing now, trying to calm himself.

"Do you want children, Kane? I thought that would have been important to you."

"I don't know—" Kane began, but Avery cut him off.

"Bullshit! You do know!" Avery was back in his face, calling him on that blatant lie. Kane had grown up considering himself a family man.

"Avery, please calm down," Kane tried again, but now his voice was monotone. Kane was fully in his passive, relaxed, anxiety mode, and again, it sent fire coursing through Avery's veins. He thought he had not only broken through that shell but that Kane had abandoned those walls a long time ago.

"No! I won't calm down. You would make a wonderful father. I see how you are with the children at church. You glow and gush all over them. I want that for us! I want to watch you hold our babies and glow and gush over them. I want to watch you care for our children. And now we have a fucking chance to make that happen. I want this, Kane." Avery shoved the folder into Kane's lap and got right in his face as he spoke. Through it all, Kane stayed quiet.

"Goddammit! I can see it in your eyes. We aren't wrong. My love for you isn't wrong." Avery flung his hands in the air and stormed out of the room. His anger fueled each of his steps as he pounded down the stairs and out the back door, letting the screen door slam in his wake. He had no idea where he was going, but seconds later, he'd jumped in his Corvette and peeled out down the driveway. He needed to get away. Kane was so frustrating. After everything he'd done, everything he'd given, Kane still didn't believe in them enough to extend their family and that realization hurt. *Damn!* He slammed his fist into the steering wheel, and pressed on the gas, picking up speed until he hit the highway. What more could he have done?

* * * *

The house was dark, all except the lamp Kane had on as he sat on the sofa, waiting for Avery to come home. The grandfather clock chimed twelve forty-five in the morning, and with a frustrated sigh, Kane reached up to pull the lamp drawstring, plunging the living room into darkness. His great plan for making Avery grovel, the one he had spent the last few hours formulating, was falling apart with each passing minute. Avery had been gone far too long.

Kane kept the lights off and went to the kitchen sink to get a glass of water. He willed himself to calm down. His heart had been pretty much broken since the minute he heard the back door slam shut and Avery's car revving up then tearing down the driveway. He closed his eyes and exhaled deeply before taking a big drink of water, wondering how badly he'd messed things up between them.

Regardless of what Avery thought, all the accusations flung at him, their problem today was that he'd just been caught completely off guard.

Avery's stuffed file folder of information on the possibility of a test tube baby showed he had tracked every bit of progress on this birth, yet Kane had never known Avery was even interested in having children. Something that important to Avery and Kane had never known. How was that even possible? Avery knew everything about him. He kept no secrets, but Avery had.

It took hours after their fight for Kane to even work himself up to his own thoughts on raising a child as a gay couple. Without question, he wanted children. If things had turned out differently in his life, he'd have had a house packed full of children. But he was a gay man. Even after racking his brain, he couldn't come up with any other gay couple he knew that had children, unless they had them before they came out. Reason told Kane he wasn't wrong in needing to take this slow. Avery should have been more patient with him. He had just needed to catch up, but Avery hadn't offered that as a possibility.

Those thoughts had dominated everything until the clock struck midnight. Then all his thoughts centered on why Avery wasn't home yet. Emotion came forward. Kane had messed up every relationship he'd ever been in because of his stupid personality and crazy beliefs. He'd grown too complacent with Avery and let his guard down.

Avery never stayed out this late. Fear gripped him. His mind raced and his stomach churned at the prospect of what Avery would say when he came through that door. Would it be tonight? Maybe tomorrow? Would he ask Kane to leave?

He prayed he hadn't messed things up too badly. Over the last few hours, Kane had even imagined letting himself hold his own baby. He loved the idea of having a son who looked exactly like Avery. Those thoughts warmed his heart and sent spine-tingling pulses of happiness running all over his body. What he wouldn't give to have children to raise. He loved children and wanted them with Avery. He had just never thought he could have something as basic as the American dream being a homosexual.

Now he'd ruined that perfect dream.

Moments later, two lights shone through the front window blinds and tracked the back wall of the kitchen. Kane held his breath until he heard the garage door opening. Relief hit hard. Right then, he decided to hold his ground. If Avery wanted out, for the first time in his life, he wouldn't go easy. He'd fight to keep them intact, he'd fight for Avery. They were good together. He went back to his spot on the sofa, pushing all those desperate thoughts aside as he heard the kitchen door open. Kane steeled his spine and let resolve blanket his soul.

* * * *

Avery entered the house through the garage, as he always did, but for some reason it felt wrong that night. Maybe it was the guilt he carried playing tricks on him. He saw the house was dark as he drove up the driveway. That wasn't abnormal for this time of night, but still felt wrong. He had to remind himself Kane's car was parked in the garage. He had to be in this house somewhere. That should have given him peace, so he tried hard and worked at pushing the bad vibes away. They spent most of their time in their bedroom when they were home alone. The darkness shouldn't have intensified his gloom, but dammit, he felt like such a heel for starting their fight.

Avery kept the lights off and walked through the kitchen. He was almost through the living room when a lamp light clicked on. He had a small heart attack right there, as he whipped his body toward the sofa. Kane sat only a few feet from him. The file folder of information spread out around him.

"You scared me to death," Avery said, taking the minute to catch his breath and calm his pounding heart.

"It's late," Kane responded. His face calm and passive, giving Avery all the information he needed to know that things were still bad between them.

"I'm sorry," Avery immediately said and moved toward the sofa. Kane's face tightened as Avery stepped forward.

"For what?" Kane finally asked, and that made Avery give a small smile. It was just like his mister to need clarification before he gave in. God, he loved this man.

"For flying off the handle earlier," Avery replied, now standing directly in front of Kane. He prepared to drop to his knees to beg for forgiveness. Kane paused again, but his stare never faltered. Avery held his ground, waiting.

"We can go talk to this doctor you found. I also want to talk to a psychologist about the effects on a child being raised by two fathers. If we move forward with this, I want you to go first. I want our children to look like you and I want to pick the mother carefully. She has to be smart and well-rounded, not just anyone will do. I want nothing left to chance," Kane finally said.

Avery let out the breath he'd been holding. Relief poured through him and he couldn't help the smile that spread across his lips as he dropped to his knees in front of Kane. He reached out for Kane's hands, grabbing them, trying to thread their fingers together. Kane didn't return the hold. Kane always took his hand; that wasn't a good sign, but he held on to the hope Kane's words gave him. Avery kept eye contact and tightened his grip. He'd hold Kane's hand tight enough for them both.

"Thank you. I was so worried you wouldn't want this for us. I agree with everything you said, but I wanted you to go first. I want your baby," Avery replied, resting back on his heels. Thank God! This so wasn't what he'd expected to walk into. His Kane was always so full of surprises.

"No. I want you to go first. And I want to know the legal side of things before we make a firm decision. I don't want either of us left unprotected. If we do this, we're a family through and through," Kane stated firmly.

"All right, that's fine," Avery answered. Kane rose from the couch with Avery still kneeling in front of him. He stepped away, leaving Avery alone on the floor. Kane never reached out to touch him before making his way to the stairs. Avery slowly stood, watching him go. He'd gotten his agreement, and that was halleluiah good, but the tension between them was thick enough that he could almost reach out and touch it. What did that mean? They should be celebrating now. Yet Kane was walking up those stairs by himself and didn't show any signs he wanted Avery to follow. He was uncertain about what to do in his own home. Once Kane got to the top of the stairs, Avery decided, "*fuck the tension*," and started to move forward, but stopped as Kane spoke.

"You're wrong, Avery. I don't doubt us. I'm proud of us. I never pray for anything but for you to stay in my life. I'm just worried about the science of it all, and I never thought about us having children because it wasn't an option, until today. You should have given me a minute to catch up. You're so wrong in what you think about me." Kane's voice lowered on the last few words as he disappeared inside their bedroom. Avery heard their bedroom door shut firmly, closing him completely out. He supposed he deserved that, but did this mean he'd been relegated to the sofa?

As if Kane had read his thoughts, he opened the door and yelled out, "Yes, you're on the sofa. You should've called to let me know you were okay, but you didn't, you stayed gone and that's not right." The bedroom door shut again, and Avery smiled, running his fingers through his hair. Kane knew him too well and they had finally had their first big fight. He was sleeping on the sofa tonight. He guessed it was better than a hotel. He could use the guest bedroom, but he looked around and, though he hadn't noticed them before, saw his pillow and blanket on the sofa. The sheet was already tucked across the seat cushion where Kane had been sitting when he came in.

Avery began to undress, resigned to his makeshift bed for the night. He deserved this, but his heart couldn't get too far down. Even when angry, Kane still took care of him. He had made his bed for the night. His mister always took care of him. He stretched out on the sofa and lay there for several long minutes, thinking about all the possibilities.

No, he wasn't wrapped around Kane, but he did fall asleep with the smile still on his face.

Chapter 16

August 1979 ~ Minneapolis, Minnesota

Avery sat with Kane in the small, sterile hospital waiting room. His concern landed squarely on his shell-shocked husband. The minutes ticked by and the whirlwind experience of the last several months came down to rest in these last few hours.

As it turned out, everyone was ready to jump on board the fertility bandwagon. Kane and Avery were excellent candidates. Not because they were gay men, or because Avery brought a certain notoriety to the procedure, but because they could pay and that made them perfect.

Today's procedure would implant the in vitro fertilized eggs into their donor's uterus. Approximately a month from now, they would know if any of the embryos took to create a viable pregnancy.

The process to get them here hadn't taken nearly as long as they'd expected. The medical community sat ready and waiting to make the same miracles happen for infertile couples across the world. Both the doctor and donor were in Minneapolis, meaning Avery and Kane would get to be involved with each step of the pregnancy until their baby was born. All they needed now was for the fertilized egg to take, and apparently that had been the tricky part in other cases.

Kane had won the battle and Avery went first. Avery had actually held on to his desire to have Kane be their first biological father until he slept on the sofa for a second night in a row. He didn't like being kicked out of their bed or at odds with Kane.

Interestingly enough, it hadn't been a porn magazine that helped him ejaculate into a cup, but Kane right there in the room with him. Kane had been his own personal porn show. It hadn't taken much—never did when Kane was around.

They were matched almost immediately with a female. She was a young, highly-educated physician in the same practice as their doctor. She was eager to make her mark on history. When they first met, they had spent hours talking with her and her husband, who, believe it or not, actually supported her decision to be their surrogate. A close friendship had grown over the past eight months and they couldn't have been happier, and everyone knew exactly where they stood in all of this.

Sophia Richardson was tall and blonde with an athletic build. She could have been Avery's sister, they looked so much alike. She met every one of Kane's long list of requirements in a donor and Avery personally worked out all the legalities. He covered each point Kane insisted upon, and many Kane hadn't thought of, until their budding little family was as fully protected as the law would allow.

Although gay adoption was still an uphill battle, the consensus amongst psychologists was clear—any children they had could turn out as well-adjusted as children in traditional families and Avery made sure Kane was legally protected if anything happened to him.

The only noise in the waiting room came from the large white and black clock hanging high on the wall. Avery bit at his fingernail and looked over at Kane who sat there, pale and quiet. Avery imagined he looked pretty much in the same condition. He forced himself to stop worrying his fingernail and reached over to thread his and Kane's fingers together, bumping Kane in the shoulder with his.

"What're you thinking?" Avery asked. Kane looked over at him a little dazed and confused.

With no hesitation, he whispered, "I honestly didn't know this would all come together so quickly."

"I hoped it might," Avery replied.

"If this takes, we'll have a baby in nine months," Kane whispered.

"But we can't get our hopes up, Kane. You know that. They said it rarely takes the first time. Maybe the fourth or fifth time, but not the first time," Avery explained. Even though Kane spoke in a whisper, Avery used his regular tone of voice, trying hard to manage their expectations.

"It's really expensive to do this over and over," Kane responded, his voice even lower than the whisper now.

"I know, but it'll be worth it," Avery said. Kane nodded and looked forward again. They'd made a joint agreement that they would be a part of every doctor's appointment, every pregnancy milestone until their baby was finally placed in their arms, no matter how long that took. The decision had actually been a joint one between Avery, Kane, Paulie, and Rodney since they would be picking up Kane's slack at La Bella Luna.

"I know I said I didn't doubt us and I don't, but are you sure you believe this is gonna be okay on our baby? I mean it just seems wiser to have the mother in the mix," Kane asked softly, his eyes downcast now.

"Honey, you know the answer to that," Avery said, trying to get Kane to look at him.

"Hmmm," was all he got back, and Kane started worrying his lip.

"Baby, you were meant to be with me. We have so much love, so much to offer a baby. We can do this. We can. Look at me, Kane." It took a moment, but Kane finally slid his eyes back to Avery. The worry there warmed his heart. His honey always took everything so seriously, it was exactly the reason he knew they would be good parents. "I promise this is going to be all right. I promise you. You're going to be the best mother/father combination on the planet. Trust me, okay?"

Kane said nothing, but turned his head back to the closed door where the procedure was taking place. Other than the biting of his lip, he sat so still he could have been a statue, a true sign of Kane's anxiety. Nothing Avery could say or do would help relieve Kane's concerns until this was all done. "Are you praying?"

"Yes," Kane replied instantly, his eyes back on Avery's.

"Then ask God to give you peace, because I totally have it in this deal. I have no doubt we're going to raise happy, well-adjusted children. Or as well-adjusted as they can be in today's world," Avery said. Kane didn't have time to reply as a compact Paulie came busting through the main doors like a bull in a china shop. Avery grinned like he always did when he saw Paulie. He never got over how much attention the small built man commanded.

"You never called! I couldn't stand the waiting. What do you know?" Paulie asked, ripping the well-worn cap off his head.

"Nothing. We're still waiting," Kane said, letting go of Avery's hand as he started to rise.

"Nah, don't get up. How much longer?" Paulie asked, taking the seat directly across from them.

"Your guess is as good as mine," Avery said, lifting up, sitting straighter as Kane sat back down beside him.

"Damn doctors always make you wait!" Paulie grumbled, sitting fully back in his seat, clearly there for the long haul. That was all they said, although Paulie gave several grunts, and eye rolls with each passing minute. They waited the next hour and a half until the doctor, dressed in light green scrubs, stepped inside the waiting room.

"Everything went well. Took a little longer than expected, but there were no complications, Sophia's doing good. We have her in recovery, she's awake, alert, and just a real trooper." Avery stood first, Paulie a close second, and Kane was slower to get to his feet.

"Is her husband here?" Kane asked. Avery looked back and noticed his honey's coloring had drained from his face as he stood nervously tucking his hands in his slacks pockets. He couldn't help but want to comfort him so he reached out and wrapped an arm around him, anchoring Kane against his side.

"He's with her now. She gave me two thumbs up to send out here to you two," Dr. Palmer said.

"Now, we have to wait about a month to know for sure?" Paulie's gruff voice piped in.

"Yes. Now it's in God's hands. A prayer wouldn't hurt," the doctor said. Avery chuckled, drawing all eyes to him as Kane gave an overstated nod, agreeing with the physician. That was something Kane had down. There would be no shortage of prayers over the next month.

"Let Sophia know if there is anything she needs, we'll get it taken care of," Avery reassured.

"I will. Get some rest, this is the first of many steps," Dr. Palmer said, letting that be his goodbye as he retreated back through the waiting room door. That left the three of them alone again. Avery was so much lighter now that they had made it through the procedure.

"Thank you for coming. We need to celebrate!" Avery said, shaking Paulie's hand, who surprised him by reaching up and embracing him in a solid, back-whacking hug instead. Kane still didn't look good. "Honey, you okay? Are you hungry?"

"I'm gonna throw up," Kane said. Avery narrowed his eyes and looked closer to see if Kane was joking or serious. He was much paler than before and maybe had a little greener tint to his skin. He untangled himself from Paulie's hold and they both went to Kane who landed back in the seat with a thump. His head dropped down between his knees. After a moment, Avery decided Kane probably wasn't going to pass out and helped him up, pulling him back against his side.

"You think this is bad. You just wait until that baby comes home the first night. You're gonna be a nervous wreck!" Paulie announced, completely not helping.

"Come on, babe. You'll be all right. Have you already started the prayers?" Avery asked, motioning Paulie ahead of them as they left the waiting room. Kane bumped up against him as they slowly made their way down the corridor.

"You know the answer to that," Kane replied, taking a deep breath.

"Good, then everything will be fine." Avery pushed the button for the elevator and held the door for Kane and Paulie when it arrived. After the doors closed, Kane turned toward him, laying his head on Avery's shoulder.

"This is all so emotional. I hope you're right."

"I know I'm right," Avery stated, kissing Kane's forehead.

"I love you," Kane professed, lifting his lips for a kiss.

"I love you, too," Avery declared as he looked deeply into Kane's eyes.

"Good God, does it ever stop with you two? It's way too sweet in here! You're making my teeth hurt. Come on, I'll fix you something special at the restaurant. You know it wouldn't kill you to go ahead and work tonight. You'd think you were having this baby yourself..." Paulie started as he exited the elevator, leaving them in his dust. Avery listened halfheartedly as he kept Kane close and headed toward their car. He'd have to manage his own excitement, play it cool for Kane, but he found himself praying too—for this procedure to take, for them to have their baby.

* * * *

Avery anxiously paced, wearing a path in the brown shag carpet in the back of the physician's office. They had become intimately familiar with these four walls. Dr. Palmer kept a tidy, neat desk with a large stack of magazines at their disposal. Kane had kept a steady tempo, flipping through most of them in the hour or so that they had been waiting. Avery's steps never faltered in the steady route he followed. The rustling of his clothing filled the silent room as he restlessly marched back and forth. It was the only noise they'd made since they'd arrived.

Today was their one month exam to see if any of the fertilized eggs had taken.

Kane had emotionally prepared himself for a no. His brain told him to expect a negative response, but his heart seemed to have a mind of its own. No matter how hard he had scolded himself, he couldn't quite work the hope out of his system. Now, as he sat waiting, he pulled deeper inside himself with each passing minute. Good Lord, how he wanted Sophia to be pregnant.

The accumulation of anticipation every day for the past month now resulted in nothing more than another apprehensive waiting game. The last few weeks had been torturous. It seemed the daytime hours ticked by slowly in expectation of their nightly phone call to Sophia. Avery dropped by La Bella Luna every evening after work. Kane always stopped whatever he was doing and they retreated back to his office to check in on her progress. As each day passed and the one month mark closed in, the three of them grew cautiously excited. Kane hid the eagerness clawing at his gut. He had secretly grown to crave the idea of having a little baby to complete their family.

For Sophia, with her scholarly and professional mind, she'd wanted to explore and participate in this newfound territory of fertility. She was a true scientist, through and through. Her excitement over being a donor, knowing firsthand with real time experience how the pregnancy played out, seemed a dream come true for her. She was documenting and journaling everything for the American Medical Association. It seemed they were all impatient to get this ball rolling. For Kane, they were a match made in heaven.

The interesting thing was the more Kane spoke to Sophia, the more he liked her, and that helped solidify everything for him. They had known each other for almost a year now. The connection he felt with her was the root of why he allowed himself to secretly hope they could pull this off. In his mind, he couldn't have asked for a better surrogate. She fit them perfectly, while being genuinely and completely at ease with his and Avery's relationship. Avery was taken with her as well, or so he'd said many times over the past months.

All of them had become fast friends, even her husband, Thomas, sometimes got in on the nightly phone calls.

This wasn't Sophia's first pregnancy. She was happily married with two children of her own. She specialized in fertility treatments in her medical practice. When they all met for the first time, Avery thought Sophia would be their physician. She was young, progressive, and had just turned thirty. She had studied under the top physicians and researchers in the field. But as their first meeting progressed, it became clear the scientist in her wanted to be more involved, and after the initial tests were run, she became both their surrogate and egg donor. She worked closely with Dr. Palmer in every aspect of her care.

Both personally and professionally, Kane knew Sophia understood the signs of pregnancy, but she would always fall just short of saying those confirming words. She'd stop herself, and no matter how hard Avery tried to talk around her to get her to reveal her suspicions aloud, she never would. Instead, she'd laugh at him, tease Avery about being an excellent prosecutor, and say she didn't want to jinx them. Those moments were the true reason Kane's heart had a little more hope than his brain would allow him to admit to.

He never told Avery, but he listened intently to how she spoke. He learned everything he could about her, trying hard to digest how his children might turn out. She was fun, smart, easy to speak to, and Kane grew to love the idea his babies might share in her personality. Kane could even see that if things were different between them all, she would have made an excellent wife to Avery before he came into the picture and botched up his political career. She matched him on every level, from her tall, sunny blonde looks, to her dynamic wit and charm. They were lucky to have such a compelling woman as his and Avery's child's biological mother.

Lost in thought, Kane startled as the physician's office door opened suddenly. Dr. Palmer entered with Sophia right on his heels. They were both in lab coats, carrying on a deep discussion. Neither paid any attention to him or Avery. Avery came immediately to stand behind Kane's chair, resting his hands on his shoulders and squeezing. He used his thumb to lift Kane's chin, guiding his head up, and back until he looked into his eyes. Avery bent forward and whispered in his ear, "No matter what the test shows, we'll work through this. I love you. This will happen for us."

Kane tried for a reassuring smile, but his anxiety levels were too high, and the narrowing of Avery's eyes told Kane he wasn't buying it. Instead of letting the moment linger and having Avery focus just on him, he cut his eyes back to the doctors.

"Gentlemen, I'm sorry this has taken so long. Dr. Richardson wanted to be here when I shared the news. I won't draw this out. We have a viable pregnancy," Dr. Palmer said in a matter-of-fact tone, like he hadn't just changed their entire world with those five small words. Although his demeanor never changed, Sophia's did. As she stood right beside him, she broke out in a big grin and threw her arms in the air. Avery was around Kane's chair, dragging him up as the room busted out in handshakes and hugs all around. Kane couldn't stop his tears as he was wrapped in a solidly tight three-way hug, sandwiched between Sophia and Avery. He wasn't alone in his emotions though, Sophia was in full blown crying mode.

"The first trimester is already a concern before you factor any of the unknown complications that may arise from this type of a procedure. We need to manage our excitement levels and keep a good eye on Dr. Richardson," Dr. Palmer advised in a somewhat fatherly manner while standing on the outside of their embrace.

"But it worked!" Kane declared, reaffirming the obvious. Avery tugged Kane closer. He was beyond happy as he tightened his hold. He gave Avery a quick peck, closing his eyes as he wrapped his arms tighter around him. Their world was about to change, and he couldn't wait for the next chapter to begin.

"We did it," Avery whispered in his ear, keeping him pressed head to toe against his body as he kissed the side of his neck.

"Yes, we did," Kane said. His voice broke and Avery pulled him in tighter.

"Hey! I played a part in this," Sophia teased. Kane had to angle his head awkwardly to even see her, because Avery wouldn't let him go.

"A big part. How do you feel?" Avery asked. He finally loosened his hold and let room in between them. Avery kissed his cheek, gave him that deep soul searching look he had become accustomed to, and then kissed him again on the mouth, his warm lips lingering this time. Kane was certain his cheeks were bright red as Avery broke the kiss and anchored him again against the side of his body. Avery Adams had no social filter; how had Kane just realized that in all these years?

"I feel great, not a problem at all! You two are so sweet together. The love you have for each other lights up the room and fills it with such joy. You're both going to be such great parents," Sophia finally answered after she got their full attention. Kane's tears started again. He needed her validation, and he clung to her words.

"We need to keep you feeling great. Thank you so much. This baby will make our lives complete," Avery said, tugging Kane closer to him, if that were even possible. "So what's the next step?"

"We're going to watch her closely. She knows what to look for. For now, we'll have bi-monthly checkups," Dr. Palmer said.

"When's the due date?" Kane asked.

"May tenth is the anticipated date. We'll know more as the time comes," Sophia answered, her mannerism changing as she slowly returned to her professional mode again.

"That's a great day for a birthday," Avery added.

Their baby's birthday. Turning to Avery, Kane gave his brightest and biggest smile as he silently said his prayer of thanks. They exchanged that knowing look, the one that made it clear Avery was right on board with whatever thought was racing through his head. He tucked in closer around Avery, wrapping an arm around his waist and absently listened to Dr. Palmer's exit, and then Sophia's as she went to schedule their next appointment. Kane wrapped his arms tighter around Avery's waist, stepping around to face Avery.

"We need to call Paulie and your mom." Kane laid his palm on Avery's cheek, hoping to convey every emotion running through his body in that moment. "Thank you, Avery," he whispered and leaned up for a light brush of lips to seal the moment.

Chapter 17

December, 1979 ~ Minneapolis, Minnesota

For Kane, the months ticked by slowly in a never-ending stream of doctor's appointments. He and Avery attended every one of them. They happily experienced most parts of Sophia's pregnancy. Her great initial heath didn't hold. She got a severe case of morning sickness about midway through the second month, and so did Kane. The bouts were so bad, she was forced to stay close to the bathroom for much of the first trimester until she was finally admitted to the hospital for fear of dehydration and malnourishment.

Kane, in sympathy, continued this pattern and experienced every symptom Sophia had as if they were on the same cosmic plane. Every time Sophia became ill, so did Kane. Avery became so concerned that he had Kane in their physician's office, trying to find the answers as to what might actually be going on. When that didn't help, Avery finally got on board and worked hard to help relieve Kane of the constant nausea he experienced in her honor.

From the beginning, Kane refused to allow Avery to buy anything for the baby. Kane finally asserted his power over Avery and placed all sorts of new rules on their relationship. Kane had never limited Avery before, but now, all of the sudden, he kept Avery on a short leash where this pregnancy was concerned. Kane left nothing to chance. Even extending his belief system to include every superstition or old wives tale any woman, or man for that matter, told him about.

The doctor's magic number for the pregnancy was twenty weeks. Kane required them to wait until then before he would breathe a sigh of relief and believe this might actually happen.

To celebrate that pivotal point, Avery arranged for their entire family to attend the two-dimensional ultrasound reading. Avery's mom, as well as Paulie, tagged along to discover whether they were going to have a little baby boy or girl. It took every bit of Avery's power of persuasion to convince Kane modern technology had its advantages and it was okay to know the gender of their child before birth. Truth be told, the blow job probably had more to do with the ensuing yes Avery obtained, not his communication skills, but he'd taken the approval and run with it, not letting Kane back out.

When they arrived at the doctor's office a few minutes late, they were escorted inside a standing room only exam room. Every member of the staff stood anxiously waiting the first glimpse of this little baby.

During the last few appointments, Avery had started a betting pool that currently sat at three to one odds that Sophia was having a little boy. Avery bet on the opposite side, so did Kennedy, because they were convinced it would be a baby girl. Avery always made it clear he'd be spending their hard earned money on his little princess when they teased and talked about the bet in the office. For Kane, he never called a gender. He stayed out of the bet. His prayers were for the health and well-being of their baby, nothing else mattered.

As they entered the room, the ultrasound technician was already on one side of the table Sophia lay on. Her husband, Thomas, who now worked for Avery full time, stood at the head of the small exam table. Thomas was an attorney and a tremendous support system for Sophia. It hadn't taken Avery too long to give him a position in his law firm, with an obscene salary to match, all in an effort to make sure they both knew how grateful he and Kane were for everything they were enduring to give them this child. Thomas hadn't let Avery down. Besides his unwavering support of this pregnancy, per Avery, he always proved his worth at the office as well, time and time again. Avery even spoke of offering Thomas a partnership in the next few years.

"How are you? Still craving those sweet pickles and ice cream?" Avery asked, drawing chuckles from the staff. Paulie and Kennedy quietly took places along the back wall, but Avery didn't, drawing Kane in beside him next to the table. From this vantage point, they were able to stand right up front, close to the monitor, and could see everything.

Avery took Sophia's hand. He had the most sexy, charming grin on his face, and the full force of that grin was aimed at Sophia. Avery's charisma added to the excitement in the room. Kane watched as she relaxed, smiled up at Avery, and kept a little silly grin lighting her face too. Avery had that way about him. He just owned the room every time he entered. Kane let it happen, stayed quiet, dropping his hands inside his slacks pockets to hide the nervous energy coursing through him. Since the first mention of this baby, Kane found his calm attitude had slipped away. Having a child created a nervousness he had never encountered in his entire life.

"No, it's peanut butter and anchovies now. Who eats that way?" her husband responded when Sophia didn't.

"It's delicious. You have no idea what you're missing," Sophia retorted, rolling her eyes as she looked back at her husband who gave her the universal grossness gesture of sticking his finger down his throat. Kane laughed along with everyone else in the room.

"Kane, did you get through Dr. Spock's book, *Baby and Child Care*?" Sophia asked, ignoring her husband altogether.

"I did," Kane said. The subject change helped his anxiety level. Kane loved that book.

"He's read it twice already," Avery added, now grinning at him.

"You have? That was quick, we just talked about it!" Sophia said.

"Our bedroom's become a small library. Any book he can find on raising children, he reads," Avery stated. Kane heard pride in Avery's voice, at least he hoped so, and Avery loosely wrapped his free arm around Kane, drawing him closer.

"We read them together," Kane said in his own defense.

"You read out loud. I fall sleep," Avery tossed back, winking at Kane.

"Yeah, that's about how it was when Sophia was pregnant. Those books can put you to sleep faster than a long-winded evangelist at a week-long revival," Thomas said.

"Those damn books are all we hear about at the restaurant. He's talking about that natural diet now," Paulie piped in from where he had stationed himself against the back wall. That got another round of chuckles from the entire room.

"I've been thinking about the organic diet. Making my own baby food. Maybe using cloth diapers instead of the plastic ones," Kane said, his gaze staying focused on Sophia. Out of everyone there, this was something the two of them shared and had in common. He knew she'd be on board with this kind of diet.

"Oh, Kane, that's an excellent idea. I love that we did that with both our girls. It's a lot of work, but so beneficial," Sophia agreed, beaming up at him now.

Kane smiled at her praise, even as Avery gave a slightly condescending chuckle. He chose to ignore that little laugh. Avery wasn't as on board with the whole organic theory to life, but Kane had resolved they were doing this. He had read all the studies on the benefits of natural versus processed foods. They were in a time of research, modern medicine was a marvel, and with Avery's father's side of the family all dying of heart disease early in life, to Kane, it seemed the best way to fight against those odds. Avery didn't yet know he was going to be included. This was going to be a whole family lifestyle change, not just one for their baby. Kane had decided this would probably be their second fight, so he'd wait to drop his nutritional bomb until he knew he could win.

"Ready to get started?" the ultrasound tech asked as Dr. Palmer entered the room. The lights were dimmed, and he wasted no time squirting a thick liquid gel on Sophia's exposed belly. He flipped on the equipment and immediately began to rub the wand through the gel. The monitor lit up and static filled the screen. All the conversation came to an abrupt end, everyone's eyes focused at the monitor. Kane had no idea what they were supposed to see because all he could make out was black and white static, yet the entire practice seemed absorbed and fascinated by what they were viewing.

Dr. Palmer's normal bedside manner didn't change. He was very dry, matter-of-fact, and all about work. As the wand moved around, he started right in, marking patterns he saw on the screen. The sound of the baby's heartbeat filled the room. The fast whooshing sounds always excited Kane. It was proof their little one was doing all right.

Slowly, with the help of the doctor's markings, Kane began to possibly make out a foot, and then maybe, he saw a second one. The rest of the room seemed to have no problem counting toes and fingers easily. *Yeah, right!* So, he kept his eyes glued to the screen. Sophia had her professionalism back in place, asking specific questions, guiding the technician along as they spoke clinically, losing Kane even more. The confusion must have shown on his face, because Avery pulled him in tighter against his side.

Two things happened at once. A third foot was identified and marked at the same time a second, very faint, somewhat slower whooshing sound became audible. The room erupted in cheers, Paulie and Kennedy were suddenly there beside the table, but Kane's confusion continued. Whatever was happening had the room filled with excitement, and he focused harder on the screen, trying to understand why they were happy that his baby had three feet. The technician continued moving the wand. Kane ignored the dull background conversation, mainly because of the defect his little one showed. The pounding of his own heart rang louder than the noise in the room until the tech's voice announced a head, a heart, another heart, and a fourth foot.

Kane finally got it. He understood what everyone else in the room had already picked up.

"We have twins, babe," Avery whispered, hugging Kane, kissing him in the crook of his neck.

"There's two," Paulie's gruff voice sounded. Kane could feel Paulie at his back, giving him some sturdy pats. Kennedy was right there beside him, smiling up, and the four of them were enveloped into a tight family hug. Kane was on autopilot because his entire world had just suddenly stopped, only to jolt forward again at an amazing speed.

He finally took a deep breath, exhaling the pent-up tension. Two hearts and four feet did mean twins. Avery was right, they were having twins. Their family was growing by two, not one. Avery finally let him go and gathered his mom up in the huge bear hug. Paulie stayed right there beside him and all Kane could do was focus on the screen.

Somewhere in the back of his mind, he heard Sophia and Dr. Palmer talking with the technician, but his eyes were glued to the monitor willing himself to make out any of the shapes, other than just flat black static.

The moments of intense numbness faded seconds before overwhelming joy filled his heart. His body shook and tears threatened to fall. *Twins!* They were having twin babies.

"Can we tell their gender?" Kane thought to himself, and only realized he'd said the words aloud when every head in the room turned his way. Okay, so maybe he'd said the words rather loudly by the looks he got. Avery was right there, a concerned expression on his face.

"Are you all right?" Avery asked.

"I don't know. Are they healthy?" Kane asked. He could hear the desperation tainting the words, and he cocked his head past Avery, his gaze moving between the ultrasound technician and the doctor.

"We're going to see what we can see. The two heart rates sound strong. One is slower than the other but still strong," Dr. Palmer said. The room settled down, listening to everything said, and the tech began moving the wand back over Sophia's stomach with purpose.

"How did we miss this before?" Kane asked.

"Most likely the position the babies were in. Are you sure you want to know their sex if I can find it?" the technician asked, giving Kane a concerned look. He could feel the heat in his face. His voice was edgy, and he probably carried a corresponding expression on his face. He schooled his features, gathered himself, and rolled his shoulders as the tech angled the wand differently across Sophia's belly.

"Yes, we do. Right, babe?" Avery asked. For the first time since the announcement was made, Kane remembered Sophia. Avery stood right there, still clasping her hand. Knowing Avery and his constant encouragement, he'd probably never let her go through the happy shock of their discovery.

"Yes!" Kane said immediately. "Do you? Please say yes." That drew a laugh because Avery had clearly just affirmed they wanted to know.

"Of course I do," Avery agreed, and it took a few minutes more of the technician moving all around her belly. The electricity in the room was tangible. Everyone focused on the screen.

"Right here. Do you see it?" the technician asked the doctor. "The first baby looks like a boy."

"Do you see him?" Dr. Palmer asked, looking directly at Kane as he circled something on the screen. The room busted out in a cheer, that meant Avery was paying up. As much grief as he gave them about knowing he was having a little girl, they were all giving back to him now. Based on the screen, Kane just had to take the doctor's word on it; he saw nothing that looked like anything distinguishable, let alone boy parts.

"It's a boy? You're sure?" Avery questioned back loudly over the whooping and hollering. This Avery was the attorney, challenging the doctor's observation. He had been so certain he was having a little girl. There had never been an option of anything else.

"Pretty sure. He's hiding the other one… Protecting the other baby. He's facing the world," the technician said.

"Then he's got Avery's personality," Kane said, and Kennedy beamed up at him. That seemed to settle Avery down, he took pride in that and kissed Kane, clearly pleased Kane thought such a thing about him.

"Try on this side," Sophia suggested patting her left side, back around her hips. She tried to turn over, angle her oversized belly better, and Avery was right there, helping her turn.

"Hang on, grip onto my hand, I'll turn you," he said. The technician stayed on her, moving the wand, adding more gel.

"Wait, turn for me a bit… Right here. Do you see anything?" the technician asked, who knew who he spoke to. "Yes! Right there. Do you see?"

"I think we may have a girl," Sophia said, beaming back at Avery.

"I believe you're right," Dr. Palmer seconded.

"Yes!" Avery exclaimed, and Kane went numb again for the second time in a matter of a few minutes. They were having a boy and a girl. Avery was so excited, beaming from ear to ear as he drew Kane up and hugged him tight, actually lifting him off his feet.

"Two, babies. We're having two," Avery said. Kennedy and Paulie were gathered in the hug. Hugs were again shared by everyone. Avery couldn't hide his enthusiasm as he made sure everyone knew his little girl was in there too. The small, confined exam room overflowed with joy and laughter. It seemed their family had just grown to include everyone in that room.

"Are they healthy?" Kane quietly asked Dr. Palmer as they stood in the center of all the commotion.

"From what I'm seeing right now, I'd say yes. We need to run some tests. They're small, but that's expected with twins and explains a lot. Let me get my hands on these reports, but they seem good, Kane. Celebrate this, Son. It's a good day for you," Dr. Palmer said, breaking out of his normal stone-face to give him a grin and handshake across Sophia's belly.

Kane let a breath out, shook the doctor's hand, and the tears he'd been trying so hard to hold back welled in his eyes. He'd never expected twins. This just seemed too good to be true. Not one baby, but two. He and Avery were having twins. Surely, God wouldn't bless them like this if they weren't suited to be parents. Kane watched Avery celebrating out of the corner of his eye. He was so excited, so animated in his actions. The feeling was starting to settle into his soul, they were going to be fathers, and the emotions were overwhelming. The tears spilled down his cheeks, clouding his vision. Even if they were tears of happiness, he didn't want anyone to see him cry. He excused himself to the restroom. He needed to pull himself together. He barely made it out the exam room door before he heard Avery behind him.

"Wait, Kane. Baby, you're crying," Avery said behind him, stopping him before he could get to the restroom and clean himself up.

"I'm not crying," Kane said, turning his tearful eyes to Avery.

"You are! Baby..." Avery said, drawing Kane up against him and gently brushing at the wetness on his cheeks.

"I'm just happy," Kane confessed, the tears now spilling onto Avery's dress shirt. "You stay in there with everyone. I'm going to the bathroom to clean up." When it looked like Avery was going to argue, Kane stopped him, lifting a finger to Avery's lips. "Stay here with Sophia and our babies. I'll be right back." Those were effective words. Kane pulled free of the hold and was down the hall before the hiccups started. He couldn't even take a full breath. This was even more than he'd ever hoped for. They were going to have a family, he couldn't believe it.

Twins!

Chapter 18

Avery swirled the Chivas and water, letting the ice clink in the small cocktail glass before he downed the contents in one large swallow. The sound of laughter filled the living room as he stopped by the wet bar, pouring himself another drink. Kane caught his eye. It was funny how in tune they were with each other, and Avery turned in his direction. The look Kane gave made it clear he was keeping an eye on Avery, even though he was occupied with a house full of guests. Avery grinned and lifted two fingers, wiggling his eyebrows. He'd been placed on a strict, love-filled health regime, and Kane watched him like a hawk, because without question, Avery would cheat on his diet given the opportunity.

Today, Kane allowed him two alcoholic drinks, and out of nothing more than teasing Kane, he reached up and pulled another taller glass from the rack, pouring himself a double. That would earn him a lecture later, and he'd play dumb, saying he'd only had two drinks, but Kane had never said a thing about what glass he could use. Avery would go round and round with Kane, and by the end of the discussion, Kane would feel guilty for reprimanding Avery so solidly. He was certain to get one of those Kane Dalton Adams fan-fucking-

146

tastic blow jobs to help ease his pain and hurt feelings. Avery's smile grew and his body stirred, thinking over the possibilities. God, Kane still had him completely under his spell.

It was only another solid round of laughter that had Avery leaving those thoughts and schooling his body's reaction. They had a house full of guests, and it wouldn't do to have a hard-on tenting his slacks for the next few hours until he could finally get Kane alone.

Avery had thrown Kane a baby shower, inviting just about everyone in their day to day lives. The whole thing was really more a party. Everyone invited brought a guest, which allowed for a solid mix of both men and women to celebrate the twins who were soon to arrive.

They were still approximately six weeks from the delivery date, but Kane had spent so much time and energy creating the perfect nursery, Avery felt compelled to show off his handiwork. Kane had worked meticulously, trying to create the perfect design for their children. After much debate, he chose Mickey and Minnie Mouse, having matching layettes made for each child. Kane agonized over the decision. He spent hours and hours going over materials and designs. Many of their nights were spent lying in bed well into the morning hours, talking about nothing more than drapes, colors, polka dots, and accessories for the twins' room. Finally, after weeks of contemplation, Avery gently nudged Kane into a decision, hoping bedtime could be more than nursery talk again.

Funny though, once the nursery was complete, Kane's attention turned to the all-consuming project of choosing the safest car seats for the road. After another few weeks of agonizing, Paulie stepped in and made the decision for Kane. He bought the latest in car safety and made a show of dropping the car seats at the house then leaving in a disgruntled huff. Avery guessed Paulie must have heard it all day at the restaurant, like he'd heard it all night at home. Kane didn't even seem fazed. Instead, he spent the remainder of the day installing the car seats in the vehicle, making sure they were a secure fit. Avery grinned, taking a small sip to hide his smile. God, his mister was going to make a wonderful father to those children, just like Avery had always known he would.

Avery wound his way through the living room, taking a seat closest to Sophia. She was thirty-four weeks along, with her belly growing bigger by the day. She made good progress, which they considered nothing but good news, and they were hopeful she would remain pregnant another few weeks. The babies were a nice size and by all accounts seemed healthy. Avery could easily see they were a load on her slender frame. As a testimony to the thought, she'd just announced that she had quit seeing patients until after delivery. She stopped short of saying she was on bed rest, but she was going to be taking it easy in an effort to draw the pregnancy out.

Another huge turn of events had happened over the last few months; they had finally made the headlines. However, two close to full gestation in vitro babies seemed less important than the fact he and Kane were the first gay couple to get this far in the game. Avery doubted either guaranteed a headline. He suspected it was more the tie to his heritage that kept them front page news across the country, but regardless, they were heavily debated on the national news and hands down their decision was widely criticized, especially in the Deep South. Yet, here in Minnesota, the community seemed to protect them. No one cared anything more than that an Adams was back to having babies and that excitement superseded anything else that could matter.

Avery tried to keep all the negative national media from touching his husband. Paulie seemed as determined to shield Kane as well. Together they made a pretty impressive team, but for the most part, Kane seemed immune to it all. They had made the decision not to watch television, which was paying off. Kane's only focus was preparing their home for the twins' arrival. Avery loved how resilient his honey had become. He was accepting who they were as individuals and who they were as a couple. That pleased Avery most of all.

"No, I hired a registered nurse to come over this week and make sure we're set and ready to go. She's going to work with us on the care of the twins. They have these life-like dolls now. They called them interactive, and we'll practice everything with them," Kane said, telling Avery's mom all about the dolls he'd found and the classes he had arranged for them. She sat right next to him as he opened the presents the guests brought. Kane's comments caught Avery's attention, just as Sophia's hand came to rest on his thigh.

"He's doing so well. He's so excited," she said quietly. Avery didn't miss the amusement in her eyes, and he gave her a showy eye roll.

"The nurse and classes are news to me," Avery said back in little more than a whisper. He didn't want to squelch Kane's enthusiasm.

"It's admirable. He's determined to care for these two without any help. He's trying, you have to give him credit for that," Sophia said, patting her round belly. Avery couldn't help the laugh that slipped out at that thought. He was absolutely certain Kane would pull off taking care of the two babies, but as someone born with a nanny waiting in the wings, he was breaking all sorts of new ground for himself.

"Things have changed so much since Avery was a baby. Pampers are from God. I remember the days of cleaning those cloth diapers," Kennedy said as Kane unwrapped a box of disposable diapers.

"I think we're going to give cloth diapers a try," Kane said and immediately looked down at the gift in his lap. He was too much of a gentleman to not try and make that right. "But we've decided to use disposable diapers when we go out. We think that will be the simplest way to care for them." Avery chuckled at Kane's expression as he tried to reassure their guest that he loved their gift.

"Is that true?" Sophia leaned in, whispering to Avery after he hid a more serious laugh by taking another sip.

"Hell no! Kane is earth friendly, environmentally aware, and ecologically safe all the way now," Avery whispered back, hoping no one heard him.

"That's the impression I got," Sophia quietly said.

As fun as sitting in the living room, opening all these gifts and listening to the hundreds of stories about raising children was, Avery couldn't help but give in to curiosity and take a peek at what was going on in other rooms in his house. He slanted his head to the right to see if he could get a good look inside the game room.

From this angle, he could see some of the men shooting pool. For the most part, the men had gone straight to the game room when they'd arrived, while the women stationed themselves inside the living room. Paulie was the last stray to hang on, and without question, it was only to show support for Kane, but after so much "women talk" Paulie finally bailed. Avery was left all alone, listening to the Pac-Man arcade game ding in the background, calling his name to join them.

Both groups seemed to be having a great time. He kept telling himself that was all that mattered.

Avery sat on their blue velvet sofa and watched as Kane opened the gift from his mother. He was as surprised as Kane, and cut his eyes to her, a little stunned and completely uncertain as to how she accomplished such a feat. She had baby pictures of both Kane and Avery framed together.

To Avery's knowledge, Kane had nothing of his past, and the moment Kane's eyes landed on the photo, they shot back up to meet his. The same shock pooled in Kane's eyes as he turned the framed photos toward Avery. Kane was the happiest he'd ever remembered seeing him.

In that moment, Kane's emotion took his breath away. He could do nothing more than stare. He had become so lost in the happenings of day to day life, he'd taken for granted he'd married the most handsome, kind, gentle man he'd ever met. Kane's soul whispered and reached out to embrace his. Good God, he loved that man. Their connection was so strong, he didn't want to take his eyes from Kane.

"Oh no!" All the heads in the room whipped around to Sophia, who sat on the edge of the couch clutching her stomach. The bewilderment left most of their faces, kicking everyone into action as it became clear the spot where Sophia sat was saturated. She struggled to stand. Her pants were soaked, and the liquid pooled on the hardwood floor beneath her feet.

"Get Thomas," she said urgently and gripped her stomach. Avery was up, holding on to her as she doubled over in pain.

"We need to get you to the hospital," Thomas said, appearing by Sophia's side, taking Avery's place.

"I'll call Dr. Palmer," Paulie said, moving faster than Avery had ever seen him move.

"The contractions are coming fast. We must hurry," Sophia said, looking straight at Thomas, already walking toward the front door. The living room filled as their guests crowded in to offer their support and advice. Everyone rushed about, but no one could actually do anything to help. For the first time since Sophia's water broke, Avery looked around for Kane. He was nowhere to be found.

"Mother, where's Kane?" Avery asked, sure she could hear the panic in his voice. This wasn't the time for disappearing; they needed to get to the hospital.

"The answering service is getting the doctor to the hospital," Paulie bellowed from the kitchen door. Avery fished around inside his pockets for his keys. By this point, everyone from the party was in full panic mode. Chaos ensued, if nothing more than in Avery's head, and he needed Kane. They needed to follow Sophia to the hospital.

"I've got the car out front, ready to go," Kane shouted, busting through the front door. "I packed a second hospital bag, just in case you needed it! I'm glad I did," Kane stated matter-of-factly, calmly moving to Sophia's other side, and carefully, but quickly escorting her across the porch and down the stairs to their new, baby-safe Volvo.

Avery made it to the front door, as Kane closed the passenger side door. Thomas slid in the backseat.

"Come on!" Kane yelled at Avery. There was even a moment of clear frustration on his face when he spotted Avery still at the front door. Through all the confusion, Avery realized that Kane must have planned for this too. The just in case. He couldn't have been more proud.

"Avery, go. I'll make sure we get everything closed up. Paulie and I can ride to the hospital together," Kennedy said. Kane honked, waving his hand, yelling out the window for him. The sound of the car being put in drive gave Avery the distinct impression he'd be left behind if he wasn't in that car in a matter of seconds. He took off down the steps, running, and jumped in next to Thomas. Kane was already speeding down the drive before he even shut the car door.

* * * *

"You were spectacular getting us here," Avery said, carrying Kane's backup overnight bag through the hospital halls. Kane seemed to innately know his way, and Avery followed a step behind, just trying to keep up and stay out of Kane's way as he turned corners here and there, never stopping to ask his way. Sophia had agreed Kane could be her labor coach for the birth, and his mister wasn't wasting one minute. No one else would be in the room, just her and Kane and the medical staff. He had even attended Lamaze classes with her.

"I practiced driving here just in case. From both the house and the restaurant," Kane said. He must have realized what he'd just revealed, because for the first time since entering the hospital, he cut his eyes to Avery. "Don't laugh!"

"You saved the day. I'm not going to laugh," Avery said, a huge smile on his face. Of course Kane would have done something like that. Since they started this whole birthing thing, everything he knew about Kane had flown out the window. His ultra conservative, very reserved husband was a ball of nerves that'd evidently left very little to chance. What he couldn't work through, he learned about until he knew every single detail there was to know.

They had made it to Sophia's hospital room, and Avery grabbed Kane's arm before he entered. "Keep me posted. I'll be in the waiting room. Take care of them, Kane," Avery said, leaning in for a quick kiss.

Kane gave him a quick peck before pushing through the swinging metal doors. The door closed, only to reopen before Avery had a chance to even turn away. Kane reached for the bag. "Stay close." And with that Kane was gone again.

He and Thomas were relegated to the waiting room two doors down the hall. Minutes felt like hours. Slowly, members of the baby shower began to trickle in. It wasn't too much longer before he heard Paulie's booming voice asking about the babies at the nurses' station. He sounded as impatient as ever, but that was Paulie's manner. Avery spotted him and his mother about the same time Sophia's hospital room door opened unexpectedly. Sophia lay on a gurney and was being pushed out of the room. Kane followed behind the doctor and nurses solemn-faced and resigned. Resigned to what?

Thomas jogged the few steps to the gurney, and Kane walked immediately to Avery. "Her blood pressure's too high. They have to take the babies."

"What happened? She's been doing well this whole time?" Avery questioned, watching Thomas stand at the other set of swinging double doors his wife had just been pushed through.

"It was high when she got here and spiked higher while we were in there."

"What's happening?" Kennedy asked Avery while she watched Thomas as he stood looking lost, staring at the closed doors.

"It's her blood pressure," Avery replied. He left his family and made his way straight to Thomas. He'd promised to take care of Thomas while Kane handled Sophia. It was the only thing Sophia asked of him, and he wasn't going to let her down.

"She'll be fine, come back to the waiting room with us," Avery said, wrapping an arm around his shoulder as he took in Thomas's clearly worried face.

"She never had this problem before," Thomas said and let Avery slowly turn him.

"She's got the best possible care. You know that," Avery offered, now guiding him back to the waiting room.

"She said it's normal," Thomas added, his worried eyes now searching Avery's.

"She would know, wouldn't she?" Avery calmly stated, trying to hide his own concern. Thomas only gave him a nod. Paulie, God love his soul, took over, because that was all that Avery could muster in the way of encouragement. Avery was worried too. They had come so far with such smooth sailing. How could this be happening now?

The small waiting room was packed with their family and friends. Time seemed to slow to a snail's pace, with each sound of the clock's ticking filling the silent room. Kane stood by a window, his eyes stayed focused on something unseen. After a while, Avery left his seat next to his mom and went to his Kane. For one of the first times ever, Avery felt the need to respect Kane's public displays rules—probably because of the worry rolling off him in waves.

"It's been too much time," Kane said. He never looked back at Avery. Avery stood there, taking in Kane's stance, his arms tightly crossed and his head bent down.

"Baby, it's only been thirty minutes," Avery said quietly back.

"Avery, it doesn't take this long," Kane stated. Avery could see his husband's reflection through the windowpane and knew he'd closed his eyes.

"Don't bring worry into this yet. We don't know anything," Avery advised. He broke the restraint he been showing and reached for Kane, but before he could turn him, Kane flipped around, railing at him.

"Exactly! How come we don't know anything, Avery?" This was a first. Had his partner really just raised his voice at him in the middle of the crowded waiting room? For the first time ever, something had finally broken through Kane's well-placed calm façade. And Avery realized it was the fear that something might happen to their babies, his papa bear was protective over his unborn cubs.

Kane's frantic eyes slid away from Avery's, and he stepped forward, leaving Avery to do nothing more than try and catch up with all the moods Kane was tossing his way. Dr. Palmer had come inside the waiting room, pulling his surgical cap off his head. Stress showed on his face, but Avery couldn't read anything more. Thomas was there, standing next to Kane, with Avery right on their heels.

"How is she?" Thomas didn't wait for the physician to begin.

"She's made it through and is in recovery now—" Dr. Palmer started.

"How are the babies?" Kane asked, interrupting the doctor. Apparently Kane's behavior was a surprise to them all, because every eye in the small waiting area was on him. Paulie had even made his way over to Kane, worry on his face.

That few seconds, waiting for the confirmation, had Avery's heart dropping to his feet. He didn't think he could take much more as he balanced on pins and needles for the doctor's answer. He released a shaky breath, in hopes of calming himself, not wanting Kane to pick up on his distress; his nerves were getting to him. He reached out for Kane and wrapped an arm around his husband's waist for comfort. The feel of Kane's body pressed next to his seemed to have a calming effect he so desperately needed at that moment. After the initial confusion faded, Dr. Palmer gave a weary smile.

"They're doing well. They're premature, but a nice size. They were bigger than we originally thought and that's plus for them. Both are in neonatal now, being checked out, they weren't too happy with us and were voicing their opinion loudly when I left them."

"When can we see them?" Kane fired right back while Avery, along with everyone else in the room, gave a deep sigh of relief at the initial good news. Of course, his wound up honey had to see those little ones for himself before he'd believe anything.

"We'll get you in as soon as possible. The doctor's with them now. Let them get through their assessment and fully checked out. Thomas, if you'll come back with me, you can be there when she wakes up." Kane nodded, somewhat resigned, and turned, pressing fully into Avery's waiting arms.

"We have our babies," Kane said, wrapping his arms around Avery, tucking his face in the crook of his neck.

"We do," Avery whispered, before lifting his head to the doctor and catching a glimpse of his retreating back as he called out, "Tell Sophia we're here and thank you!" Avery got a thumbs up from the doctor. Thomas looked relieved, but completely exhausted. Everyone was drained and the room filled with so many emotions. Avery tugged Kane tighter to him. They stayed just like that for several long moments until Paulie spoke up.

"If you can tear yourselves apart, I think we have some congratulations for you!" Paulie said in his typical rough-edged way. Kane was the first to release their embrace, only to tilt back and greet Avery with the biggest smile ever. He got a quick kiss before his mom was there with tear-filled eyes, hugging them both tightly.

Chapter 19

The twins' names came easy after Kane sat with each baby the first day. They named their daughter Autumn Kennedy and their son, Robert Paul. For some reason, those weren't names on the endlessly long list they had made over the last several months, but were the most fitting nonetheless. And Autumn and Robert were perfect. Both had thick, full caps of blond hair and perfectly shaped lips. They were absolutely adorable.

Kane couldn't actually touch either baby, but he stayed right there with them every day they were kept in the neonatal unit. After the first twenty-four hours of Avery trying to get him to eat or leave for sleep, he arranged for them to have a private family room where they both stayed for the entire length of time their children were in the hospital. Paulie ran the restaurant and Avery went back and forth between his practice, the restaurant, and the hospital, making sure everything kept running as smoothly as possible, leaving Kane the sole task of staying vigilant over their babies care.

Almost a month to the day of their birth, the four of them were able to leave the hospital. Most of the media hype from their birth had died down. Kane's adamancy about staying at the hospital had allowed him a certain amount of immunity from the mass frenzy of news reporters stationed out front. Early on, Avery gave a press release on the children's birth and their health. He even broke one of his long-standing rules and addressed the media directly, but it still took weeks of speculation on every aspect of their children's lives before reporters found something new to fill the hours between the morning and six o'clock news.

Sophia stopped by regularly, checking on everyone's progress, but she allowed them the time they needed to connect as a family as well. For Kane, the parental bonds formed immediately. He couldn't believe how much he already loved both babies, yet somehow every day that love grew to new and boundless proportions. Avery had been so right to do this for them, and Kane tried hard to show his appreciation.

He never held himself back anymore. No matter where they were, he invited Avery's touches and small caresses. For the first time in their long relationship, he even initiated some of them. Kane held a level of love for his newfound little family that he could barely contain. He'd never dreamed he would ever have any of this or be so completely fulfilled.

"Robert's asleep," Avery whispered. He sat rocking Robert while Kane sat next to him rocking Autumn. They had been home for a few hours and hadn't put either baby down since they'd arrived.

"So's Autumn," Kane whispered back, looking between both the babies and Avery. His whole world was right here inside this nursery.

"We should put them down," Avery whispered. He never took his eyes off Robert.

"I'm glad they're home." Neither made a moved to rise.

"Me too," Avery said, still rocking.

"They look like you, to me," Kane stated, now fully focused on Avery.

"You can't tell that," Avery replied.

"I can. Thank you for doing this for us," Kane confessed. Avery looked him straight in the eyes and slowly brought the rocker to a stop. There was such love in his eyes that Kane slowly rose from the rocking chair, carefully holding Autumn in his arms, and bent over to kiss Avery's upturned face.

"You're my always. I love you so much. I'd do anything to see you this happy," Avery whispered, and the warmth of Avery's words touched Kane's heart, making his smile grow sweeter.

"I'm glad I found you," Kane said quietly, stepping back as Avery stood.

"I think it was more like me finding you, handsome." For Kane, the sentimental memories were so strong; all he could do was stand there as they held their babies, thinking about their lives, their future, and his love for Avery.

"I can't imagine my life without you," Kane proclaimed sweetly.

"Good. I don't want you to. Come on, we need sleep. They'll be awake in a few hours to eat." Avery was the first to turn away. He carefully placed Robert in his crib and went to Autumn's baby bed to whisper a silent goodnight to her. Kane felt strong hands gently pulling him away. Avery wrapped an arm around Kane's waist and guided him from the room. They didn't shut the door. The nursery was right across the hall from their bedroom and Kane had made sure the monitors were on as they quietly made their way out.

"Now that they're home, you need to sleep when they sleep. I've been worried about you," Avery said as he began to disrobe.

"I can sleep later. They're only little once," Kane stated as he undressed quickly. His suitcase was on his side of the closet, still packed, and he ignored it as a yawn slipped out. He tossed his robe on the end of the bed and set the alarm for the feeding before he slid between the sheets.

"Did you check the monitor to see if it's on?" Kane asked, flipping off the light of the lamp on his nightstand. Avery met Kane in the center of the bed. The spot they normally shared. Kane had on his pajama bottoms, Avery wore nothing, and Kane's eyes connected with his.

They had made love every single night until the babies were born. How had he already forgotten their routine? They really hadn't had alone time while they stayed in the hospital. Kane had followed the same schedule as the babies, back down in the nursery every two hours for their feedings. Too many people were in and out, and he knew Avery didn't count quickies or blow jobs as proper alone time.

"It's on. You checked it a hundred times already, remember? And I checked it too. Have you thought any more about a nanny?" Avery asked. Kane saw him look up to check the monitor, so did Kane. The red flashing light gave him all the reassurance he needed. He leaned in and kissed his husband on the lips and wrapped him tighter in his arms.

"Not yet. I know we'll need one soon. The restaurant won't keep running itself, but not yet. Let's take care of them by ourselves a little while longer," Kane said, pushing his pajama bottoms down.

"We should still start accepting applications. If I know you, it'll take us interviewing about two hundred people before you decide on one." Kane didn't deny it, Avery was probably right. He felt sure Paulie would be in on the interviewing too. He had a keen sense and could pick up a fake with just a glance. Kane kicked his pants down to the end of the bed and spread his legs in a blatant invitation. Avery never missed much, thank heaven. Kane smiled to himself, relishing the feel of Avery's weight as he settled in on top of him. "What are they going to call us?"

"Dad?" Kane questioned. They'd had this conversation before, never really deciding anything for certain.

"We both can't be dad." Avery chuckled. Kane pressed against his warm firm lips, but when he tried to deepen the kiss, Avery pulled back. "Father's too formal for either of us, don't you think? How about Dad and Daddy?" Avery asked, anchoring his elbows under Kane's shoulder, keeping distance between them.

"Will it confuse them?" Kane asked

"I don't think so. I want you to be their Daddy." Avery smiled at him and he nodded. For some reason, this was an emotional decision. He'd called his father Daddy when he was a child and always envisioned his children using that word with him.

"Then it's settled. I'm truly happier than I've ever been in my entire life. I need you to make love to me tonight, Avery." He held Avery's gaze with his, fighting the emotion running through him.

"I want to make love to you, but I'm also content to hold you and let you fall asleep in my arms. You need sleep. I've been worried about you," Avery said, his weight shifting as he rolled himself beside Kane, until their heads shared a pillow.

"I'm fine," Kane started, but Avery placed two fingers across his lips, silencing him.

"Good night. I love you."

"I love you too, Avery." Kane ran his hands down Avery's back. God, he wanted this man inside him tonight. He needed the feel of Avery's skin sliding against his. It had been way too long. And Kane could feel the evidence of Avery's desire pressed against his thigh. Like always, Avery sacrificed his own needs for Kane's or in this case what he thought were Kane's needs. He loved that about Avery, always making sure he was well taken care of, always worrying about him. Kane turned his head on the pillow, looking at Avery's closed eyes, and he listened to him breathe.

"I'm not tired. I need you to make love to me, Avery, please. I've missed being with you." He slid his hand along Avery's hip and around to grip the thickening cock at his thigh. Avery pushed into his fist, and he couldn't help but smile when he heard Avery's low groan and mumbled protest.

"Shit! How can I say no with you touching me like that?" Avery's mouth was on his before he could complete the second stroke. He loved the way Avery took control, sweetly kissing him, pressing him into the mattress as he settled back between Kane's thighs. Avery's lips worked against his. His husband's probing tongue pushed inside his mouth and his senses were flooded with the sweet taste of Avery. He kissed Avery back with desperation. His hands now fisted in Avery's hair as he tried to convey his feelings through his kiss. Kane lifted his hips grinding his erection against his lover's. His dick plumped and ass tightened at the feel of Avery's hand sliding between their bodies and wrapping around his aching cock.

"Yes, this…I missed this." Avery knew just how to undo him, make him lose all control. He widened his legs, giving Avery's fingers room to explore. "Get the lube. I need you inside me, now."

"Hold on, let me open you. I don't want to hurt you," Avery warned, his fingers continuing their pursuit.

"I don't want to wait! Make love to me, Avery. I need to feel you stretching me, moving inside me." He bucked his hips as he pleaded against Avery's ear, sucking the lobe between his lips. He grinned to himself as his mister's weight suddenly lifted from him.

Kane watched eagerly as his husband pushed back, sitting on his heels, and reached over to the nightstand. Avery opened the drawer, grabbed the bottle, and settled back in between his thighs. He poured a generous amount of lubrication on his fingers, and then gave his hard length a few tugs. Kane's ass clenched and his cock jerked in anticipation at the sight of Avery's palm wrapped around his own leaking cock, his well-defined abs flexing with each breath.

"You're so beautiful, Avery. I'm so lucky…"

Avery shushed him as his warm palm slid down the inside of his thigh. He pressed back, opening Kane wider. Avery looked down at him, his amber eyes darkening with lust. He felt his face flush as Avery watched him like a hungry predator, waiting to devour his prey. Just seeing that lust-filled glint bore into his soul proved Avery needed him as much as he needed Avery. Warm strong fingers circled and pressed against his hole, and he lifted his hips, wanting the feel of them inside him as Avery drove him insane with all the teasing.

"Babe, please...Ahhh!" Avery surprised him and shoved two thick fingers deep into him, and he just about came from the delicious sting the action created. Avery always identified what he craved, knew his body so well. He played him like an old guitar. Avery worked him, slowly pumping those long fingers in and out of him. His knuckle brushed against his prostate sending zings of toe-curling electricity coursing through Kane's veins. His blood boiled hot, his eyes slammed shut, and only his panting and the wet sound of Avery's fist now working his cock filled the silence. God, it felt good, so good.

"Now, please...Avery, I want to come with you in me," Kane begged as he concentrated on not shooting his load. He was already skating a fine line.

"I love when you beg, Kane. Sounds so sweet." Avery's grip tightened, but the rhythm on his dick slowed to long deliberate strokes. "Just like your ass. You want me in your ass, don't you, Kane?" Avery teased, sliding his thick cock head down Kane's crevice and up again before pressing against his rim. Kane whimpered at the sensation.

"God, please...yes! Avery, I need to come..." He opened his eyes and stared up at Avery. His needy ass clenched, wanting to be filled by his lover. Kane gripped the back of his thighs, pulling them toward his chest, opening himself for Avery. Waiting.

"And I want to give you exactly what you need, babe." Avery took his time positioning himself; Kane knew the man did it to drive him insane. Avery did everything with purpose. The stroking suddenly stopped, and he looked up at Avery who gave him a wicked grin.

"Avery, ple—" He gasped at the welcomed burn as Avery pushed past the contracting ring of muscle, sliding in deep with one long thrust. Avery's thick cock stretched him wide, making him moan. Avery froze above him, letting him adjust to the fullness. He wiggled his hips, and Avery began to move, slowly dragging along his passage. The fullness eased as he withdrew and returned as he pressed back in. And Kane lifted his hips to meet each one of Avery's torturous thrusts.

"You're so tight, so hot, you look so fucking good like this, with me fucking you, Kane," Avery growled, his eyes heavily hooded with lust. Avery's words made his dick twitch, and he felt the wetness of his own pre-come leaking onto his stomach. Kane lifted his head and glanced down their bodies to where he and his husband were joined, watching as Avery's cock disappeared in and out of his body. Nothing felt as good as Avery making love to him. He was complete when he was in Avery's arms.

"I love you so much, Avery." He pulled Avery down to him, sinking his fingers into Avery's thick hair as they kissed slow and deep. Emotions flooded him, overwhelming him. His dreams were now a reality because of this man. His tongue danced against his lover's as he tugged his knees closer to his body, wanting Avery deeper.

"I've always loved you," Avery whispered into his mouth.

Avery picked up the pace. His hips moving back and forth, thrusting in and out of Kane, hitting his spot and pushing him closer to the edge with each pump of his hips. He writhed as Avery's skilled hand slid back between their bodies and stroked him in time with his thrusts. His thumb spread Kane's moisture across the head of his cock, stopping only briefly to delve teasingly inside his slit. No, it wasn't going to take him long tonight.

"I'm-m…gonna come." Fire gathered in his spine. His balls filled and drew up as the intense heat finally exploded, engulfing him and robbing him of his breath as his hot come shot between their bodies. "Avery," was all he managed before his ass contracted in speech-stealing and mind-numbing spasms.

"God, yes! Kane, oh God, yes…" Avery choked out in deep grunts. He plunged in one last time and his whole body tensed. Kane's ass continued to clench and constrict around Avery, while his husband's cock jerked and twitched inside him. Avery flooded him with liquid warmth. His body involuntarily shuddered at the amazing feeling of rapture. His ass tightened around Avery one last time as his lover collapsed on him. Kane gasped for breath, kissing Avery's sweaty skin, willing his heart rate to slow. He was weak with pleasure, his body limp with contentment.

They lay, totally blissed out, with Avery's full weight resting on him. Neither spoke. Kane always loved this moment of just being, of knowing they were one. Their heartbeats were in sync as their bodies slowly returned to earth. Avery's sweet lips pressed against his as he slid out of him, drawing him from his thoughts. Their bodies were no longer connected, but their souls were. He loved this man. He loved the life they shared and the future they were building, His heart filled with joy as he thought about the two sleeping babies in the nursery.

"Hold on, babe. Let me clean us up, stay right there," Avery said, breaking the silence as he pushed from the bed, placing a kiss on Kane's chest before heading to the bathroom. After a few minutes, he returned with a warm wet towel and cleaned them both. Avery tossed the towel to the floor and crawled back in bed, pressing the length of his body along Kane's. Kane turned to face Avery.

"I'm so incredibly happy. I still can't believe it's real. Our family's finally complete." Avery's arms slid around his waist and pulled him closer.

"This is exactly what I've wanted since the first time I kissed you. I love you, Kane, and I love our family."

Chapter 20

December, 1989 ~ Minneapolis, Minnesota.
La Bella Luna

"I can't believe you pulled this off," Avery said, holding Kane close as they danced together on the makeshift dance floor covering half of La Bella Luna. Seventy-five of their closest family and friends were gathered for Avery's surprise fiftieth birthday party.

"So you were surprised?" Kane grinned, proud of his accomplishment. It was a rare day to get anything past Avery Adams—especially when he lived in the same house—yet somehow he'd made this surprise happen. They were dancing to "Your Song" by Elton John. Avery always called it their song. Kane wasn't sure they had an official song, but Avery always said this particular tune reminded him of them. The slow melody allowed for intimate moments, while still being appropriate in front of their family and children. Kane suspected that was more than likely the true reason Avery chose this song as theirs.

"I must be slipping in my old age," Avery shot back, waggling his eyebrows.

"Yeah right!" Kane snorted. "You're sharper than ever. This wasn't easy for me to keep secret. You made me work for it."

"I can't believe I didn't figure it out when you made me wear a tux to the theater," Avery said, swaying to the music.

"You know I love you in this tux." He grinned up at Avery. Age had been kind to his husband, Kane loved the sprinkling of gray hair just beginning to show and how the fine lines formed around the corner of Avery's eyes as he beamed back at him.

"I was just thinking I was gonna get lucky tonight if I wore it. I was surprised it still fits." Avery drew Kane closer, and Kane laid his head on Avery's shoulder. The exact move Avery had been angling for since they'd started dancing. They were pressed together from head to toe, and he loved the feel of Avery's firm body, warm and solid, against his. Avery brought their entwined hands up, tucking them between their chests as he slid his hand inside Kane's suit jacket, keeping them tightly together.

"You haven't changed that much over the years," Kane said in little more than a whisper. Avery lowered his head, laying his cheek on Kane's head. Lord, did Avery have a way of making him feel special. Kane wrapped himself tighter around his husband.

"How does it feel to be married to a fifty-year-old?" Avery finally asked. Kane lifted his head, mischief in his eyes.

"Now that you say it like that, I am just a babe in the woods!" Avery snorted and gave an indulgent grin.

"My original plans for the night were to put the children to bed early and show you what someone of my advanced age could still do to a body like yours. Since, those plans have changed, and this is the first few minutes I've had alone with you, I think you need to lay your head back on my shoulder, whisper how much you love me into my ear, and remember your day is just around the corner."

"I'm a young forty-seven," Kane said, following the directions with the help of Avery's hand lowering his head back down on his shoulder.

"Your ass is still hot and firm as ever," Avery said. He turned them in a slow circle toward a darkened corner and slid his hand down Kane's ass, squeezing as he leaned in to place a light, soft, lingering kiss on Kane's lips. "Thank you for tonight."

"You're welcome," Kane replied, and that earned him another kiss, this time just below his ear. Kane actually shivered in response. He could feel his body harden and his cock plump. Avery was probably doing it to him on purpose. He needed to do something, anything, to change the direction his body was taking in this dance.

He'd be tenting in his slacks before long, and Avery would totally have him talked into a quick romp inside his office. No way would that go unnoticed.

"And the kids didn't know either?" Avery asked. Thank God! A platonic conversation, just what he needed to settle himself down.

"Of course not. There would be no way Autumn could keep this quiet," Kane said, lifting his head so Avery could see him rolling his eyes.

"She knows when to tell her dad what he needs to know," Avery grinned. Autumn was Avery's shadow where Robert was more content to be on his own.

"Exactly why they couldn't know." No question, Autumn would have let the whole party slip and feel terrible about it for many months to come. If Robert would have known, he would have teased Autumn until she brought Avery in on their fight, and again, Avery would have masterfully pulled the information from Robert. No, for this to work, neither could have known.

"You're tricky to keep such secrets," Avery said, narrowing his eyes at Kane. That caused him to laugh out loud as he lowered his head back to Avery's shoulder. Avery began to move Kane backward in slow determined steps. It was late in the night. The party was slowly winding down. They'd had dinner, a fun little roast in Avery's honor, and ended the night with drinks and dancing. Both Autumn and Robert had gone home about an hour ago with their Nonnie, Avery's mom, and even going home then, they were well past their bedtime.

"Why are you guiding me to the kitchen?" Kane asked, keeping easy steps with Avery.

"You know why," Avery said and pressed his hardened cock against Kane's. At the same moment, Avery dipped his head, swiping his tongue across the seam of Kane's lips. So much for them trying to keep it casual.

Kane felt the electric shock shooting through his body. His dick swelled up instantly and his steps faltered. Avery still had that effect on him after all this time. He knew where this was going, but he needed to put up a little fight, for appearance's sake. Plus he knew how much Avery liked to talk him into doing these bad things.

"We shouldn't. I'm the host. You're the guest of honor..." Kane said, stopping dead in his tracks, but Avery kept moving, and he was forced to fall into step or be pushed over.

"I don't care. It's my birthday and I want my present," Avery growled just as Kane felt the kitchen doors at his back. Avery lifted his hand, opening the doors and propelling them inside. Under the darkened light of the now closed kitchen, Avery slid his palm to the back of Kane's neck and pulled him forward, capturing his mouth in an urgent, demanding kiss. Kane opened immediately, kissing Avery in a frenzy of lips, tongue, and teeth. Avery never stopped their forward motion. He kept guiding them toward Kane's office, until he pushed open the door and shoved Kane inside.

"Baby, we shouldn't. Our guests..." Avery latched on to Kane's neck and ran his hands down his chest, finding and gripping his now rigid cock through the material of his trousers. Avery massaged him with purpose while freeing his belt buckle and sliding the button to his slacks free.

"You know this won't take long, and it'll be like old times," Avery whispered in his ear. Seconds later, Avery took his lips again, driving his tongue inside, licking and exploring the depths of his mouth. Avery exhaled against his lips, sending shivers down Kane's entire body. "Let me do you like we used to. Before the kids came, before I got so old... Come on, baby."

"You aren't old, Avery." Kane drew back to look Avery in the eyes. Uncertainty lingered. There was a flash of insecurity in his usually overly-confidant husband's gaze. Kane slammed the office door shut and grabbed Avery's hand, trying to guide him inside the personal restroom he'd had built into his office.

Avery was on him in an instant. Kane didn't get halfway to the restroom before Avery had his jacket off, his slacks shoved down, and a finger probing between his ass cheeks.

"We need lube," Avery said, latching onto his neck again. Kane's back was against his chest, and Avery teased his ass while reaching around to stroke his dick.

"It's in the...bathroom." Before Kane knew it, he found himself shoved forward, bent over a chair, his head hanging between his shoulders. He closed his eyes and a deep moan escaped his lips as Avery's deft fingers massaged him with determination. "To the left... Yeah..."

"Come on." Avery anchored an arm around his waist, dragging Kane the few feet to the bathroom. They were awkward steps until Kane finally bent over, laughing as he pulled his slacks back up his legs to help with movement. The bottle of lube was old, but exactly in the same place they'd left it back when they used to do this every night. Nowadays, Avery was home with the children at night, while Kane took the morning shift of getting them ready for school and back home again. The memories of the past flooded Kane, and he turned in Avery's arms, wrapping himself around his lover's body.

"You're so hot," Avery said, and the emotion was clear on his face. They had to be thinking the same thing.

"I'm not," Kane said, kissing Avery's parted lips.

"You're still the best looking man in the room. Any room," Avery declared. Kane slanted his mouth over Avery's and kissed him with everything he had. Those words stroked his heart and turned him on every single time he heard them. Avery fought for dominance in the kiss, pushing Kane against the sink. Kane worked to remove Avery's clothes as Avery worked the cap off the lube, coated his fingers, and slid them deep inside his ass. The delicious burn and stretch had him abandoning the kiss and tossing his head back as he let out a deep groan.

"Feels so good…" He pressed his hips against the sensation, wanting more. Avery's fingers worked him, dragging across his prostate, making him shudder. He pushed his hips forward, lined up their crotches, and reached down to grab both their cocks. He held them together and started stroking. He was already panting and so was Avery. They could work each other into a frenzy in no time, and with Avery's fingers working his ass like they were, it didn't take long.

"Turn around, baby." Avery's husky voice barely penetrated his hazy thoughts. The things Avery was doing to him felt too damn good. Minutes passed as Avery continued to stretch Kane, massage him. Kane gathered the beads of moisture from their cocks and stroked them harder, faster, rougher. Avery's head dropped to Kane's shoulder. His breath was hot and heavy against his ear as he moaned. Avery jerked his hips in uncoordinated strokes as he shoved himself deeper into Kane's palm.

"I need you hard. You hear me? Hard," Kane commanded, loosening his hold and turning in Avery's arms. Avery never released him, he stayed pressed against his back and gripped Kane's hip. His strong fingers dug deep into his skin as the wet tip of his husband's cock nudged along his crevice. Avery's wide head breached his rim in one mind-blowing thrust, stretching him in an exquisite burn. "Ahh, yes…babe, that's it….love you so much."

"Fuck! You're so hot. Love you, Kane." Avery hissed, drawing back and ramming himself forward. "It's not gonna take long."

"You can draw it out. You feel too good," Kane whispered. He gripped the sink as Avery's thrusts grew in intensity. His hooded gaze met Avery's in the mirror, and they both grinned wickedly back at the other's reflection.

"Our guests... Kane, how are you so fucking tight..." Avery pistoned his hips, driving Kane into the edge of the vanity with each snap of his hips. The moment was perfect, too perfect. Kane reared back, arching his body, and met Avery thrust for thrust.

"You've been...ah...bottoming the last few times," Kane groaned. Avery closed his eyes and gritted his teeth. His husband always did that when he concentrated on holding his load. Kane kept his eyes open, looking at their reflection in the mirror. He loved watching Avery make love to him.

"Keep going." Kane lifted his dress shirt up and over his head. He tossed it across the top of the toilet and began stroking himself. He was close, very close, and Avery never stopped pounding away at his ass. He tightened his grip, desperately wanting to come, but trying hard to keep it at bay.

"Feel good?" Avery's voice was deep, breathy.

"Yeah," was the only thing he could manage at the moment.

"So good. Fuck, Kane, I could do this all night."

"Avery...yes." Kane strained to hold back his orgasm. He rolled his hips then pushed back, grinding against Avery, taking him deep inside. Avery responded just like Kane imagined he would—his lover's eyes opened, and shot straight to their reflection in the mirror, meeting his. Avery's heated gaze pierced Kane to the core.

"Come for me," Kane whispered.

"You're so beautiful. You're mine. You're *always* mine." Avery's eyes stayed locked on his. Avery gripped Kane's hips tightly and bucked harder, nailing his spot over and over. Fire surged through Kane's veins. "Come with me!"

"Now!" Kane loosened his tight grip on the sink to stroke himself faster, dropping his head down on to the counter as his body tensed and his ass contracted hard around Avery. His release jetted from his body, painting the cabinet and floor with ribbons of white, taking his breath, and buckling his knees with pleasure. He was barely conscious of missing the slacks pooled around his shoes. He closed his eyes as loud moans escaped his lips. He savored every second of Avery's pulsing cock filling him with liquid heat from the inside out.

"I can still fuck you like I'm thirty," Avery whispered, his weight resting fully on Kane's back. Kane's body was amped up. His heart hammered in his chest, his lungs and ass burned, but in the best possible way. His release had hit him hard; just what he'd needed. Avery moved to wrap his arms tightly around Kane's waist. The feel of Avery's damp skin across his back made him shudder and his ass contract, causing Avery to groan. Neither moved again for several minutes. His knees were weak, and he was worried they might not hold the combined weight. He wasn't sure how long Avery held him, but their breathing returned to normal and his heart had slowed to a steady beat before Avery slipped free, and Kane felt Avery's essence seeping down his leg.

"Babe, I've gotta get cleaned up," Kane said.

"I wanted to come on your back, but your ass felt too good." Avery nipped the back of his neck.

"Yeah, it felt real good, but you gotta get off me. We need to get back out there," Kane said, pushing himself back, forcing Avery to stand up straight. The look on Avery's face made it clear he would rather have stayed right where he was. Kane reached over for a hand towel, swiping it up his leg before Avery took over the task. He cleaned Kane, like he always did. Several minutes passed as they set themselves as close to right as possible.

"You really are still the most handsome man I've laid eyes on," Avery said. He finished dressing and rested with his hip against the counter, waiting for Kane to finish tying his necktie. Kane stopped working the knot and cut his eyes over to Avery, watching him for a minute.

"That's the third time you've said that in the last hour. What're you hiding?" Kane asked.

"Nothing." Avery chuckled. "You still look young."

"I do not. What are you hiding?" Kane said, finally finishing his Windsor knot, before his eyes were back on Avery's.

"You think you know me so well?" Avery fidgeted with his cuff links.

Avery was definitely hiding something. Kane's heart dropped a little. He'd enjoyed the night, loved their bathroom time. Did Avery have a purpose in all this? Kane matched Avery's stance, crossing his arms over his chest and asked one more time. "Avery. What is it?"

"Baby..." Avery stepped closer to Kane and embraced him. When Kane didn't immediately wrap his arms around his husband, Avery made a show of uncrossing Kane's arms and draping them around his waist. Kane guessed Avery was getting the hint he wasn't backing down and tried for a joke. "At least pretend like you love me."

"Just tell me," Kane said.

"They want me to run again." Avery stopped playing the game and said what he needed to say. Except Kane didn't really understand what those words meant. He paused for a moment, unsure of what he'd heard. After a minute, he had no choice but to ask.

"What do you mean?" Kane furrowed his brow.

"For senate. They approached me earlier today," Avery said.

"What? You didn't tell me?" Kane pushed out of Avery's arms, putting as much distance between them as the small bathroom would allow. Avery followed, moving with him, and he had to put out a hand, stopping Avery from getting any closer.

"I was going to, I just knew you had big plans for tonight, and I didn't want to mess that up. How did you pull this off?" Avery asked, pushing against Kane's extended arm as he stepped forward. He didn't touch Kane, but most definitely invaded his personal space.

"No. There's no changing the subject. What did you tell them?" Kane searched Avery's face. He crossed his arms over his chest again in an effort to hold his pounding heart inside.

"That I needed to talk to you."

"And what else?" Avery grinned at his question and gathered him, crossed arms and all, back in the circle of those strong arms. He ignored the irritation and concern radiating from Kane and kissed him sweetly on the lips. Kane didn't kiss back.

"It's good you know me so well. It's always been that way between us. It's one of the reasons I love you so much. I told them I was interested, it was you that would need convincing."

"We're so public in this community, Avery. They won't be able to hide us," Kane worried out loud. How had he gone from feeling a million miles high, to being buried with doubt? Now the desperation was creeping in, he heard it in his own voice. He hated the feeling of no control, hated feeling like he needed to hide what they'd built. Kane loved his family and didn't want to hide any of part of who they were, but the hate they would face would be a huge obstacle.

"We're a package deal. There's no hiding us. We're a family, a unit, and I would run with us intact," Avery said. This time when Kane pulled free, Avery let him. He had to process this fear racing through him.

"Avery…" Kane began with only the slightest shake of his head. This wasn't good. People outside of their small, secluded world didn't accept them. Autumn and Robert had been taught from the time they were babies to ignore the hateful verbal slaps hurled their way whenever they left Minnesota.

"No, honey, listen! Stop squaring your shoulders and putting up all those walls. Talk to me. The demographics in the area largely support us. The incumbent isn't running. All the polls have been done. They're certain I can win." Avery grew serious, and he refused to let Kane walk away from him.

"Even with us?" Kane questioned, doubt edging his words.

"Yes! That's what I just said," Avery assured him. Kane was quiet, watching Avery closely. "We don't have to decide right now. I want you to come in and listen to what they have to say. If you don't want us to, then I won't. End of story." Avery gave a small shrug, blowing the whole thing off.

"But you would run if it was just up to you?" Kane shot back.

"I would've already run, but I chose something far better, I chose you. Of course you know all that. Baby, you know how I feel about this." For Avery, the conversation appeared to be over and there was no need to say anything more on the subject. He picked up his suit coat and slid it onto his shoulders, straightening his dress shirt. For Kane, this was so far from over, they had only just begun.

"What about the restaurant expansion?" Kane asked, refusing to take his jacket from Avery's outstretched hand.

"Nothing changes for us. Come on. I shouldn't have brought it up tonight," Avery said, wiggling the jacket until Kane gave in and took it.

"No, you shouldn't keep secrets from me. It's just you haven't ever said another word about running for office. I didn't know you were still interested." Kane tried to read Avery's face as he slid his arms in his jacket.

"It's in my blood, you know that. I just never thought it would be an option after I came out. Now it seems to be an option. Fix your collar." Avery smiled, stepping up to straighten Kane's collar himself. Avery also adjusted his tie and dusted off his tux jacket sleeve before they locked eyes. "You are gorgeous."

"Stop saying that. We can talk to them. Set up a meeting. And we need to talk to the kids' school counselor. I want the children safe. If it's too much for them, I don't want to do it. Our responsibility is to them. We have to shield them as best as we can." Kane looked Avery over before he opened the office door.

"You and the children are always first." Avery walked past the open door, briefly stopping to kiss Kane lightly on the lips. "Thank you."

"Avery, you don't have to thank me. What you want is what I want. You just caught me off guard, that's all," Kane said, following along behind him. Avery reached back and wrapped an arm around Kane.

"That's enough serious talk for tonight. Someone's going to notice we're gone and you'll get flustered. I'll think it's sweet that after all this time you still get embarrassed over sneaking away, and then I'll have to work you back in here to have my way with you again, thereby proving I am still a young man in this old man's body!"

"Come on, birthday boy. You're clearly in a mood tonight." Kane chuckled, hoping to hide the apprehension about Avery's political future still lurking in his thoughts.

Chapter 21

Avery sat, kicked back in his home office desk recliner, his gaze focused on a birdfeeder Kane had placed in a tree right outside his window. He had to admit, he'd spent hours in this chair, staring out at the birds, contemplating whatever case he currently worked. He'd found solace here in this spot. Today, there wasn't a bird to be seen. Something about the dead of winter and inches of newly fallen snow had a way of keeping the birds at bay.

His office door, which was also his bedroom door, stood open—as it generally did. He listened to the activity going on in his house. He craved the noise, loving the sounds of his family. If he took a guess now, he would say Robert was teasing Autumn about something in just the manner she was growing to greatly dislike. Her voice was rising, and Robert laughed. An argument was certain to break out soon. As expected, Kane's voice intervened, trying to stop the impending brawl before it took root.

The almost silent beep of his direct telephone line caught his attention. He'd been waiting for this call. She was late, but traveling the world had a way of messing with your time. He picked up the phone as he started to rise from his chair.

"Mother, hang on a moment." Avery crossed the bedroom and shoved the door closed. "I'm back."

"Hello, my darling son. Before you tell me to hang on again, please remember this is costing us a fortune," Kennedy scolded, amusement in her voice.

"What's costing us a fortune? Your trip to Greece?" Avery teased.

"No, this phone call. I'm assuming the children and Kane are fine. If there was an emergency, I'm certain the call wouldn't have been scheduled. How are you, my son?" Kennedy's voice turned warm and loving. She usually reserved that tone of voice for Kane and the children, only on occasion was he on the receiving end.

"I've been approached," Avery said, not beating around the bush.

"I wondered when they would pull their heads out of their self-righteous asses and do the right thing," Kennedy said.

"You saw this coming? I didn't. I truly believed I'd lost my chance," Avery's eyes gravitated back to the brightly-colored bird feeder.

"You regularly underestimate yourself," she said.

"So you think I should go for it? I'm nervous for Kane and the kids." Avery lowered his voice several octaves. He didn't want Kane to hear his concern. He never let Kane know he worried about their situation.

"Son, you hold the power to make it a non-issue. You run on your own merit. Your personal life is never to be discussed. It's truly as simple as that," Kennedy said, with her usual air of confidence.

"Is it worth upsetting the balance of my life?" Avery asked.

"Only you can decide that, but I've seen the change in you. Kane's helped settle you. You're a force and I believe in you and I will support you with whatever path you choose. If you decide your answer is yes, you should speak to Sophia. Even with you not discussing your life, she will be approached," Kennedy said.

"Thomas is going to talk to her this weekend. We'll all get on the same page before any announcement's made," Avery assured her.

"Then let me know what you decide."

"Of course I will. Mother, at the time, I think I took this for granted, but you were always so accepting of me. After knowing Kane and being a father myself, I can only imagine the concern you had for my life," Avery said, his voice going even lower.

"I've always believed in you. Since I first held you in my arms, I knew you were destined to do great things. You make me proud, Avery. I love you, Son," Kennedy stated.

"Thanks, Mom," Avery began and stopped mid-sentence when he realized he was talking to dead air. She'd disconnected the call which was something his mom would totally do. She had said what she needed to, so the call was done. As he laid the phone back in the cradle, he heard the doorbell ring downstairs.

* * * *

Kane knew right from the beginning that he had very little chance of resisting when their home was overrun by the team known as the Democratic Party. They brought out the masses, even the big names, all there to talk Kane into letting Avery run in this year's senate race. Standing flow charts littered the living room. Men and women, all dressed in severely tailored business suits, stood ready to jump in and throw numbers at Kane whenever a point needed validation. They'd clearly left nothing to chance and were quite skilled in the power of persuasion.

Kane's only defense didn't seem to matter. He was a staunch Republican with no plans to change. But they beat him down in that area too. Kane slipped up when he said he'd vote for Avery no matter what platform he ran on. That sealed the deal. They wanted Avery, wanted him badly, and were prepared to do whatever it took to get Kane to agree.

They were back to the future, back to where they began. The whole reason Avery had even moved to Minnesota in the first place. Avery had inadvertently done everything required to get him in the running, and Kane wondered if perhaps those steps might have been done in meticulous order. La Bella Luna was still the place to be seen. Avery was a regular there, so regular he had built a significant social foundation. When you looked for Avery Adams, it was a sure bet you'd find him in the restaurant. Avery had also designed his law firm to specialize in two major areas: helping the indigent and going after big business that took advantage of the ever-increasing labor laws. Union leaders throughout the district were already hinting they would back Avery in a possible run, as Avery had backed them time and time again.

Avery scoffed at Kane's concern over the legality of their marriage. When he wouldn't let it go, Avery grew intense, determined, and refused to hear another word, saying they were bound together by God. The campaign team lining the living room ate that up, loving Avery's stance.

As uncertain as Kane stayed, Avery's resolve grew stronger. After three hours of meetings, Kane was no closer to wanting the run, but Avery's enthusiasm kept him quiet, until he finally relented. Dread filled his heart, but he hid it. Avery had stood by him through all his quirky attitudes; he'd do the same for Avery and pray things would work out for the best.

As the day wore on, Autumn and Robert became the only concern Kane wouldn't give on. Personal decisions between Avery and Kane would have to be made as to how involved the family unit would be in this run. For Kane, he wanted to plan the best ways to protect them from the backlash. The children had been taught from the beginning that families came in all different shapes and sizes. They'd been questioned about their fathers since they were old enough to communicate, but they were sheltered. They had never been exposed to the brutality and hate aimed at the homosexual community. Kane and Avery were also very hands-on parents. Avery would be on the road, Kane would be left to hold down the fort until he returned. How could he keep the restaurant going and the children in their normal routine?

After several long meetings and watching Avery's energy and excitement grow, Kane slowly relented, deciding to leave the decision to their children. If they thought they could handle the possible backlash, then Kane would agree to give the run a try. The campaign team departed within six hours of their arrival, and Avery didn't miss a minute before he called the kids downstairs.

"Family meeting!" Avery called from the bottom of the stairs up toward Autumn's and Robert's bedrooms. Autumn was first out her door. At almost ten years old, she was the image of Avery—tall, slender, naturally graceful with beautiful long blonde hair flowing as she bounded down the stairs. Robert easily overtook her as he ran full throttle. This year, he'd hit a growth spurt, reaching five foot three, and could easily navigate the stairs two at a time.

"Beat you," Robert said as Autumn stepped off the last step. His voiced echoed as he said the words and pushed the forever aggravating piece of thick blond hair off his forehead just as he spotted Kane already in the living room. "What's going on?"

"Nothing, we just wanted to talk to you two." Kane tried to appear relaxed. His children were smart, well-adjusted, and incredibly perceptive. They would pick up any discord he might be feeling.

Kane watched both their expressions change as they took in the scene around them. He quickly looked up at Avery, but he was already off to the bar, pouring himself a drink. He rarely drank in front to the children, but with his back turned, he hadn't noticed the change in them. Kane patted the sofa next to him. The natural choice would have Robert sitting by him and Autumn by Avery, but tonight they both came to sit by him. So he clearly looked worried enough to spark their concern.

"Why are you both home? Daddy, you said Granddaddy Paulie needed your help to run the restaurant," Autumn started, but Kane quickly interrupted her.

"There's no need to look so concerned. This is not the end of the world. Get those looks off your faces." Avery came and sat directly across from them on the coffee table.

"Babe, you ask them," Avery said, watching them intently with elbows on his knees, the glass resting between the palms of his hands.

"Your dad's been approached by the Democratic Party to run for the United States Senate. We haven't made a decision yet, we wanted to talk to you two first and see how you feel about it," Kane said, sliding an arm around each child.

"But you're a Republican, Daddy. Are you going to vote for Dad?" Autumn asked Kane. That made him smile, and he looked over at Avery who actually laughed. It had been years and years of heated arguments about their difference in political views that caused the worry from his daughter.

"If we agree to do this, I'll vote for your dad," Kane promised reassuringly.

"So you're gonna change your vote?" Robert asked, clearly not believing it for even a minute.

"I will for him, honey, but that's not the issue. This is gonna affect each of us, and we all need to be a part of the decision whether he moves forward with this or not." Kane pulled in both arms he had around their shoulders, drawing them in for a hug. He was so proud.

"But you never vote Democrat." Autumn's upturned face looked so confused. She participated in the hug, but she hesitated, her eyes were squarely focused on his, waiting for his answer.

"Autumn, this decision isn't about who I vote for, honey. It's about whether your dad runs. If he makes it, we'll have to move to Washington with him," Kane explained and that changed everything.

"We have to move?" Robert exclaimed, sitting up, somewhat alarmed.

"That's jumping way far ahead, but yes, if I win, we'll spend time in Washington DC. It would mean you guys would have to attend school there. There's a great private—" Avery began, but Robert cut him off.

"So we have to change schools?" These weren't the issues Kane thought they would talk about right now.

"Yes, but there are great schools in Washington DC. My old alma mater is there—"

"Daddy, I don't know if it's a good idea to switch schools in the middle of the year. I wanted to try out for cheerleader next year," Autumn announced, and Kane quickly stopped them, tried to focus them in on the more important issue.

"Wait, you two. Listen to me. This is a much bigger step for all of us. It's not just moving and how to vote, we have bigger things to think about. You know we're a different family. If we enter into this, we could be targeted pretty badly. Worse than anything you've seen before. This could potentially be hard on all of us," Kane said, looking between Autumn and Robert. Avery's concern showed, too, as he reached out and placed his hands over the children's legs. As protective as Kane was, Avery was tenfold.

"We don't care about that. Right, Autumn?" Robert said, cocking his head forward to peer around Kane so he could look at his sister.

"It'll be different than anything you've experienced before," Avery said.

"It's okay, Dad. We're different, but not wrong, no matter what anyone says. Right, Daddy?" Autumn asked.

Robert didn't wait for Kane to answer before he continued, "So, if you win, when would we have to change schools? I want to play school basketball next year." Kane glanced between the two and then looked up at Avery who had a sly smile on his face. It sure seemed he'd be running for office. Neither Autumn nor Robert cared one lick about anything other than their school activities. They seemed a little self-absorbed to Kane, but he also reconciled that to mean they must be raising normal, well-balanced kids and that filled his heart with pride.

"We'll time it where everyone is where they need to be for tryouts. You can play ball, Son. And Autumn, if want to cheer, that's fine too. None of that changes. If I make it, and that's a big if, then we'll move you during off season," Avery clarified to the relief of both children. Robert nodded, but now that things seemed normal again, Autumn got up and wormed her way into the small place beside Avery, sliding under his arm, so she could sit next to him. He wrapped his arm around her as her big blue eyes focused on Kane.

"I thought you never would change your vote. Nonnie says you're wrong, but you won't ever give. You have to give this time, Daddy. We support each other all the time, remember?" Autumn was most likely to follow in Avery's footsteps. It was just very undecided where her political beliefs were headed. She was all over the place, picking and choosing so her views were based on the issue, not the side. Avery just hugged her tightly as they both stared at Kane. Avery grinned bigger and nodded at him.

"You will have to vote for me. And no opposing candidates' signs in the yard this year," Avery said.

"No, Daddy! You can't put up signs for another candidate, that would be wrong," Autumn exclaimed.

"He already said he'd vote for Dad," Robert jumped in on Kane's defense. This was something new. While they'd not had sibling fights much before, that had changed as they entered this school year. The fights were coming faster and they were becoming more argumentative with each passing day.

"So we're moving forward. I can let them know we're running for office?" Avery asked before Kane could. He was an expert at diverting their attention where Kane stumbled a bit sometimes. Funny how that worked. He'd come from a large family, Avery an only child. It should have been the other way around.

"You'll have to be gone a lot, I bet. I'm gonna miss you," Autumn said, laying her head on Avery's shoulder.

"You guys can come with me as much as possible, and when I'm not home, I'll call." Autumn nodded. Robert came to sit by them, sliding under his other arm.

"What about La Bella Luna?" Robert asked.

"The expansion's changing everyone's role. Kane can do more on the road now," Avery said.

"And Daddy has his portable computer," Autumn said, as if that solved everything.

"Paulie, Rodney, and I will work everything out. It'll be okay," Kane reassured Robert.

"Granddaddy Paulie won't move with us?" Autumn asked, a little alarmed.

"He hasn't decided yet, but I'm working on him, I promise. So what's the vote?" Avery asked.

"I vote go for it, as long as I get to play basketball," Robert said.

"I'm fine with it. I think it's up to you. You have to do all the work," Autumn agreed.

"We'll all have to help him," Kane said, and Autumn's eyes lit up.

"Do we get to help in the campaign? I love when Nonnie tells us about working on Great-Granddaddy's campaign." She was all smiles and eyes on Avery. She so knew exactly how to work him. She couldn't have said anything better.

"Absolutely! You can do it all," Avery said, kissing her forehead.

"Yay!" Autumn jumped up and bounded up the stairs. "I have to call April and tell her!"

"Hang on! You can't tell anyone yet. Not until I announce it," Avery called out after her.

"Okay," Autumn yelled back, but she was already in her room, the door shutting loudly behind her.

"So that's it, then. You freaked me out a little, you looked so serious. I thought someone died," Robert said. He rose, stretching out his back as he followed his sister upstairs. "I'll make sure she doesn't tell. I'll listen on the phone."

"No listening to her on the other phone, Robert. She needs her privacy," Kane called out as his son walked up the steps.

"I just pretend to listen. It makes her crazy," Robert said from the top of the stairs.

"And you wonder why you two fight," Kane said. All Robert did was laugh as his door slammed shut behind him.

"Well, I guess that's it then. I'm running," Avery said, moving from the coffee table to the sofa, wrapping an arm around Kane's back.

"I guess you are," Kane nodded. He let Avery draw him into a small snuggle.

"So, are you changing your vote for me?" Avery teased, sliding his hand under Kane's sweater, letting his fingertips graze the bare skin of his stomach.

"I don't know. You'll have to work for it. Convince me." Kane leaned in to capture Avery's lips with his. There was only a small swipe of tongue before he pulled away, conscious of the kids being home.

"Oh, I'll work for it. Come upstairs and we'll start now," Avery suggested, waggling his eyebrows.

"Tonight," Kane said. He moved away from the hold, and it cost him to do so, but he pulled Avery up with him. "I think it's a pizza kind of night, and we need to call your mom and Paulie. They'll play a huge part in this. We need to tell them the big news."

"Kane…" There was a distinct whine to Avery's voice. "Babe, I like my idea so much better…"

Chapter 22

Late January 1990

Before Avery had even announced his intention to run, the campaign committee evaluated every part of their lives. Individually and as a family, they were tutored, trained, and reset for the public eye. All new clothes were bought, which Autumn loved more than Kane or Avery had thought possible. Preset answers were drilled into all of their heads, ready to pull out of their back pockets at any given moment.

As much as Avery argued, Kane pulled the plug on the restaurant expansion. He and Paulie held a private meeting a couple of days after Avery decided to run, and they agreed Kane's focus and attention needed to be on the children and Avery. In Paulie's infinite wisdom, he pushed Kane to be home more, while moving Rodney, their bartender, more fully into the role of manager. He'd been Kane's right-hand man and backup for years. The decision was absolutely the right one to make, but Kane's heart hadn't quite separated from the restaurant.

It hurt to see their plans squelched, and it was a hard lump to swallow thinking about stepping away from the restaurant. He hid all the inner turmoil of the decision from Avery. As much as it bothered Kane, Paulie had an easier time with the decision. For Kane, he knew how much Paulie loved him, but Paulie took that love to a whole new level where the twins were concerned.

Paulie had even gone so far as asking Kennedy Adams to make Minnesota her full-time home. She'd traveled between Minnesota and her New York flat for years now. Paulie called her and talked her into moving back, so the two of them could tag team each other to be a better help to Kane in Avery's possible absence. All those discussions happened behind Kane's back because Paulie left nothing to chance where his family was concerned.

Avery's political campaign ran like a well-oiled machine; all they needed was their candidate, and as predicted, Avery Adams took to politics like a duck to water. Being gay seemed to play very little part in the voters' decisions in November, because Avery refused to allow any questions about his personal life. For Avery, his family wasn't open for speculation and that stance seemed to work.

Avery won his senate race in an easy landslide, and set off to Washington DC, grudgingly leaving his family behind to finish out the school year. It wasn't until then that the national news began to take notice.

"Daddy, Peter Jennings is talking about you again!" Autumn yelled from her perch in front of the living room television set. She'd given herself the job of media specialist, a position she'd created, which meant she tracked every bit of press on Avery and their family that she could get her hands on. In her sweet eleven-year-old way, she scrapbooked all the information for Avery, putting colorful hearts and kisses on each page. For the information not in print, she took notes and wrote them up every night in her journal, adding them to the scrapbook in chronological order.

"What's he saying this time?" Kane asked absently, somewhat distracted in the kitchen. He never stopped his flow of making dinner as he flipped the faucet on, letting the pasta cool in the colander.

"That you and Dad aren't really married," she yelled back. Kane heard what she said and gave a sigh. He didn't answer back right away. Their marriage was always the fallback story when news was slow around the world and nothing else was going on.

Since Avery had been in Washington, the national news covered the homosexual issue, and then children being raised by same-sex parents, now they were back to the beginning—the legality of their union. Avery would always laugh it all off, saying their family was so intriguing they drew in high ratings anytime they even got a haircut.

Autumn and Robert loved thinking they were so special, but for Kane, it was already getting old.

"Honey, do you think you should be watching all this?" Kennedy asked from the doorway between the kitchen and living room.

"It's okay, Nonnie. I know they're married by God, and he's more important than anything," Autumn said. Kane had moved in behind Kennedy to check on Autumn, but she was bent over, taking notes, completely oblivious to them standing there watching her. Kennedy wasn't letting it go. She'd disagreed with Avery for allowing Autumn to be this up close and personal with the media coverage, and her irritated, steely gaze cut to Kane, making it clear she wasn't happy at all.

"I agree, it's getting a little worse, but nothing too terrible," Kane replied, trying to keep the worry from his eyes.

"This is no surprise. We knew it would, Kane," Kennedy said, looking back at Autumn, still bent over, writing as the newscast continued.

"It was just so easy here in Minnesota. I'd hoped that would last," Kane said, leaving the doorway to turn the water off. "I'll talk to Avery when he calls. She just takes it all so serious. Maybe it'll come to an end soon."

"Kane, you know it's not going to. The whole bottom half of this great country thinks your marriage is an abomination. I'm not sure she needs to keep such a close eye on this." Avery's mom came to stand directly in front of Kane. She was holding firm, and Kane agreed with her. But with Avery already gone to Washington, and Kane, Autumn, and Robert still in Minnesota finishing the school year, it just gave Autumn something to keep herself connected to her Dad. Avery called her every day and let her tell him about what she found. He just wasn't prepared to put a stop to all that.

"Dinner's ready," Kane called out. Kennedy was such a force when she got something stuck in her head. He would deal with her later.

"Daddy! Your dad's having a live interview," Autumn yelled. "And your brothers and sisters are there too." Her pitch became higher as she clicked the volume up several notches.

Kane dropped the colander back in the sink and rounded the kitchen island to the door in a matter of seconds. The sound of his father's voice caused his heart to stutter. It was something he hadn't heard in thirty years. The man's voice was older, but still bellowed in his deeply Southern accent. Kane slowed as pain lanced his heart. He'd thought he was past this. He'd reconciled these feelings with these people who he had spent more time without than with. He hesitated at the kitchen door as his father came into view.

"He doesn't look like you at all," Autumn called out, but Kane ignored her. His eyes remained riveted to the television screen. In Kane's mind, his father hadn't changed. He was still the same man who had kicked him out of his house all those years ago.

In the most recent letter he had received from his family, they had written and asked for money, saying their father was in poor health, but the man on the screen was anything but sickly. He looked robustly healthy as he spewed his opinions at the reporter who seemed to cower under the older man's vengeance-filled words.

"Those children are an atrocity! That boy is No. Son. Of. Mine. Corinthians 6:9-11, do not be deceived. Neither the sexually immoral, nor idolaters, nor adulterers, nor men who practice homosexuality, nor thieves, nor the greedy, nor drunkards, nor revilers, nor swindlers will inherit the kingdom of God! The devil owns Kane Adams's soul and the State of Minnesota should be wiped off the planet for allowing those children to live in that den of debauchery."

Kane sat down on the edge of the sofa completely stunned. His heart pounded in his chest. He barely registered Kennedy removing Autumn from the living room. What had he truly expected from his family? How had he not better prepared for this day?

Did he honestly believe they had all worked out an agreeable solution, that he could give them money to help overcome his sins? Yes, he did believe that, and he had to sit down because his heart thundered in his chest and his knees grew weak. He could feel the heat climbing in his cheeks as horror and embarrassment took its grip on his body.

Kane stared at the television as the screen went dark a moment before Peter Jennings image took shape, and the reporter looked momentarily astounded. "Ladies and Gentleman, those are the views of Pastor Dalton, not of this station..." The news cut immediately to commercial. Kane sat there, staring at the screen. After a second more, he let out his pent-up breath, evaluated the pain in his heart as not a possible heart attack, and ran his shaking hands over his face. The home phone started ringing.

"Honey, it's Paulie. Paulie, hold on, call waiting's beeping in. Hello, yes, honey, he's here." Kennedy was apparently back in the living room and had answered the phone. Both children had been ushered upstairs but were sitting on the top step looking down at him with sad, concerned eyes. Kennedy always sent them to their room when things got rough, but they weren't those kind of kids. The four of them were a unit, a little team.

Kane waved them back down to him as he reached for the remote control, turning the television off. Autumn and Robert raced down the steps; Autumn almost knocked him over as she tackled him in a hug.

"I'm so sorry, Daddy. I wouldn't have told you if I knew he would say those things," she whispered in his ear as she kept a death-grip hug wrapped around his neck. Robert stood less than a foot away, until he bent in, too, wrapping himself around Kane and Autumn. Tears were in his eyes.

"Guys, it's okay. I know how they feel," Kane said, holding them both tightly in his arms.

"It's wrong. You're a good man, Daddy," Robert said, holding him tighter.

"Kane, here talk to Avery. He's worried. Paulie's on his way over," Kennedy said from behind him. He managed to take the phone, situate the kids beside him, and remove most of Autumn's long blonde hair from his face as he lifted the cordless to his ear. He didn't speak as he listened to Avery barking out orders on the other end.

"I hear you breathing," Avery finally said.

"Autumn heard it all," Kane replied.

"That's okay, baby. They have us to help process it all," Avery said.

"My grandfather thinks I'm an atrocity," Autumn yelled close to the phone for Avery to hear her.

"Tell her that's not her grandfather. He's a thief and bigot and you're better off without him." The venom was back in Avery's voice. Kane couldn't speak the words. He couldn't say anything. He just hugged the children closer and let Kennedy pat his shoulder. There had been enough said in front of the children tonight.

"You guys stay here, I need to talk to your dad alone. No more TV tonight," Kane said. After a moment more, he left them sitting there and made his way to the far reaches of the kitchen.

"Kane, please talk to me," Avery finally said.

"I'm sorry," he mumbled and dropped his head inside his hand as he took a seat at the kitchen table.

"Sorry for what?" Avery asked, his tone clear that Kane had nothing to be sorry for.

"That was national news. Everyone all over the country heard my father's hatred toward us. I can't believe he brought the kids into this," Kane said.

"Honey, I don't care about that. I'm worried about you. He didn't look like he was too much on his deathbed. That was an awful nice house they were standing in front of," Avery said, his tone turning harder.

"I send them money every month," Kane confessed.

"I know, and he sure cashes those checks. He didn't mention that, did he?" Avery asked.

"They've been lying to me this whole time," Kane whispered. How, after all this time, was his heart still completely broken over anything that concerned them?

"Baby, I'm coming home," Avery said.

"No, Avery, stay there. I'll be all right." That kicked Kane into gear. Avery had just settled in. They'd found a house on one of Kane's weekend trips to Washington, and Avery had the house furnished.

As a freshman senator, Avery had hit the ground running, taking Washington by storm and already making a name for himself. He needed to stay and continue the foundation he was building, not drop everything and run home to him because of his callous family.

"I hate I wasn't there for you tonight. I'll catch a flight out as soon as I can." Avery sounded distracted, but determined to move forward with his plan.

"Avery, no. Listen to me. I'm all right. Don't rush home, it's a waste of your time. Besides, I need to go check on Robert and Autumn," Kane said, already rising. On a last thought, he blurted out an unfiltered, "Honey, are you sure we should move them from here?"

"I can give this up, and I will if you think it's best, but what does that teach Autumn and Robert when our first real hint of adversity has us packing it in? We're doing something, Kane. Something bigger than politics. We're functioning happy people, living normal lives, working for the greater good of our country. We need to be together. We belong together. It doesn't work if we're apart, honey." Avery had repeated the same speech about fifteen times since he'd won the office.

"Avery," Kane started. He got the 'greater good' concept, and he even believed in it, but not at the price of Robert and Autumn's well-balanced life.

"Dammit, Kane! You know I love you more than anything. I hate to see you hurt. I hate they still have the power to hurt you, but that doesn't change who we are or what we're doing," Avery said, clearly frustrated. "If you were here, we could have dealt with this together. But now I'm a million miles from you. I should come home."

"Daddy," Autumn said. Kane lifted his eyes to see both Robert and Autumn standing in front of him. His children were growing so big. Autumn wrapped an arm around him, Robert followed her lead and Kane smiled at each of them.

"Is that the kids?" Avery asked.

"They just came in the kitchen. They're worried about me," Kane said. Talking to Avery, having Autumn and Robert with him, he was starting to feel better.

"Is my mom in there, too?" Avery asked.

"Yes, she's hovering close by," Kane said, looking up to see Kennedy taking the seat across from where he stood at the table.

"Good. Let them give you love until I can get home. We'll finish this conversation then," Avery said.

"No, stay there. I'll be fine. I promise," Kane said, his voice strong now.

"Then let's get you guys moved here, now. We shouldn't be apart when these things hit," Avery said.

"We need to stick to the plan. We'll be there when school's out," Kane said firmly.

"Dad's coming home for my first game, remember?" Robert added excitedly, referring to Avery's promise to attend his son's home game three weeks from then.

"Avery, they're waiting for you downstairs," Kane heard Janice saying in the background.

"Babe, I need to go. Tell Robert I'll be there. Are you sure you don't want me home tonight? Everything I have can be rearranged," Avery asked.

"I'm certain, Avery! Go to work. Thank you for calling. You made things better." Kane looked up at his anxious children. He needed to pull his thoughts together, focus on them, and move them all past this moment. This was just another extension of the day his father kicked him out of the house. Just like then, he had to pull himself up and focus on the future. All his dad had were words and those should have stopped hurting a long time ago.

"I love you, Kane. I wouldn't be here without you," Avery said, his voice husky with emotion.

"I love you too," Kane whispered quietly.

"I love you, Dad," Autumn called out, breaking their moment.

"Me too," Robert yelled. Kane took the moment, handing Autumn the phone.

"I'll take care of Daddy, I promise. I love you," Autumn said, and handed the phone to Robert as she wrapped an arm around Kane again.

Kane could hear Avery on the phone. Every word helped heal his heart like nothing else ever before. He could hear Avery's words to Robert. "Son, call me if anything happens, okay? And keep an eye on your sister and father for me. I love you."

"Yes, sir. I love you, too," Robert said a little sedately. Robert's eyes were trained on his as he handed Kane the phone. Kane hid the small smile forming, easing his heart even more. Robert was their serious one, and he could see that his son just gave his oath. Nothing would stand in his way. His children were absolutely precious.

"Honey, I'm going to arrange to have security on the kids as a precaution. I want someone on you too, but I know you won't let me," Avery stated. "I'll have them start right away."

"Avery, I already know you have people on us. They don't have to hide anymore," Kane said.

"Dad, we know. They aren't very good at hiding. They wait right out front of the restaurant every day," Autumn called out. "Granddaddy Paulie thought they were reporters and yelled at them real good."

There was silence for several moments before Avery responded. "I knew you were against bodyguards, Kane. I wasn't keeping secrets. You're just too important to me to take chances with, and this world's too hard a place. Besides, it'll just be easier if they don't have to hide."

"Stay safe. I love you," Kane responded, and he could hear Avery's sigh of relief on the other end.

"Kane-baby, I'll *always* love you. Thank you," Avery said, and the husky tone was back.

"It's all right. We know we're good, that's all that matters," Kane said. Avery made a kissing noise on the other end of the phone—it was his standard goodbye to Kane—and Kane ended the call.

"What's for dinner? I'm starving!" Robert asked, clearly over everything. Kane laughed as audible sounds were heard coming from his growing boy's stomach.

* * * *

Avery sat, fuming in his office. He fought hard to keep the intense hatred he felt toward the Dalton family from blistering through his veins and manifesting in some outward display of contemptible retribution, but his resolve was only so strong.

Janice came through his office door, her mouth opened to speak as their gazes met. Her eyebrows shot up, she closed her mouth, and backed quickly out of the room, the door closing with a tenuous click in her hasty departure.

A heartbeat later, his will broke and the contents of his desk went violently flying across his office. Anger rolled off him in repugnant waves as he gripped the sides of the brand new mahogany desk and dug his fingers into thick wood. Nothing pissed him off more than having Kane fucked with, and he was damn tired of that detestable family getting the best of his husband.

Reason! He needed reason. A reason to take their vile fucking asses down! *No!* He couldn't lower himself to their level...or could he? *Fuck!* He needed sound reasoning ability to filter through this intolerable and nauseating disdain robbing him of his capacity to think rationally.

The constant sound of the annoying dial tone in an otherwise silent room brought Avery's focus back to his surroundings. He glanced around the office, his papers and files lay jumbled in scattered heaps, along with the loudly buzzing phone on the floor. Avery reached for the cord and pulled the receiver back to his now empty desk. He shouldn't let that family get to him, but damn, Kane was too good a person to be treated like that. He methodically placed the phone in its cradle, hanging it up, only to have it immediately begin to ring.

"Avery, it's Sophia. Thomas is right here with me. We've been trying to reach Kane, but the phone's busy. Have you talked to him? Are they okay? Thomas was just about to head over there," she said, her voice just as frantic as everyone else he'd spoken with since the newscast aired. Avery scrubbed a hand down his face and took his seat, trying to gather his composure.

"Yes, they're fine. A little shaken up, but they're all together. My mom's there too. Autumn saw the whole thing," Avery said. Thinking about Autumn watching that awful man spew his hate and bigotry had his gut twisting again.

"I can go there, Avery," Sophia suggested.

"No, stay home. I'm sure Paulie's on his way. Can I talk to Thomas?" he asked. A second passed before Thomas was there.

"I can stop him if you'd let me," Thomas stated emphatically. He sounded just as pissed off as Avery felt.

"No, handling this through the courts would cause too much press. I've got something I'm thinking, I just need time to pull it together. Listen, I'm increasing security on you, Sophia, and your girls. I'll also call you in the morning. I want full, current background reports on every member of that family. Use anything available to find out everything on them. I want it all. And if you and Sophia could help keep Kane and the kids occupied, that might help, too. He's adamant I'm not to come home," Avery said.

"No problem, Avery. For what it's worth, I'm really sorry. You guys didn't deserve that," Thomas said, and he could hear Sophia agreeing in the background.

"Kane's been too good to them. He certainly didn't deserve it. I'll call you in the morning." Avery disconnected the call and dialed his security company. They needed to double their watch. He wanted his family protected until he could figure this out.

* * * *

"That man hasn't shown his face for thirty years. You've supported that entire family for years, and he disgraces you like that? But your money's good enough to take?" Paulie came through the back door without knocking, straight into the kitchen where they were having dinner. "It's not right! Did anyone tell that reporter that your dad put you out of the house at eighteen years old with nothing more than the clothes you were wearing? What kind of father does that to his son?"

"Paulie, it's all right. We're past it. Grab a plate, sit down, and eat." Kane tapped his fork on the table in front of the empty chair Paulie usually sat in.

"Your father did that?" Robert asked. Kane had never shared that story with his children. They were too young, and the story he felt was far too harsh. He only wanted them to know that parents stood by their children, not tore them down.

"Kane Adams! You've sent him thousands of dollars, and that man sure didn't look like he was hurtin' like all those letters said he was." Paulie was on a roll, not even taking his seat at the table, letting everything out to Avery's mom and the kids.

"We send him money?" Autumn asked. Her face visibly changed. She put her fork down and stared at Kane.

"Honey, keep eating. It's the right thing to do to send money to your family when they are down on their luck," Kane said, now tapping the side of her plate.

"I don't think it's right, not if he talks about you like that," Robert said.

"The boy knows what he's talking about," Paulie piped in, still on his roll.

"I don't want us to send him any more money," Autumn said. "He's a bad man, Daddy!"

"I don't want us to either," Robert agreed.

"Me either!" Paulie sat down in a thump in Avery's empty chair right next to Kennedy.

"For the record, and since we seem to do everything on a family vote, I'd prefer we don't send them any more money either," Kennedy added, dabbing her mouth with a napkin. Kane just stared at Paulie. The rant had been substantial, but already fading. Paulie looked older in that minute than he'd ever looked before, and Kane reached out a hand, clasping his. Haggard, worn eyes met his. This had been an argument they'd had many times over the years. Tonight, Paulie won.

"I'm sorry, I should've considered they didn't know," Paulie said and clasped Kane's hand tighter. "It's just wrong, Son. Tonight they crossed too many lines."

"We don't turn our back on those in need. We walk in love, and live the life of a good Christian regardless of what anyone else does. That doesn't change, but I agree. They didn't seem in need to me either." Kane wiped his mouth and began picking up plates to take to the sink. They all spoke the truth, and Paulie hadn't said anything more than Avery had, but this wasn't a conversation to have in front of Robert and Autumn.

"Did you see the report?" Autumn asked.

"Yes, honey, I did. That man needs to rot in hell. Your Daddy hadn't eaten in days—" Kane held up his hand and cut Paulie off.

"Did you know Daddy's father before?" Robert asked. Kane flipped on the water, running the dishes under the faucet, realizing this conversation was taking place whether he wanted it to or not. Honestly, he was in too bad an emotional place to judge whether this discussion was a good or bad idea for his kids.

"No, Son, I met your dad a few days after he was put out of the house. It was one of the best days of my life," Paulie said, adding a little force to the word by slapping the table with his hand. Paulie looked up at Kane, when he glanced over his shoulder to the table again. Loving eyes met his and warmed his heart. If he were honest, it was Paulie who taught him what love meant—gave him the tools to become a caring, supportive father—not the family who had raised him.

"How could anyone put Daddy out of the house? He's a good man," Autumn exclaimed, and now they were all looking at Kane. Thankfully Avery's mom was pensively quiet, one less person to dissuade from the conversation.

"That's enough. No more talk of the past. That time's done and over and we can't change anything. Autumn, did you finish your science project? Robert, you have a math quiz on Friday. You won't have time to study tomorrow night. You have a scrimmage," Kane stated firmly, finally feeling on even ground, and trying to switch gears, get them back to normal.

"Okay, I'll be quiet, but I still think it's wrong," Robert mumbled, digging back into his second plate of spaghetti. He was the only one left eating at the table and back to shoveling the food.

"I think Dad will handle it," Autumn whispered to Paulie, who gave her smile and patted her head.

"Someone needs to handle this," Kennedy said as she cleared the plates from the table.

Chapter 23

Lost in thought, Avery added up the air miles he'd traveled as he sat on his mother's private jet. He didn't usually pull strings, opting instead to fly commercial most of the time, but not today. Today, he was taking the long way home from DC, by way of Alabama. His briefcase sat close by. He'd traveled light—only one file filled the case.

He had gathered a lot of information on Kane's family for years, and he'd never told anyone, never brought it up. The data he'd pulled over the last few weeks since that horrific news report featuring Kane's father told him far more than he'd expected. His steely gaze narrowed. He knew all their names, ages, and marital statuses. He'd found out where they worked, how they lived, and all Kane's nephews' and nieces' names. He knew about every letter they'd sent to Kane, knew all the coercion they used to manipulate his husband, and it had worked every single time. He also knew Kane didn't send them small amounts of money occasionally, he sent large amounts every month.

Kane had kept this from Avery, and he didn't like it, but let the process happen, knowing his mister was too good a man to abandon his so-called family no matter what they'd done to him. He also

194

wondered if Kane paid them not to hate him. His kind, loving husband was paying his family not to hate him...that broke his heart the most.

How could a family turn their back on their own blood, but take the money he worked so hard for? Avery had also wrongly assumed the money would keep Kane's family quiet if they were approached. That turned out to be a huge underestimation of both their intelligence and their level of hatred.

Over the years, Avery estimated hundreds of thousands of dollars had been sent to this hateful, lying, backwoods blood connection that had just shoved his husband through a weeks-long public ringer. They hadn't shut their fucking mouths for the last three weeks. Every overeager news reporter across the world now played clips of the venom spewed by Pastor Dalton.

No matter what brave face Kane put on, Avery knew he was deeply hurt and couldn't take any more. He shouldn't have to. Those people needed to pay for what they had done.

Avery prepared for his arrival in Alabama, with intimidation as his goal. He hoped the two large bodyguards he'd hired, who sat directly behind him on the private plane, might give the visual he wanted, but regardless, he needed to shut that damn family's mouth and move them out of the picture. He'd use the full force of the law, as well as his large bank accounts to silence them, forever.

Kane would be angry at him for getting involved. And this wasn't for him, because Avery couldn't give a shit one way or another about what they had to say, but it bothered Kane too much. He could hear the stress in Kane's voice every time they spoke. Kane sounded more and more down, withdrawing into his carefully constructed shell. The very one that had taken Avery years to pull him out of, and that just wouldn't do at all.

For whatever reason, Kane cared what those awful people thought about him. So they needed to shut the fuck up as soon as possible.

Avery and his crew landed as close to Ashland, Alabama as they could. He drove first to Pastor Dalton's residence. The house was far nicer than it appeared on television, but regretfully, no one answered. Prepared for that eventuality, Avery drove to the local church, one he'd learned the man had pastored for the last forty years.

The church was simple and quaint. The congregation couldn't be too large, given the size of the building, but by the looks of things, the ambiance was that of a true Southern Baptist church.

The massive hellfire and brimstone scripture on the billboard out front and the dramatic crucifix on the front doors all showed a church clear in its interpretation of the bible. Hellfire and damnation all the way. Avery never paused as he walked straight up to the small church. He grabbed the handle and jerked. Denied. The building was locked up tight.

"I noticed a Cadillac parked out back as we drove by," Tyrone, one of the bodyguards, said from behind him.

"I can get in there," Marcus, the other, much quieter bodyguard, said from behind him as he pointed to the locked church door. Avery turned to give Marcus room, and the man pulled a small black bag from the inside of his jacket pocket. Within a minute, maybe less, the front doors popped open.

The church was dark and surprisingly smaller than it looked from the outside, with the altar as the chapel's largest feature. The pews were outdated and solid wood. They looked uncomfortable as hell. And deep red carpet and equally as red velvet drapes closed the whole place in. No light filtered into the small room, making it feel oppressive. As they made their way closer to the altar, Avery could hear talking from somewhere in the rear of the building. They headed toward a door at the back of the altar, and he could make out both a woman's and man's voice.

The conversation seemed intense, maybe a little frantic. Avery followed the sounds. Tyrone and Marcus were on his heels. Evidently the offices of the church sat in the back of the building. They entered the well-lit hallway, where they could see a single back door, barred shut. An office door sat directly to the right, completely closed but clearly the location of the voices they'd all heard.

"Let me touch you again, Helena," a deeply Southern, husky voice said. Avery recognized the voice and knew instinctively what was happening. Catching Pastor Dalton in a compromising situation would just be the icing on the stay-out-of-our-lives-forever cake. Avery quickened his steps while looking over his shoulder, putting his finger to his lips. He wanted to catch him off guard.

"But I don't like it, Pastor Dalton. You said I would, but I don't. You're scaring me." *Shit!* That wasn't a woman's voice after all. The door was locked and Tyrone didn't miss a beat, not waiting for Marcus to work his magic. He reared back, and in one swift kick, the door caved in. The light from the hallway streamed inside the dimly lit office. Everything inside Avery hardened as he caught sight of Pastor

Dalton on a small sofa with a young woman underneath him. She couldn't have been much older than seventeen or eighteen. She wasn't completely undressed, but close, and looked scared. She actively fought off his hands. Tears streamed down her face.

Tyrone and Marcus never paused and were on the situation without a second thought or instruction from him. Marcus ripped the aging pastor off her and Tyrone had the young woman up and covered, removing her from the office. They were both off-duty Washington DC police officers and understood the need to quickly subdue the perpetrator and remove the victim from the threatening situation.

"Tyrone, keep her in the chapel," Avery called out.

"Unhand me!" The pastor struggled until his eyes landed on Avery and recognition set in. "What the hell are you doing here? This church has no place for the likes of you..." Avery ignored the rant and went to the desk telephone. The pastor lunged for him, Marcus eagerly cut him off, tossing him back on the sofa with a solid punch to the gut. The pastor was red-hot mad, spewing his venom until the hit landed, and he doubled over in pain, gasping for breath. Avery dialed 9-1-1.

"What's your emergency?"

Avery anchored his hip on the desk and looked directly at Pastor Dalton when he spoke. "I'm at First Baptist in town, and I've witnessed a crime. I need assistance, please," Avery said, and the pastor finally found his voice. He went nuts. The old partially naked man again flew off the sofa and began a violent rant so nasty, Avery had a hard time hearing the operator on the other end of the line.

"I can do this all day long," Marcus said, after tackling Dalton again and violently throwing him back on the sofa. "Get up again, I dare you." Marcus got right in the pastor's face.

"Marcus, keep him in here. The police are on the way." Avery left the phone on the desk, letting the recording capture everything the pastor screamed, and strolled out of the office with a casual gait he truly didn't feel. His mind raced as he made his way back to the chapel where Tyrone stood guard over a weeping, still somewhat frantic, young woman. Tyrone had taken off his coat and wrapped it around her. Her shirt must still be in the office.

"I just need to go home! My parents are going to be so angry," she bellowed, collapsing against Avery as he sat down beside her.

"Sweetheart, I've called the police. They'll make sure you get home safely, I promise. Are you all right?" Avery asked. The pews were equipped with small boxes of tissues. Avery pulled several and handed them to her as the tears poured down.

"I thought I was coming to babysit for a meeting this afternoon after school. I didn't want to do that," she cried.

"You need to tell the police officers the truth of what happened when they get here. It's the only way to keep this from happening again," Avery said, handing her another tissue.

School-age had to mean she was younger than eighteen, right? What a seriously sick old man. For the first time since he'd walked in, Avery considered what he'd just witnessed and hugged the girl closer, thinking of Autumn. The thought made his blood boil. He hoped Marcus was getting a few extra punches in for him.

"They won't believe me," she sobbed, blowing her nose into the Kleenex.

"They'll believe us," Avery said as the police sirens neared. Less than a minute later, several officers entered the front door of the chapel. Weapons were drawn, clearly uncertain as to what they would find. The young woman crying in his arms looked over her shoulder and, if it were even possible, began to sob harder. Avery watched one of the officers look confused, lower his weapon some. The girl bounded out of his arms and stumbled forward, down the aisle toward the officer.

"Daddy, I'm so sorry!" she said, jumping toward the man in uniform.

"Shit," Tyrone said and immediately raised both hands in the air.

"Take her outside, Pebbly. Hands in the air," the lead said, aiming his weapon between Tyrone and Avery. He finally understood what Tyrone must have already known and raised both his hands, wondering how long this was going to take. Robert's first basketball game was in seven hours.

* * * *

Cheers erupted from inside the gymnasium. Avery was late. Since every parking space had been taken, he had been relegated to the back forty, parking sloppily just to get inside the building a little faster. No way Robert or Kane would understand why he missed tonight, and he prayed as he jogged to the front doors that he'd at least made it there before halftime. That was when Autumn wouldn't forgive him for missing her halftime performance as a cheerleader.

Avery'd had to pull some strings to get out of Alabama. His men were still there, detained for the next few hours. Since Tyrone and Marcus were moonlighting as private security, their real profession came in handy. Tyrone was a corporal with the Washington DC police force, which was probably the real reason his strings were even allowed to work. Pastor Dalton had a good reputation in that God-fearing town. No one wanted to believe the clear truth.

Another big negative weighing against him was that he hadn't told Kane his plans to go to Alabama. But who would have ever thought things would turn out the way they had? He'd only called home briefly from the flight, asking Kane to keep Autumn away from the television. It wasn't hard to do tonight. Their private school hosted the basketball season opener. Autumn cheered, Robert played, and Kane headed up the parent booster club committee this year. For the first time since he had left all alone to go to DC, Avery was glad they were busy and not able to focus on anything else.

He paid the five dollar event fee and entered the gym just as another set of cheers erupted. He hoped the home team was winning. It would make for a far better weekend if they won tonight, maybe help smooth over what he'd done this morning.

He scanned the crowds, looking for Kane, but he spotted Autumn first as she cheered for the crowd. Avery looked up three rows, and there was Kane, sitting directly in front of her. His brilliant husband had strategically placed himself so he was high enough to see Robert play, but low enough to watch Autumn cheer for the team. Avery smiled—he missed his family.

He nodded at a few people he recognized as he made his way around the gym. His Kane was such a good father. He took such good care of their children. All those years ago, when he suggested they have Autumn and Robert, he'd had no idea how much pride he'd experience with his family. Avery was so focused on Kane that it wasn't until the cheers of the crowd erupted again that he realized he'd completely missed the dunk Robert had just made.

Avery worked his way over to Kane, who stood clapping excitedly. He excused his way up the bleachers, past the other cheering fans and parents. Kane's face lit when he spotted him, and Avery's heart tripped in his chest, along with his foot as he misjudged the step and fell forward into the space Kane was saving for him. Kane bent down to help him, and he took the opportunity to kiss those lips that were so close to his. The blush came, searching eyes were next to see who might have witnessed that public display, but Avery didn't care. He'd missed Kane while he'd been in Washington.

He tried to be strong, put the needs of his family above himself. They agreed to let the kids finish out the year here in Minnesota, but he hadn't spent this much time away from Kane since they'd met. He wanted Kane with him all the time, because even after this long day, his body naturally relaxed with Kane there with him.

"How's he doing?" Avery asked when Kane settled down beside him.

"Twenty-four points," Kane said over the roar of the crowd, "now, twenty-six points."

"Ah! That's great. He'll be excited. Autumn looks good," Avery said, smiling down at his daughter as she beamed up at him.

"She's tumbling on the hard floor. She spelled out Panthers in back handsprings. She said she would do it again when you got here," Kane said. Avery kept his grin fixed on Autumn as she finished her cheer in unison with the other girls. When the chant ended, she smiled bigger and waved at him before turning back to the game.

"Paulie's videotaping him from up in the bleachers," Kane said, turning back and pointing up. Paulie was as high as he could get with a tripod video camera following the game. He worked hard moving the camera back and forth as the boys ran down the court.

"Where's Mom?" Avery asked after seeing it was impossible to catch Paulie's eye, as he was so focused on the game.

"She's on the other side videoing Autumn." Kane pointed and Avery spotted her with the camera trained on Autumn. She waved in his direction. That overwhelming pride swelled more as he loosened his tie and undid the buttons at the top of his neck.

"We should have had more children," Avery whispered, dropping his tie in his side suit coat pocket. He wasn't sure why he even put the tie back on after his flight, except he knew Kane liked him dressed up, and he wanted to please him after not seeing him for so long.

"No. I'm glad I stood firm. They're perfect just like this," Kane said, his eyes back on Robert who was running down the court, dribbling the ball.

"I miss you guys," Avery said, watching Robert too.

"We miss you," Kane whispered, leaning in, playfully bumping a shoulder against Avery's, but keeping his eyes focused on Robert.

"Shoot, Robert!" Kane yelled, standing and wildly clapping his hands as the shot slid right through the net. Avery was up beside him, maybe a little slower, but with two fingers in his mouth, whistling loudly. That caught Robert's attention, and he looked up, grinning at a smiling Avery.

Okay, today with his family was worth whatever cost they might endure. Avery was truly a very lucky, lucky man. As Kane's strong arm slid around his waist, he realized things were just about as perfect as they could be.

Chapter 24

"I like Georgetown," Kane said from the bathroom door of their home in Stillwater. Avery stood over the sink as he finished brushing his teeth, glancing into the mirror to see Kane perched against the doorjamb, his pajama pants on and his shirt off. Both Robert and Autumn were gone for the night to sleepovers. Kane and Avery were alone in the house or as alone as they could be with the team of security Avery had watching over his family. Avery finished up at the sink, and Kane turned away from the door, heading toward bed.

"Are you sure we need so much security, Avery?" Kane asked.

"Babe, I don't want to take any more chances with you guys. We can tone it down when you get to DC, if things settle some."

"I can't see that my father would seriously try and hurt us, Avery," Kane said. He lifted the bed covers and started to shove his pants down.

"Honey, about your father…" Avery's tone, more than his words stopped Kane in mid- motion. "No, don't stop. You're still sexy as hell, and it's been a long month. Push 'em all the way down. I've missed you, Kane." Avery gestured with his hands before taking his robe off and dropping it at the end of the bed. When the kids weren't home for the night, they always reverted back to their old ways of sleeping—no clothes.

"No...*you* keep going. What about my father?" Kane kicked out of the pajama pants, but sat on the bed, facing Avery, concern clear on his face.

"Babe...Listen. I'm just going to say it. I went down to talk to him today," Avery confessed, making his way back around the bed to Kane's side.

"What? Avery, you didn't." Kane's brows narrowed, watching every movement he made until Avery stood directly in front of him.

"I did. I should have told you, but I'm tired of him hurting you, and I didn't want you to stop me." Avery kept his eyes locked on Kane's.

"So you went there and gave him more ammunition to use against us?" Kane scrubbed his hands over his face. He reached back for his pajama pants, but Avery stopped him.

"Kane, I thought about that, but the way he milks you for money, I thought I could pay him off. That's it. Maybe intimidate him a little and pay him off," Avery said, stepping back with Kane's pajama pants in his hands, refusing to let his husband add any physical barriers to the emotion-filled conversation.

"He's my problem, not yours. You don't even know them!" Kane was up on Avery, grabbing at his pants. "You shouldn't have even known about the money I give him. How did you know? Do you watch everything I do?"

"Of course not! It comes up on the taxes, Kane, and he's our problem. We're married, it's our money you're sending, and besides, he isn't going to be much of a problem anymore. Well, in the normal sense. I think he's going to be a huge problem, but not like before," Avery said, letting Kane snatch his pants back, but he'd lost some of his steam as the words settled in.

"What does that mean?" Kane asked.

"Honey, your dad apparently has a thing for young women," Avery said, now taking a step toward him.

"What?" Kane said, balancing on one foot until he abandoned putting the pants back on and just stood there staring at Avery, apparently letting the words sink in.

"I caught him with a young woman. She turned out to be barely seventeen, a police officer's daughter. I guess there are more your dad's been with in his parish." Avery watched the confusion cloud Kane's eyes.

"More?" Kane asked. Avery knew he must be struggling as he tried to comprehend what he heard. "Did you go alone? Could you have seen it wrong, Avery?"

"No. I took two of my security guards with me, but the girl was very upset and spilled to the police. It's the only reason I was so late to Robert's game." Avery reached out and gripped Kane's hip, but otherwise kept his distance.

"Is she all right?" Kane stepped into Avery, concern clear in his voice.

"I believe so. I know what I saw, but I don't think things got that far. Your dad was arrested immediately. He was still spouting Bible verses as the police car door closed and they drove away. We left soon after. The sheriff and arresting officers agreed to keep this quiet for now, but with him being as vocal as he's been lately, I didn't want to take any chances and rushed home. I didn't want you to hear about this from anyone else. This is something we'll have to deal with soon enough. I want you prepared. Our public relations people are ready to field any calls we get."

"Avery, this is…I can't believe it. I had no idea," Kane said, visibly shaken as he tried to step away, but Avery held on tight.

"I know you didn't. And I'm sorry I had to tell you. We'll deal with it together just like we always do. Come to bed. I've missed you. I don't want him to affect us ever again," Avery said and slowly began to walk Kane back toward the bed.

"Is the girl okay?" Kane asked again. Avery pulled Kane close and pressed his lips to his husband's forehead.

"She is, I promise, and I'll stay involved, but I don't want you connected. Let me handle this. Come to bed and hold me. I've missed you. It's awful sleeping alone. I think that might be the worst part of our separation," Avery said, trying to draw Kane to bed. He'd missed Kane and having to come home and tell him the latest news about his father gutted him. And they called themselves Christians? The man led a congregation for Christ's sake, yet he'd been stealing money from his son and forcing himself on young women. Kane was strong, but Avery hadn't been sure how he would handle the news. Now, all he wanted to do was comfort Kane and keep him from worrying any more tonight.

"Honey…come to bed. I'll check in with the police department in the morning. Your father's not going to hurt you, or our children, or anyone else for that matter, anymore. He's done. That's what we need to focus on." Avery threw back the covers, climbed in bed, and scooted to the middle. "Come on, come join me, I need you."

"I can't believe you went there. Thank God you did."

"I'd do anything to protect you, Kane. You have to know that by now," Avery said, whipping the bed covers over Kane as he came to settle on Avery's chest.

"I'm lucky to have you. I can't believe all of this. It completely changes everything." Kane finally turned, lifted a little as his gaze slid down Avery's body. Avery responded to Kane's intense stare, growing hard under his sensual inspection. He forced lingering thoughts of Kane's family from his head and focused all his attention on the man he loved. Avery reached over, pushed open the hidden compartment in their headboard, grabbed the bottle, and dropped it beside him on the bed.

"I love you, Avery. I've missed you. I don't want to talk about them right now. All I want to do is make love to you." Avery leaned in and kissed his husband softly on his lips.

* * * *

Kane nestled against Avery's chest and leaned in to kiss the skin right above Avery's ear. When Avery told him about his father's arrest, he'd had so many emotions running through him he hadn't known how to respond. The news came as a total shock. All this time he'd tried to do what he believed was right, but they had used him, and his feelings, against him. He carried enormous guilt over letting them down. Now that everything was out in the open, he could already feel that weight lifting. In its place was the complete love and protection of his little family.

Kane lifted, smiling that love down to Avery. He raised a hand, tangling his fingers into Avery's thick blond hair, keeping his mouth closed and crushing their lips together. Avery held him there, not letting him break from the kiss. Kane's smile broadened as he moved his hand to cup the back of Avery's head, holding him in place. Kane loved to play this game and flicked his tongue out, slowly licking along the seam of Avery's lips. He knew it was Avery's favorite move.

Avery's lips parted, and he deepened the kiss. His body heated and every nerve ending heightened as Avery's body pressed against his. He'd missed this. He missed the closeness he and Avery shared. He attacked Avery's mouth thoroughly. Kane pulled Avery closer, needing the feel of this man's skin against his own. Kane didn't wait, couldn't wait, his hand went straight to Avery's hardened cock, and he wrapped his fingers around his husband's erect length. He began working him from tip to base, taking his time and circling his thumb around Avery's weeping head.

"I missed you," Avery moaned, pulling from the kiss, pushing Kane's head toward his exposed neck. "I'm trying to buck up and be strong, but I don't like being without you. I'm not sure I would have agreed to run had I known you wouldn't be with me in Washington right now."

"I miss you too, so badly. But we'll be there soon, baby. Just a few more months. The kids need to get through the school year," Kane said, breathing into Avery's ear as he kissed and nibbled his earlobe.

"I'm such a wimp without you," Avery said, tugging Kane's hair, forcing him to look directly in his eyes as he said the words.

"No, you're not. You're the strongest man I know. Nothing gets to you." Kane scooted the covers out of the way and kissed his way down Avery's body. He drew Avery's nipple between his lips and nipped the small bud with the tip of his teeth before flicking it with his tongue. Avery moaned and writhed under him as he continued to kiss and lick a path down Avery's stomach then across his hip bone. Kane pressed his nose against Avery's skin and inhaled deeply, he loved the scent that was all Avery.

His mouth watered needing a taste of the man he'd been dying for ever since Avery walked into the gymnasium earlier that night. He gripped Avery's cock, stroking a few times as he lowered and placed a kiss on the mushroom head before sliding his tongue across the small slit, tasting the bead of moisture gathering at the tip. Kane sucked Avery's arousal deep into his mouth, his eyes watered as Avery's hard cock slid across his tongue and the thick head hit the back of his throat. Avery shuddered, arching his hips as his hands slid into Kane's hair.

"Shit, baby," Avery groaned.

"Mmmm…so good," Kane mumbled around Avery's thickness, while rolling his balls in his palm.

"I haven't jacked off since I left for Washington. I don't know if that was wise." Avery raised his head, his eyes piercing Kane's soul as he spoke.

"It was our deal," Kane purred against Avery's perfectly cut head, teasing the leaking slit with his tongue before leaning over to grab the bottle of lubricant. "You haven't gone more than a few days without sex since I met you. You haven't been with anyone else, have you?"

"No! I wouldn't. I've told you. It's only you, Kane." Avery's brows furrowed, and he reached out to stroke Kane's cheek with his knuckles.

"Even there in that world with all the willing interns?" Kane didn't let it go. He hadn't even known he had this insecurity until the questions poured from his lips.

"Not in any world, not ever." The words Avery spoke touched and eased his heart, but the emotion on his lover's face completely embraced his soul. Avery stared down his body at Kane where he lay poised between his parted legs. There was no doubt in his mind Avery spoke the truth. Why had he even questioned him? The whole situation with his family had him second-guessing everything, and he had just doubted the person who always stood by him.

He pushed those thoughts from his mind, not wanting to contemplate them again. What he and Avery shared was solid, real, and he was grateful to be married to such a wonderful and caring man. He leaned in and kissed Avery's thigh, before pushing up so he was kneeling between Avery's splayed legs.

He popped the top on the lube, making sure his fingers were well-coated. He needed to make love to Avery. He needed to be buried inside his husband, making love to him, because in those few moments, they were truly one. He felt the safest he ever felt in his life wrapped completely around Avery. Making love to Avery comforted and eased his soul like nothing else ever could.

Kane trailed a fingertip down Avery's heavy sac to his circle and teased the rim. He slowly inserted his thumb, just the way Avery liked it. He found the gland as he began to stroke Avery's thick cock with his other hand. He worked another finger inside massaging Avery from the inside out.

"Baby, just like that." Avery squirmed against his hand.

"You're tight." He continued slowly making love to Avery with his fingers, twisting and turning them so they brushed against his spot. Kane reveled in the fact that every slide of his fingers drove Avery a little further, caused him to whimper a little more. Avery's lips parted and his eyes squeezed shut as he tried to force himself harder onto Kane's fingers, seeking as much sensation as he could.

"Kane, your touch—"

He stopped Avery midsentence. "Open your eyes and look at me, baby." He wanted to look into Avery's eyes as he entered and made love to him. He needed that open honest connection that always came when they were together. Avery eased his soul, and Kane needed that moment tonight.

Kane guided Avery's legs back toward his chest and palmed his aching cock. He lined up with Avery's entrance and pushed into the tight passage, never breaking eye contact. Avery arched his body, tugged his legs free, and wrapped them around Kane as he began to move in and out of his husband. Kane dipped his head and took Avery's mouth with his, kissing him with all the love and devotion coursing through his body. Avery kissed him back with just as much ferocity.

"I'm not gonna last, but don't stop. Don't ever stop." Avery threaded his fingers through Kane's hair and urged his head to his neck. Kane latched on, suckling and licking his way up to Avery's ear.

"I don't want you to ever be with anyone else. You belong to me," Kane breathed.

"Baby, it's only you for me too, I swear." Avery clenched his ass and Kane lost it, his balls churned, drawing up tightly against his body. He couldn't stop, didn't want to stop. Avery's body felt too good wrapped around his.

"I love you," he ground out through clenched teeth as he pushed deeper into Avery's tight ass one last time as his seed spilled from him, filling the man he adored.

"Fuck, Kane, I love you, too." Avery shuddered and tensed beneath him. Hot ribbons of come splattered across his stomach and chest as Avery's orgasm shot from his body.

Chapter 25

1992 ~ Washington, DC

The school semester ended June 5, 1991, and by June seventh, Kane, Autumn, and Robert joined Avery in DC, and he couldn't have been more happy. Avery barely let them catch their breath before he thrust them into the world of Washington politics. With each passing day, Avery's political popularity grew. He'd become a much sought after commodity, especially at the many social gatherings held by DC's political elite.

Avery made his reputation clear; he was a family man through and through. He had Kane with him always and Autumn and Robert attended as many events as appropriate. Avery's charisma and charm smoothed any awkward moments they encountered as a gay couple, even though Kane still shied away from the attention and cameras. That was mainly due to his father's trial and all the legalities that complicated what could and couldn't be said.

As suspected, Kane's name was dragged through the mud throughout the court proceedings. Cable court television was a new thing, something no one had really ever heard of before, and they were making a name for themselves by televising Pastor Dalton's trial in real time, all day long. When the cable networks weren't in court, they spent hours a night discussing the events of the day, dissecting every part of the trial and making every possible assumption on the outcome until the jury returned the verdict. His father was sentenced to twenty years for multiple counts of sexual abuse to a minor. In all likelihood, with his advanced age, he'd never again see the light of day, which Avery thought was a fitting punishment.

For Avery, apparently bad press was still a very good thing. To have his name on the nightly news just propelled his political agenda. As for Kane, not so much. Avery had to work hard at keeping him from sliding back into himself and hiding there until the whole thing played out.

In politics, Avery quickly became the rookie rebel, shaking things up. Over the next year, he worked his way into becoming the congressional hope of the Democratic Party. He had a way of making everyone comfortable, regardless of their views on homosexuality, or any other view for that matter.

Benjamin Taylor, the current presidential hopeful, hosted this event where he would certainly name his running mate for the 1992 presidential election. That made this the perfect place for the 'see and be seen' portion of Avery's job.

"Did you get enough to eat?" Avery stepped in front of Kane, who looked rather bored but mouthwateringly handsome holding the small plate of hors d'oeuvres.

"Why are you looking at me that way?" Kane asked, eyeing him closely.

"I'm just thinking about the first time I ever saw you. I remember thinking what a sharp, sophisticated man you were, how you would look good on my arm if I ran for office," Avery said, stepping in a little closer. "Plus you're still the best-looking man in the room."

"I'm almost fifty years old, I'm not sneaking off to have closet sex, or bathroom sex, or whatever dark corner, nook, or cranny you might find sex," Kane whispered very quietly back to him.

"There are so many places we could explore here..." Avery started, but a hand clamped down on his shoulder before he could continue the direction he was headed. How did he already feel denied when he had only just begun to persuade Kane to an empty room.

"Son, you remind me of your granddad," Senator Taylor said, coming to stand next to them, shaking Avery's now outstretched hand.

"I'm hearing that more and more. It's a true compliment, he was a great man. I'm not sure I could ever fill his shoes."

"Well, I disagree. I think you'll make your own mark soon enough," Senator Taylor said, turning to Kane.

"Hello, sir," Kane said, quickly wiping off his hand before shaking the senator's.

"You all gettin' settled in all right?" Senator Taylor asked as they shook hands. They were both Southern boys, and Avery would swear Kane's accent grew stronger whenever they spoke.

"Yes, sir. Our children love their new school. That was a great relief," Kane answered.

"Good, good. I'm glad to hear it. They seem like great kids. Listen, I won't keep you two. Everyone here thinks I'm gonna announce my running mate today. I'm not. I haven't even asked him to run yet, so I'm fixin' that right now." The senator turned and looked directly at Avery. "Avery, I'd like you to think about running with me. It'll be a battle, but one I think we can manage for the betterment of this nation. It's time to get this country back on track. You're the only person I have in mind that can help me make a difference. Think on it, you two talk, and take all the time you need, but come see me tomorrow and let me know what you decide," Senator Taylor said and again clapped him on the shoulder for a short squeeze, then left as quickly as he'd come.

Avery could only stare at Kane and mouth, "*Vice president?*"

"Was he serious?" Kane finally whispered.

"I don't really know," Avery answered, a little breathily as he snaked an arm around Kane's waist and drew him closer. This time it wasn't so much about coercion, but needed support. Avery felt a little light-headed. Senator Taylor was going to be the next president. There was no question there. He was the clear frontrunner and every poll had him moving into the White House come January.

Never in a million years did Avery see himself as anything more than a United States Senator. What was Taylor thinking?

"Avery, I can see you want this," Kane started, but Avery cut him off. He discarded Kane's plate on a random tray and pulled him away from the gathering without even telling anyone goodbye. He wouldn't allow Kane to say another word until they left the house and were safely tucked inside their car, heading home.

"You want this," Kane tried again, his eyes on Avery's as he sat in the passenger side seat.

"I honestly never considered this could be a possibility. I thought the Senate was as far as I could go," Avery said, linking his hand with

Kane's as he navigated through the Washington streets toward their home. "Fuck, Kane. I mean, damn, this is big."

"Watch you're language, Avery. Nothing's changed. We don't talk like that anymore," Kane scolded him, and all Avery could do was smile and bring their joined hands to his lips for kiss.

"I'm sorry. How do you feel about it?" Avery ventured a gaze over at Kane who was still staring at him.

"I think it's a family decision, Avery. If you do this, they'll spend the rest of their childhood as the children of a vice president. You'll have to explain it all to us. What it will mean for all of us," Kane said. His tone was firm, not really negative, but definitely not enthusiastic. And with each passing mile, Avery's excitement grew. Vice president! What in the world?

* * * *

Three days later, Kane, Autumn, and Robert were dressed in their finest as they stood by Avery's side during the televised announcement introducing him as Senator Taylor's vice presidential running mate. In Kane's estimation, Avery did the Democratic Party proud during his acceptance speech, outlining his goals for the future and his support of the presidential nominee.

The fanfare was high, the room seemed only momentarily stunned that Senator Taylor had chosen Avery, making this one of the best kept secrets in Washington, but the Adams political charm and appeal held true. It didn't take long for the room to erupt in one of the biggest shows of support Kane had ever witnessed. Since he'd prepared for the worst, all the support that exploded around him took a minute to process.

Kane attempted to remain discreet and unobtrusive. He stayed as far away from Avery as he could while remaining on the same stage. Robert and Autumn, on the other hand, stood right beside Avery, waving, smiling, enjoying every part of the experience. They were absolutely perfect and played the part of what they truly were, loving children, proud of their father. Avery quickly and completely owned the room. Avery was funny, sharp-witted, and explained politics on such a basic level that he could easily connect with the everyday man or woman.

Once Avery realized Kane wasn't standing on the other side of Robert and Autumn, he very clearly, and publically, corrected that mistake. He made a show of going to Kane, grasping his hand and waving their joined hands in front of the crowd. Kane was certain he was ten shades of red. The heat of the blush crept up his cheeks, but Avery tugged him out of his hiding place to the front of the stage, and they stood there, letting the audience cheer them on. Any lingering signs of worry about his and Avery's relationship were eased as Senator Taylor and his wife came out to join them.

Those next few days passed in a blur. Before he knew it, the whirlwind days became weeks, and weeks became months of Avery traveling the country and winning himself a place in the people's hearts. The conservatives came out in abundance, picketing every event Avery attended in the Southern United States. Kane tried to create some semblance of normalcy for Autumn and Robert. His only stipulation in this entire campaign was that he remain out of the limelight. Even when coached, he didn't feel comfortable with the press. Those times were hard, too hard, and he shied away from the exposure. Avery refused to be anything but himself, keeping their standing date nights going, and continued his show of being out and around town with Kane, which forced him more and more into the public eye.

In September 1992, the frequent parties and social gatherings all came to an abrupt halt. Kane was in Washington when he got a call letting him know Paulie had had a heart attack and was in critical condition. Kane barely stopped long enough to leave a message for Avery and arrange childcare before he was on the next flight out in a panicked race to get back to Minnesota.

Chapter 26

"Avery..." Janice whispered in his ear, sliding a folded note in front of him as he sat in a round table discussion at the Midwest Governors' Conference in Chicago. He nodded once, but continued to listen to the discussion going on around him.

"Sir, it's important," she whispered again, tapping the note with one of her well-manicured fingernails. When Avery still didn't give, Janice did something she'd never done before; she lifted the note and put the paper in front of Avery's eyes. That got his attention. The words were simple, and everything around him faded away as he read Paulie had been hospitalized and Kane was on his way there now. *Shit!* He crushed the note with his fist and abruptly stood, effectively ending any discussion going on around him.

"I need a car," he said to Janice.

"There's one waiting, sir," she said from behind him.

"Gentleman, I've had a family emergency, please continue this without me." He never looked back as he left the room, eating up the distance to the front door.

"What have you found out?" Avery asked, hearing Janice's high heels clicking on the polished marble floor behind him, trying hard to keep up with his long and hurried strides.

"He's not well. They don't expect him to make it through the night," Janice said as he hit the front door. A driver stood by a Lincoln Town Car, holding the backdoor open for Avery.

"Where's Kane?" Avery asked, sliding inside. Janice jogged around the side of the car, ducking in next to him.

"He should be boarding his plane now. He called me from the airport," Janice said, looking down at her watch.

"How did he sound?" Avery asked, but Janice's non-answer was enough. Kane must be frantic. Damn, he should have insisted Paulie move with them to Washington.

"I've chartered you a plane. A car will pick you up, take you to the hospital. I took the liberty to have your schedule cleared. It wasn't a popular decision with the campaign organizers," Janice said, her portfolio now spread out on her lap. Avery was lost to it all; her words drowned out by his thoughts of Kane as he stared out the side door window, focusing on nothing but his husband's indubitable loss. Paulie was an old man, well into his eighties. He'd lived a good long life, Kane had made sure of that. He knew this day would come, but he'd hoped not for a few more years.

This would give Kane one less family member, and for a man who lived for his family, that loss was a tragedy. Avery's heart hurt with the grief Kane would feel. Scrubbing a hand over his face, he did what he knew Kane was doing right now. He said a prayer. "Please, God, let Paulie hold on until Kane gets there."

* * * *

Sometime late in the evening, Kane stood in the hallway outside Paulie's hospital room. His red-rimmed eyes stung. He wore his heart on his sleeve and tried to steel his emotions as he pushed open the door, but he broke at the sight of Paulie lying there, not moving. His frail worn-out body hooked up to machines. The medical equipment kept a steady beep in perfect time with Paulie's old heart. Kane ran his hand through his hair, gathering himself. The sterile smell of the hospital room made his stomach roil. He hated the stark white walls that surrounded the man he considered his father. He hated knowing what would come of this, but most of all, Kane hated being powerless over the whole blasted situation.

Avery sat directly in front of Paulie, holding his hand, steadily talking to him. "He's coming. I promise he's coming. Hang on, Paulie," Avery pleaded.

"I'm here." Kane forced himself the rest of the way into the room, going immediately to the other side of the bed. Paulie's eyes cracked open, nothing more than slits as he stared up, causing Kane's heart to break. His strong, invincible Paulie, looked so old, so helpless. He grasped on to Paulie's hand. He looked small, frail, and in a tremendous amount of pain. Kane couldn't help the tears that slipped free and rolled down his cheeks.

Paulie fought the oxygen mask, but couldn't work it off his face. Avery helped, lifting the mask from his mouth as tears formed in Paulie's eyes. "I love you like you were my own son."

"I love you, too, Paulie. You can fight this," Kane said, tears rolling down his face as he leaned in closer, running his hand over Paulie's almost bald head.

"Not this time," he whispered, sucking in a deep breath.

"He wouldn't allow them to give him any pain medicine. He was afraid he wouldn't wake up when you got here," Avery informed him.

"Paulie, take the medicine, please, don't do this to yourself." Kane brushed his thumb across Paulie's forehead.

"Son, you made my life better. You gave me a reason when I had none. You and Avery take care of each other. Love each other. *Always*," Paulie said in a harsh whisper, gasping for shallow breaths as he spoke. The few sentences seemed to exhaust him. The medical equipment connected to him went wild as Paulie fell unconscious. Those were the last words he ever spoke. Paulie never woke again.

Kane flew Paulie back to Alabama to be buried next to his wife and son. Avery canceled his entire schedule and never left his side. Kane didn't argue, needing Avery to lean on. Paulie was an old man, and Kane thought he'd mentally prepared for this day, but not a day had gone by over the last thirty years that he hadn't talked to Paulie in some way.

After the burial, Avery took Autumn and Robert to pick out flowers for the headstone while he stayed tucked away inside their hotel suite. Kane cried like he had never cried before. He missed Paulie more than he ever thought possible.

Paulie left a formal Last Will and Testament and required an official reading attended by only Kane and Avery. He left everything to Kane—his shares of the restaurant and all his most cherished belongings, which pretty much consisted of the memories of his wife and son.

After a few days, Kane pushed Avery back out on the campaign trail. His husband resisted, but Kane needed the time. He sent Autumn and Robert back to Washington with Kennedy, and he flew to Minnesota. Kane had decisions to make. La Bella Luna had been his heart and soul for many, many years. Avery changed all that. The restaurant was no longer his life. He'd kept it going for Paulie. Years ago, Kane had made the decision to follow Avery no matter what course he chose. There was no room for the day to day operations of such a busy restaurant. If he tried to hang on and manage La Bella Luna, his time with Avery, Autumn, and Robert would be sacrificed and Kane couldn't stand for that. Avery and his children were his life now. He knew what he needed to do.

He drove from the airport straight to the restaurant, choosing to enter from the front, not the back. No one would be around if he came in this way. So much of the restaurant had changed. They had remodeled more than once over the last fourteen years. As he looked around, he realized he wasn't even sure he had been in the decision-making process of this last round of updates. He couldn't remember ever seeing these color schemes before.

In the back, a new young man worked the bar. Kane supposed he was the new hire who took Rodney's position. Kane didn't know him, and the bartender glanced his way, only to look away, and then straight back at him.

"Can I help you? The restaurant's closed," the young man said, coming to the end of the bar.

"Kane Adams," Kane said, sticking out his hand for a quick shake. He barely slowed as he made his way toward his old office.

"I'm sorry, sir. I didn't know," the bartender said, stumbling all over himself. "I'm real sorry about Paulie."

"Thank you," Kane tossed over his shoulder as he entered the kitchen. The mood was somber. Paulie's head chef was hard at work, prepping for the day. No one paid any attention to him entering, and he didn't comment. Instead, he walked straight back to the office. The office it seemed was the only room in the restaurant that hadn't changed. Without doing much more than going on instinct, Kane booted up the desktop computer and connected the dialup to send two short emails. The first was to Avery.

> *Avery, you have to know by now that I didn't return home with the children. I'm in Minnesota. I've decided to sell the restaurant. It's not fair to you, the kids, or any of the staff if I try to keep it. I thought I'd have your office here handle the paperwork. I wasn't going around you, I just didn't want you to worry about anything more than what you are dealing with right now.*
>
> *I love you always, K*

Kane read and reread the message. Short, sweet, and to the point. He hit send, making sure everything stayed connected and the email actually left the outbox. Next was Rodney. As he opened a new message and began to type, there was a knock at the door.

"I heard you were here, boss," Rodney said, sticking his head in the office. "It's good to see you back, man."

"Come in. I was just sending you an email," Kane said, motioning for Rodney to take a seat.

"You get Paulie all squared away?" Rodney asked softly, his eyes showed the pain of their loss. Rodney carried that same somber mood as everyone else.

"I think so. Look, I'm here to let you know I'm selling La Bella Luna," Kane began, and the shock showed on Rodney's face. He started to speak, but Kane stopped him, raising a hand. "And I want you to buy it."

"Kane, man, I can't afford this place. And I don't have the credit to get this kind of money," Rodney said. He was up and on his feet, panic now replaced the shock.

"Trust me, you can afford it. And I'll carry the note. Avery's firm can draw up the papers," Kane said, realizing for the first time in a long time his super-calm facade was back in place. "I want you to have the place. It's the only way I can let it go."

That stopped Rodney in his tracks. His face again went through a variety of changes, until uncertainty settled in. "Can I handle it?"

"I think you can. You already do most of the work now. I can stay on as your consultant. Talk you through anything you need help with.

I'll also handle the paperwork transfer and be your lender. Paulie would want you to have it," Kane added, nodding his head now.

"Paulie kept this place going just in case you ever wanted back in," Rodney said, dropping down in his seat with a thump, the somber mood back in place.

"I know. He was always watching out for me since the first day I met him," Kane said, he fought the instant tears that threatened to blur his vision.

"He loved you, Kane. Like you were his son," Rodney said, holding his gaze.

"I was his son, and I think he'd approve of this decision. You need to just say yes. Let me clean out this office, and get the paperwork started." They were silent for several long minutes staring at one another. Kane nodded, knowing this was the right decision, while Rodney sat there looking unsure.

"I'm taking your silence as a yes," Kane said, feeling weirdly relieved when Rodney didn't immediately object. Rodney would treat La Bella Luna with the same care that he and Paulie had. "I'm heading over to the firm now. We'll draw up the paperwork. Once you sign, I'll start the transfer. The only thing I ask is that for the time being, we keep this all on the down low. Everything we do is supposed to be approved through the campaign. It's not going to change what happens, I just want Avery brought up to speed."

"I don't know, Kane. Do you think I can handle it?" Rodney rose from his seat when Kane did.

"I have the utmost faith in you, Rodney. I'm moving forward and heading over to Avery's office to get things outlined. I'll be back to get Paulie's things, and we can talk more then." Kane rounded the corner, giving Rodney a giant bear hug. This was abrupt, possibly not thought completely through, but he wasn't taking no for an answer. He was ripping the Band-Aid off, getting things done. As he let Rodney go, the office phone began to ring.

* * * *

The restaurant telephone line rang until voice mail picked up. Avery aggressively disconnected the call only to hit redial, letting the phone ring again. He must have read it wrong. Kane surely had not just made such a monumental decision as selling his beloved restaurant without talking to him first. And what the hell was up with an email? He didn't warrant high enough on the food chain to even get a phone call? Hell, he'd just spent four full days with the man, why hadn't Kane mentioned any of this to him then?

"Dammit!" Avery hissed, disconnecting the call again, only to hit redial for the second time. This email had to come from the computer at La Bella Luna. There wasn't enough time for Kane to have taken Autumn and Robert home and return to Minnesota. Who was with his children?

"La Bella Luna," Kane answered on the fourth ring.

"I honestly don't even know where to start," Avery said as all the frustrating thoughts jammed his mind at one time. "Yes, I do. We'll start at the end and work our way back. You can't sell La Bella Luna, Kane. We'll make it work."

"Rodney, will you give me a minute?" he heard Kane say on the other end of the line.

"Sure thing, boss. Oh, sorry," Rodney said in the background. What the hell did that mean?

"Avery, I knew if I told you, you would fight me on this," Kane started explaining.

"Why are you trying to sell?" Avery asked, even though he was really more stuck on why Kane hadn't discussed any of this with him. He talked everything over with Kane.

"For the reasons I mentioned in the message, Avery," Kane said, and this time he sounded sad.

"Babe, that's your place. It's our place..." Avery began, but Kane cut him off.

"Not anymore, and it hasn't been for many years. We're in Washington now. That's our life. I can't run the restaurant from there," Kane stated.

"Yes, you can. And you can go home more. The kids are getting older. We can hire a nanny, they can live without you for a few days a week," Avery countered.

"Honey, you know you're gonna win. It's inevitable. If I don't do this now, I'll have to eventually. It's better to tie up all these loose ends while I can still be in control of them. I thought I'd have your office draw up the papers. I've already talked to Rodney about buying the place. Besides, I don't want to be here during the little bit of free time you have. It's too rare to miss," Kane reasoned. Avery could hear the fatigue, and his heart hurt for Kane. He'd had too much pain in his life already.

"Are you lonely?" Why had he asked that? Or, better question, why hadn't he considered that before right this minute? Kane always stayed so busy with Autumn and Robert. But they were new to town, no real friends yet, and Kane hadn't found a church like the one they had at home. Damn, why hadn't he thought about this before?

"Sometimes, but it's okay. I knew what I was agreeing to when we moved. Besides, selling the restaurant has nothing to do with that." Kane's voice dropped an octave, and Avery thought he might have heard a hint of underlying sadness in his tone.

"I don't want you to be lonely, Kane." Avery gripped the phone tighter, the restaurant completely forgotten. He wished he could be there with Kane and have this conversation face to face.

"I know you don't, but it's the nature of the beast," Kane stated matter-of-factly.

"I can be home more."

"No, you can't," Kane shot instantly back, and then there was silence.

"I don't want you to be lonely, Kane. I never wanted you to be lonely. You three can move back to Stillwater. I'll make that my base," Avery said, his mind racing, trying to find the answer to this problem.

"No, we can't move back to Minnesota. The kids are in a new school, they've started new lives, and besides, we made these decisions together. I know my place. It's there, waiting for you to get home," Kane said.

"Baby…I should've given this decision more thought. I don't like the hurt in your voice at all." How had this conversation turned so quickly into a realm they had never discussed? Avery went from being irritated to guilt-ridden in a matter of a couple of minutes. How had that happened?

"Avery, listen to me. I'm going to be fine. I just wanted you to know before I have the paperwork drawn up. You have a little over one month before the election. You focus on that, I'll take care of this," Kane specified, his voice firm, resolute, definitely in control.

"I feel like I need to be with you right now, honey," Avery tried again. He couldn't let this go.

"But you don't. I've got this," Kane affirmed.

Avery went silent, and he knew that silence spoke volumes. He so didn't like the answers Kane gave him. He scrubbed a hand over his face, closed his eyes, and let the thought of Kane not needing him settle across his heart. That was what all this was about. It wasn't the sale of the restaurant or the alone time for either of them. Once Avery had decided to run for office, he'd inadvertently distanced himself from the most important person in his life. Dammit, why was he just now realizing this? Kane was everything to him. His always. What had he been thinking? Did he expect that Kane would just sit and wait for him? Yeah, actually that was exactly what he'd thought.

"Avery, you're needed in Ballroom A. They're almost ready for you," Janice said, poking her head inside the door.

"Give me minute, Janice," Avery began, but Kane cut him off.

"Go, don't make those people wait. I'll see you in Ohio next week. Autumn and Robert are coming with me. I love you. This was not a conversation I wanted to have right now. I'm hanging up," Kane warned.

"I love you. Always. You know that, right?" Avery whispered quietly into the receiver.

"I do, but I like the reminder. And I feel the same. My love for you has never been in question. Now go kick butt in your speech," Kane said and hung up without saying goodbye. Avery was slower, lowering the phone to its cradle before again scrubbing his hand over his face for the second time in less than two minutes.

"You're being introduced," Janice stuck her head back inside his hotel room's makeshift office. After taking a good look at his face, she walked inside, shutting the door behind her. "Are you all right?"

"No, not at all." He stood, his mind still reeling from his and Kane's conversation. He straightened his suit as he stepped past her, opened the door, and headed toward the podium in Ballroom A. She was right on his heels, but he ignored her. He had to hide this heavy heart, put on a confident face, and make these people believe in him. He'd worked too hard to keep his sexuality out of the public eye and make politics the main focus of his campaign, but now his heart was flying across the country, making life-altering decisions without him. All of the sudden, he wasn't certain the overall price was worth the outcome. Squaring his shoulders, he plastered the smile on his face and took center stage. As he waved to the clapping hands, his heart lurched. He'd have to do better by Kane. In no way did he ever want a repeat of today.

Chapter 27

"I want you there with me, Kane. I don't care what anyone else thinks is best. It's tradition, and you need to be there. I can't believe we are still even having this conversation," Avery proclaimed, early on inauguration day morning. And definitely much too early for the tension that filled the room, if you asked Kane. Avery exited his closet, fully dressed, shrugging his suit jacket on over his shoulders, with an irritated look on his face. And all his ire seemed to be focused directly on Kane, even at four o'clock in the morning.

"Babe, why are you doing this? It's tradition for legally married couples to appear together during the inaugural events. I'm not legally..." Kane lowered his voice, mumbling the last part, dressing at a much slower pace than Avery.

"Kane, dammit! I want you there. You're every bit as responsible for this as I am. Look, if you aren't there, it looks like we're hiding. I don't want that to even be a possibility for the future." Avery followed Kane inside his closet. A knock on their bedroom door interrupted them. Thank God, because Kane was past tired of this argument. Public opinion had reservations about Kane being there beside Avery today, so did Kane. Why couldn't Avery see that?

Not waiting for them to let her in, Autumn flung the door open, clearly upset and full of award-winning drama and total over-the-top theatrics that only an almost teenage girl could pull off. "Daddy, Nonnie says I have to wear the pea coat today, but I don't want to! It makes me look like a little girl. I want to wear my long coat. It still matches, see," Autumn argued.

"Baby, please just wear what they asked you to," Kane started, but Autumn threw in the tears, drawing Avery's attention off Kane and directly to her.

"I'm tired of this. What's wrong with you people? If we would have listened to public opinion, we would never be moving into the vice presidency to begin with! Autumn, wear the coat you want to wear. Kane, you're beside me all day. I'll hold the whole ceremony up if you continue to buck me on this," Avery asserted, and just as dramatically as Autumn had entered, Avery fled the room, slamming doors and pounding across the hardwood floors as he headed away to meet security for his ride to the White House.

"What's wrong with Dad?" Robert asked from the bedroom doorway.

"Daddy got him mad," Autumn said, checking her reflection in the dresser mirror. She was beautiful, long flowing blonde hair to match her long, lean frame, and seemingly completely unfazed by Avery's dramatic display of anger.

"I think you contributed your fair share, young lady. Now, come here, both of you. Let me take a good look at you," Kane said, pulling his suit coat on. Both Robert and Autumn came to stand in front of Kane. His heart swelled with pride. His children. Both so similar, there was no question they were twins. Robert was already five-ten, and Autumn was an inch or so shorter than him. Avery had the clothes they wore today made for them, and they fit perfectly. Robert's suit made him look a few years older, where Autumn went with the styles of the season. Her shoulder pads were thick and pronounced. He was so in love with their children.

"You two pass. Now, remember your manners all day. Do everything you learned. We need to represent today, and today more than ever—ignore the hate. It's their problem, not ours," Kane said, turning off the bedroom lamps. This was their last day in this house for the next few years. All their furniture was being stored as they moved in to the vice president's residence. "Get your things. We need to be on time this morning."

"Yes, sir," Robert said, turning immediately to do what was asked of him.

"Daddy, are you going to stand with us today?" Autumn asked, lingering at the bedroom door.

"I guess so, if that's what Avery wants," Kane said, moving to stand in front of her. "Go get your things, honey."

"I think you should. Dad likes to hold your hand when he gets nervous and he's really nervous today. I'm not supposed to say anything," Autumn confided.

"Is he nervous?" Kane asked, smiling now. Of course Autumn would tune in to that.

"Yes, he told me last night when he told me the school's going to approve this absence today even though we aren't sick." Kane's smile grew. Autumn would be worried about missing school today to stand beside her father.

"Don't worry anymore about it. I'll be there with him whenever he wants. Now, go get your things. The cars are waiting out front for us." Kane smiled again, watching Autumn's retreating back as she dashed away with the same flair with which she'd arrived.

Chapter 28

Avery left the closed-door meeting in the president's office with a deep scowl on his face. The president's top advisors flanked Avery, none of them speaking to him. He didn't bother speaking to them either. They were at odds, yet again. He shouldn't be surprised, their primary differences as people played a big part in their inability to come to any kind of workable agreement. Avery also suspected their disagreements really had more to do with personal agendas. If any of them had the heart of a true statesman, there wouldn't be such discord every time they met for these private advising sessions.

Why didn't the president speak directly to him? They were so in sync. They shared fundamental beliefs and both kept the American people's true interests at heart. As Avery let the thought linger, he also conceded the president needed outside opinions. Besides, Avery's strengths were sadly also his weaknesses. The people he tried to protect against government bureaucracy were the very people that set up daily pickets outside the vice presidential residence, damning him to hell for all eternity. The president needed a broad cabinet to help direct him, and Avery understood that, so he would just have to let what happened at these sessions roll off his back.

Janice stood off to the side. Her ever-present clipboard rested in her arms, along with a cordless phone ready in her hand. Avery concentrated on her, instead of the men surrounding him, and made a beeline to where she stood. He rarely liked whatever made her stand waiting for him, but in this case, he was certain he'd prefer whoever might be waiting on the phone to those senior cabinet members he was growing to hate.

"I have Kane waiting to speak with you," she said, handing Avery the phone. That confused him. Kane never interrupted his day, even when Avery begged him to do just that. Then Avery's eyes connected to Janice's as panic gripped his heart, and he brought the phone to his ear.

"They're fine, everyone's fine," Janice said, then mumbled something he didn't quite catch.

"Kane?" Avery asked, turning away from Janice. The phone's reception surprisingly held as he headed back to his office on the White House grounds. First, the irritation of the last hour, then the panic of the last thirty seconds, caused the beat of his heart to accelerate, and the constant indigestion that had plagued him since the day he took office made its presence known once again. Avery absently rubbed his belly, before sliding a hand across his heart. He'd left his packet of Rolaids at his desk. Dumb move since he lived on those things.

"Avery, why are you ignoring your physician?" Kane asked. Janice's hand appeared out of nowhere, producing his antacids. He snatched them from her and shot her a disapproving look. Why had she shared that with his overprotective husband?

"Babe," Avery said, lowering his voice as he passed a throng of interns heading the opposite direction down the long hall to his office.

"Do not babe me. I've scheduled you a doctor's appointment for this afternoon. They'll come to your office here. I'm having Janice cancel your weekly conference call with the secretary of state. You two don't discuss anything important anyway. "

"I'll see to it when I—" Avery started but Kane cut him off.

"When you get back from Asia? In ten days? No. And I'll be here with you this afternoon when you talk to the doctor. You shouldn't have kept this from me. I have half a mind not to go with you tomorrow. I can't believe you wouldn't handle something so important as your health, Avery Adams!"

Avery didn't say another word until he entered his office, closed the door, and lowered the internal blinds that faced Janice's office. He'd deal with her later. Once he was in the privacy of his office, he took the seat closest to the door and dropped down on the soft leather sofa, letting his head fall back as he closed his eyes.

"Don't be angry. I hate when you're mad at me. I honestly just kept forgetting," Avery said.

"I don't believe that's possible. Janice would have said something to you before she called me," Kane shot back.

"Honey, how can I possibly listen to everything she has to say? She's like an overbearing warden with her schedules and appointments." Avery loosened his tie and unbuttoned the top button of his dress shirt, waiting for the Rolaids to begin working.

"We're meeting here at your home office at two," Kane instructed, not giving Avery any sort of break.

"All right, that's fine. Now, tell me you love me," Avery coaxed, smiling as the pain in his chest began to ease.

"I love you, but stop being an ass where your health is concerned," Kane fired back.

"Was that an obscenity? Did you just use your first bad word with me?" Avery laughed. Kane always eased his stress, even as he heard the other end of the phone disconnect. He was slower to end the call, a smile on his face at the love he felt from Kane.

* * * *

"Heart disease isn't the death sentence it once was. With some lifestyle changes, new medication, and regular check-ups we're encouraged, even with your family history," Dr. Lee said, sitting across from Kane and Avery. All Avery's medical records and recent tests were spread out across the coffee table separating the two of them.

Kane felt adrift and scared, gripping on to Avery's hand like he held the only golden life preserver available on a sinking ship full of thieves.

"So this isn't just indigestion?" Kane asked, even though the doctor had just painstakingly answered that question in great detail.

"No, sir, but I don't believe surgery is needed at this time. That's very encouraging for a man of his age, with his family history." Kane looked over at Avery and mouthed the word *surgery.*

"This isn't a surprise to either of us, Kane. We knew the very real possibility was here," Avery said as though trying for reason.

"And clearly we should have been seeing a doctor regularly like I've asked you, over and over, for years!" Kane said, eyeing Avery before he turned to focus on the doctor. Kane released the hand-lock and leaned forward, speaking directly to the physician as if Avery weren't even in the room. "This won't be left to him any longer. I want to be involved in every step of his care from this day forward."

"Of course, as long as Mr. Vice President agrees," the physician acknowledged, gathering the paperwork and tests back into the file folder. Kane cut his gaze to Avery, who was still lounging back against the sofa like he didn't have a care in the world. Kane narrowed his brow, waiting the heartbeat or two until Avery answered.

"Of course," Avery said, grinning at Kane who immediately turned back to the physician.

"What kinds of medications does he need?" Kane asked.

"We'll begin with something to help lower his cholesterol and then a combination to help slow the progression of coronary artery disease. Mr. Vice President, we have a packet of information; it would be in your best interest to re-evaluate your diet and begin a fitness program," the doctor advised, looking over at Avery, but Kane situated himself directly in the man's line of vision to bring the doctor's focus back to him.

"I can have the kitchen prepare low-cholesterol, low-fat meals," Kane added, and Avery gave a groan. Kane just lifted his hand shushing his husband. The physician smiled, but Kane was all business. If Avery didn't take his health seriously, then Kane would have to do it for him. "And we have a workout facility here in the house. We can start that today," Kane stated.

"Good. It sounds like he's in good hands," the doctor said, rising. Avery's chart was tucked under his arm as handshakes were given.

"Thank you for taking the time to come here," Avery said.

"This is very common, and really no problem for me to come to you. I'll have the pharmacy deliver the prescriptions to you within the next few hours," Dr. Lee assured. Kane stayed silent as he shook the doctor's hand and watched as Avery opened his office door, ushering the man out. He tried to control his fear, not letting it turn into the rolling anger he felt sliding over his body.

"Now, that's taken care of..." Avery started as he closed the door, but Kane cut him off.

"No! You've known about this for a while, haven't you?" Kane accused, rounding on Avery.

"I've only had suspicions. I didn't know anything for certain," Avery defended himself.

"And you still put this off? Is that all I mean to you?" Kane's anger turned quickly to hurt. Avery was too young, they were both too young. If something happened to Avery... The thought was too much. Tears filled his vision, threatening to spill down his cheeks, so he turned away grinding the palms of his hands into his eyes. Avery was there at his side, turning him around, forcing his face up. Avery didn't allow him the moment he needed to gather himself, to rein in his overflowing concern.

"We're changing things up, Avery. You're starting a solid exercise program that you can take with you on the road, and your diet's changing completely. No more sweets. You have to trim up, get healthy. Promise me," Kane said, gripping onto Avery's upper arms. He didn't wait for answer. "I want to meet with your staff myself. And I want a family meeting the first chance Autumn and Robert have, and everyone *has* to get on board with this."

"Honey, I don't need to give up all sweets." For some reason Avery's words grated on Kane's last nerve and something snapped.

"Is that seriously your only response? Of course there are no sweets! No more fatty foods, Avery. You have to play a part in this. You're already to the point of needing medicine. Did you not hear him say surgery? That was his word. Surgery. So yes, you will give up all sweets." Kane tried to pull away, but Avery anchored an arm around him, drawing him closer.

"I love how concerned you are, I really do. But have I told you how deliciously sweet you look in this suit." Avery's lips were only inches from his as he spoke. "I don't want to give you up. Maybe you'll be enough of a sweet treat for me that I won't need the others. Now, kiss me before I have to go to my next meeting," Avery said as warm lips descended down on his. Kane wouldn't participate in the kiss. Instead, he held himself as stiff as a board, keeping his own lips pressed tightly together. No amount of Avery's persuasive tongue could get him to open up. Just as Kane's willpower began to waver, Janice knocked on the door and stuck her head inside.

"Ambassador Ezekwesili is on line one, and your translator is here to sit in on the call," she said. Avery gave a dejected sigh and Kane pulled away.

"Janice, his blood pressure is too high, and they're worried about his heart. He's having prescriptions delivered in the next hour. Make sure this hard-headed man takes the medicine immediately, or call me. I also have to schedule time with the kitchen, the sooner the better. His diet needs to be altered. We're heading to Asia tomorrow, and I need to get started on his menu. Avery's life is about to dramatically change." Kane tossed the last bit in for effect before he stepped out of Avery's office, not bothering to look back. Janice appeared as concerned about Avery's health status as Kane was, and she followed him out. How could Avery allow himself to get in this condition?

Chapter 29

"A treadmill in the bedroom? Seriously?" Avery tugged at the knot in his tie. They'd just arrived home from their ten day tour of Asia. He was exhausted, maybe a little irritable, and actually pretty damn hungry. On top of it all, Kane blatantly ignored his mood and continued putting out all those happy vibes when clearly he was indignant about every part of the health regime his mister forced on him.

"So you don't have to dress and go downstairs." Kane had the nerve to smile at him, after he thanked one of their staffers for bringing the piece of equipment up to their bedroom.

"I think it's so you can keep a better eye on me and you don't have to get dressed to go downstairs and make sure I'm working out." Avery lifted his hands in a very clear what the hell motion at his head of security who stood on call outside his bedroom door. The guy just shrugged and gave him an apologetic look. They would definitely be having a talk about this in the very near future.

"Avery, it's ten o'clock. You're exhausted, I'm exhausted. Can we talk about this later or preferably never again, because it's not leaving this room," Kane declared.

"I get a bedtime snack, Kane, and I want my snack! You're starving me to death." Avery sat on the end of the bed, staring at the newest piece of what he considered torture equipment that had been added to their bedroom, as Kane disappeared in his closet.

"You should have asked for a snack when we got in. It's really a little late to be eating now, honey. You've lost nine pounds, you only have seven more to go, so stay focused and get ready for bed," Kane yelled back. His eyes shot to the closet door as he finally pulled the knot free and stood. He dropped the silk tie on the dresser and unbuttoned his dress shirt as he stalked across the room to Kane's closet.

"I have a better idea since you're being a hard ass about it all. I'm in the mood for something more satisfying than carrots or an apple anyway." Avery bumped into Kane as he exited his closet, pulling a T-shirt over his head. His mister's nightly wardrobe always consisted of a soft cotton shirt and pajama bottoms, which he promptly removed before he crawled into their bed. Avery slid his hands up Kane's chest, keeping Kane from pulling the cotton material down the rest of the way, and leaned in, swiping his tongue across the exposed nipple.

"Avery," Kane began, but Avery wasn't interested in listening to anything else his husband had to say on the matter. He grabbed Kane's face between his palms and silenced him with a demanding kiss. Kane responded immediately, melting against him and returning the kiss with such ferocity that he swore he tasted the coppery tang of blood on his tongue. Kane had always been responsive to his advances and that always turned him on, but just knowing Kane still craved his touch after all these years made his dick twitch and swell painfully against the binding material of his trousers. Avery broke from the sweet taste of Kane's mouth long enough to draw the shirt up over Kane's head and toss it to the floor.

"You're still such an unbelievably good-looking man. I need you, Kane." Avery watched lust darken his husband's eyes.

"You sure changed your tune mighty fast." Kane's hands were busily tugging his dress shirt from his slacks. His knuckles accidently brushed against Avery's throbbing hard-on causing him to screw his eyes shut as an all-consuming need coursed through his veins. He couldn't help but let out a groan as those same knuckles skated up and down his length again; this time, no doubt, with deliberate intent. Kane knew exactly how to push his buttons and bring his body to life. In a matter of seconds, his husband managed to get him out of his shirt, undo his pants, had his slacks pushed partway down his thighs, and had a hand down the front of his silk boxers.

"Is this what you had in mind?" Kane's mouth settled on his, and that familiar warm hand curled around his cock, stroking him as he was pushed backward from the closet door and across their room. Oh, yeah, it was exactly what he had in mind. He wanted Kane to take control, tease him, suck him, stretch him, and then pound into his ass till neither of them could move. His needy ass clenched tight at the decadent thought.

"Oh, God... Fuck." His hips bucked forward into Kane's warm palm, seeking the friction. Kane complied and tightened his grip. Kane smiled against his lips. The man knew exactly what he was doing. Kane licked a trail along the seam of his lips, drawing him closer. He pressed their bodies firmly together as Kane's wet tongue dipped into his mouth. Avery instinctively opened wider, deepening the kiss. His tongue brushing and curling around Kane's as they fought for dominance. He moaned at the heat and pressure of Kane's body crowding against his, and he moved him across the large space. Avery tilted his head, finding a better angle, and submitted to the kiss, allowing Kane to devour his mouth.

God, he loved this man, always had. Avery's world had been tilted on its axis the day he laid eyes on Kane. His soul had found its other half; he'd been told 'when kindred souls meet, they were destined to be together, always.' And there was no doubt he'd met his kindred soul in Kane. He let his husband continue guiding him toward the bed, careful not to trip over the dress slacks that were now pooled around his ankles. The edge of the bed stopped his backward motion, and he finally took the time to rid himself of the annoying pants, kicking them across the floor. "Make love to me, Kane. I need you."

Without a word, Kane sank to his knees in front of him and dipped his head, swallowing his length in one smooth motion. The gesture forced the air from Avery's lungs. He sank his fingers in Kane's thick dark hair and thrust forward, driving himself deeper into the hot, wet tightness of Kane's throat. Avery watched, mesmerized, as Kane's head bobbed up and down on him, sucking then licking across his swollen tip before taking him deep into his throat, over and over again. Kane's blue eyes lifted to meet his and held him there with that intense gaze. Kane's large hand slid up the inside of his thigh and cupped his balls. His husband tugged his sac away from his body and rolled it gently in his palm as he sucked Avery's cock between his lips. Avery smiled at Kane and ran his fingers down along his open jaw.

"You're so beautiful like this." And he was, his blue eyes hooded with desire and his full lips stretched wide around him. Kane hummed around his sensitive dick and went back to work. The hot wet suction of Kane's mouth threatened to undo him. He rolled his hips, pushing deeper, and began to fuck his husband's face with vigor. Heaven. Yes, heaven, that was exactly how he would describe the draw of his lover's skilled mouth. He closed his eyes, Kane's mouth felt so good, too good, and now he was torn between pulling away or coming down the moist cavern of his throat.

Kane took the decision from him when he suddenly released the mind-numbing suction on Avery's cock and flattened his hand against his chest, pushing until he tumbled back onto the mattress, legs splayed wide. He heard the bottle hit the nightstand next to them and opened his eyes to see Kane coating his fingers and ridged cock with lubrication. Kane leaned down and took his mouth in a bruising kiss, he could taste himself on Kane's tongue as it was pushed between his lips and deep into his mouth. He greedily sucked him in, enjoying the mingling of the flavors melting across his own tongue. Kane's mouth was the only part of his partner's body touching him. And God, he loved that mouth, but he craved skin on skin. Avery cupped the back of Kane's head and tugged him forward begging for more of this man against him. Kane broke from the kiss and stood watching him, an evil glint in his eyes.

"On your stomach, babe." Kane urged him over, and before he could fully get his knees under him and his ass in the air, Kane sank a long slick finger into his channel. He clenched around the digit and pushed back against Kane's hand, seeking more. Another finger quickly joined the first, and he moaned at the feel of the thick fingers scissoring inside him. His lover withdrew his hand, and he whimpered at the loss.

"Kane, I want you in me now." He wiggled his ass, begging to be filled.

"Not just yet. I'm enjoying watching you squirm." Kane pushed three fingers back into him and slowly pumped them in and out of his entrance, twisting and dragging them against his prostate with each stroke.

"Jesus," Avery groaned and pushed his upper body off the mattress, forcing his weight back, and began fucking himself on those wicked digits.

"Now, Kane. Fuck me...now," he demanded and tried reaching behind him to stroke Kane's length, hoping to set them both on even ground, but his teasing husband kept what he was searching for just out of his reach. "Dammit, Kane, don't make me beg."

He swore he heard a low chuckle as a warm hand palmed his balls, then moved to his leaking cock, gripping and stroking in long tight pulls from root to tip.

"Kane, I'm gonna come if you don't stop."

"Isn't that the idea?" Kane growled and continued his delicious assault.

"Yes, but I need you buried inside me when I come. Please." He heard a strangled groan, and the maddening fingers pulled free from his ass, causing his entrance to clench hungrily, trying to draw them back in. Kane released his cock and gripped his hips, pulling them back and angling them against his body. The wet tip of Kane's length slid along his crevice, making him whimper, while the warmth of Kane's groin pressing tightly against his ass caused him to tremble with need.

"It's gonna feel so good to be inside you." Kane teased his ass with the thick head of his cock, then suddenly pushed into him, stretching him, filling him in one swift thrust. The slight burn in his ass still so sweet even after all this time. Kane began to move in and out of him, each thrust going deeper than the next. Avery dropped his chest to the mattress and gripped the sheets as his husband moved inside him. There were no words to describe the feeling overwhelming him. His nerves fired, sending electrical impulses shooting from the base of his spine and settling firmly in his groin every time his husband's length banged against his gland. Kane's fingers dug into his skin as he drove himself into Avery. Without a doubt, there would be bruises tomorrow, but the exquisite pain was exactly what he needed right this minute.

"Ahhh, babe, that's it." He panted, arching his back and fisting the linens tighter. His knuckles turned white as he held on while Kane pounded into his ass, driving him into the mattress with every powerful thrust.

"Yeah?" Kane grunted behind him and pulled out. A small sound escaped his lips as his lover flipped him to his back. "Need to watch your face when you come, babe." Kane panted and grabbed his leg, placing it over his broad shoulder before pressing himself back into his entrance and setting a relentless pace. The heady smell of sex filled

Avery's senses, and the sound of flesh slapping against flesh resonated throughout the room.

He moved his legs to wind them around Kane's waist, pulling him forward as he dug his fingers through the silky strands of his lover's hair, urging his head down for a kiss. Kane's mouth descended on his in a frenzy of teeth, lips, and tongue. Kane nipped and bit, licking into his mouth in a fevered exploration, sucking his tongue roughly then softly between his firm lips. Avery straightened his tongue and fucked Kane's puckered lips in the same rhythm their bodies collided with one another. The passion and need in the scorching kiss clawed at him, bowed his body tight.

Avery gripped his knees, pulling them back, opening himself wider for his lover as he slid in and out of his body. He writhed as Kane drove deep, plunging into him, banging against his spot with each thrust of his hips. "God, yes, Kane!" His vision blurred, he wasn't even sure he could form coherent words—fuck, he didn't even care. All he could concentrate on was the delicious pounding Kane was giving his prostate.

The spiral of heat continually building at the base of his spine burst free, traveling like molten lava through his body and churning heatedly in his balls, drawing them up tight, before exploding in thick creamy ribbons of warmth across his chest and stomach.

"Kane," he hissed, staring into his husband's eyes as he came. The name was uttered as the last bit of air left his lungs, driven out by the waves of pleasure seizing his body. Avery's ass clamped greedily around Kane and shuddered uncontrollably while his heart thundered loudly in his ears. He was lost in Kane's gaze, completely caught up in those blue orbs. The love and devotion he saw reflected in their depths embraced his soul. He had never felt closer to Kane than he did in this moment.

"Avery," Kane moaned, his mouth remained open, but no sound was made as the force of his driving rhythm faltered. Kane's dick twitched and jerked deep in his ass, liquid warmth flooded his insides, drawing a final shudder from him. His husband's frantic thrusts slowed and finally stilled before Kane collapsed against Avery's chest. Avery lay there, not moving, quietly willing his racing heart to settle.

Each beat echoed through his body as he tried to catch his breath. It took longer these days for the gripping pressure in his chest to calm and the tingling he felt in his fingers and arm to subside, but he'd never mentioned any of this to Kane. Knowing that information would worry

Kane even more, and his fretful husband would make him swear off sex. He'd given in to Kane's demands for the most part, but sex with Kane was something he wasn't willing to do without.

"Damn, I needed that," he professed, still out of breath and completely sated from their love making, and only faintly aware the pounding in his chest had ebbed.

"Me too," Kane said, staring down at him with a big grin plastered across his handsome face. Kane slipped free from his body and rolled partially to his side, kissing Avery's chest as he curled in against him.

"I love you more than life, Kane."

"I love you too, Avery. And I don't want to live without you, ever. I want us together always," Kane whispered, his head resting on Avery's chest, his arms tightening around Avery, drawing him closer as he spoke the words.

"Baby, I'm not going anywhere, I promise." Avery placed a kiss on Kane's damp hair.

"This is too much. I know I agreed to all of this and I'm proud of you, but Avery I don't want you to run for president. I know it's a long way off, but it's too much stress. I've been reading, stress is a leading precipitator of heart attacks and heart disease. Please let this be enough. We aren't young men any longer, we don't have a lot of time left on this planet, and you've forged ground no one thought you could, " Kane said, lifting his tear-filled gaze to Avery. "I've followed you for years, asking very little. Please let it end here."

Avery's heart lurched in his chest. Kane was his everything. One heartbeat passed, and then a second, before Kane's tears began to spill from his eyes and roll silently down his cheeks. He recognized what he thought might be uncertainty and apprehension in his husband. Kane started to pull away from him. Knowing his partner felt so much anguish over his position almost slayed him where he lay.

"No more. I promise this is it. We'll see this through and then we'll bow out," Avery reached for Kane, pulling him back reassuringly against his body.

"Thank you!" Kane's expression lit up, and he climbed back on top of Avery, placing random kisses all over his entire face. "Thank you!"

"All right, all right," Avery said and rolled Kane onto his back. There was a time they would have gone again, making sure Kane knew who the real boss was, but not so much anymore. Instead, he looked down at his smiling love. "But I believe I burned a few calories, so can I have my snack now, please?"

Chapter 30

2004 ~ Georgetown, Washington, DC

Avery sat in his usual place, directly across the kitchen table from Kane, the house phone stuck to his ear as he gave the occasional and unsure 'yes' while Autumn eagerly explained her new Christmas plans. The ones that differed from any other itinerary they had discussed before. This year's plans gave him pause as he stared at Kane, trying to figure out how his husband would feel about this latest development. Kane loved Christmastime with their family. He looked forward to the weeklong festivities leading up to the big day.

As if he already had a clue something was up, Kane kept his gaze glued to Avery, never rushing the conversation, but waiting for his turn to talk to their daughter. Autumn was in her final year of graduate school at Yale while Robert had chosen Duke, and they were both very busy and excited about their chosen careers.

"Dad, you tell Daddy for me. I have to go to class. I'm late," Autumn said hurriedly.

"Wait a minute. No way, you tell him," Avery immediately shot back, breaking his standard uh-huh response.

"I don't have time. Besides, he'll take it better from you," she said, but Avery wasn't buying any of that, he knew his husband too well. No way would he be stuck with the task of breaking Kane's heart.

"Kane, she has to go," Avery clicked the speaker phone on so Kane could hear her.

"Daddy! I love you! I'll call you tomorrow. I'm late for class," Autumn yelled into the phone, making sure she was heard. Then came her signature giant smack from the other end of the line—Autumn's kiss goodbye to both of them.

"I love you, too. Study for finals," Kane called out, but she had already ended the call and the phone went dead. Damn, she'd left Avery holding the bag! He hadn't been fast enough at seeing where her sneaky, middle of the day phone call was headed. He should have known that something was up when she sounded surprised they answered the phone, and then insisted on talking to him first.

"What was all that about?" Kane asked as Avery reached forward to click the phone off.

"Well, honey, it seems neither of our children can make time for us this Christmas break, but they both still plan to be here for Christmas day. They don't want us to be alone while unwrapping presents, can you imagine that? Anyway, Robert evidently has a mini-mester and Autumn is traveling to meet her current boyfriend's family before heading to New York City for New Year's with her friends. We'll apparently be the stop in the middle of her jaunt," Avery announced, watching Kane closely, worried about his reaction. Kane had dedicated his life to raising their children, and now it appeared they were back to just the two of them at home.

"She's like you, go, go, go," Kane said, picking up the empty sandwich plate taking up space in front of Avery on the table.

"I can call and ask them to come home," Avery started but Kane stopped him as he placed the dish in the sink.

"I think we should go to Aspen this year," Kane surprised him by saying. Avery watched him even closer as he turned on the faucet and washed the dish. Had he heard him right? He had been certain the holidays without the children would have depressed Kane.

"Why are you looking at me that way?"

Avery rose, trailing a finger around the center island as he walked toward Kane. He kept his gaze focused on his husband, trying to figure out why the man was okay with a change of plans this year. He wrapped his arms around Kane from behind and kissed his neck before he answered. "I've always wanted to go to Aspen for the holidays."

"I know. I think it's the perfect time," Kane stated, leaning his head back to look at Avery.

"What about the children?" Avery asked cautiously.

"They can come there for the day, just like they can come to Georgetown. They're twenty-four years old, they're moving on with their lives, and it's back to just us now. It's time for them to leave the nest. We have to let them jump. It seems they're past ready to spread their wings and fly," Kane said, shutting off the water and drying his hands before he turned in Avery's arms.

"So does this mean No-Clothes-Thursday can be added back to our weekly schedule?" Avery gave Kane a grin and waggled his brows.

"I'm old enough to collect Social Security, Avery, I don't think anyone wants to see me naked," Kane replied, leaning in to give Avery a small kiss before pulling away. Avery wasn't having any of that. They were going to have the house to themselves again. Kane was settled with their children creating their own lives away from home, so Avery found this the perfect moment to reinforce how much he loved his husband. Because Kane was very wrong, his need for this man had never faded, it had only grown stronger over the years.

"Whatever! You're the hottest, silver-haired fox around. I want you naked all the time." Avery tugged Kane back against him and slid his hands underneath Kane's shirt. "Actually, why wait till Thursday, I want you naked right now…"

"Baby, you have to get ready for your speech tomorrow…" Kane began, but Avery cut him off by tugging his shirt over his head.

"And you have to lead a Bible study class in two hours. We need to get started so you aren't late." Avery captured Kane's lips with his and pushed his man backward through their home, to the bedroom, where he purposefully left the door open.

Chapter 31

Present Day

The waiting was the absolute worst. For Kane, the minutes ticked by incredibly slowly. The hospital staff stayed vigilant to his needs, as did Autumn, who'd sat in the same chair by the waiting room window, holding his hand, for the last few hours. Autumn worked hard to keep Kane talking, never letting the crazy, scary thoughts of Avery's surgery take too much root in his mind. She helped, even though he never stopped the ongoing prayer running through his head. *God, please keep Avery safe and here with me. Please.*

"Daddy, I was thinking of redecorating my living room. I like the fall colors this year. I think I could live with those for a few years. What do you think?" Autumn asked, drawing his attention back to her.

"I think you should have gone into interior design instead of law," Kane said, patting her hand with his own.

"Probably, but I wouldn't have gotten to work with Dad had I done that," she said and cut her anxious eyes up to Kane's. The entire afternoon she had concentrated on keeping the topics of conversation flowing and not centered just on Avery. She was perfect that way. It was also why she had made such an amazing assistant district attorney. Avery had been proud of that accomplishment.

"It's okay, baby. I wish they would give us an update. I don't know why this is taking so long," Kane said, and as if on cue, the waiting room door opened. Like so many other times today, Kane steeled his heart, bucked up his spine, and prayed there were positive, smiling physicians there, not the hospital aides coming to check on them again.

He got one part right.

A team of doctors came through the door still dressed in scrubs from head to toe. Each entered, holding the door for the one behind them. Robert was nowhere to be seen. Autumn stood first, and Kane rose at a slower pace, his eyes staying trained on the doctors. They wouldn't make eye contact with either of them. What did that mean? Kane's breath hitched, he tripped, stumbling when he tried to get to his feet. Robert had been the last physician to enter the waiting room. He was tugging the cap off his head when his red-rimmed eyes connected with Kane's.

Kane stopped. He held his breath as everything around him stilled as if he were standing alone in the middle of the waiting room instead of surrounded by people. Everything he never wanted to hear, never wanted to know, was held in his son's gaze.

"Daddy, I'm so sorry. They did everything they could. He didn't make…" Robert started, but his voice broke, unable to say the last few words. The weight of Robert's unspoken words registered in his mind, crushing him. Avery. Oh, God, his Avery…gone.

Surprisingly, his legs held him upright. Although, he wasn't sure how long that would last. Instinctively, his hands went to his face, covering the flow of tears that erupted as his heart dropped from his chest and shattered into a thousand little pieces on the beige and honey-limestone floor of the waiting room. Pieces that Avery had held together, pieces that could never be put back right, pieces that would remain lost forever.

No, this wasn't real! This couldn't be happening. They had so much planned, so many dreams still ahead of them. No…No! Kane could see the doctors and his family advancing on him. Could see their mouths moving, but no sounds penetrated his ears. Silence. Deafening silence consumed him. He became dizzy, confused, and he stepped back a step or two, needing air. He reached behind him, feeling for a chair. He needed something to steady himself, because he was sitting down, even if that meant on the cold hard hospital floor. Hard plastic met his hand, and he dropped into the seat, lowering his head between his legs as he gasped for breath. He couldn't pull enough air into his lungs. Did he even want to? He'd lost his everything; he'd lost his reason to live.

He'd lost Avery.

"Daddy, I'm so sorry," Autumn said. He could hear the tears in her voice and accepted the hand trying to grip his. She was on her knees beside him, her tear-filled eyes searching his. Those were Avery's eyes, Autumn had Avery's eyes. He reached out, drawing her into his embrace.

Take care of our family... Avery's last words to him echoed in his head.

He looked up to see Robert standing close by, his hands clasping his and Autumn's shoulders. The three of them were now alone in the waiting room, everyone else had vanished at some point after the news had been given. Kane lifted an arm and pulled Robert down into the hug he shared with Autumn. The hold was intense, heartening, needed, and they stayed like that for several long minutes, not moving, just existing. Robert was the first to break from the hold. He left only to immediately reappear, tissues in hand.

Autumn remained tucked under his arm, holding him tightly. Tears poured from her eyes, streaking down her cheeks, but her sole focus was on him. She seemed more concerned about his welfare than hers.

"Was he in any pain?" Kane asked and took a small drink from the water bottle Robert insisted he hold.

"No, sir," Robert said. Kane nodded through the tears.

"Good. I wouldn't want him in pain." Kane wiped at the tears that blurred his vision even as more tissues were shoved into his hand. "Has anyone called Kennedy?"

"No, sir. I was waiting on you first," Robert answered, finally standing, but keeping Kane in a tight embrace against his side.

"Okay, I'll call her, or go to her house. I don't know." Kane knew he sounded confused. He was so lost he didn't know what to do or who to call, everything seemed to be imploding at once. The door to the waiting room opened again, and Avery's nurse stood there, solemn-faced. Kane could see she'd been crying.

"They've cleared the area. It's safe to leave, whenever you're ready," she said. Kane wasn't sure he could do this. Avery had been his lifeline, his world, and now he was left to deal with the aftermath—the press, the questions, their children—alone. He would go back to their house, to the life he and Avery built together…alone.

"Thank you, Doris. Daddy, come on," Robert urged, helping Kane up. The three of them walked the long hall, arm in arm. As they made their way out, the hospital staff slowly and quietly aligned themselves along the hall, nodding, with their eyes downcast, as they passed by. Everyone seemed to feel his loss; he could see the reverence in their stance as he walked past the staff. Avery was such a good man and had spent so much time in this very hospital where Robert worked as a cardiothoracic surgeon and Sophia was now the chief of staff. Avery had been so proud of his son. He'd been so proud of both of their children.

His soul mate had left him, Avery was gone.

Chapter 32

Everything blurred the days following Avery's passing. Their home in Georgetown filled with mourners and well-wishers before they even had a chance to make it home from the hospital. Avery had been well-loved and highly-respected by most everyone he came in contact with.

Kane had moved Kennedy straight to his house. She was ninety-six years old, and still a little spitfire of a woman. She ran his home, orchestrating the hundreds and hundreds of visitors stopping by the house each day. For Kane, she was a godsend because she freed him of those responsibilities. He rarely participated in anything going on inside his home since the loss of his husband, instead tucking himself away in his and Avery's bedroom, sitting in Avery's things, as he tried to come to terms with what life was going to be like without his Avery there every single day.

Through executive order, Avery received a state funeral with every bit of pomp and circumstance offered to his political rank. United States flags were immediately ordered to half-staff and a national day of mourning was called. Military personnel were assigned to remain by Kane's side until the funeral actually took place. He paid no attention to any of it, instead staying inside himself, working only to keep his tears at bay. He was rarely successful.

Kane allowed all funeral protocol to take place as mandated. The only part he refused to allow others to handle was the flower selection for the casket. He chose those arrangements with care, making sure they represented the man beneath them.

He instructed Autumn to participate in handling the weeklong schedule of events. He learned keeping Kennedy and his children busy allowed him time to sit uninterrupted beside Avery inside the funeral home. He only left when the funeral home closed for the night, and returned early the next morning.

Kane remained beside the casket even as they shut Avery inside to prepare to take him for the twenty-four hour lying in state vigil. Kane broke protocol for the event and stationed himself beside the casket as thousands and thousands of people filled the capitol rotunda and walked by to pay their final respects. This was where he belonged, where he had always been, where Avery wanted him to be, right there by Avery's side.

"Daddy, you have to get some sleep for tomorrow," Autumn said, coming to kneel down in front him. Kane had no idea of the time, but he was surprised to see her. He looked around to find the room quiet. The only people remaining were the honor guards standing watch over Avery's casket.

"You look so much like your father at this age. You've got that same determined set in your eyes. He was just a little older than you when I met him," Kane said, patting her hands that were folded across his knee.

"We need you to come home and sleep for a few hours before the funeral tomorrow," Robert said, and Kane looked up, startled. He hadn't seen Robert there.

"I've arranged to stay here tonight. You two go home and get some rest. You've done a good job for your dad. He'd be so proud of you. When they take him to get ready for the processional, I'll go home and get cleaned up, but I want to stay here tonight." He patted Autumn's hand before placing his palm back on Avery's casket where it had been most of the day.

"Daddy, before you got to the hospital, he made me promise we'd take care of you. You aren't a young man anymore. You can't do these things," Autumn started, but Kane stopped her.

"This is my last night with Avery. I'm not leaving him." Kane tried to be as stern and forceful as he could, but he thought he may have fallen short when Autumn shook her head and started to speak again. Robert placed a hand on her shoulder, effectively stopping her.

"I'll stay here with him. You go home and stay with Nonnie. I'll get him home as soon as I can," Robert said. Kane began to argue, but watched as Autumn started to stand and decided to let it go. Robert could stay if he wanted.

"Do you have a ride home?" Kane asked, reaching for his wallet to give her cab fare.

"They have cars for us. Daddy, there's a car out there for you and Robert. When you get tired, please come home." There were tears forming in her eyes, and seeing them tugged at him. He didn't want her to worry, but he couldn't leave Avery. Not yet. Tomorrow night, he'd deal with remaining in a life without Avery, but he didn't have to do that today. After a moment, he rose, handing her the tissue he'd worried in his hands for several hours and gave her a tight hug.

"I'm okay, baby. Just give me this," he whispered into her ear, hoping to ease some of her concern. "After tonight, it's all over. Just give me this last night." Autumn nodded against his shoulder, letting out a small sob as she hugged him tighter. "Robert, please take her to the car."

Kane released his sobbing daughter to his now crying son. All he wanted to do was continue sitting here just being with Avery. Robert did what he'd asked and came back, giving Kane room to do what he needed, where Autumn would have crowded him in her desire to make things better.

The guard in charge provided Robert a place to sit, where he could wait with Kane until the honor guard came to escort the casket to the funeral procession. When the military pallbearers arrived the next morning to execute their duties, they were denied at the door by the guard.

"Sir, they're here to take Mr. Vice President. I'm clearing out the room to give you a moment alone. They won't wait long," a younger sounding guard said. Kane never saw him. The man spoke from behind Kane's back, and then immediately turned and left the room again, drawing the doors closed behind him with a soft click. Kane stared at the casket. This was it, his last time with Avery. He stood; his tired gritty eyes roamed the top of the closed mahogany box. He wished he had one last look at Avery before they took him away. Kane placed both hands on top of the coffin, his eyes filled with tears. Tears that just wouldn't stop flowing.

He leaned in, placing his forehead close to where he thought Avery's would be, and he softly whispered, hoping Avery could hear his words, "I have to leave you now. I know you would fight this, but you have to do this part alone. They have so much planned to honor you today. It's exactly the way you would have wanted it. It's what you deserve..." Kane closed his eyes tighter, saying goodbye to Avery was the hardest thing he'd ever had to do. He took a deep breath, trying to get through everything he wanted to say. "I love you, Avery. Always. You completed my life. You made me whole, gave me hope, made me a better man. For me, you were everything right in my life. And I know you're in heaven smiling down on us. You're too good a man to be kept out because of me. I know you have to be one of God's special angels. I know you're there, and I'm happy for you. I just miss you so much already. I'm trying to pull myself together here, but I'm failing, and I'm sorry. I'm just lost without you."

"Daddy, they need to take the casket." Robert's voice came from somewhere behind him.

"I love you, baby. Forever and always." Kane pressed his lips against the top of the casket, his tears falling freely on the polished mahogany box. This was it, they were taking Avery. It felt so wrong to leave his side, so final. How would he find the strength to go on without him? Kane kissed the coffin again before he forced himself away. Robert materialized beside him, handing him a handkerchief—one of Avery's—and he cried a little harder when the scent of his favorite cologne wafted from the soft fabric. Kane stood, watching the guards, Robert's arm wrapped around his shoulders, holding him up, as Avery was taken from the room. Kane followed closely behind the casket, waiting until they loaded Avery inside the hearse to transport him to the funeral events of the day.

Chapter 33

One week later

"Kane honey, you have to eat. I've told the children you're eating more and bathing. Please don't make a liar out of me," Kennedy said from her perch at Kane's kitchen table. He'd only come out of his room for a glass of water and a couple of Advil. He honestly didn't even know what time it was, a little surprised to still see daylight through the open curtains.

At the sound of her voice, Kane looked down at his clothing, relieved he wore his robe. He closed the lapels, tightened the sash, and he ran his fingers through his messy, dirty hair. He'd have thought she would have gone home by now. Kane grabbed the bottle of Advil, shook the last two pills into the palm of his hand, and reached for a bottle of water from his refrigerator. They were all gone.

Avery needs more water bottles, he thought to himself, before the realization of Avery's absence slashed across his heart on a level he'd never experienced before this last week, yet was growing painfully accustomed too. He'd had this same experience about nine hundred times a day since Avery's funeral. It was interesting how much anguish the heart could take and still continue to beat.

As the days since the funeral passed, and the house became depleted and unkempt, Kane naturally thought of how Avery would feel with his favorite soft terry bath towels still dirty from the morning he'd last used them, or how his toothpaste cap still lay discarded at the sink. Kane hadn't allowed housekeeping inside their bedroom; there were so many things Avery would have balked at after all this time.

Now, as he stared at the empty refrigerator, he thought about how Avery had been a complete water snob. He'd only drink a certain brand of water, and Kane had gone out of his way to keep the house stocked to encourage Avery to drink more. That brought tears to his eyes, ones he successfully fought as he turned away, settling on a glass of water from the sink.

He swallowed the pills down, dumping the rest of the water into the sink, and reminded himself all this was normal, no matter how bad he felt. Avery had occupied his head, heart, and soul for the last forty years. Of course he would continue on like this, probably until the day he died, and just like every time he thought that way, he said a small prayer wishing that day would come sooner rather than later.

The doorbell broke into his thoughts, making him aware Kennedy still chatted away behind him. He hadn't heard a word she'd said. Actually, he'd completely forgotten she was in the kitchen. Kane turned away, not interested in trying to catch up with her conversation as the doorbell chimed again insistently. He tightened the sash at his waist, ran his fingers through his hair again, then headed for the front of the house. He opened the door just as the delivery driver turned away to retreat back down the steps. The young kid waved a good-bye and hopped back in his van. A bouquet of calla lilies sat at Kane's feet. A smile tugged at his lips. His favorite flower—and these were tipped in the lightest of pink. They were beautiful.

Kane picked up the vase and brought the flowers to his nose, breathing them in. Most people said calla lilies had no fragrance. He always disagreed, picking up the faintest of clean, sweet, floral scents. Pain slashed again across his heart as he recalled sending a similar bouquet to Avery after his first dinner at La Bella Luna. The tears started to roll down his cheeks as he looked closer at the blooms. There was no way whoever sent them could have known this arrangement was his favorite or that it had been the one he'd chosen to use when he'd apologized to Avery all those years ago. The pain of Avery's loss rolled through him again, becoming too much. He closed the front door behind him and set the flowers on the nearest end table, grabbing a tissue from the box beside them. It was then he noticed a notecard hidden among the flowers, having missed it amid the beautiful blooms.

"*Kane*" was scribbled across the front of the envelope—in Avery's handwriting. His heart stopped in his chest, and his hands shook as he opened the card.

My love,

If you're reading this, that means I'm no longer there with you and that worries me more than you know. The idea of leaving you is almost more than I can bear, so I'm going to leave that thought right there and move on to more important things.

I've told you so many times how much I love you. Please remember that every single day for the rest of your life. You are my everything, you hold my heart and carry my soul. You made my life better. My only regret was not meeting you sooner, so we could have had more time together in this life.

Please make sure Autumn and Robert have what they need. I've taken care of them financially, but I'm sure you know that by now. Let them know how much I love and cherish them, how much I love our family, and how proud I am of who they've become as people. Please look in on my mother. She won't allow you to take care of her, but please visit her often. I love her very much, too.

These flowers will keep coming so you know how much I truly love you. I tried to come close to the ones you sent me all those years ago. I'm not sure if you even remember them, but I do. What a special memory that has been. And what a beautiful life I had the honor of sharing with you.

I know I'm waiting for you. Take your time, do what you need to do there, but I know I'm wherever I'm supposed to be, waiting for you to walk beside me again for all eternity. You are my soul, my always. Never doubt that for a single moment.

I'm crying, Kane, and I haven't even left you yet. I'm not afraid to die, but I am afraid of leaving you.

I'll be waiting.

I love you always,

A

Kane read and re-read the note before he stared disbelievingly at the paper in his hand.

"Son, what is it?" Kennedy said from behind him. It took a minute, but he handed her the note, his eyes focused on her face as she read each word. He recognized the minute she read Avery's words to her. The poised, always together matriarch of the family began to cry. When she was finished reading, she turned away, hiding herself as she handed the note back to Kane.

"Thank you for staying so long, Kennedy, but I think you should go home now," Kane said, gathering the flowers and holding Avery's note tight against his chest.

"I believe I should too," Kennedy said. Her voice broke as she walked away from him, back into the kitchen. "He loved you, Kane. You can never doubt that, but you have to find a way to go on, Son. Avery wouldn't like seeing you like this."

She was right. Avery would hate to see him this way, but he couldn't seem to find a way to move on. He didn't respond to her. Instead, he went back into his bedroom, shutting and locking the door behind him. He placed the bouquet on his nightstand and kept the note in his hand, reading the words over and over again.

Chapter 34

Seven weeks later

Kane sat on his back porch, listening to the birds chirp and letting the cool spring breeze blow across his skin, ruffling his hair. He tightened the sweater around his chest. Avery's latest bouquet had arrived this morning, about the same time Autumn had come to check on him. She called the unexpected visit 'time alone' with her father, but Kane knew her true motivation. These unannounced visits were growing in frequency, and the frowns were more pronounced each time the children stopped by. Kane tried to care, tried to ease their worry, but apparently no matter what he said or did, they had their own thoughts and nothing seemed to make them feel any better once they'd arrived.

"Daddy, come eat," Autumn called from the kitchen. Kane was slow to respond, apparently slower than she liked, and she stuck her head out the back door. "Would you rather eat out here on the patio?"

"Baby, I'm not hungry. I told you I wasn't hungry," he said, not bothering to move from his seat.

"Daddy, you're losing too much weight. You have to try to eat," she reprimanded, then disappeared back inside. Kane went back to biting at his thumbnail, watching the birds play at one of the birdfeeders in the yard.

"Daddy, you have to eat more. Your refrigerator's completely full of food. None of the dinners being sent over here are being touched, so that means you aren't eating. You're going to make yourself sick. Here's your favorite. Potato soup and a Havarti with turkey sandwich. Come eat," she said, placing a tray on the patio table close to him. Her eyes now pleaded with him to move to the table. She was right. He needed to eat more. He needed to do a lot of things more, but what he really wanted was for her to go, so he could make his daily trip to Avery's gravesite and then tuck himself away for the night with Avery's latest note. It had been eight weeks since Avery death, and he had seven bouquets and two handwritten notes from Avery. God, he missed that man more than he could bear. Tears sprang to his eyes.

For nothing more than to hide them, he rose and made his way across the patio to the table and focused on the food. His stomach turned at the sight, making him feel weak, but he hid that too. Instead, he reached for the water bottle on the tray. "Thank you, honey."

"You're welcome." She kissed his cheek as he swallowed the water. "Please eat it all. I talked to your pastor this morning. He says he hasn't seen you in church since Dad died. He's tried to come over, but you aren't home, or you're not answering the door." Kane didn't respond as he reached for the mustard, spreading it across the bread. Everything she said was true, so there was no point in denying it. Under her close inspection, he held his stomach and took a bite of the soup.

"Thank you, Daddy," she said, kneeling beside him and kissing his cheek again as he forced the warm soup down. Autumn could be blunt and straightforward one second, tender and sweet the next. She was so much like Avery in that way. The thought touched his heart and brought a beloved memory forward.

"I remember when your dad and I found out we were going to be parents. Avery was so sure we were having a little girl he started a betting pool with the physician's staff. Everyone had their money on us having a boy, but not your dad. 'His little princess', that's how he referred to you from the very beginning. Of course Avery had been right, but so had everyone else; none of that mattered to your dad. You should have seen him gloating in the doctor's office that day. Your dad always did like being right, probably about as much as he loved getting his way."

Kane smiled as he recalled the joy in his heart, and the triumphant gleam on Avery's face, the day their doctor announced they were going to be parents of not only a boy, but also a baby girl. Kane softly brushed a loose strand of blonde hair from Autumn's forehead. "I hope you know how proud I am of you, how proud you made us as parents and what joy it's given me to watch you grow into a remarkable woman. I couldn't have asked for anything more. You and your brother are such blessings. You helped make my life complete. I love you, Autumn." Kane spoke slowly, trying to calm his quivering voice and give his words meaning as he reached out and took her hand.

"Daddy, I love you, too, but I need you to start taking better care of yourself. You don't look good." Autumn's eyes stayed trained on his as she spoke. He saw her concern, and the pain he caused her, but he didn't know how to reassure her everything would be okay.

"I need to call Robert. I'll be back." She stood abruptly and left him sitting there while she walked down off the back porch and sat on the bottom step. He sat quietly, staring down at the food, thinking about how many times he and Avery had eaten their lunch in this very spot. This was their favorite time of year. The flowers were just beginning to bloom and Avery had made sure their backyard was packed with every type of flower he could find.

The strategically placed bird feeders kept their backyard buzzing with hummingbirds, blue jays, and cardinals all springtime long. How could someplace that had given him such peace just months ago cause him so much pain now? The tears he'd been fighting sprang free, and he lowered his head to his hands, scrubbing his face, angry he wasn't able to pull himself together better than this.

"Robert, he's *not* good. You're not listening to me. He needs help. I don't think it's a good idea he stay here. He has to have lost another five pounds just since you've been here," Autumn said, her conversation filtering over to him.

He apparently hadn't hidden his emotions or himself as well as he'd hoped. This wasn't good. Kane pushed back in the chair and picked up the tray to take it into the kitchen. He had no desire to stick around and hear anything else she had to say about how bad he looked or how little he was participating in life. He'd been subjected to that same refrain for weeks now. Instead, he placed the tray on the counter, and took the keys to Avery's car off the key rack by the back door. He left Autumn there at his house without a second thought and drove straight to Avery's grave.

The bench he'd had installed waited for him, just like every day. He spent the next six hours there, talking to Avery, telling him all his thoughts until the darkness of night forced him away.

Chapter 35

Four weeks later

"Mr. Adams, you aren't taking care of yourself," Dr. Connors said, dropping his stethoscope back into his bag. He was young, fresh, and one of Robert's friends who was willing to make house calls. Kane let out a cough that hurt badly as it racked throughout his body. The doctor pulled out a syringe, filled the barrel with an unknown substance, and lifted Kane's arm to give him a shot. "You should be in the hospital, sir."

"I want to stay here," Kane said, his throat raw and his voice gravelly. He let out another long bark. By the time this coughing fit was through, Autumn sat on the other side of the bed, up on her knees, crying. Robert was beside her, the same concern etched across his face.

"You keep saying that, sir, but you're not doing what needs to be done to get you well."

"Daddy, please," Autumn said. When Kane shook his head no, Autumn grew visibly angry. "You have to. There isn't a choice anymore. You're wasting away! We have to stop these flowers from coming, and you need medical help and counseling, Daddy. This isn't right. I can't take care of you if you don't take care of yourself!"

"Autumn…" Robert started as Dr. Connors took his bag and quietly left the room. Kane felt like Dr. Connors probably supported his daughter's thoughts on his care, and Robert, most certainly, thought she was correct, and if he were honest, she wasn't wrong, but he wasn't leaving this house.

"No, I can't take this Robert. He's killing himself, and it's happening right in front of us," she ranted. Her tears were full-blown now, and she hovered right over him. He started to speak, planning to tell her he would be fine, but another round of coughing gripped him, stealing the breath from his body.

Thank God Robert stepped in, dragging Autumn from the room, talking to her as he pushed her out the door, closing it behind her before returning to Kane's bedside. This time the coughs were longer to get through and exhausted Kane. He could feel the medicine taking hold as he lay back, trying to catch his breath, reaching for the oxygen mask laying on the nightstand. Robert took over, helping Kane adjust his position.

"Daddy… Here," Robert said, his tone soothing as he helped him lie down on his back, placing the mask over his nose and mouth. "You aren't taking care of yourself, and you're stopping us from taking care of you. Dad would hate this. We're failing him because you won't let us help you."

Kane shook his head again, carefully breathing in the oxygen. The medicine the doctor had given him was putting him to sleep, and he welcomed the oblivion. Sleep meant Avery would visit him. He'd been visiting more and more in Kane's dreams. He closed his eyes, breathing in as deeply as he could and slowly fell asleep.

* * * *

"This isn't right, Robert!" Autumn said, rounding on him as he came into the living room. Her arms were crossed over her chest. The tears were there, but anger was the most dominant emotion pouring off her at the moment.

"He's lost his will to live, Autumn. Medicine can only do so much." Robert scrubbed his hands down his face as he came to stand in front of her. Dr. Connors was there too, waiting to be told the plan of care. Clearly, he was on Autumn's side, ready to transport Kane into the hospital tonight. And hell, he completely agreed, but the little boy inside him struggled with the man he'd become. In the end, his father's wishes won out over his common sense.

"Screw that, Robert! You know better than that," Autumn yelled at him. Dr. Connors came for Autumn, wrapping an arm around her, and Robert narrowed his brow at the familiarity. Were they a couple? When had they started dating? Shit, maybe he wasn't paying enough attention to his family if he didn't know something like this.

"Robert, it would be in your father's best interest to move him as soon as possible. He's not well, you have to know that," Dr. Connors told him. Autumn stayed tucked in his arms, her gaze begging him to do the right thing—at least as she saw it—but he also knew his father's current condition had very little to do with bronchitis. He just couldn't figure out how to make his father want to live again.

"I'd like to give it a few more days. We have registered nurses here with him around the clock. I want to try to get him well, and then move him into some serious inpatient counseling—" Robert started, but Autumn cut him off.

"We're past that point, Robert. He's past that. He's lost thirty pounds in three months. He's sicker than he's been in his entire life, and I want these stupid flowers to stop coming! What was Dad thinking? We should even move him out of this house. He has to live, Robert. Dad made me promise to take care of him." Autumn was frantic, more so than he'd ever seen her before. In his silence, she grew angrier, picking up last week's bouquet and tossing it across the room before she flung herself out of the house in a disgusted rage. That left Robert and Dr. Connors staring at the door she'd just stormed out of. It took a second, but his friend took off after her. Robert let them go, and he stayed right where he was, trying to come up with anything to help this situation and make everyone happy.

When nothing came to mind, he decided to clear his schedule and stay with his father for the next few days. Which meant he wouldn't be working. Not work? That almost sent a panic through him. He hadn't ever taken a vacation before, but he didn't take time to think about it as he promptly called his office to leave instructions for them to rearrange his schedule until further notice.

* * * *

Carrying a tray of soup, Robert rounded the corner, heading back to his father's bedroom. He was in day three of his overnight stay, and he was absolutely certain he hadn't made any difference in his father's mindset at all by being here. His father was still sick, lethargic, and becoming unresponsive. In Robert's best estimation, he was certain the last two had nothing to do with his illness.

"I have chicken broth for you," Robert said, managing to open the door while holding the tray. "Priscilla, I've got this," he said, looking at the nurse sitting by Kane's bed. She nodded, quietly excusing herself.

"Here we go," he said, putting the tray over his father's lap. He learned early on not to give his father an option. Instead, he scooted the chair up to the side of the bed and started spoon feeding the soup to his mouth. Like normal, his father took a bite or two willingly, then maybe another one unwillingly before rejecting anything more.

"Daddy, I'm concerned about you. You can't go on like this," Robert said, putting the spoon down, and wiped Kane's mouth. His father didn't reply.

"You're wasting away. You have to make the decision to live, because at this rate, I'm very worried for you. I can't see how you're going to last much longer." His throat clogged as he said the words. He moved the tray and lifted his frail father, adjusting the pillows behind his back.

"I've always been so proud of you," Kane said in a labored, gravelly voice, looking up at Robert as he shoved another pillow behind him. For the first time in months, his father's blue eyes didn't look hollow, and that gave Robert hope. "You were protecting your sister in the womb. We didn't know she was there until we got one of those fancy ultrasounds."

"I love my family. I love you. I've wanted you to be proud of me," Robert said, bringing the blanket up, tucking it tightly around Kane.

"I never knew if we were really doing right by you and your sister. I tried to make up for things you might be missing. I'm glad Sophia stayed in your life. You followed in her footsteps," Kane managed, only coughing once or twice as he spoke.

"I have no complaints about my life, Daddy. I had a great childhood. I was lucky," Robert declared. He paused in taking the conversation back to his father's current health. This was more discussion than they had had in a long time. Maybe his father had made a turn, perhaps the memories of something other than Avery would help him, spur him back into the world of the living. Robert took Kane's hand out of the blanket, holding it tightly until he linked their fingers together.

"Is Dr. Connors seeing Autumn?" Kane asked. That made Robert smile. His father seemed so lifeless, but he had picked up on that even when Robert had completely missed the subtle signs.

"Seems that way." Robert chuckled. "He's a good man. I like him."

"What about you? Who are you seeing?" Kane questioned. The talking was getting to him, and he had a solid fit of coughing, gasping for breath between each spasm. Robert gave Kane several sips of water and rubbed his back until he settled down. When he was done, Kane looked at Robert expectantly and it took a second to remember his question.

"No one. I'm not seeing anyone," Robert said, sitting back on the chair, still holding Kane's hand. Having two gay fathers had made his own coming out incredibly easy. His grip tightened when he considered how accepted he'd always been in his life compared to many of his gay friends who still struggled to this day.

"There are lots of single professional men in this town, Son," Kane started, his voice raspy and low.

"I know, Daddy. I'm not settling for just anyone, not until I find what you and Dad had," Robert said, stopping himself as sadness crossed his father's face. His eyes returned to that hollow look again. Damn, why had he said that?

"Robert, take me to Avery's grave, I have to go," Kane pleaded, his eyes searching Robert's face.

"I don't think that's a good idea," Robert said, shaking his head. "It's cold outside. You're sick…"

"Please, Son. I haven't been," Kane asked again and began to cough. "Please, I feel him there."

Robert stared at his father's pleading gaze. He was a shell of a man, lying listless and frail. It wasn't a good idea to consider taking him outside. Robert searched his brain, trying to come up with a viable reason to say no, or at least one his father would agree to. Nothing came to mind.

"We're taking a wheelchair. I want you bundled up, and you promise, if I take you, you will take your medicine and turn this around for us. Promise me, Daddy. We can't keep watching you wither away to nothing. You have to stop this." Robert pulled the covers back, helping Kane to the side of the bed. "Promise me."

Kane nodded his head, taking short shallow breaths. He was weak and much smaller than Robert had realized as he helped place each of his father's feet on to the floor. In that moment, Robert knew he was going to have to go against Kane's wishes. Autumn was right, he needed intensive, constant care. Nothing had changed, nothing had gotten better with Robert staying here. His father deteriorated with each second that passed by. He had to stop thinking emotionally, and take care of his father like he was any other patient at the hospital.

He would let Kane stop by the gravesite one last time, and then he would take him to the hospital. He'd stalled long enough.

"Stay here, I'm getting your house shoes and some warmer pants." Kane nodded, and Robert saw it took everything inside his father just to stay upright. Dammit, why had he let this get so far out of hand? Robert rummaged through Kane's things, grabbing a pair of sweats, house shoes, and a coat. He called the nurse to prepare the wheelchair. He dressed Kane as the chair was wheeled in.

It took quite a bit of time to load Kane, first from the bed to the chair, and then the chair to the car. Robert had to reach over and strap his father in with the seat belt. Kane was exhausted and winded just getting himself inside the car. Robert fought his need to drive straight to the hospital, but he wanted to honor this last wish before getting his father the help he needed. The ride to the cemetery was quick, but Kane seemed to weaken by the minute.

Robert pulled the car as close as he could to his dad's grave. He put it in park, got out, then pulled the wheelchair from the trunk. He hoisted his father into the chair because he was too weak to lift himself. His father's eyes focused on Avery's tombstone, and nothing more seemed to exist for him.

"Daddy, we aren't staying long," Robert said as he began to wheel Kane forward. Kane's only response was more coughing. Robert parked Kane close to the headstone, locked the wheels in place, and made sure Kane was completely covered before he left him to go back to the car to make plans with the hospital for Kane's arrival. He paced beside the car, making phone calls, keeping a watchful eye on Kane. He'd give him fifteen minutes, and then they were gone. After he set all the wheels in motion, his last phone call was to Autumn, letting her know to meet them at the hospital as soon as possible.

Chapter 36

Kane struggled for air, taking shallow breaths as he kept his eyes focused on Avery's tombstone. The words he wanted to speak wouldn't come; his mind was so muddled, he couldn't think. It was all he could do to hold himself upright in the chair. Could Avery know what he was thinking? He needed to say the words out loud, wanted them to be heard. Needed to tell Avery how much he loved him. He was so afraid of losing the bond he'd felt here, so close to his soul mate. The connection was all he had left of Avery.

Closing his eyes, he tried to open his heart and mind. He didn't think about his struggles for breath, he ignored the vise-like pain gripping his chest and held on to his thoughts of Avery, knowing Robert wouldn't let him stay long. He had to do this, had to tell Avery. After a moment, he felt the first stirs of Avery. His Avery. The cool air faded away. In its place was warmth that caressed his soul. He felt Avery's presence there with him, this time stronger than any time before. He could feel Avery missing him as he missed Avery, and he smiled.

"I love you," Kane said as the weight of his body slumped forward. His voice somehow seemed richer than before. In an odd sensation, Kane felt lighter and Avery's presence grew stronger. His chest no longer hurt, his vision was clearer than it had been in years as he floated weightlessly, experiencing a comforting peace he'd never known before.

In the distance, he could see a brilliant white light. Something wasn't right. Movement below him caught his attention, drawing his focus away from the peacefulness of the light. He watched Robert running, but not from the ground where he'd been earlier, but from where he now hovered above. That confused him. Almost like watching a movie playing before him.

His gaze followed as Robert ran toward the toppled wheelchair. Robert yelled as he grabbed the frail body, flipping it over. The realization dawned on him that he looked down at himself, but he wasn't afraid or frightened. He felt...serene, as if he'd been wrapped in a blanket of tranquility. Kane watched curiously as Robert began CPR on his old lifeless body, which caused a sharp tug to pull at him, drawing him back down toward the empty shell Robert so frantically worked on. Kane resisted. He felt no connection there, but the pull was too strong. No...No...*No!* He slowly floated back down, away from the warmth of the light until there was nothing but darkness.

"Babe, open your eyes." Kane swore he heard Avery's voice, stronger than ever, and he tightened his eyes, keeping them closed, trying to hold on to that precious sound. "I'm right here, Kane. Open your eyes. Reach out and touch me."

Kane inhaled deeply and held the breath inside his body, trying to keep Avery's scent with him. He had to be dreaming, but this was the best dream he'd had since Avery died. He braced himself for the expected discomfort at the thought of Avery's death, but the pain didn't slice across his heart or wake him up sobbing in grief. Kane gave a diminutive smile in relief. "I miss you."

"Oh hell, Kane, open your eyes. I'm not allowed to touch you until you look around, but you're killing me. I need my hands on you, I need to touch you," Avery barked. Kane sensed him close to his face, felt his breath caress his skin, and he fought the tears. This was the way Avery had always woken him in the mornings, right up in his face. Slowly, he cracked his lids. That same intense bright light he remembered from earlier blinded him and had him shutting his eyes tightly again.

"Try again, Kane. I'm here," Avery coaxed. A dark shadow passed over his face and Kane cautiously opened his lids again to see Avery grinning down at him, only inches from his face. It wasn't the Avery he regularly dreamed about, the one he'd grown old with. Instead, he was young. All Kane could do was stare. His Avery was such a beautiful man. Kane reached up and pushed that stray piece of hair off Avery's forehead just like he'd done thousands of times over their lives together.

"I don't want to wake up from this one." Avery gripped his arms tightly and leaned all the way in to kiss him. Kane parted his lips for Avery's and was rewarded when his beloved's tongue slid across the tip of his before Avery's soft lips pressed firmly against him in a tender kiss. Just as Kane relaxed into the kiss, Avery pulled away.

"I've missed kissing you. I tried to be patient and wait. That bullshit about a minute up here is like a lifetime down there is all wrong. These last few months felt like years waiting for you, but it's all right. You're here now. Sit up. You'll adjust to the light faster if you sit up," Avery said, and out of nothing more than Avery lifting his arms to pull him forward, Kane came to a sitting position and a celestial world opened to him. He saw his backyard times about a trillion. There were no words to describe the beauty before him.

"Where are we?" He had to ask, but somehow he already knew the answer.

"I think you know, babe," Avery said and smiled at him.

"You're so young." His eyes were back on Avery's face, then his hands followed and began exploring Avery's distinct features. Avery felt so real. He wasn't sitting next to Kane; instead, he was crouched down on the balls of his feet. Avery started to stand, slowly pulling Kane to his feet, barely allowing him time to get his balance. Avery took Kane into his arms, love and contentment filled his heart as his husband embraced him tighter than he ever remembered. Kane held onto Avery as if his life depended on this embrace.

"I told you we were meant to be together," Avery whispered into his hair.

"I miss you so much."

"Me too, but not anymore." Avery's voice grew excited. "You have to listen to me, Kane. This isn't a dream. I'm not going anywhere. You've left Earth, and you're here with me now. Do you remember when I told you how I knew from the beginning you were meant for me? How we were destined to be together? I was right, and I always knew it! I always told you, but I don't think you believed me. And guess what else, you got part of the afterlife right, but you got lots wrong, too," Avery announced, trying to pull free of Kane's hold. He had a death grip on Avery, and as far as Kane was concerned, his man wasn't leaving his arms. If he held on as tight as he could, maybe he could keep Avery with him in this dream world forever.

"Interesting how you're so hard-headed even in this life." Avery chuckled. "Kane, let me go. This is the transition. I have so much to show you." With a slight struggle, Avery managed to slip free of his hold, but kept their hands linked together.

"I'm going to kiss those lips I've missed so much, but you can't grab me again, not until later when were alone, I don't have the willpower to deny you. Oh, and from what I understand, *that's* like a million times better up here. So I really can't wait until later. Damn, I missed you!" Avery's lips took his in a quick chaste kiss...then another. Kane eagerly kissed him back, but his husband's hands were on his arms, keeping him from drawing Avery to him again.

"Come on, come with me," Avery said, breaking their kiss.

"What about the children?" Kane was hesitant to leave this spot for fear the illusion would dissipate.

"They're fine. I promise. I've seen bits and pieces of the future. Autumn has five children, she marries the doctor who treated you. Robert struggles a little more, but I've met his other half. Remember the handsome honor guard from my funeral?" Avery asked. Kane just stared blankly at Avery, not knowing what to say. A slight smile curled the corners of his husband's lips and an amused look crossed his handsome face, and he just kept right on talking. "You'll like him, I promise. Come on, Kane." So classically Avery, never giving him a chance to catch up with his own thoughts.

Kane looked over his shoulder and reluctantly took a step forward with Avery, ignoring the dull draw still tugging at his back. Behind him, the pain and darkness from before still existed. In front of him, light and hope enticed him into taking more steps. Okay, Avery was the true motivator in getting him moving. The more steps he took, the less the dark vortex pulled at him, and the more clarity finally settled inside his soul.

"Are you saying we do belong together? This is heaven?" Kane tightened his hold on Avery's hand. Avery glanced over, giving him an indulgent look.

"You aren't listening to me, are you? Funny how that trait came across, too. I hope the doting on me attribute came with it. I need some of your tender lovin' care." The flowers and calla lilies actually separated as they stepped through the fragrant grassy meadow. Kane loved that, never fond of the idea of seeing a precious bloom trampled on.

Avery gave him a wink as he came to a stop halfway through the field, in a spot where they were surrounded by the flowers he adored, finally letting Kane take him back in his arms. "Listen to me, babe. This is important. Parts you got right, and parts you got wrong. The only thing I'm saying right now is that I got *us* right, just exactly like I told you over and over again. You should have had more faith in me. You were meant for me. You're my other half, my soul mate destined to walk with me through eternity. You're my always and forever. Now that you're here, I'm complete again. The rest is easier to understand if I show you instead of tell you."

Avery was gone from his arms again, pulling him forward. "Oh, and you're hot. I mean, you were a good-looking older man, but this is just how I remember you the first night I met you. Damn, I'm a lucky soul. And don't look at me like that. I'm working on the language, but apparently that's my cross to bear, it's what I brought forward with me."

The light and the meadow faded and a heavenly realm opened into something Kane again had no words for. Never could he have even imagined something so awe-inspiring and stunning. And his Avery was right there beside him, wrapping an arm around him.

"See? It's so much better here. We're completely accepted and loved. That bullshit hate down there has some of the big guys really pissed off." Avery grinned sheepishly. "And I seriously need to watch my language, don't I?" Avery chuckled, pulling him against his body.

"I love you, Kane. Now let's go begin our *always*," Avery whispered as familiar lips descended on his.

The End, or The Beginning,
whichever you prefer.

Books by Kindle Alexander

If you loved *Always*, then you won't want to miss Kindle Alexander's bestselling novels:

Double Full
The Current Between Us
Texas Pride
Up in Arms

* * * *

Coming Soon:
Full Disclosure

The word is out on Double Full

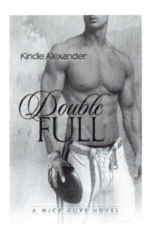

"Kindle Alexander knows the rules of romance and she applies them good."
— *Elisa My Reviews and Rambling*

"You can't help but love Jace and Colt and suffer their heartbreak right along with them."
—Tanis, *Scandalicious Book Reviews*

"I was drawn into this book from the first paragraph!"
—*Dirty Hoe's Book Blog*

"These two hunky men had me in tears, their love for one another is magically."
— Jennifer Robbins, *Twinsie Talk Book Review*

"It's a really steamy story, and I put this on my GRL TBR list and was everything I hoped."
—Jessie Potts, *USA Today*

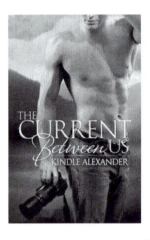

"Loved this book!!! This is the second book I've read by Kindle Alexander. The first one was *Texas Pride*. I was hooked right from the beginning. It's an amazing love story." —Brenda Wright, *Twinsie Talk Book Review*

"This book is an excellent love story, where even the most hardened heart and disillusioned soul can find the romantic streak hidden deep within and see it blossom into something neither thought possible. I fell in love with the author, her writing and the characters... just go read it!!!"
—Monique, *Sinfully Sexy Book Reviews*

"This is my first book by Kindle Alexander and I have to say that I loved it! I am a fan of the m/m genre especially when there is a beautiful and touching story behind it."
—*Three Chicks and their Books*

"If you enjoyed Texas Pride you will love *The Current Between Us*!"
—*Swoon Worthy Book Reviews*

What readers are saying about Up in Arms

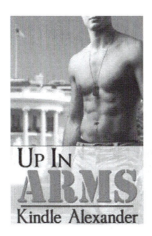

"*Up in Arms* is a compelling, fascinating drama that honestly explores the conflict of love in the military without taking away from an enchanting romance." —*Joyfully Reviewed*

"This story not only follows these men's love affair, which is sweet and sexy, but we also see the aftermath of how they deal with tragedy. I love these boys, how they interact, how they overcome, how one of them blushes *sigh*." —*The Bitches of Eastwick*

"This is a tender love story…. She taps all the sensory elements that binds a romance reader to the narrative, characters, conflicts and resolutions." —*Blackraven Reviews*

35001988R00162

Made in the USA
Lexington, KY
26 August 2014